Rose May
may romance
bloom!

JENNIFER'S GARDEN

Dianne Venetta

Acknowledgements

When writing a book, you never write it alone. You always depend on the support and patience of those closest to you. In my case, it's my husband and two children. Without their understanding and full-fledged belief in my dream of writing a novel, none of this would have come to pass. Sure, I would have written stories, passed the time with my garden blog and various creative outlets, but completing an entire novel (or several) would never have become a reality.

And it doesn't stop at the front door. From the praise and encouragement my mother lavished upon me for creative writing in elementary school to the steadfast and faithful support of my step-mother today, I am buoyed by people who love and care about my endeavors. This includes a sister who edited and re-edited on my behalf while the other focused her photographic talent on making me look good, plus two brothers willing to engage in my shameless promotion, not to mention a mother-in-law willing to read *anything* I write. Included among my devoted and indispensable beta-readers are Sheri and Joanie—thank you!

But as the last word slips off the keyboard, it's my family to whom I owe the most gratitude.
Thank you one and all.

Dedication

This book is dedicated to my daughter.

"Given the proper care and feeding, a woman will bloom in time; her own sweet time."

Chapter One

Jennifer Hamilton glanced at her mother again, sweeping her pencil across crisp white paper as she outlined the seated figure before her. "Gosh, it feels good to have a pencil in my hand again," she said, her fingers never stopping as she sketched in a horizon line, her point of reference to denote distance and space. "It's been *years* since I last picked up pad and paper." Yet it felt so natural, so second-hand.

Beatrice Hamilton smiled. "Med school has a way of doing that to a schedule."

Jennifer sighed. "Residency, private practice..." She laughed. "Sometimes it feels like I have time for nothing else!"

Her mother smiled. "Wait until you add a husband and children to the mix. Talk about no time, my goodness!"

The mention of Aurelio Villarreal warmed Jennifer's mood a degree. A gust of wind lifted the hair from her neck, the cool air a welcome break from the late afternoon heat. Casting another glance toward the Coral Gables Mediterranean-style building, Jennifer framed-in the main structure, arced a few lines to represent windows and doorways, emphasizing the contrast between the dark brown of their casings against the vanilla-colored stucco, then lightly smudged the lead for a shadow effect. A few waves across the top and she had the beginnings of the barrel-tiled rooftop.

Though she hadn't drawn in years, her ease of motion felt as though she'd never missed a beat, drawing every day of her life. And the release. Drawing opened her spirit, unleashed her imagination. It gave her a sense of freedom, of inhibition.

Next she focused on the trees. With a few choppy strokes, she depicted the natural fall of oversized palm fronds swaying heavy in the wind, their bowed trunks lazy yet strong—strong enough to endure the hurricanes that whipped through this city every year! But living in South Florida, one became accustomed to such thrill.

"Time management," she declared, feathering in the wispy tips. "I'll just have to make sure I'm on top of my time management skills."

"You will be, darling. If anyone can juggle career and family, I know it will be you."

Jennifer stopped. She peered at her mom. "You've always been my biggest fan, haven't you..."

"Number one."

Jennifer smiled. No question, no doubt. Only love. Which made her mother's impending passing all the more difficult. Thrusting her pencil back into motion, Jennifer didn't want to dwell in thought. She wanted to continue, to enjoy their time together and this catharsis of sketching. It reminded her of days gone by, time lost in the sand wriggled beneath her toes. Hours and minutes felt the same, afternoons drifted into the ocean as she drew—what she saw, what she felt.

What she wanted.

Scrutinizing the emerging scene, Jennifer was pleased with her progress. Ready to trace the delicate features of her mother's face, she settled in for a closer look. Age had nothing on her mother. Blue eyes shone bright and her skin glowed, flushed with healthy tones of pink. Hers was a beauty that persisted in graceful defiance. Why, if you didn't know better, you'd swear she was the picture of health.

"Dr. Hamilton."

Both women turned.

Jennifer stiffened as Dr. Roberts drew near.

Fully gray, balding in the middle, his mouth was set in a stern line. "They told me I'd find you out here." Placing folded hands behind his back, he glanced at the pad in Jennifer's hand with disapproval. "If you can spare a moment, I came to discuss your mother's medications."

Jennifer rose from the stone bench. Lowering pad and pencil against her body, she replied, "Yes?"

"We need to increase dosages."

"Why?"

"According to the nurses, she's been experiencing more severe pain. At this stage, I suggest an increase to encourage rest."

Jennifer hardened her gaze. *Put her to sleep*, you mean.

"It's not unexpected at this stage."

"It's not what she wants."

"The nurses are with her twenty-four hours a day." He pulled his arms forward and crossed them over his chest. A wiry man, he barely put a dent in the starched white lab coat he wore. "I think they know best."

"My mother knows full well the ramifications of her meds."

"Under the circumstances—"

From her wheelchair, Beatrice cleared her throat. "I'm *right* here."

Jennifer discarded pad and pencil and went to her mother's side. "Mom, is it true? The pain's getting worse?"

She gazed at Jennifer before responding to the doctor. "I'm fine, Al. I told the nurse it was nothing to worry about."

"Your bones are decaying, Beatrice. They are vulnerable to serious breakage."

"My bones are working fine," she raised her hands, turning them back and forth for inspection, "as you can see. It was an isolated incident."

Dr. Roberts frowned and dipped his head forward. "Your condition is serious, Beatrice. Breaking your bones can lead to complications. You of all people should know the risks."

"I do."

"What are you talking about?" Jennifer blurted between them. "What incident?"

He turned and addressed her forthright. "Your mother injured her wrist while getting into her bed last night."

Jennifer gripped the padded armrest of her chair. "Why didn't you tell me?"

"I didn't want to upset you." She patted Jennifer's hand. "I told you, I'm fine." Then to the doctor she said, "As to medication, my current prescription is adequate."

Adequate? Jennifer stood. She didn't like the sound of that. And she didn't like her mother keeping things from her.

"It's my body and my choice."

Dr. Roberts shook his head in resignation.

"You heard her, doctor," Jennifer defended, though part of her wanted to discuss the options, the alternatives. The thought of her mother in pain didn't sit well at all.

Wielding his full focus on Jennifer, he asked, "Is this what you want? Are you okay with what you're doing?" He eyed her pad on the bench with naked contempt. "What you're asking her to do isn't helping."

It took every speck of control she had not to reach out and slap him. He had no right to speak to her this way. "You heard her," Jennifer said. "She understands the clinical repercussions. Despite what you or I may advise, she's made her choice."

He scowled. "Somewhat under duress, don't you think?"

Jennifer didn't appreciate the insinuation, or the nasty smirk forming on his lips. "She's made her decision and I intend to respect it. As her physician, I suggest you do the same."

He stepped back, clearly displeased with her response. But both of them knew his hands were tied. Dr. Roberts would not override the wishes of a physician patient. "Yes, of course. You understand, I have a Hippocratic duty to uphold."

"You've said your peace." She breathed in deep and slow and added, "Now if you'll excuse us, we'd like to get back to enjoying our visit."

His glare mocked her, but he said nothing. When he glanced at her mother, his expression softened. "Are you sure?"

"This is the best medicine for me, Al. Being outside in the fresh air, feeling the wind on my face, hearing the sounds of life... I'll be all right, really I will."

"I want you to be comfortable."

"I am." She angled her head and added, "With my daughter by my side, I'm better than ever."

Dr. Roberts grunted beneath his breath. "Very well," he replied, his voice tight and controlled. Without another glance toward Jennifer, he retreated back along the manicured path he came.

Once he was out of earshot, Jennifer withdrew her hands and linked them across her chest. "I do not care for that man."

"Don't let him get to you, Jenny. He means well."

She stared after him. "His attitude is horrendous."

"He's very good at what he does."

"His bedside manner sure leaves a lot to be desired."

"Not everyone can be adored by their patients like you."

Jennifer turned to her mother and was met with a wink. *Ergh.* She flung her arms open and went to her mother's chair. Stooping to a crouch she heaved a sigh. "I don't like it. Any of it."

"It's life, darling." Beatrice held the younger in her gaze, and reaching over, brushed Jennifer's hair to one side.

The small gesture reminded her of when she was a girl. When she came home from school, exasperated by some kid, some teacher...her mom consoled her. She always had the answers.

"Things are what they are. No sense in fighting."

"He thinks I'm pushing you. That it's my fault you're..." She couldn't finish the thought.

"He's wrong."

"We don't have to wait. Aurelio and I can get married tomorrow. Here, at Fairhaven."

Annoyance flickered in her mother's eyes and she waved the suggestion away. "I'll have no such thing. You'll be married in fine Hamilton tradition. Like your father and I."

Jennifer closed her eyes. Guilt simmered deep inside. *But at what cost to you?*

As though sensing her thoughts, Beatrice replied, "Don't worry about Dr. Roberts." She ran her hand lightly over Jennifer's head, gliding down her cheek and then cupped her chin. "It's his job to worry."

Jennifer opened her eyes and stared out across the grounds. Beyond the canopy of oaks, the sun shimmered gold, casting the nursing home in luminescent tones of peach and rose. Quiet, gentle, exterior lighting glowed in and around the landscape. Opulent, welcoming, it seemed more like a private estate than a medical facility specializing in end-of-life care.

"I'm fine, really. But more importantly, I want to be there when you and Aurelio take your vows. I want to be a part of this monumental step in your life. You promised."

Looking into her mother's eyes, there was no room for argument. She would be held to her promise. Even if it killed her.

Chapter Two

Jennifer slowed her black BMW for the entrance to the historical mansion and eased down the long and winding drive. Located off Old Cutler Road, Michael Kingsley's home had been renovated and restored to its original grandeur and grand it was, with its oak-lined driveway, salmon-colored azaleas in full bloom ringing their base. Exposed stone walls and coral-formed arches, weathered to a soft patina of gray. Elaborately molded ironwork trimmed balconies along the second-floor, while more of the same outlined the grounds.

"We're here for an appearance, for Michael's sake."

Jennifer managed a small smile. An appearance. She knew this was the last place Samantha Rawlings wanted to be. Fiery brunette, hotshot attorney—party was her middle name, not social commitment. Yet here she was, willing to drive halfway across town for a quick shot of pleasantries. Because her friend needed her.

Jennifer nodded and slowed the car beneath the *porte-cochere*, careful to avoid the formally clad young men waiting to get their doors. Above them, a magnificent lantern hung from the rounded ceiling, inlaid with shells and mosaics, an eclectic mix of all things Old Miami, bathing the area with light.

Jennifer took a deep breath and released, suppressing a fresh rush of nerves as she glanced through the open front doors. "For Michael's sake."

Michael's daughter was getting married. Springtime seemed to be that time of year when brides surged to the forefront of attention and like any proud father would, he was hosting an engagement party. Any other time she would be delighted to be in attendance, but under the circumstances, it only proved a sad reminder.

"Try to enjoy yourself," Sam said, patting Jennifer's thigh. "You could use the diversion."

Diversion. Wary reluctance pulled at her. Like Sam, this was the last place she wanted to be, but obligations were obligations and she wouldn't shirk a single one. "I will."

Jennifer placed the car in park. As Sam slid out the passenger side, she caught her reflection in the rearview mirror. Determined blue eyes reinforced: *We're in, we're out.* Michael was a good friend and it wasn't every day your daughter became engaged. Not every day the family stood witness. A sliver of grief pinpricked her heart. No, not every day. Time didn't wait on anything, or anyone. She closed her eyes. Even when you begged, pleaded. Time offered no reprieve.

"Jen?" Sam ducked her head into the car. "You coming?"

"Yes." Of course she was coming. Shaking her head, she scolded herself. Stop. Stop this nonsense right now. This isn't about you. It's about Michael and his daughter. It's a happy day.

A celebration.

Tears pushed at the back of her eyes as a young man waited by her door, the one he held open. Embarrassed she hadn't noticed him there, Jennifer shook her head once more, quick and sharp. Enough. In one smooth motion, she rose from the car and snapped the lens of her mind closed. Tonight was about new beginnings, rejoicing in the future. Two young people were beginning their lives as one. *Could there be a happier day?*

Circling around the car she caught up with Sam.

Sam froze mid-stride. Lanterns of light swam in her dark brown eyes. "You sure you're okay 'cause you don't look so good."

"I'm fine," she replied, swallowing hard against the tender swell in her throat. Maybe if she said it enough times, it would be true. Maybe if she focused on others, she would forget about herself. Maybe Sam was right. Tonight, she could use the distraction.

Diversion. Shut the lid on her life and focus on Michael's. "Really, I'm fine." She tried to back it up with a smile, but abandoned the effort.

"We can leave right now." Sam glanced sideways and back, her feisty auburn waves swinging in sync. "Ditch the scene before anyone's the wiser. Tell them you were called to the hospital."

"Nonsense," she said, waving the notion off as entirely unacceptable. "We're not going anywhere." With a brief fuss to her hair, Jennifer started toward the door—before second thoughts sent her running.

Sam nodded. "Good girl." Linking an arm through Jennifer's, she reassured with a squeeze. "Don't worry. You'll get through it."

"Of course I will."

Jennifer heaved a sigh. It's what I do.

In the expansive foyer, they were greeted by an enormous arrangement of bird of paradise, anthurium, ginger, and a spray of delicate purple blossoms. Perched on a pedestal of mahogany and centered beneath a glimmering chandelier, it was exotic and vibrant and though predominantly Hawaiian by nature, felt completely Miami tropical.

"That is some kind of gorgeous," Sam murmured.

Jennifer nodded dully. Everything in Michael's home was gorgeous. From the baby-smooth leather furniture to the glossy wood and polished stone floors, he'd spent a veritable fortune to make sure of it.

Several guests mingled in the main living area and to their left, a few huddled near the wide doorway into the kitchen. Arched and trimmed in heavy dark wood, intricately carved, it was a superb piece of craftsmanship. But Jennifer's attention was drawn outside. Through floor to ceiling windows amidst a tangle of palm and ferns, she could see the main party gathered by the pool, the area lit by a flicker of torches.

Sam stopped in place. Glancing across the keystone flooring, from artwork to furniture, she let out a soft whistle. "That patio is unbelievable. If I didn't know better, I'd swear we were smack in the middle of wild jungle." She flipped her gaze to Jennifer. "I may be no fan of the mosquito fest it presents, but I have to admit," she hitched a thumb toward the back, "that's enticing out there."

Jennifer willed the soft clink of glasses, the easy rhythm of light conversation to work magic on her mood. "Yes. Michael and Laurencia have done a spectacular job."

As the two meandered toward the patio, Sam pointed to a colorful painting of a cottage prominently displayed on the dining room wall. It was a watercolor of a house trimmed in shutters of yellow, bordered by pink hibiscus, its small porch leading to a secluded stretch of sandy shoreline. Nothing else existed in the painting but blue sky and blue water. "Now that scene makes me want to toss the legal pads and head for the islands!"

Buoyed by the sight of it, she smiled. "It does, doesn't it? Aurelio gave that piece to Michael...as a housewarming gift."

"I'm surprised it appealed to him."

Jennifer tensed. Sam didn't care for Aurelio and changing her mind was a game of fools. A game she no longer cared to play. As Sam turned away and headed outdoors, Jennifer cast a glance toward the painting. She had been with Aurelio when he selected the piece and both agreed it was perfect for Michael. Both had been right.

Jennifer joined Sam outside and the warm evening air coated her skin in an instant. The woodsy, spicy scent of ginger filled her senses, the fragrance made richer by the nearby saltwater clinging to the air. The combination helped cleanse her thoughts of negativity. An associate from the office caught her eye and she waved. He returned the gesture with a smile.

As she and Sam glided between bodies, a light Spanish tune swirled around them, mixing with the din of conversation. She recognized this particular piece as Flamenco; her preferred selection of music.

Sam neared the edge of the pool. Almost black in color, it appeared more lagoon than pool, and dotted with small lights. It blended seamlessly into the natural stone waterfall cascading down the center, overflow splashing into basins on either side.

"Damn," Sam murmured. "I feel like I'm stepping into another world." Her gaze trailed off down a hidden pathway which disappeared behind a burgeoning mass of philodendron. "The house may be an architect's dream, but this...this rainforest is the real jewel." She turned to face Jennifer. "I sure as hell hope you got your referral for landscaping from Michael, because this man knows what he's doing."

"I did indeed," she replied, heartened by Sam's approval. "As well as from a few other physicians at the hospital. He's scheduled to come by the house tomorrow morning."

"Yes, well..." She pivoted on her heel. "Perfect. Now let's get a drink."

"Yes. Let's."

Trailing her to the nearest makeshift Tiki bar, Sam's voice picked up as she slowed. "Ah... I think we've found the popular man this evening."

Doling out drinks and a smile, the bartender's movements were fluid and swift as he served the guests clustered around him. Medium-build, average features, Jennifer thought his tanned skin seemed all the darker against his white cotton Guayabera button-down.

But it was his hair that garnered the most attention. Swatches of sandy blonde thrust upward and sideways—every which way, in fact. "Sam, there are all of three bars and a group upwards of a hundred people. I daresay all the men have their hands full."

"God, *don't I wish*—but this one... This one's setting fire to my loin as we speak!"

Jennifer sighed. "Don't you ever tire?"

"No and if I do," she quipped, "they make drugs for that."

She shook her head, but duly followed as Sam jaunted off to capture the latest target of her lust. Well-skilled in the art of flirtation with her fiery bronze eyes and wavy auburn curls, black fitted dress cut high above the knee on her long bare legs, Sam was an eyeful herself at nearly six foot, let alone *hand*-full. Jennifer had no doubt she'd add this man to her list of conquests before all was said and done.

"I'll have a gin martini straight up, three olives," she ordered, then added with a smile too large to be innocent, "and make it dirty."

"You got it."

Jennifer wondered if Sam really enjoyed her drink as such, or was she simply after shock appeal. Probably the latter she mused, and plugged herself into the spirit of fun as best she could. "Oh, and by the way Sam, those little blue pills you're counting on... Don't. They're for men only."

Jennifer took satisfaction at the bump in the man's eyes.

Two could play at this game.

Sam gave her a gotcha smile. "Good thing I know a few tricks."

He grinned and winked. "I'll bet you do," he said to Sam, but his gaze landed on Jennifer.

"You are so delicious."

Despite being well-accustomed to Sam's take-no-prisoner approach to flirting, the comment caught Jennifer off guard.

But not him. "You're pretty sweet yourself," he passed back to Sam, though his gaze remained uncomfortably on her.

"Not really," she replied with a throaty chuckle, "but I am downright tasty."

Jennifer was amazed. Not only by their salacious banter, but the fact the man poured her martini without missing a beat, skewered three plump olives, slid them in, pinched a napkin from its cradle and handed off the finished product—all with a smile.

"As," he said, extending the oversized triangular-shaped glass to her, "is this."

A warm, friendly, unaffected smile.

Sam retrieved the drink. "Damn, you're good."

"That's what they pay me for." He turned to Jennifer. "What's your pleasure?"

"I'll take a white wine spritzer, please." She preferred red, but tonight was warm; ice-drinks preferable.

"You got it."

Avoiding his gaze, she ran her hands down the backside of her navy skirt, smoothing material that needed no smoothing. Her white button-down suddenly felt too warm. She wished she had worn a dress like Sam, but coming straight from the hospital, she had no time to change into more suitable attire.

Sam sipped her drink in silence while behind the bar strong, lean arms covered by a sparse layer of sun-bleached hair went to work on the spritzer. Jennifer's gaze drifted to his chest, noting the top button of his shirt was open, exposing another mass of hair. This section was thicker and darker, more a golden brown than the rest.

"Tasty, isn't it?"

Feeling the blaze of Sam's grin, Jennifer swung her head around, the skin of her cheeks flushed hot, like a school girl getting caught looking at dirty magazines. Her throat went dry and she scowled at Sam, daring her to push.

"Here you go." Splashing in some soda, the man dropped a wedge of lime in and with equal proficiency handed her the glass.

She cleared her throat and managed a proper, "Thank you." Taking the drink, she stepped away from the bar.

"You're welcome." Sable soft eyes closed in. "If there's anything else I can get for you two ladies, don't hesitate to ask."

"We won't," Sam assured.

Moving out of hearing range, Jennifer snapped, "How do you do it?"

"What?"

"How do you come-on to complete strangers?"

Sam smirked. "It's a natural gift."

"I'm serious." Her brow furrowed. "Don't you ever want more?"

"Of course I do. What do you think I was trying for? I'm not interested in stopping at that delightful smile of his—no ma'am. I want more, much more!"

"Stop. You know what I mean." She glanced around for onlookers. "You're thirty-seven-years-old, Sam. You're not getting any younger and despite those 'tricks' you think you have in store, there's a lot you're missing out on."

She took a long swallow of the ice-cold martini. "Like you and Aurelio?"

"Yes. Like me and Aurelio." With a reflexive glance toward the bartender Jennifer continued, her aggravation heating. "We're getting ready to begin one of the most rewarding chapters of our lives and you should take a page from our storybook for yourself."

Sam shifted weight to her back heel and cocked her head. "What are you proposing, Jen? That I find myself a wonderful man who can take care of me, add me to his collection of trophies on a shelf and put my libido out to pasture?"

"I'm *suggesting* you find someone to settle down with, someone to love until you're old and gray, and maybe..." she added, though knew it would receive protest, "someone with whom to have children."

"Now I know you've gone mad." She eyed the glass in Jennifer's hand. "I think that gorgeous man spiked your drink."

Sensitive to prying eyes, Jennifer lowered her voice. "You may change your mind one day."

"About kids? I think not." She gave a cursory whip to her head. "I'm a little too fond of my freedom and sanity, thank you very much."

"Children do not denote insanity, Sam."

"For some. I know women you'd swear their brains leaked out with their breast milk—a feat that would end my legal career in about the same time it takes a shark to rip through its prey." She gave an exaggerated shudder. "No thank you. I've better uses of my time." Then she turned the spotlight on Jennifer. "And you?"

"Me?"

"You've settled for a man who fits your bill of sale, rather than a man who sets fire to your heart."

"I have not." Self-conscious of onlookers she whispered, "I love Aurelio and he loves *me*."

"You may love who he is, but I'm not convinced you love him, you know, the for-better-or-worse kind of love. I think he fits your image of what a good husband's supposed to look like—which has nothing to do with what actually makes a good husband." She paused. "And I think you've settled."

"And I think you're crazy. This," she scoffed, "from the woman who's most extensive experience in the mating department comes from a twelve month cohabitation."

"Jeremy and I were sharing some space. I wasn't interviewing him for a position as my husband."

"I'm not *interviewing* anyone." Jennifer smiled at a couple of women glancing their way, then forced a sip from her wine.

"That's exactly what you've been doing. You have an ideal mate in your head—successful, well-educated, good-looking—and you compare each guy you meet to your concoction of perfect."

Patience frayed, yet Sam continued, her tone ever-so-polite while dark eyes held sharp and steady. "But no one is perfect, so you make a list of the prospective suitor's pros and cons, then decide if enough of them fall onto the appropriate side of the T-bar before rendering your final decision."

"I do not."

"Yes you do." She paused again. "Most women do. Forget the fact you're an accomplished physician in your own right, you're still out looking for that knight-in-shining-armor fellow to sweep you off your feet and take care of you. You know, big strong man meets small helpless female. Every damn fairy-tale I ever read, the woman looked *up* to the man." She tipped her chin up and declared, "Subliminal sabotage, if you ask me."

"You're reaching, counselor."

"I don't think so." Sam relaxed into a grin and posed the challenge. "You would no sooner accept a date from the sinfully handsome bartender that plied you with wine than you would a ride home from a stranger."

"I am *not* dating a bartender."

Sam raised her brow and glass in unison. "I rest my case."

"By the looks of him..." She looked back in his direction. "He probably spends more time at the beach than he does working." A little rugged for her taste, he wasn't bad looking. "How does someone like that support himself?"

"Hey," Sam knocked back. "I hear bartenders make pretty good money. Unlike you and me, he doesn't need to slug through long hours to manage the big bucks."

"Be serious, Sam. Dating a bartender is like asking me to give up filet mignon for hamburger."

"There's nothing like an all-American juicy hamburger in my book," she pumped with a smirk, laughter swamping her eyes. "It's one of my favorite meals!"

"I prefer steak."

"You might be surprised." Sam pulled the sword of olives from their gin bath. "Me, I'd take him solely for his looks." Plucking one off the end with her teeth she chewed, her eyes dancing in delight.

Jennifer's gaze hardened. "I don't date men simply because they look good. I want a man with whom I can stand shoulder to shoulder, see eye to eye. A man I can respect." She stole another peek at the happy-go-lucky fellow dispensing drinks to a couple of guests. Animated, he conversed with them like they were old friends, knew each other from way back.

She turned a shoulder. "I'm a doctor, for heaven's sake. I've worked hard to get where I am. My life has direction, purpose. I'd last two seconds with a man like that, at most."

"It would probably prove to be the hottest two seconds of your adult life!"

"Would you stop." Jennifer admonished. She scanned the immediate vicinity, certain someone had overheard. "You're supposed to be helping me tonight, not antagonizing."

Like a flash of steel, Sam cut the humor. Grizzly turned doe as she reached across the divide, her tone rendered tender. "Look. I'm not trying to embarrass you. I'm simply trying to point out that beneath the surface of your calm exterior exists a mountain of passion, churning like a volcano, dormant in a sea of control."

"What exactly do you have against Aurelio, Sam? What has the man done that you dislike him so?"

Chapter Three

"He is a wonderful man," Jennifer defended. "He's kind and loving, intelligent and yes, he's successful—*very*—for which there's not a thing to be ashamed."

Sam drew a sip of gin and regarded her pal with a weighty stare. "You got me there..."

"Then what," she demanded. "What is wrong with him?"

"Jennifer."

She turned.

"Hey, is everything all right?" Michael's physician assistant appeared by her side. She narrowed her gaze. "You seem upset."

Jennifer's pulse jumped. *How long had she been standing there?* "No, no, I'm fine."

The woman rubbed a hand up and down Jennifer's arm, as though she knew better. "It's okay. I understand." She flicked a glance toward Sam and said, "I just wanted to say hello and see how you were coming along."

Jennifer stepped back, uncomfortable with the close contact. "I appreciate that. Things are well." She gestured toward Sam. "This is my friend Sam. Sam Rawlings. Sam, this is Carly Tucker. Michael's P.A."

"Nice to meet you."

"You too," Sam replied.

"I hope I didn't interrupt anything..." She returned her full attention to Jennifer. "But I didn't want to miss you."

"No, you're fine. You didn't interrupt anything."

Sam raised a brow at the lie as she sipped from her drink.

"We were merely catching up."

"Well, good." She lingered, creating an awkward silence. "Okay, so maybe we can talk later?" She nodded, encouraging Jennifer to agree.

"That would be nice." Carly was familiar with her situation. It was kind of her to make an effort.

She smiled. "I'll go on and let you two get back to your discussion."

While it was the *last* thing Jennifer wanted, Carly excused herself before she could stop her.

"So where were we?"

"Nowhere. Forget I asked."

"Jen."

"There's nothing wrong with Aurelio."

"Except he doesn't crack lightning through your heart."

Jennifer stilled.

"Or break waves across your soul. He's not ocean vast or mountain high." She sighed. "There's no intensity to him Jen, no depth." She paused, a hint of pity entering her eyes. "I'm sorry, but Aurelio is duck-pond still."

"I don't need waves, Sam. I'm not like you." She hated the falter in her voice, the desperation, but she needed to be heard. Sam needed to understand. "You thrive on the highs and lows, but not me. I get enough turmoil on the job, I don't want it at home, too. My home is my sanctuary, my peace. I need calm waters, not raging."

"C'mon on, Jen. Storms aren't necessarily a bad thing." She leaned closer, but didn't touch her. No predictable wrap of her arm around the shoulders, no hand to her back. "They're Mother Nature's rumbling—a growling need, gathering dark and intense along the horizon." She motioned to the sky above them, licks of a nearby torch jumping in the reflection of her dark eyes. "She sways and rocks, giving herself to the passionate throes and then explodes, high above the landscape in a spectacular light show, releasing herself in a thunderous downpour, bathing the earth with her riches."

Indignation refueled as she grasped hold of Sam's underlying meaning. "Remind me to take my umbrella next time they forecast rain."

Undaunted, Sam said, "I'm talking about tossing the agenda, Jen. Feel your way through life, like you used to. Embrace the highs and lows instead of 'allotting' for them." Sam inched closer, checking for nearby eyes with ears and lowered her voice. "Let go. Let yourself be courted by desire, not success. Toss the schedule into the trash, leave the pen and paper on the desk and follow temptation. *Give in.*"

"You're in the wrong courtroom."

"Am I?"

"Marriage isn't about sex, it's about love."

"Passion."

"Same thing."

She cocked her head to one side. "Are they?"

"Yes," she said, though Sam clearly disagreed. "They are." Jennifer gave a slight shake to her hair. "You don't have a case here."

"I think I do."

"You don't.   And whether you like it or not, Aurelio and I will be married."

"It's too soon."

She tightened her grip on the glass in hand.   "Are you forgetting about my mother?"

With quiet determination, Sam replied, "No."

"Then why would you ask me to wait?   You're not making any sense!"

Sam slid her eyes to the turn of heads to their right.

Heat flushed into Jennifer's cheeks.   "You know what's at stake.   You know how much this means."

"I know marriage is for life.   Your mother will understand."

Her heart steeled.   *Famous last words*.   "I need to find Michael."

"Give it some consideration, Jen."   Sam's eyes deepened, steeped in concern.   "It's the least you can do."

"I'll catch up with you in a little while."   Without waiting for a response, she left Sam to fend for herself.   She would be fine.   She always was and tonight would bear no different.   Most likely she'd end up with a phone number and a promise and for Sam, it was enough.

But it wasn't enough for her.   She needed more than a good time and she didn't need to consider anything.   Hadn't she learned enough about need?

If the experience with Tony taught her anything, it was that need disappointed.   It worked you up like an addiction then dropped you like a withdrawal. Worse than a patient trying to kick the habit of smoking, need for another human being acted like heroine. When you had it, life was great. When you didn't... You wished you were dead.

Winding her way through guests, she continued to stew over the exchange. There's nothing wrong with Aurelio. A decent, hardworking man, intelligent and sophisticated, loving and kind... He was perfectly suited for her, and she him. Unlike Sam, freewheeling love had never been her style. Except that once. But she had learned her lesson. Whether shame had been her teacher or plain good sense, was immaterial. She had moved on. She and Aurelio wanted the same things from life, shared the same outlook and now it was time for marriage.

The marriage her mother wanted to witness.

The stab to her heart was quick and severe. How could Sam ask her to walk away? How could she be so insensitive?

At a sudden loss of direction, Jennifer stopped. She looked around, gained her bearing, and searched for any sight of Michael. Laurencia. Anyone related to the family.

But she saw no one. Met by a sea of faces, a blur of happy and content, Jennifer hurried into the house.

Where misery followed. Beatrice Hamilton wanted her daughter married and in a lovely garden surrounded by family and friends, much like she and Jennifer's father had done. It was the one thought that gave her mother peace. The one thing she could look forward to other than pain and nausea.

Surely she could give her that much?

"Jennifer."

"*What*—" She whirled around. "Michael," she responded in a rush of breath. The man of the hour.

Dressed more casually than she expected in a floral button-down and dark slacks, inky brown hair curling at his collar, his temples touched by gray, Michael Kingsley's gaze was charged with concern. "You okay?"

"Yes." She worked to calm the thud in her chest. "Fine." It would not do to have him sense her distress. She was his guest, not some spectacle of emotional unraveling. Struggling to even her voice she said, "You startled me is all."

His smile was instantaneous. "I apologize. Hey, thanks for coming. Laurencia's been asking about you all evening."

"I'm sorry I'm late."

"No, no, you're fine. She just wanted to ask about your mother." His change in tone was swift. "How is she?"

"Fine. No change."

As a physician, Michael understood the deeper significance. "Do you need anything? Anything at all?"

I need my mother back to full health she thought grimly, but knowing that was a dream, she shook her head. "No, but thank you. You and Laurencia have been wonderful."

"We love you like a sister, Jennifer. You know that."

She nodded. Before she had moved on to her fellowship in cardiology, Michael had been instrumental in her internal medicine training. As a resident under his tutelage, the two discovered they shared a soft spot for children. It's all it took. They'd been friends ever since. "You've done more than enough already."

"Dr. Roberts towing the line?"

She poked the lime in her drink with the tiny red straw. "He's doing what he feels is best."

"He's old school, Jennifer. You have pain, you treat it."

Unless the patient refuses. She faced him head on. "Yes, well, at least he listens to my mother."

"Anyone with any sense listens to your mother."

She laughed softly. "True."

"She's in good hands. If she needs something, she'll get it."

"I know." In no small part, because of this man. "Thank you."

"Don't thank me, I'm just the messenger!"

Manager more like it, but he wouldn't accept any more. He was too humble.

"Jennifer!"

Both turned toward the direction of the woman's voice.

Laurencia Kingsley waved. Encircled by several elegantly dressed women in a kitchen large enough to service a restaurant, she shone in her pantsuit of lustrous gold hues and beaded trim, which set off her brown skin beautifully.

Mother-of-the-bride was radiant. From joy, Jennifer mused.

A conspiratorial gleam lit up Michael's eyes. "You obviously haven't made the rounds, yet."

"No, I haven't."

"Well then, you'd better get to it." Michael laughed. "She's invited two hundred of our closest friends tonight, and this is only the first engagement party. She has three more scheduled later this month!"

Jennifer held her best smile in place while the energy drained from her limbs. "Does she now..."

"*Trust* me. You'd be wise to move along. I learned early on, you don't want to keep the mother-of-the-bride waiting for anything."

"No," she cast a reluctant glance toward Laurencia. "I most certainly don't."

Nearly three hours later, Jennifer returned to the area where she left Sam only to find no sign of her. She groaned inwardly. She was ready to leave and leave now. Turning about, she searched the crowd. We should have set a meeting place and time for departure.

At this point, there's no telling where she might be.

Jennifer continued to scan faces, and felt more conspicuous with each second that passed. She wanted to go home. She was tired. Drained. And thirsty.

Water. She needed water. Turning, she headed for the nearest bar but suddenly remembered the focal point of Sam's lecture; the bartender extraordinaire. Before she could switch course, the man had secured her in his sights.

And smiled.

Her pulse skipped.

All-American juicy hamburger.

I'd take him solely for his looks.

Well not me, her thoughts hammered in revolt. I have everything I want in Aurelio, despite what Sam thinks. Anxious to avoid reminder of her friend's inflammatory commentary, she considered her options. She could fake a wave and head in the opposite direction. She skimmed her gaze past him and he waved.

And stared. Thoughts of escape evaporated. To walk away now would only pique his curiosity. She exhaled a heavy sigh. *Whatever*. The man was oblivious to their callous use of his person in their discussion. It had no bearing on the moment, so long as she permitted none.

Calming the momentary skitter in her chest with a deep breath, she straightened her shoulders with an indiscernible shake and walked over to his bar.

"What can I do you for?"

Jennifer stiffened.

"Another white wine spritzer?"

"No, thank you. I'd like a glass of water, please."

"With bubbles or without?"

"Without."

"Coming right up."

Jennifer noted that he smiled the entire time it took him to grasp a tumbler, fill it with ice, twist open a bottle of spring water and dump its entire contents into the awaiting glass. Pulling a white napkin from the top of the pile, he slid it under the glass and handed the ensemble over the bar counter.

"Here you go."

"Thank you."

"So, your friend told me you're an associate of Michael's."

"Yes." Uninterested in idle conversation, she glanced around.

He waited. With a smile.

The darned thing never seemed to leave him! And with no excuse for a hasty departure, she was unable to ignore him. "We're not exactly associates. We do work together, but he's one of my referring physicians."

"So you're not an internist?" he asked, wiping down the counter in front of him.

"No. I'm a cardiologist."

His eyes came alive with interest as though it was a significant fact, but he let the subject of specialties drop. "Mike's a great guy."

Jennifer thought it a bit presumptive of him to speak of his employer in such familiar terms. "Yes. Dr. Kingsley is a wonderful person and one of the most *respected* in his field."

He chuckled. "That he is."

Ready to move on from the conversation, she scanned the area, surprised the party remained in full swing. She checked the slim gold watch on her wrist. Wasn't it time to wind things down? And where was Sam?

Edging away from the bar, she made way as another guest placed an order for a *mojito*. Once again, the man went to work with an ease and fluidity that amazed her. She sipped from her drink. Watching him, she imagined he could serve drinks in his sleep it came so natural.

Working on the second cocktail, her thoughts fell back to Sam. He wasn't bad looking really, though she couldn't imagine what he and a date discussed over dinner. Bartending? The beach? By the looks of his tan, it was obvious he spent a lot of time outdoors. Boating? Fishing? That's what men did in their spare time, wasn't it? Volleyball in the sand?

Then golden hair seemed to leap out from his chest, ensnaring her attention. Before she could help herself, her vision rolled right over his collarbone, up along his neck to his well-shaven jaw line where she found herself wondering if his brown skin would feel as soft as it appeared. Inching further up, she bumped into his gaze.

He was staring at her expectantly. Knowingly.

"I should have known I'd find you here..."

Jennifer's pulse skipped—at least three beats—and she swallowed hard. Hot with embarrassment, she sliced her gaze to the floor. *What was she doing*?

Sam waltzed up, an empty martini glass in hand. "I've been looking all over for you."

"Yes, well," she said, her pulse slowing to a pound. "I doubt that very much but I *am* ready to go."

Had she really been checking out the bartender? Jennifer deposited her gaze into the glass of water. It must be the wine. Talk of Tony. She had one too many and it was affecting her behavior. Had to be.

Save for one minor detail.

She'd only had one.

"Oh, pooh." Sam slapped her empty martini glass on top of the bar. "Just when things were starting to pick up for me." She turned to the bartender and said, "Thanks for the drinks Jax, but it's time for Cinderella to return to her castle."

"Any slippers I should be looking for?" He responded to Sam, but again his eyes hovered about Jennifer—as though she had *encouraged* his attention. She glanced away.

"Not tonight. My Princess Charming here is driving me home and she's a stickler for loose ends. Broken crystal really gets under her skin if you know what I mean," Sam whispered loudly, followed by a wink.

Jennifer glared.

"Egads," Sam pulled back in mock alarm. "It appears I might be spending some time in the dungeon this evening!"

"Better you than me, Sam," he replied with pronounced relief, but the merry grin on his face belied any concern.

Refusing to play along—and wondering why her friend was on a first-name basis with the bartender—Jennifer set her water glass on the bar. "Let's go Cinderella. Your pumpkin is about to burst." She seized Sam by the elbow and steered her toward the door, a slew of mixed emotions colliding in her chest.

Chapter Four

Standing on the edge of the patio, outfitted in her standard fare of suit and heels, the sticky morning air served to thicken Jennifer's aggravation. Some friend.

Her mood knotted as strands of anger and exhaustion wound through her body. It was Sam's fault the dream was back. Nearly two years without a wink from the man, but last night her tycoon and his yacht had returned. Mostly distant references, spotty images of the Greek interspersed with those of Tony, the bartender from last night and some men she had never seen before in her life—it had been enough to rattle her clear out of rest.

And why?

Because Sam felt compelled to stick her nose where it didn't belong. She had no right to criticize Aurelio and no business comparing him to Tony. They had been kids, for heaven's sake! Wild and crazy yes, but with no responsibilities and no demands, of course they could act out in the moment. It was expected of teenagers, but not of adults.

And why her tycoon fellow entered the picture was anyone's guess. Especially considering she had Aurelio. According to her psychologist at the time, the dream suggested her need to open up and let someone into her life; her heart. She had spent too many years with her guard up, preventing her from realizing a deep and meaningful relationship; something Jennifer wanted more than anything. Having achieved the status of practicing physician, she wanted to develop the personal side of her life.

Heeding the analysis, she worked to open up her heart and reach out to others, pleased to then discover Aurelio. A good friend of her senior partner, the man had been there all along.

Now, engaged to be married, it made no sense the dream was back though it was ironic, she thought at once, struck by the similarities. Aurelio and her tycoon did resemble one another. Her mind narrowed in on the visions from last night. More than their light olive coloring and rich black hair, their mannerisms were quite similar, calm and sophisticated, subtle in speech. Both shared a taste for fine art and champagne. Both were affluent, amassed money well beyond their need...

Relieved by the commonalities, her thoughts picked up steam. *Perhaps it was a sign.* Not one for crediting the unconscious with more power than it deserved, but Jennifer found it intriguing how dreams could parallel real life. Almost comforting, as hers seemed to validate the decision to marry Aurelio.

Irritation flared. A decision Sam had better get used to. It simply won't do to have her husband and best friend at odds for the rest of her life. "Beauty meets beast" should be limited to the movie screen, not the dinner table.

She expelled a sigh. Much like her yard. Jennifer's shoulders slumped. Alongside the meticulously restored home and the recently refurbished pool, her yard was a wasteland of dirt. Sandy gray, mounded with anthills, the grass overrun by weeds. It looked like a junkyard.

Her stomach twisted. It was no place to host a wedding.

From above, a rapid burst of tweets pierced the quiet, fusing into two long slow chirps, followed by another higher-pitched tempo which cut across the tree tops. Then silence. From the distance slid in a long low whistle.

Then again, silence.

A symphony of nature.

The favorite expression of her mother's dropped Jennifer into the hollows of morning. With a thud. There had been a beautiful garden, a host of roses and gardenias, hummingbirds and butterflies, all working together in complete harmony. Jennifer easily recalled the vivid fragrance of gardenia which drenched the yard in spring, followed by the heavy perfume of jasmine. Throughout summer her mother's roses took center stage, an endless supply of fresh cut flowers for the home.

But more than anything, Jennifer remembered the birds. From every corner they stood watch, peering out from their birdhouses, fluttering about their perches. The image of her mother fussing over them like children drew a small smile from her lips. The garden had been her personal retreat. *Her little secret*, as she was fond of saying, proclaiming it was the simple joys that created simple pleasures, and simple living was the key to a good life.

Her father agreed, but from the comfort of a garden bench. Something her mother didn't seem to mind. She didn't need him to share her devotion. His mere company was enough.

Jennifer inhaled, deep and full, the motion soothing as she longed for the same connection. Today, as she prepared for her new life, she wanted to capture the same spirit of love in her yard and in her life. She and Aurelio would make this their home, beginning each and every day with the same devotion, in harmony with nature.

Jennifer emptied her lungs in a ragged breath. But the yard was nowhere near ready. She swung her wrist up and checked the time. Eight thirty-nine.

And it never would be, if she didn't get started and soon.

The sudden sting on her ankle bone snapped her attention in two. Ants. Stepping back, she searched for the source. Located at the base of a post she noticed a small pile of sand forming, a trail of dark brown bodies moving toward it from the patio steps in a near straight line. She groaned aloud. Enough already. Jennifer whirled around and marched into her house, slinging the French door closed behind her.

Where was he? Didn't he understand she had a schedule to keep? She had patients to round on, a cath scheduled for ten. If this tardiness was a sign of things to come, she may be forced to reconsider her choice of landscaper.

A luxury she could ill afford, but may find necessary.

She strode over to the kitchen counter, grabbed her leather bag and contemplated leaving. She'd leave a note for him to call and reschedule, perhaps come back this afternoon. She dumped her purse onto the stone counter and spewed a sigh.

She couldn't do it this afternoon. She had a dinner with Aurelio and tomorrow was Sunday. If she left now, she'd have to wait until Monday before even getting started.

Her hand tightened around the strap of her bag and she pressed her lips into a firm line. *Darn him.* She was stuck, and she hated that she was stuck. If she didn't need this job started *yesterday*, she would leave this minute. Call someone else and fire this man before he drew his first breath of protest.

She glanced at her watch again, reality thrashing her threats to pieces. But she couldn't. There was no time.

At the sound of her doorbell, Jennifer blew out her breath.

She shoved the purse aside and crossed the living room in seconds. We'll make this quick and to the point. I know what I want. I'll convey it in clear and concise terms and be on my way.

Inhaling a chestful of air, she tried to regain some of her calm. Losing her patience with the man would not serve her. Calm, she reminded herself. Cool. Grasping the handle of her door, she controlled the release of her breath like Sam taught her and regained control. *Sam.* Spits of irritation flew. There was another must-do. She deserved an earful and would get it the first minute she could give it to her.

Inhaling once again, she forced the stress to loosen its cranky hold and opened the door. The sight of him shot holes through her composure. "What are *you* doing here?"

Surprise filled his eyes. "What...?"

This was the last straw. If Sam thought she was being cute, Jennifer was going to wax her scalp and rub it with alcohol. "Look," she said, clenching her hand around the door knob as her jaw tightened. "I don't know why you're here or what my friend Sam has up her sleeve, but I am expecting someone at the moment and I cannot deal with you right now."

"*What are you talking about?*"

The bartender from the night before stood firm, his confusion appearing to be genuine. "I'm talking about you and Sam—last night at the party?" she reminded. "You two were carrying on about who knows what, but what I *do* know," she underscored, "is that I have an appointment to keep."

His expression revealed nothing.

"Listen, if you're here to ask me out, I'm sorry but you've wasted your time."

He chuckled.

Her irritation curdled. "Something amusing?"

"You. This." He gestured about the courtyard entry, brushed a hand through his tangle of hair, then centered his gaze on her. "I'm not here to ask you out on a date—though if the thought ever were to cross my mind, you've made your answer quite clear." Quietly self-assured, he laughed again and rested hands on his hips. "I'm here on business."

"Business?"

"I'm Jackson Montgomery. The landscaper." He smiled, pride brightening his expression. "I'm your appointment."

"*Landscaper?*" She gaped, feeling the complete idiot. "You're not a landscaper, you're a bartender!"

"Only on the side."

Jennifer didn't mean to insult the man, but facts were facts. You serve up drinks at a party, you're a bartender. She grazed over his appearance. Dressed in jeans and a golf shirt, he didn't even attempt to portray a professional image—if that was indeed his goal, though she'd still venture to bet Sam had something to do with his being here. The woman could be a pit bull when she aimed to cause trouble.

"I'm sorry." She shook her head and stepped back. "There must be some kind of mistake." Darn if this wouldn't set her back. Images of her mother flashed across her mind, mixing with those of her barren backyard, dead leaves floating across the pool's surface, the awful air of desolation...

"No mistake," he replied with a smile. "Montgomery Landscape, at your service."

"Look," she said, breaking from the gloomy scenario, her manners waning fast. "I'm in the market for a landscape architect, not a lawn service."

"I'm him. Michael told me what you needed and I can deliver."

Michael. Reality crashed. She had trusted him. How could he do this to her? Swimming in turmoil, she stared blankly at the man on her threshold. The desperate part of her was tempted to accept him and move forward. Lawn guy, landscape designer, what was the difference at this point? She needed grass and plants and she needed them now.

But as usual, the sensible part of her took control. No, she couldn't settle. This job was too important to make do with less than the best. It had to be right and it had to be perfect. "I'm truly sorry. There must have been a miscommunication." But how? Michael understood the details of her mother's condition, he understood her motivation to get this done. *How could he have sent this man?*

"Is there a problem?"

She blinked. Jackson stood, casual and confident.

He was waiting.

Yes, there was a problem and time was wasting. "Listen," she said, brisker than she intended but under the circumstances, it couldn't be helped. "I'm sorry you wasted your time, really I am, but I'm running late for the hospital." She held up a hand between them before he could object. "Don't worry. I'll let Michael know you stopped by and while I appreciate the effort, things didn't work out."

He shifted forward, the first hint of discomfort settling in his soft brown eyes. "Can we talk for a minute? If you give me the chance, I think I can clear this up."

Jennifer understood. He was flustered. He probably didn't want to lose the job, the money a big deal in his scheme of things. While her heart went out to him, she knew direct and honest was the best course of action. "Mr. Montgomery, is it?"

He nodded, and she in turn smiled. "This is a big job. I need a skilled designer to create a master plan for the entire property. It entails rendering drawings using an in-depth knowledge of plant and foliage selection, color and placement..." Her line of thought coasted off-message as anticipation surged in his eyes. Rather than appear disappointed, the man seemed encouraged. "It's a complicated situation," she clarified. "I need the job done in a hurry."

An added stress, surely to overwhelm the likes of you, though she'd never say as much. "I need a guaranteed finish date. There is no room for error," she said, her intent clear: you would be held completely accountable if the job didn't progress as specified.

"I'm your man."

"But you tend bar," she blurted.

"I'm a landscaper," he corrected. "My bar-tending is part-time."

"Yes, of course..." She gave a quick nod, regretting the insensitive slip. He seemed nice enough. If he wanted to work on the side to earn extra money, fine. Good for him.

But not on her time. It was too valuable. Summoning her most polite smile, Jennifer retreated further into the house with a feeble wave. "Well, like I said, I have to get to the hospital. But thanks for coming by..."

"That's it?" He held his hands up in question. "You're not even going to hear me out?"

She shook her head, and her smile floundered. "I don't think so, I'm sorry." When he didn't move, she began to close the door. "So if you'll excuse me—"

"Mike really missed the mark on this one."

The door stopped.

"He said you'd be a pleasure, a real exception to the word client." Jackson dropped his hands to his sides. "But I guess I'll never get the chance to find out." Turning his back on her, the man took his leave.

Michael. Jennifer squeezed her eyes shut. He insisted he had gone all out to get this landscaper for her. Called in a favor, were his exact words. Said it was the same man who did wonders at his place. He was certain he could do the same for her.

Opening her eyes, she watched as Jackson Montgomery climbed into the beat-up old truck, slamming the door closed. *But how could he be the guy*? It wasn't possible, was it? That fellow couldn't landscape a child's sand box let alone an incredible estate home like Michael's.

Could he?

And how was she going to explain her refusal without offending Michael? Uh, sorry to pressure you for a referral, but I've decided against it. *Against him*.

Jennifer heaved a sigh. The truck sputtered to life and accelerated in her drive, wheels screeching out onto the street. Hope flattened as she closed the front door. Now what?

# # #

Jax gunned the engine of his 1984 pickup, and peeled out of her driveway. Now there's a surprise. Mike bragged this Dr. Jennifer Hamilton was a notch above the rest. She'd be an easy job, though it was to be done in a hurry. But none of that resembled the woman who had just dismissed him. She was as judgmental as they came, prickly as a rose bush.

As beautiful, too, particularly those incredible blue eyes. They had jumped out at him last night. Add creamy white skin combined with her dark brown hair...the combination made her appear fragile.

Until she opened her mouth. Crisp and curt, he bet she didn't have a fragile bone in her body. And it was clear what she thought of *him*. He was a bartender trying to earn a buck on the side. A guy who cut grass—not a professional designer, a man who created works of art; living, breathing master-pieces. She may be good-looking, but dismissing him before he had a chance to explain?

That was unacceptable. With a hard turn to the right, he closed the short distance to Dixie Highway and with an over-acceleration, punched the truck into the flow of traffic.

Yanking the cell phone from the clip on his jeans, he punched in Mike's number.

He would leave that thorny job to someone else.

His call was answered on the second ring. "Jax."

"Hey Mike."

"How's it going?"

"Not so good. I had my appointment with Dr. Hamilton this morning, but I don't think it's going to work out."

"What do you mean? The job isn't that involved, is it? Jennifer assured me she only wanted grass, a few plants and some flowers."

"We didn't get that far. She refused my services."

"*What*?"

Jackson chuckled now, his anger dimming with every mile he placed between himself and the good doctor. "I know. It's hard to believe there's a woman alive resistant to my charm," he continued, his sense of humor buoyed by the familiar camaraderie of friendship. "But I think we've found one."

"What happened?"

"Seems she remembers me from last night, and isn't convinced a bartender can handle the job."

"Didn't you explain?"

"She didn't give me a chance."

"That doesn't sound like Jennifer."

"Actually..." He paused. "She stopped me cold."

"I don't get it."

Jax did. She has an image of what she wants in a landscape architect and he didn't match up.

"Let me talk to her. I'll see her at the hospital later this morning and we can straighten this whole thing out."

"I appreciate it Mike, but don't go to any trouble on my behalf. I've got other jobs going right now. I'm okay if I lose this one."

"Hell, it's not you I'm worried about! It's Jennifer. She needs this job done in a hurry and there's no one better to make that happen than you, Jax."

Though pleased by the vote of confidence, he wasn't so sure. Dr. Hamilton was not going to be an easy woman to work for—or around—as the case may prove, especially under the pressure of time.

"Let me think about it, Mike."

"Jax—I need you to do more than think about it. She needs you."

He laughed, and let go of the earlier insults entirely. "She doesn't need me. There are plenty of good landscapers out there who can handle the job, but thanks for the good word. I appreciate it."

Mike spoke to someone on his end then said into the phone, "Listen Jax, I've got to run. Tell me you'll reconsider."

Jackson took pause, ambivalence churning in his gut. He wouldn't be where he was today if it weren't for Mike's referrals. And he was damn close to where he was going.

Because of this man. "Okay. If it's that important to you, I'll do it."

Let's just hope I don't regret it.

Chapter Five

Jennifer dialed Michael's number on the way out her door, her stomach tumbling with nerves. It was imperative she apologize for declining his recommendation—though she still couldn't accept that Jackson Montgomery was the person responsible for Michael's gorgeous landscaping. His yard was incredible! How was it possible?

Impossible. The man who showed up at her door wasn't a professional. He didn't carry a notebook or portfolio. He wasn't conducting a true business operation.

Something must have changed. Michael's yard had been done years ago. There must have been a partner at the time, someone who made all the decisions, unbeknownst to Michael, for which this fellow took all the credit.

Frustration eased. Poor Michael. Trusting as a new fawn, he was out waving this Jackson's banner, bringing him more and more clients to bilk without the first clue he was aiding and abetting a con. She slipped the phone against her ear and awaited his answer.

Far be it from her to drown his good deeds with cold water, but she had no intention of falling prey to Mr. Montgomery's swindle.

"Michael Kingsley."

"Hello, Michael."

"Jennifer—I talked to Jax. What happened over there?"

So, he was a step ahead of her. Her stomach cinched tight. God only knows what his version sounded like. But it was irrelevant. Her task was to make Michael understand the underlying issue—the man's obvious lack of expertise—and to do so without insulting him, her friend. She would assure Michael the setback was not a problem. She would find someone else.

A daunting prospect, one looming heavy on her mind.

"We didn't get off to a good start, Michael," she said, forging ahead, proud of the calm and professional ring to her voice. "But it's just as well. It wouldn't have worked out between us, though I appreciate your help with—"

"Why not?"

The million dollar question, she mused.

"Jennifer." Michael's voice picked up strength as he barreled forward, "Jax is the best in the business. I've seen other jobs he's done and he's amazing. He can finish your place ten times faster than anyone—and he'll do it right, for a fair price. Trust me, you need him."

Bless his heart, he was only trying to help, but she didn't *need* this Jackson. If he could get it done, so could someone else. Time constraints or not. "I'm sorry, Michael, but I think I'd feel better if I knew I was dealing with a larger firm," she said, hoping to defer any insult which he may take personally. "Aurelio has a few names." Aurelio knew no one, but she would not succumb to the half-baked efforts of

this Jackson fellow. They'd just have to find someone.

"But please, don't worry. I'll get it done. I just
wanted you to know how much I appreciate your and
Laurencia's help. It means a lot to me, really."

"I don't understand, Jennifer. What happened?"

"Nothing happened," she said, her discomfort
mounting.

"The bartending thing? It was a favor to me.
Jax's a good friend of mine and offered to fill in when
the catering company came up short on staff."

Good friend? Surprise kicked at her chest.
Favor?

Michael rolled past her pause. "He used to
bartend for hotel banquets, back when he was
establishing his landscaping business. That's not a
problem, is it?"

"Of course not," she answered, before realizing
that is exactly what she had used against him.

"Your job isn't that big, right? You said you
were only looking for a couple of small plants and
flowers?"

"Yes, but..."

"He's the guy, Jennifer. Jax has contacts with an
established nursery and can guarantee fast delivery—
unless you wanted something special."

"I don't really..." she heard herself say.

"Then all he needs is an idea of how many plants
you want. He'll take it from there."

While she knew Michael's aim was pure, she felt
backed into a corner. For her to say no now would
most definitely cause offense, something she could
not do.

Not to this man. Her heart fell. "You're a life-saver, Michael."

"Anything for you, Jennifer. You know Laurencia and I are there for you."

"Thank you," she said, but there was no pleasure in her gratitude. Only ambivalence, tinged with regret. "I know you are and I appreciate it so much." She paused, nowhere left to maneuver, to escape, she said, "I'll call him. He can stop back this afternoon."

"Let me do it for you. Will five work?"

"Fine." *Perfect*, she rued.

But four o'clock that afternoon found Jennifer getting ready to start another case. And while she hated to cancel last minute, she had to reschedule. From the darkened quiet of the cath lab control room, she dialed Jackson's cell number. Rubbing her forehead to ease the headache building within, she avoided eye contact with the staff on the other side of the glass partition. Busy working to move her patient onto the operating table, what did they care she was skulking back, tail between her legs.

As she waited for him to answer, Jennifer felt her nerves rev up in anticipation. If he chose to be cocky and shove an attitude her way—something he may feel entitled to do—it would only make matters worse. Eating her words did not suit her well and had she been firmer with Michael this morning, she wouldn't be in this position at all.

Nor would she be any closer to getting the job done.

"Jackson Montgomery."

"Hello. This is Dr. Hamilton calling."

"Hello Dr. Hamilton."

She detected no animosity in his voice, no gloating. "I apologize," she began with steady resolve, "but I need to cancel our appointment for this afternoon. I'm still at the hospital and won't be able to get away for at least another hour, probably more."

"No problem. Should I come by at seven, or hold off until tomorrow?"

She balked. Laborers didn't work on Sundays, did they?

Michael must have insisted, she thought at once, feeling a wave of obligation wash over her shoulders. He knew she was pressed for time and must have compelled Mr. Montgomery to be available. Jennifer winced from the quick stab of guilt. She wasn't the one pressed for time. *It was her mother*.

Too tired to brush the despair from her voice, she agreed, "Tomorrow, if it's all right with you." She expelled a sigh. "Say around ten?"

"Ten it is."

As Jennifer hung up the phone, she was struck by his professional tone, his willingness to accommodate. Neither was consistent with his surfer boy image.

Placing the phone in her pocket, she was tempted to call Aurelio and cancel their dinner tonight. But she couldn't. It had been over a week since their last.

# # #

Aurelio reached over and squeezed her hand, the gesture warm, reassuring. "It will be fine, sweetheart. The yard will turn out better than you expect, you'll see."

Staring down at the gold-rimmed china, chunks of lobster covered in cream sauce, Jennifer wanted to believe him. Hopeful, positive, he sounded so sure.

"Michael's a stickler for details. If he thinks the man can handle the job, then I'm inclined to agree."

She glanced at him, and relaxed into her first real smile of the evening. Michael was certainly particular with a penchant for detail. "Of course," she replied, willing the silky glow of the restaurant to ease her doubt.

Aurelio had made reservations at her favorite Chez Vendome, a Coral Gables institution, but its rich, indulgent atmosphere was no match for stress she felt over the wedding.

Aurelio smiled. "You know what you want. Communicate it to him and all will be well. Trust me."

Gazing into dark brown eyes, she sighed. "Do I have a choice?"

"None." He laughed. "Absolutely none."

She tried to laugh with him. Almost two years ago Aurelio Villarreal had walked into her life and changed it for the better. He never wavered over the last year, during the worst of her mother's diagnosis, and he wouldn't waver now. "None, he says. Absolutely none. Well, that is reassuring!"

But like it or not, Aurelio was right. She had no choice.

"Michael hasn't let you down yet, has he?"

"No," she murmured, and cast her gaze down toward her plate. That much was true.

But still. Preparations for the wedding were crushing her calm, her mother's condition providing the crank. It was a lethal combination, but to admit as much made her feel like a heel. Like a thundercloud looming over her big day, it undermined the joy she should be feeling and instead, made her feel like a schoolgirl wearing a new dress. One who must continually glance over her shoulder in her rush to avoid the downpour, keenly aware of the emotional meltdown that would surely follow if she didn't make it to class on time.

"Sweetheart, relax. Everything will turn out, you'll see."

Jennifer dragged her gaze back to him. Was she that transparent?

"Now listen. I want to discuss the opening."

Grateful for a change in subject, she brushed her own thoughts aside.

"We've added a few artists to the list."

"Really?" An avid art collector, his latest venture was a gallery specifically geared to showcase new and upcoming talent. Prominently located in South Beach's art deco district, *Illuminations* offered the chance of a lifetime for budding artists. Not only to display their work, but to meet Aurelio's extensive clientele.

It was a priceless opportunity.

"Yes. Two from Ft. Lauderdale and one is actually a student transferring down from New York."

"What type of work do they do?"

As usual, when Aurelio discussed artists his face lit up, and it was then she found him most attractive. Raven-black hair was cut in impeccable layers, a length stopping just shy of his collar. Full black brows appeared flawlessly manicured, yet were completely natural, giving his face striking definition. His features were soft, much like his fine olive skin and where his smile was quick and brilliant, his creative mind proved more of the same.

Taking his pristine white napkin, Aurelio dabbed the corner of his mouth, then returned the linen to his lap. "There have been some interesting new developments as well."

"Developments?" His expression had closed just a bit, the flicker of candlelight swayed in his eyes.

"Yes. I've scheduled a tour."

"Tour?"

"Yes. There have been quite a few international buyers expressing an interest in our project. More than we imagined."

"Excellent," she replied, confused by his reticence.

This brought a smile to his face. "Yes, it is." He reached over and took her hand. Rubbing a thumb lightly back and forth across her palm, he said, "It's been very rewarding to know my efforts are getting noticed."

"Noticed?"

"There is a well-known philanthropist extremely interested in continuing our concept, linking with some of the universities in his country."

In his country?

"He feels it is vital to the development of his nation if young artists are granted the opportunity to participate. I've been discussing the possibility of setting up similar galleries in key cities, encouraging as many amateur artists to apply as possible."

"What country are we talking here...?"

Chapter Six

"The Gambia."

Jennifer balked. *"The Gambia*?" South America, Central America, she could imagine—but The Gambia? Where was that?

Aurelio's eyes sparked with excitement. "Yes. Surprising, isn't it? Did you know the continent of Africa has seen one of the largest increases in tourism?"

Obviously not she mused, shock filtering through her limbs as she tried to absorb what he was saying. She had no idea.

"While other destinations are experiencing drops in the number of visitors, Africa is on the rise. And they want to expound upon this by raising the value of culture within their continent. For so many years, they have struggled through economic and political strife and they see this as their opportunity to introduce the new face of contemporary Africa."

Wow.

"They're raising the bar, both economically and socially." He paused. "The two really are tied together you know."

She withdrew her hand from his. Yes, it sounded reasonable, though she didn't know much about Africa at all. But she supposed, if one were developing a country, it made sense it should be a well-rounded effort.

"It's an exciting time for them and they have asked me to help."

Jennifer hesitated, unsettled by his fervent tone. "Help?"

"They want me involved at the ground level."

But peering at him more closely, she wondered exactly what did he mean.

"The first of several art galleries will be established along the coast of Africa."

First of several?

"We'll begin in The Gambia. It's a small country located on the west coast, within Senegal. A sliver of a country really, but they're working to increase their stature within the world and it's been decided to start there. Isn't it exciting?"

Exciting? "Yes," she mumbled, a million thoughts racing through her mind. Did he plan to travel there? Was it safe?

How well did he know these people? Did they speak English? Were they modern? Staring into his eager expression, eyes filled with more enthusiasm than she had seen in a long while, Jennifer couldn't help but be pleased for him. It was an exciting prospect, she couldn't disagree.

But what did it mean for the two of them?

"When do you start? I mean, do you go there? Will you work with them from here?"

"Of course my first priority is the opening of *Illuminations*. But once gallery operations are underway, I can hire someone to oversee the day-to-day business, which would free up my schedule considerably."

"Hire someone? What kind of commitment are we talking in Africa?"

He looked at her as though it were a ridiculous question. "Setting up a gallery doesn't happen overnight, darling. There is location to consider, not only in regard to the student artists, but retail areas, airports, train stations. It's an enormous undertaking to say the least. Our galleries will be at the heart of bringing art and culture to a more prominent position within their society."

"Yes, but—"

"You can't expect me to agree to a proposition of this magnitude without committing my full attention."

"No," she mumbled, abandoning the fork on her plate. "Of course not." Digesting the news of the evening, there was no room for food.

"We're building a foundation for the future. South Africa is no longer the only contemporary nation that has seen a boom. Many of the nations along the west coast have enjoyed increased prosperity as well." He paused, and held her gaze. "It's an incredible opportunity."

"It sounds wonderful," she agreed, put off by his vigor and tone, heightening with each and every word—every promise.

Wonderful, except where did she fit in? Once they were married, did he expect her to drop everything and follow him?

"The exposure alone will do wonders to raise the bar, encourage creativity and innovation. Remember, it's the youth of a nation that will dictate its direction."

Jennifer nodded. All true, but what about *their* life together? Her mother's last days?

He grasped the bowl of his wineglass and leaned forward. "Once we're married, we'll travel the continent. We'll see and visit places completely different from the states, from everything we know. Think of the discoveries we'll make, between art and music, food and drink." He raised his glass as though in toast. "Why, you'll be in veritable heaven, scouring their markets for the next interesting piece of furniture for our new home."

Our new home.

"The opportunities are endless but first, the opening of Illuminations."

Illuminations.

"Then, what do you say to a honeymoon in the Canary Islands. We can indulge in one another for a lazy week, then head south for the first of many tours across the continent."

Of Africa.

"The perfect combination of work and play."

Perfect. Somehow that wasn't the word that came to mind when she envisioned this dream he was painting. Africa. She didn't have time to travel to Africa!

He pulled her hand from the table and placed a delicate kiss on her knuckles, then another next to her diamond engagement ring. "Wouldn't you agree?"

Staring at him, reeling from the quick-fire of change he was hurling, she was struck by the glitter in his eyes. Alive, his spirit brimming with life, with passion, his eyes sparkled like the jewels in an overhead chandelier. Her gaze dropped to the ring on her hand.

The two carat stone seemed dim by comparison. "I think I need to concentrate on the wedding before I can consider honeymoon destinations."

He beamed. "May is a beautiful time of the year in the islands, I hear."

Jennifer forced a smile. "I'm sure it is." Gathering the napkin from her lap, she placed it alongside her dish and said, "Listen, sweetheart, do you mind if I head home? It's late and I have to meet the landscaper in the morning."

Aurelio sat back in his chair, moving on seamlessly to the next stage. "Of course not. I really should be getting along as well. There's still so much to do yet, before the opening next week."

Illuminations. Africa. Landscape. Wedding. A mild shudder raced across her shoulders. *Her mother*. Yes, there was still so much left to do—and discuss— but not now. She didn't have the stomach for any more grief than was already on her plate.

# # #

Showered and dressed in a plain white cotton tank and tan linen Capris, her dark brown hair pulled back into a neat ponytail, Jennifer was ready to greet the landscaper.

Again. Pulling in a deep breath, she waited outside in her front courtyard and prepared for what was sure to be an awkward meeting. She had several ideas for her landscape and hoped he was ready to listen. No need to waste time in the planning phase when there was so much work to be done. In fact, she was going to insist he start with the actual planting as soon as possible.

Startled by a loud pop, she whirled around to see the beat-up truck pull into the driveway. Her pulse quickened. Polite and firm. And smile, she reminded herself, as though coaching one on the finer points of business negotiation.

To be honest, a part of her wanted to prove his first assessment wrong. Michael had not "missed the mark" about her. Surprise had gotten the best of her, but it would not do so today. Stepping forward, she opened the narrow entry gate as he pulled around the tight circular drive, then waited on the top step. She was a professional and she'd prove it.

The engine cut off with a sputter, and the door made a horrible squeak as he opened it, causing her to cringe. He seemed oblivious, sliding out effortlessly, slamming the door closed.

He made haste in his approach. "Good morning," he said a skip to his voice. Jeans and white T-shirt, he evidently didn't feel the need to dress for the occasion. Nor did he bother to run a brush through his hair. She noted it was the same unruly mess, most tufts sticking straight up, competing with others that jogged left and right. *Did he really think the style was appealing*?

She gazed down at him from the top platform. "Good morning."

He leaped up the three steps and extended his hand. "Jackson Montgomery," he introduced, as though for the first time.

She took his hand, startled by the jarring softness of his skin. How could this be a laborer's hand? The skin was so smooth, much like his complexion. Shouldn't both be weathered from hours spent working under the sun? "Dr. Jennifer Hamilton." She saw that his smile held the same easygoing quality she remembered from the other night, completely unaffected and under no stress, despite their prior fallout.

Just as one would expect from a lawn guy who tended bar on the side. Notwithstanding, her manners urged courtesy. "Allow me to apologize for yesterday." She pulled her hand from his grasp. "I wasn't expecting to see a familiar face."

"No big deal," he said quickly. His hands went straight to his hips and settled along his belt. "Mike explained you've been working overtime. It can get to the best of us."

All business, he was very matter-of-fact. Tolerant.

Had to be. *Because of her.* Her behavior had been less than cordial and quite unlike her, though he had no way of knowing as much. He simply saw difficult and was working around her. But grateful there was no attitude with which to contend she replied, "Thank you."

Must be Michael, she mused again, gazing into friendly brown eyes. The man could be like a papa grizzly when it came to his friends.

"You have a nice place here. A large lot, by Coral Gables standards."

"Thank you." She glanced around. "Yes, it is."

"Mike said you recently completed some remodeling." He looked up at the house, took a sweeping survey, then returned his gaze to her. "I like what you've done."

Navy blue awnings, more flaps of canvas speared by black iron rods presented a pleasing contrast against the warm yellow, almost golden color of the exterior. Classic red clay barrel roof tiles coordinated with the brick driveway, and keystone blocks fanned out from the front windows and door. It was classic Gables, and when combined with the enclosed courtyard, she agreed. It made for a memorable entry.

She nodded, slightly uneasy in the spotlight of his praise. Streets flanked by spectacular red-orange Poinciana trees and lined with coral-hued haciendas, Mediterranean architecture was the norm here. "Yes, well, I wanted to keep within the style of the neighborhood."

"The house looks to have been built in the 1920's."

"1926, to be exact," she replied, suppressing her surprise. How did he know such detail? Was he from around here?

"This architecture was pretty standard fare back then," he continued, frank and unpretentious. "They used a lot of limestone and coral, forming it into arches, accents mostly of wrought iron." The man basically described her home. "Nice and private, too," he added.

"I put the iron gates in." Ensconced behind a four-foot wall, the top trimmed in keystone, her driveway was accessed through an intricately formed wrought iron gate. "Over there, as well," she said, and pointed to the driveway passing alongside the home. "That leads to a garage apartment in the back."

"You have a good eye." He flipped his full attention back to her. "It's perfectly in line with the character of the Gables and what makes this city unique, right along with Coconut Grove." He shot his thumb upward. "And that balcony is phenomenal." Jackson smiled, clearly impressed.

"Yes," she said, taken aback by the extent of his enthusiasm. "It's one of the reasons I purchased the home. The balcony and courtyard here are what sold me." Sequestered behind another four-foot wall, capped with a single row of roof tile, the small courtyard acted as an outdoor foyer, adding more privacy and charm. Coral Gables was the only place she could ever imagine calling home. She grew up here, three blocks over.

"I agree," he said. "They really make a statement. You have good taste."

Her pulse skittered. "Well," she began, smoothing the back of her pants. "I have some ideas for the yard that I'd like to discuss."

"Great. Why don't we start here, out front?"

Jennifer had prepared to start with the back, but acquiesced. About to proceed, she realized he was empty-handed. "Don't you want to take notes?"

"No, I'm fine."

Fine? How was he going to remember everything she told him to do? But with no easy way to voice her concern, Jennifer reluctantly began, by pointing to the empty space within the center of the circular drive. "For starters, I was thinking maybe one of those Sago palm trees should go there. I feel it would make a great centerpiece for the front yard."

"A Sago is a nice choice," Jackson said. "But I'd also consider a fountain. A three-tiered, Italian-style fountain with nice curves and a large basin encircling it. Around the base," he gestured with his hands, "I'd like to see a low shrub, or some flowers. I think it would add to the romantic feel of your home, yet stand out in its own right."

Startled by the suggestion, she tried to cover her surprise by fixing on the image he was forming in her mind. Italian fountain? Bushes and flowers around the base?

Jackson smiled again. "People are drawn in by fountains. Sort of an invitation to come on in and relax. Enjoy. I'd also add some flower boxes," he turned toward the house, hands outlining them like a mime. "Beneath the windows. They do wonders for bringing in warmth, both inside and out."

Romantic feel, flower boxes, warmth...

Jennifer stared at him, knocked off guard not only by his choice of words, but the accompanying sparkle in his eyes.

Was this really coming from him?

"You already have a natural wall of privacy in place there." He pointed off to the dense clusters of skinny palm trees on the opposite side of the driveway, then turned to the other side, a mishmash of plants bunched around the base of more palm trees. "But I'd like to see that area cleaned up a little. Maybe add a few ginger and ferns. Once rooted, they'll spread, and do a nice job of filling in the gaps between trees." He stopped as though a thought occurred to him. "Do you have an irrigation system?"

"Yes," she answered abruptly, honed in. "Both front and back."

"Great. It will help to establish your new plants." Glancing around one more time, Jackson suggested, "If you're ready we can head to the back."

"Around this way," she said, her mind still buzzing with images of fountains and flowers. Curious to what he would propose next, she led him to the pool area via the driveway.

"Those Oaks are some *real* beauties."

She followed the direction of his finger. "They are lovely," she agreed, steering her line of thought to one of the few positives, at the moment.

As Jackson rounded the corner and stopped dead. The smile dropped from his face. "That's depressing."

Jennifer sighed. It was one of the things she hated most about moving in before the landscaping was finished. Like living in limbo, it was incomplete; a mix of beauty and waste.

A disorganized mess. She frowned. "The same contractor who remodeled the house built the pool, so naturally they were completed together."

"Not to worry." Jackson shrugged off the brief dip into negative territory and his smile was back. "We'll get this yard in shape before you know it!"

If only she felt as certain.

"Does that wall run along your property line?"

"Yes," she confessed. Like being seen without makeup, he was observing her yard at its worst, particularly the huge blemish—the ugly, cracked back wall. "Unfortunately. It's an awful eyesore. The workers cleared the weeds from it and found the stucco is in need of serious repair. They're scheduled to fix it next week and then I plan on painting it the same color as the house, maybe put a bench or something in front of it."

She turned to him for his reaction, almost woeful at the prospect. "I could tear it down, if you think it might help."

Jackson looked aghast. "Oh no, that's a definite asset!"

She scrunched her brow. "*Asset*? How on earth do you figure?"

His expression brightened. "I'd like to put in a wall fountain, surrounded by colorful Spanish tiles and a half round basin on the ground. About midway up." Once again, his hands were working through the air as he seemed to be thinking on his feet, encouraging her to envision the project. "A splash ledge, maybe in the shape of a giant clam shell." He made a wavy motion with his hands. "Keep it simple, but elegant." He looked to her as though seeking confirmation.

Jennifer squinted, trying to imagine it as he described. "You like fountains," she said dully. While she considered herself a positive person, she found it hard to match his enthusiasm. Living with this mess took a toll on one's outlook.

"I love fountains. Water is good for the soul," he said, words flowing from him like a river of poetry. "It's a powerful cleansing force that heals anything from stress to illness and everything in between. For added texture, we can place some climbing fig on either end." He paused, as though waiting for her to catch up. "It makes for an attractive, dense wall covering."

As the sun eased past the treetops, she raised a hand to shield her eyes. The artist in her was embarrassed she couldn't keep up with his vision. Intricate, emotion-provoking, it was clear his ideas for the property were superior to her own.

"The pool is a good size, the shape simple." A rectangle with inverted corners. "Gets plenty of sunlight—an important thing to consider, as it dictates the mood of the pool." Jackson flashed an approving smile. "And a pool full of sunshine is like a party on demand!"

Yes, she nodded, thinking absolutely not. This was to be her sanctuary, not party central.

He curled a finger around his lips. "I like the paver pool deck. It coordinates well with the driveway and roof, and the keystone coping completes the look. I see a couple of statues at the far corners." He pointed out the imaginary fixtures. "Some small cherubs, nothing elaborate, or maybe some lions."

He framed the area with his hands again, a photographer assessing his shot. "I can imagine a few terra-cotta planters filled with dark green shrubs." Jackson stopped, as though it had just occurred to him to ask her opinion. "Do you lean toward a manicured look or more natural and free?"

"Natural," she replied, though he most probably took her for the manicured type. She'd always preferred the natural fall of plants and flowers, growing as nature intended them.

"I assume you're planning on using a pro-fessional yard service, to take care of the property for you?"

"Yes," she replied, taking offense to the insult she thought she detected in his voice. "I work. I don't have time to take care of a lawn." And Aurelio would no sooner cut the grass than tune his car engine. His time was too valuable. In fact, he chose high-rise living on South Beach for that very reason.

"No problem. But if you change your mind, I design a garden to live by."

She gaped at him. "What?"

"Live your garden." He slapped both hands back to his hips, slipping fingers into the front pockets.

She assumed the concept was universal, though she had no idea what it meant.

Jackson merely smiled.

Not a cloud in the sky, it was growing uncomfortably warm. While she may not know, he didn't have to know she didn't know. "Of course. A garden to live by."

"It's my own slogan."

Her pulse tripped over the blunder.

"It describes the essence of how I design. Your garden should be a reflection of you." He paused, his eyes and interest taking her in more fully. "It should mirror your image of leisure, enjoyment. It's the place where you can unwind, relax... Do nothing if you choose...or everything—depending on your personality." He smiled as though a secret was unwinding between them. "Some clients want a party atmosphere in their backyard, while others want a tranquil environment, where they can escape the hustle and bustle of the city, the office. The goal varies, but the heart of the garden is the same."

What Jackson was describing, seemed more like a slice of psychology than landscape design.

He glanced around, a quick survey of the grounds, then settled his gaze on her. He smiled and his voice dropped to quiet tones. "It should be a place where you want to spend your time. If we succeed, the job of maintenance won't seem like a job at all. Rather than a chore, you'll enjoy the upkeep of your space. Weed a little here, prune a little there..." Dancing brown eyes landed on her as he grinned. "I call it living your garden, a *must* for success."

Growing up, it was her mother who clipped the weeds and pruned the flowers. She trimmed and mulched and spent hour upon hour keeping up with the grinding chore of maintenance. All this time, Jennifer had viewed the endeavor as a backbreaking necessity. Was she wrong? Had she been "living her garden" as Jackson implied?

"Do you have an idea for what you want to see out here?"

Jennifer looked at him with what surely must have been a dumb stare. Her fundamental plan had called for trees and shrubs, some grass and a few beds of flowers. This talk of fountains and statues, and *living the garden* threw her wholly off kilter! "Oh, uh, I don't know..." She glanced around, feeling like an ill-prepared first-year resident. "Hibiscus," she murmured. "Maybe some bougainvillea..."

"Nice choices."

But not near as well thought out as your ideas. "I've always wanted a fruit tree," she added meekly.

"You certainly have enough sun for them."

Habitat; an obvious consideration, yet the thought never crossed her mind. While she may know what she liked, she had no idea if it would grow in her yard. Immobile, Jennifer suddenly felt ignorant. It was a state of mind to which she was unaccustomed. And one she didn't care for.

"Listen," he said, and gently took charge. "Let me make some sketches. That way, you'll get a better feel for what I have in mind and we can go from there."

So much for all her dictation on how things would run.

"I'll begin this afternoon."

"Will it take very long?" was all she could think to ask. I mean, because—"

He held up a hand and his eyes softened to a caramel brown. "Mike explained you're under the gun on this one. I'll draw them up today and drop them by in the morning."

Jennifer gave a double take. *That quick*? "Yes, but I leave for work pretty early."

"Will six a.m. be early enough?"

She about fell over. How on earth could he produce drawings with any detail in so little time? She hesitated, but met with a solid wall of confidence she consented. "Yes, of course..."

"All right, then." Jackson extended his hand. "I guess I better get to work."

Shaking hands, she was once again taken by the warm clasp. Firm, yet soft. Comfortable. Her senses reeled at its sudden withdrawal.

"Goodbye."

Jennifer turned to lead the way, but he stopped her. "I can find my way out."

And with a quick wave, he was gone.

Jennifer stood spellbound, her gaze trailing after him until he disappeared around the corner of her house.

For a long moment she stood, unaware she was caressing the skin where they had touched. The exchange had gone nothing like she imagined. Not once had he said "dude" or "man." In fact, he used no slang at all and instead, was rather well-spoken.

And his ideas... Some of them were really quite good!

But then again she thought, annoyed by her lingering reaction to his touch. Anyone can sound like they know what they're doing if they follow a template. His portfolio of projects probably all look the same.

With an about-face, she marched back into the house. We'll just see what Mr. Montgomery comes up with tomorrow.

Chapter Seven

"They're beautiful, Jennifer."

Organizing the flowers in a vase by her mother's bedside, she agreed and spruced them for a rounder presentation. "Rudolph's nursery does an outstanding job, don't they?"

"They do, indeed."

It had become a regular stop on her way to Fairhaven. The roses they grew were sheer perfection; long graceful stems topped with petals of red velvet. She buried her nose in the bunch, inhaling the rich, sweet perfume. "I don't know how he does it, but they are magnificent each and every time."

"It takes a loving touch to nurture such beauty."

"And you should know," Jennifer replied, heartened by the sentiment. She turned toward her mother. "Your flowers were always award-winning quality."

Light blue eyes sparkled in pleasure at the compliment. Dressed in a simple linen dress, shoulder-length hair combed until it shone a lustrous gray and held back by a pearl-lined clip, Beatrice was elegance personified. Despite the ravage within her body, she still took the time to make up her face, and receive her guests in proper fashion.

With the staff's assistance.

Fairhaven was the best assisted-living facility Miami had to offer, their reputation impeccable. The interior décor was equally lovely as creams, greens and blues were blended together in fabrics and furniture, walls were painted a buttery yellow and dotted by tasteful paintings of the Everglades. Lighting wasn't fluorescent, but instead came in the form of lamps and sconces lending a cozy feel to the rooms. The aim was quiet luxury. As patients waded through the twilight of their lives, they would do so in style.

The place was top of the line in every way, except one. It wasn't home. It wasn't where her mother should be.

But Beatrice insisted. She wasn't moving in with her daughter, despite Jennifer's pledge to provide round-the-clock nursing care, a private bedroom and bath of her own.

No. Her mother remained adamant. She wanted her independence. She wanted her own place. *Even if it was in a nursing home.*

"Come," she said, patting the cotton blanket. "Let's visit. Tell me all about your new garden."

Jennifer obliged without thinking, settling into the chair beside her. "I have a landscaper," she said flatly.

"Marvelous!"

"Maybe yes," Jennifer tempered her enthusiasm, "maybe no."

"What?"

At her mother's confounded look, she explained. "He's a bartender," Jennifer said, not bothering to conceal her concern. "On the side of his landscaper business."

"Bartender?"

"Yes. We actually met for the first time at Michael's party the other night. You remember, the one he held for Catherine's engagement? Well, this fellow was there, tending bar."

"Oh, heavens!" Beatrice exclaimed, as though this were bad news, indeed.

"It was only a favor to Michael. He insists landscaping is his first priority," she assured, placating her mother's sudden alarm. "Seems he and Michael are friends. In fact, it was his recommendation I relied on in my selection."

Beatrice's eyes expressed disappointment over the development. "Doesn't Michael understand you want a professional job done? You want design work, not someone who's going to plant a few bushes here and there."

Jennifer nodded, her mood pinched by her mother's concern. "He does, but Michael swears this fellow is the one."

"Are you certain?"

No, she wasn't certain of anything. "He came by this morning and had some good ideas. He's supposed to drop the drawings by tomorrow."

"So soon?"

Her thoughts exactly.

Beatrice eyed her warily. "I'd be a bit leery, if I were you."

"Yes," Jennifer echoed her mother's sentiment. She was bothered, too but time had clipped her wings on this one. She knew of no one else to call. "I'm willing to withhold judgment until we see what he comes back with tomorrow."

As if she had a choice in the matter.

"Do you have someone else lined up in the event his work is unacceptable?"

"Not yet." Jennifer's body sagged at the admission. "But not to worry," she assured with a confidence she didn't feel. "If it doesn't work out, I'll find someone."

But what Jennifer saw in her mother's eyes could have been a reflection of her own. Tension. They didn't have time to spare, should his promises prove hollow.

Jennifer dodged her gaze, and landed upon the fresh bouquet of roses she brought today. Sitting atop the mobile swing-table, the flowers did little to add warmth, cheer. They were merely a skimp of color to an already well-decorated room.

Her gaze drifted. The picture frames scattered across her mother's dresser and nightstand, filled with images of family and friends, didn't do much either.

While lovely memories, they were just things.

And things didn't matter. Not when illness came to call.

"When will you receive his proposal?"

"Tomorrow."

"So soon?"

"That's what he says."

Her mother didn't look pleased. "Maybe I should call someone. In the event his design falls short."

Jennifer shook her head. "Please, let's wait." This was her responsibility and she would make it happen. "His ideas actually sounded quite good this morning. He may surprise us."

Beatrice lifted her brow.

"Tomorrow I'll have a better idea and if need be, we'll call someone else." Adding more names to the list of prospective hires only added delay.

Somewhat pacified, her mother agreed. "Okay. But call me first thing in the morning. I know several people with possible connections in the landscape design business."

Of course she did. Beatrice Hamilton was a venerable institution in the Gables. If she didn't know them, they knew her. Of her. The woman was a dynamo of action when she set her mind to it.

"Now listen," she said, and reached for Jennifer's hand. "Let's not talk about that anymore. Let's talk about you." She ushered forth a grand smile. "You're going to make a beautiful bride, my dear."

Eyes bright and alert, they held the real life in her mother's fading body and shone without a hint of fear.

Unlike Jennifer. She was dreading her mother's passing.

Beatrice gestured for her daughter to take her hand, painfully slender fingers covered in a delicate pastry of skin to which she obliged, closing it in her own. Jennifer gave a gentle squeeze.

"I'm so happy for you. Aurelio is a wonderful man, Jenny."

She nodded, her response locked in the rigid swell of her throat.

Her mother eased her head back against the pillow. "Like your father. He was a good man..." she said intently. "And so good to me. Our life together was filled with love and adventure, everything new and exciting, because we were together."

As exciting as Africa she wondered, but didn't dare broach the subject. Adding to her mom's burden was something she was loath to do. This weight was one she must carry alone.

"I know you two will be as happy together as we were," she said in a wisp of breath, and closed her eyes.

Gone was the rush of panic Jennifer used to experience at the closing of those aging lids, replaced now by tired resignation. She had long since learned it was a sign of retreat; a relief for her mother to get rest, and not the final goodbye.

Not until she was ready. Jennifer dropped any pretense of strength and allowed her head to fall. The spirit was a powerful force. Journals had been written on the will to survive and she knew it wouldn't be extinguished until it was good and ready; her mother's case in point.

She had been the driving force behind her daughter's success. When Jennifer's ambition waned, when her confidence sputtered, it was Beatrice Hamilton who ignited her back to life. She kept her daughter going, kept her focused, providing soft pillows of compassion when she failed. Jennifer leaned forward and pressed a light kiss to her fragile hand, pausing over the faint scent of gardenia. There was so much she still wanted to share. Not only the wedding, but her life, her love...

Children. Something her mother had wanted so very much but now would never see. Because cancer had come to call.

Laying there so peaceful, her eyes closed, a sweet smile resting on her lips. Jennifer frowned. It was utterly deceiving. Little by little the cancer was devouring her spirit, consuming her body, until soon there would be nothing left of her.

She pulled away. She wiped the sudden tears from her eyes and blocked her thoughts. *Stop.*

Enough. It's what her mother wanted. Insisted.

But the tears refused to quit. Afraid her mother would witness the display of weakness, Jennifer brushed the hair from her face, grabbed a tissue from the nightstand and dried her eyes. *Let it go*, she urged herself. No magic potion can save her life. No miracle can keep her with you. Stop wishing for one.

Jennifer shot up from her chair. It did nothing to help her mother, or herself. Breaking down only served to distress. And she couldn't do that to her mother, not when she was being so courageous. "Mom, you need to get some rest. It's important to keep up your strength."

Beatrice barely nodded, but said nothing.

The visits were getting harder and harder on her. She seemed to lose energy so quickly these days. The doctor in her knew it was common, to be expected, but the daughter in her railed against it with all her might.

It was the pain that bothered her most. Her mother was enduring unimaginable suffering to witness her daughter's marriage, despite countless offers to expedite the process.

But her mother wouldn't hear of it. There would be no courthouse wedding or bedside ceremony for her sake. Her daughter would be married in Hamilton tradition, period. End of story.

End of story. A shiver scurried up her spine. "Mom," she whispered, and fought a fresh deluge of tears. "I have to go."

Gingerly replacing her mother's hand onto the bed, Jennifer lifted the pale yellow sheets and tucked them alongside her body. Leaning forward she added, "I love you." Placing a kiss on the top of her head, she hovered a moment to enjoy the scent indelibly etched in her soul.

Once her mother was gone, Jennifer would be alone, and this comforting connection, a thing of the past.

Chapter Eight

Jennifer was still in shock. The proposal had been delivered as promised—

And took her breath away. Not only in price, but talent. Literally miniature works of art, Jackson Montgomery's drawings depicted a garden paradise as lovely as any fairy tale.

Sitting behind her desk, finished with the last patient, she leafed through the crisp white sheets once again, marveling at his illustrations, extraordinary in both detail and color. She couldn't believe her eyes, but true to his word he had drawn a gorgeous Italian-style fountain for out front, water splashing over the ledge, capturing the sparkle of sunlight like an invitation to delight.

Both sides of her property were layered with ginger and palms, the arched lines of their fronds drawn with incredible likeness. Nearer the house, blooms spanning the colors of sunset lined the front walkway and spilled from window boxes. Out back, the wall fountain looked exactly as he described. Surrounded by bright multi-hued tiles, it was framed by rich green vines fanning out along freshly-painted stucco, a rich golden tan that matched the house to perfection.

Inside the clam-shaped basin, the water shimmered aquamarine blue. Extending outward from this area was a brick patio which he continued toward the pool via a narrow paved walkway, one accented by an overhead trellis full of purple-flowered vines. She scrutinized it more closely. Were those the Bougainvillea she had requested?

As he suggested, oversized terra-cotta planters lined the pool and two small, childlike statues playfully dipped their toes into the water. A hedge of salmon pink and yellow hibiscus separated the back driveway from the yard and on her back porch, he had sketched in a cozy fireplace.

It was remarkable; everything he promised and more.

Earlier that afternoon, Jennifer shared her impression with Michael. *I told you he was good. Good, fantastic, but not cheap.*

Yes, the drawings were wonderful. But the price tag was indeed outrageous. How did he get away with charging so much? Organizing the drawings into a tidy stack, she was more certain than ever Jackson followed a template. He must have.

Granted, her custom design didn't resemble anything of the sort, but there was no way he could create such brilliance on whim. No way he could produce such incredible detail overnight, after spending all of a half hour on-site. Impossible, unless the basics were already completed.

Or he had a team of draftsmen on call and at his disposal.

She slid the drawings back into their folder and thought well, I hope he's heard of negotiation because that's exactly what I intend to do. Masterpiece or not, Jennifer didn't take kindly to being taken. If Jackson Montgomery thought he had tapped into a vein of gold with the physician community, he had another thought coming.

Something she intended to tell him. Setting the packet aside, she dialed his number.

"Jackson Montgomery."

"Mr. Montgomery, this is Dr. Hamilton calling."

"Oh, hello Dr. Hamilton. Did you have a chance to look at my proposal?"

"I did."

"What do you think?"

"Well, it's fine but I wanted to discuss a few items with you."

"Okay, shoot."

"I'd prefer to do so in person. How does your schedule look this evening?"

"I'm pretty flexible. When were you thinking?"

"Around seven?"

"No problem. I'll see you then."

"Thank you."

Squarely past her initial surprise, she looked forward to the encounter.

# # #

Jax pulled into her driveway precisely at seven, but a wary sense of misgiving gnawed at him. Didn't she like his ideas? Was there something she wanted to add? She left the definite impression this was more than a formality to finalize terms.

Pulling around the circular drive, he cut the ignition, and its aging motor responded with a pop. "Sorry, Sue," he said, patting the crusty dashboard. "It won't be much longer before I can retire you to part-time."

Reserved solely for visits to the mainland.

As usual, the thought of his future nudged his spirit up a notch. Once he set sail, days of dealing with difficult clients would be a thing of the past. There'd be nothing but blue skies and blue waters on his horizon.

The prospect brightened his outlook and refueled his drive to handle the meeting ahead. Whatever she had coming, he was prepared. Dropping keys to the console, he pushed open the door and tossed it closed behind him.

On approach, he eyed the house with fresh appraisal. The place must have run the good doctor a cool million, easy. Best location, superb renovations, but then her type could afford such luxury. No kids, rich fiancé, she was set for life. Probably had a second and third home, too.

Not him. One was enough and a floating one, to boot. And he was getting close now. The agent swung by this morning and assured him he could cash in big, after a few cosmetic repairs. His house sat on the fringe of the more wealthy Coconut Grove section, so he had the coveted location, location, location.

Jax didn't know much about the market location. He only bought there because he liked the feel of the area. But if the woman was right, tagging the price considerably higher than he expected, his dreams of retiring were only months away.

Leaping up the three steps to the gated entry, he noted it was left open. *She was expecting him*. Passing through the small courtyard, he admired the setup. Small but charming, with a brick fireplace set in an exterior wall, a rattan loveseat and chair settled in front of it. Very nice, Jackson thought, the perfect place to enjoy a cool winter's evening.

He rapped twice on the heavy mahogany door. On second thought, maybe she doesn't need the fireplace he drew in for the back porch. Immediately his mind began to brainstorm alternatives as the door opened.

Her smile was small, cool. "Hello, Mr. Montgomery. Thank you for coming."

"Most call me Jax," he said, wondering if she was always this formal. Not only her tone and mannerisms, but she was dressed in a navy blue pantsuit, under which she wore a starched white button-down.

But, much like he noticed on prior occasion, she was definitely a beautiful woman. Cool, but beautiful. Her hair was pulled back in a shiny ponytail, sitting low at the nape of her neck, different than the higher one she wore yesterday.

Must be the business version, he mused.

"We can use the kitchen," she said and invited him inside. "It will give us a view of the back as we discuss the proposal."

"Sounds good," he said, taking in the dark wood floors as he followed her through the house. They were a near match to the tongue and groove wood ceilings. The wall color reminded him of Dijon mustard, her furnishings sparse but stylish, with tan upholstery and deep red throw cushions.

The floor rug was a blend of the same with the addition of green and pale blue accents, the effect both subtle and pleasing to the eyes. He noted with approval the fireplace, framed in by keystone. What he assumed to be family photos dotted the table tops and dominated the foyer, adding warmth to the space.

Once again, he liked what he saw. "You have a nice place."

"Thank you. I'm still working on the finishing touches, but my schedule has posed tough competition." She led him to the breakfast table where his drawings were laid across the round glass table top. He glanced at her. *In very meticulous order*, no less.

She didn't offer him a seat.

"I had a few questions before we proceed, if you don't mind."

"Not at all." He smiled, glancing into her kitchen. Wood cabinets, lighter than the floor were glazed for a pleasant almost graceful effect which coordinated well with the polished, sand-colored stone countertop. Jax wondered whether this was her selection, or had she used a professional for the interior, as well.

"I noticed you didn't include but one fruit tree in the back."

Taken by surprise, he said, "We can add more, if you want."

"The brick patio is something we didn't discuss."

"It came to me as I was sketching the fountain." Resting a hand on the back of a dining chair, he said matter-of-factly, "It gives continuity from the back wall to the pool, joining the two areas as one."

"Nor is the fireplace on the porch."

"No," he paused, instinct beginning to fire. "But it increases the intimacy of the space."

"Increases the price tag, too."

Ah... So that's where she was going with this little pow-wow. *The money.* "It does," he said, controlling his tone, "but it also adds to the overall appeal. It connects the two areas in a seamless flow, and provides a beautiful setting for a wedding." Michael told him what lay behind her haste. He had designed it with that in mind.

"Wedding or not," she snapped. "It adds to the cost."

"Yes it does," Jax answered, curious as to her sudden rise in agitation.

"And why are the plants so expensive?" Referring to his breakdown of costs versus labor, she picked up a few pages and ran a finger down the column of numbers, poking at the larger ones. "I called a couple of nurseries in town and the price they quoted me was substantially less."

The blaze in her eyes had an accusatory feel and began to singe his easygoing nature. Tightening his hand around the chair, he shifted his weight and replied, "The reason mine are higher, is because I plan on using larger, more mature plants in the back yard. I thought it would help with your plans, seeing as how the event will follow so closely behind the completion date."

"Thank you," her gaze dodged him. "But that is none of your concern, Mr. Montgomery."

One good deed never goes unpunished, isn't that what they say? He let go of the chair and placed both hands on his hips. Waiting for her next play, he was amazed by how quick ocean-blue eyes could turn to gray-blue glaciers.

"The cost of the fountain seems a bit exorbitant."

Was she just looking for things to bitch about? But he remained mute. Let her spell it out. He wasn't giving an inch.

Glaring at him, she looked down at the papers in her hand and pointed to the bottom line. "My concern is how do we modify *this*?"

"We don't," he said, before good sense had a chance to intervene. He could apologize to Michael later, but *damn it* he wasn't used to being questioned on his fees. He was worth every penny and this woman better get used to that idea if they were going to be working together. "My bids are fair and non-negotiable. You want to change the plant size, fine, but that's as far as I budge."

Jackson Montgomery stepped on his pride for no one.

Jennifer didn't say a word. She only stared. "Do you have any guarantee for your completion date?"

"I do. *Me*." He thumped a thumb to his chest. "If I don't finish when I say I'm going to finish, then you don't pay."

"Including the fountain and brick patio work, if I choose to accept the proposal as is?"

"Everything. The fireplace was an option for the future, but I can have that finished, too. If you so choose."

Indignation flared in her eyes, but at an apparent loss for a comeback, she said nothing. Slowly, she replaced the papers onto the table. When she looked back at him, the mix of displeasure and need he saw swirling in her eyes cut the legs from under him. *Damn*. Struck by her sudden vulnerability, a part of him wanted to reach out to her. This woman was on tumultuous ground. This wasn't about price.

But the larger part of him wouldn't move. Not an inch.

"Very well, then," she brushed a stray hair from her brow. "I guess we have a deal, Mr. Montgomery."

"Great," he said, a mountain of mixed emotion rumbling through him. This project was going to test him. On several different levels—if his current response to this woman was any indication.

But Michael was the kind of man you didn't disappoint. Not because he was a close friend, but because he did things for the right reasons; helping people because it helped them, no more and no less. His was a favor Jax could never repay.

If moving closer toward his goals meant working with an irritable hard-boiled silky pearl of a woman, then so be it. He could let the nastiest condescension slide right down his backside and into the toilet. At the same time, he'd have to tamp down the swell of attraction he felt toward her.

Damn the luck. "Dr. Hamilton, we have a deal."

"Can I let you know about the additions tomorrow?"

"Sure. But don't wait too long. I'll need to let my supplier know so we can get the bricks in time."

Jax hadn't meant to end his sentence with a slap, but the sharp flush to her cheeks was unmistakable.

"Fine. I'll be sure to expedite my decision and let you know in the morning. Will a call around six-thirty suffice to comply with your schedule?"

"No problem," he said, knocking the wind from her challenge. "Let me know about the fruit trees, too," he tossed back with a smile, then erased it from his face. "Have a good evening, Dr. Hamilton." Before she had a chance to react, he turned away. "I'll find my way out."

Chapter Nine

Jax arrived early Tuesday morning with a crew of three. He noticed Dr. Hamilton had already left for the day, but she had obliged his request by clearing out any personal items from the yard, such as lawn chairs and planters. His assignment today was to remove weeds and overgrowth, and prepare the ground for planting; the most laborious part of the process.

Orders for product had been placed with his suppliers and a masonry contractor was already lined up to do the fountain and patio work. An hour into the task, Jax's cell phone rang.

Setting his hoe aside, he wiped a gloved hand across his sweaty brow and plucked the phone from the clip on his waistband. He frowned at the caller's ID. Why was she calling?

Pressing the green button, he answered, "Jackson Montgomery."

"Jackson, it's Dr. Hamilton."

"What can I do for you, Dr. Hamilton?"

"I was wondering what time you planned on starting today. The pool service is coming by around nine and I wanted to be sure there was no conflict."

"We've already started and there's no problem with the pool company. We'll stay out of their way."

"Good," she replied after the briefest of pauses. "When do you expect to be finished with the first stage?"

Agitation swelled in his gut. *Was she always this controlling?* "By the end of the week," he clipped. His proposal had included a stage-by-stage time frame. All she had to do was read it.

"And then the planting begins?"

"Some of it. The back fountain needs to be installed first, then we lay the brick with the plants to follow."

Jax was beginning to get that itchy feeling on the backside of his neck, a bad omen she was going to be breathing down it. He hoped to God she didn't plan on playing pseudo-foreman for the entire project.

"Fine," she said, but didn't continue.

Was there something particular she was after, or did she simply expect him to elaborate?

One of his guys glanced at him, silent understanding in his eyes. Difficult clients were nothing new to them.

"Will there be anything else, Dr. Hamilton?" He threw in the title, just for effect.

"No, that will be all. Goodbye."

Ah, the dismissal; short and sweet. "Bye-bye," he touted softly, punching the call to an end. Sliding the phone back into its holster, he grunted and rubbed the back of his neck.

Per Mike's request, he had put this job at the top of his list, red alert on the priorities, get-it-done-at-all-costs. He was happy to do so. For a friend.

And he knew he delivered an exceptional proposal if he did say so himself, and intended to bust his butt to pull it off. What he didn't need was the complication of a client looking over his shoulder.

He knew the deal. He knew what was at stake and had accepted the terms. Terms he wouldn't have touched if he didn't think he could manage. Didn't Mike assure her she had nothing to worry about?

Probably. He was that kind of guy. Jax grabbed the metal handle of his hoe and heaving it high above his head, threw the blade down into the dirt, the sharp edge landing deep within the tangle of weeds. Despite the early hour, his shirt was soaked through. Miami was hot and there was no getting around it. During the summer months, one could only hope for cloudy days, though the intelligent man knew not to wait on them.

Besides the obvious impatience, perhaps Dr. Hamilton was the type who didn't listen very well. Or maybe she was the kind of woman who had to control everything and everyone around her.

He'd known women like that, and dated a few. Strong, independent—ornery as hell, especially where men were concerned. Those relationships had ended within weeks.

Hoisting the hoe back over his head he slammed at the ground again, working the heavy metal back and forth through the soil, ignoring the salty fluid dripping down his nose.

Jackson Montgomery was no woman's pawn. No matter how smart, rich or good-looking, he stood on his own two feet and made his own decisions. About his business and about his life.

A fact his father had learned the hard way.

He wouldn't conform to anyone's idea of what was best for him, and those who tried to force him into a mold...

Well, it spoke to their intentions, and exposed their self-centered roots. Expectations were about them, not about him. The day he'd learned that lesson was one of the most liberating days of his life.

# # #

Jennifer ended the call. Short, sweet and to the point. Let's hope he keeps it that way she thought, and threw herself into an office full of patients. It proved a typical day until one of her patients refused treatment.

"Sarah, I can't help you if you don't follow my instructions."

Seated on the padded table, her chest covered by a paper gown, the elderly woman replied with a sheepish smile, "The medicine makes me sick, Dr. Hamilton."

"Nausea is a side effect. We can try others, experiment with different medicines until we find the one that's right for you."

"My mother is not a guinea pig."

Sarah Wiley's daughter stood in the corner, arms locked in a cross beneath her ample bosom, watching the examination like a grim-faced guard.

Jennifer stared at the scowling middle-aged brunette, her skin mottled by smoking. "I'm not suggesting anything of the kind. I'm merely pointing out that patients react differently to various kinds of medications. It's best if we tailor our treatment to meet your mother's needs."

"By experimenting."

Jennifer wondered if the woman was always this helpful, or was it a simple matter of personality clash. "Unfortunately, there is no other way. We won't know how she responds to a medicine until we try it." The daughter glanced away and Jennifer returned her attention to her mother. "But you have to take the medicine, Sarah, or else we won't be able to determine which is right for you."

"Mary, what do you think?" Trusting as a newborn kitten, she would not make a move without the consent of her daughter—which at present—was being withheld.

"I think we should get a second opinion."

"Absolutely," Jennifer agreed. "Get a second opinion." Whatever you need to do to be convinced this is serious, she thought privately, do it. The alternative is almost certainly death.

"What about the surgery?" Sarah asked.

"It sounds a little drastic to me." The woman placed meaty hands to her hips and complained, "You doctors are always trying to prescribe something or perform some kind of procedure. I don't know even know if her insurance will cover this. You may be wasting your time."

Jennifer slipped her hands into the pockets of her lab coat and balled them into fists. She glared at the woman standing before her. Despite the stiff antiseptic smell in the room, she could easily detect the stale odor of smoke. In a very calm voice she replied, "I prescribe the treatment I believe to be in the best interest of my patients. My goal is to improve the quality of their life—not my bank account. If you feel the need to seek advice from

another professional, please feel free to do so."
Otherwise, *keep your mouth closed*. Jennifer turned
to Sarah. "This is your decision, Sarah. Your
condition is treatable. We can begin treatment with
medicine, but if that proves unproductive, we can opt
for a procedure to place a stent in your artery. It will
help increase the flow of blood to your heart."

Sarah nodded, but glancing toward her daughter,
it was clear she wouldn't make a move without her.

"You said so yourself, the pain isn't getting any
better." Recurrent angina, cholesterol through the
roof, the woman was a prime candidate for a heart
attack.

"I'll think about it," she said, smiling as though it
might relieve some of the tension in the room. "It's
all so confusing at the moment, I think I need time to
absorb it all." She reached out and grasped Jennifer's
arm. "But you did a great job explaining it, Dr.
Hamilton. It's just that my little old brain gets full
pretty quick these days!"

Jennifer didn't like to see elderly patients pa-
tronize themselves. They were the keepers of the
gate, the ones with wisdom and experience. She
swiped a glance at her daughter. They shouldn't be
intimidated by petulant offspring.

"I'm going to write you another prescription."
She walked to the other side of the room and pulled a
pad of paper from the drawer of her workstation. She
scribbled the name of a statin, the dosage, then signed
her name at the bottom. She handed it to Sarah.
"Take this as directed and make an appointment to
come back and see me in six weeks for your blood
tests."

"Thank you, doctor."

"And get a second opinion, Sarah. Do whatever you need to do, but don't let this condition persist untreated." She leaned closer and softened her tone. "Don't let money stand in the way, either. If your insurance doesn't cover something, let me know. We can take care of it other ways."

"She doesn't have any money," the daughter quipped. "Payment plans won't work."

Jennifer ignored the comment and squeezed Sarah's hand. "Promise me you'll do something about it."

She nodded, beaming in light of her doctor's concern. "I will."

Sliding the stethoscope from around her neck, Jennifer exited the room without a word.

Adding the last file to the stack of patient folders on the corner of her desk, all prepped and ready for dictation, Jennifer sat back in her chair. Tension knotted and twisted in her shoulders as she stared at the wall of diplomas. University of Miami. Jackson Memorial. Shands Medical Center.

She had the expertise. She had the knowledge to help. Why did people fight it? Why did they decline the treatment that would save their life?

The doctor in her knew some people chose to bury themselves in denial rather than face the truth, the scary truth that life is finite, but the daughter in her didn't understand.

Medications were prescribed every day. Catheterization was a commonly performed procedure. Yes, there was risk, but everything we do involves risk. From walking down the street to driving a car, anything can prove harmful if you think about it.

Frustration ramped higher into her neck, constricting the muscles at the base of her skull into a ball of pain. Why wouldn't you at least try? *When the alternative is sudden death*? Why would you wait?

If she could fix her mother's problems with a simple device, she would. If it meant giving her mom a few extra years, she would. She would run ten times the risk Sarah Wiley was facing if it meant keeping her mom alive. Then, she could enjoy the wedding at her leisure. She could witness the birth of her grandchildren, guide her daughter on how best to care for babies and raise them to be loving, happy adults.

Much like she did for her own child.

Jennifer's heart pinched at the memory of Sarah's daughter. Quite the opposite of loving, her selfish, distrusting attitude may cost her mother's life. The irony stung.

Chapter Ten

"Dr. Hamilton! Dr. Hamilton!"

Michael held the door to the kid's activity room open for Jennifer as she entered ahead of him. "I guess we know who the popular one is," he pronounced, not an ounce of envy in his voice.

She rolled her eyes. "Yes and I'm sure the huge box in my hands has nothing to do with it."

He laughed. "You do have a reputation, Dr. Hamilton."

She shook her head and laughed. "That, I do."

Walking further into St. Theresa's Children's Hospital's specially designed playroom for kids, they joined the youngsters gathering on the center of the colorful woven carpet. It was the heart of their play area, created for the sole purpose of bringing them together to encourage creativity and play in a normal atmosphere, one that didn't include monitors and needles, medicine or doctors.

Except Jennifer and Michael. But they weren't here in a professional capacity, quite the opposite. They were here for fun.

Dropping to her knees, Jennifer placed the cardboard box where the children could reach and as expected, little arms went crazy, grabbing, inspecting animals, turning them to and fro as they determined which was their favorite.

"I want the giraffe!"

"The hippo is mine!"

"But blue is my favorite color!"

Jennifer laughed at the raw expression of desire. "There's more, don't worry! You'll all find something you like!"

And if they didn't, she would return to her car and rifle through her stash in the trunk and find one they did, because disappointing these kids wasn't an option. Confined to their respective wards in the children's hospital, she decided the heart-wrenching battle against serious illness was enough.

Dressed in pink scrubs, she sat back on her heels and watched as they rummaged through her selection of stuffed animals while Michael played referee. "Jason, give that one back to Shana. She had it first." But as he commandeered the exchange of the multi-colored gecko, he pulled another larger one from the box and handed it to the boy as the girl popped up with her bounty and ran outside the boy's reach. "I think this one is better for you."

His eyes grew wide with delight. "It's way better!"

He yanked the lizard from Michael's grasp, most probably concerned another child might spy his prize and try to claim it for their own and admired it head to tail. Jennifer chuckled. Not a problem. She had three more like it in her car.

"Who wants to play checkers!" Michael called out.

Several boys tumbled over one another to get to him, shouting, "Me! Me!"

"I do! I do!"

"You played first last time!"

"Settle down boys. I'm here all afternoon." Michael playfully rubbed Samuel's shiny bald head. "And this time it's for the *championship*."

"Dr. Hamilton, can we have a tea party?"

She smiled at the young girl with white blonde hair, long curls pinned high to one side with a pink satin ribbon, eyes round and blue, lined by lashes so dark, Jennifer would have sworn they were false. "So long as you bake crumpets, we can."

The child peered with a curious stare. "What's a crumpet?"

Jennifer set hands to her thighs and leaned close. "I don't really know. I only heard about it and thought it sounded tasty."

"It does, doesn't it..." She placed a petite fore-finger to her lips, tinged ever so slightly blue, and pondered for a moment. "I think we should have crumpets with our tea. And I'll make them!" She giggled and raised her soft pink rabbit high in the air. "What do you say, Poppy? Wanna make crumpets for Dr. Hamilton? She's real nice and I think she'll like them."

Jennifer clapped her hands together. "Please, Poppy, *please*."

The child shook her toy and pretended to speak for the rabbit, "With pleasure and a little sugar on top!"

Laughing at her ventriloquist talents, Jennifer eased up and helped to arrange the tea set; fancy porcelain, elaborately painted with vine twisted around lavender flowers, there were enough tiny cups to go around for everyone.

Shana dutifully returned satisfied the gecko was hers, and served everyone tea. While the boys declined, Michael cheerfully accepted his cup with a gallant nod. "Why thank you, Shana. And may I ask what flavor we have today?"

"Ginger mint."

"Oh, that does sound good." Pinching the handle with his forefinger and thumb, he held his pinky straight out and sipped. "Mmmmm..."

Shana giggled. "It's rude to slurp."

"*Oops*, sorry," he said in feigned chagrin, as though it hadn't been a purposeful ploy for a laugh.

It was moments like this when she adored Michael the most. "Try a crumpet, Michael. They're truly divine."

"Don't mind if I do!" He reached up and plucked a make-believe biscuit from the tray extended before him. With great show he bit down, chewed with exaggerated motion, his mouth politely closed. He swallowed. "That's the best crumpet I've ever tasted."

"I made it!"

Michael followed the direction of the voice and spotted the girl with curls. "Her name is Beverly." Jennifer quieted her voice. "She's new."

He nodded. "Thank you, Beverly. It was delicious."

"You're welcome," she replied, and went back to her busy work at the stove, a remarkable replica in a kitchen complete with refrigerator, counter and sink, dining table and chairs. She wiped down the area around her mixing bowls, busy preparing for another batch.

Michael looked to Jennifer for explanation.

Maintaining her pleasant expression, she tapped a finger to her chest and mouthed, "Transplant."

His eyes registered the hit. He knew the odds. They were tough.

Three hours later, Michael walked Jennifer out. Strolling passed an enormous Banyan tree, the two came to a stop beneath its canopy. Long finger-like roots fell from the leaves to crawl along the ground, forming an intricate foundation around the base of the trunk. "Same time next month?"

"You bet." She smiled, picking through the contents of her purse in search of her keys.

"So how's Jax working out? Did you two overcome your differences?"

"We did." Conscious of the sensitive subject matter, she added, "He's already begun work, in fact."

"You're going to be real happy with what he does for you."

She slid on a pair of black sunglasses. "I'm sure I will be."

"You know," he glanced back at the hospital, flanked by Poinciana trees, their brilliant red-orange blooms striking against the cream of flat stucco. "I should tell Jax about this place. He might want to donate some of his time here."

"Would he be interested in such a thing? I mean, he seems to be a very busy man, do you really think he has the time for visits to the children's hospital?"

"Jax runs his own schedule. In fact, he volunteers down at the boys and girls club already and who knows," he slid brown tinted sunglasses onto his nose, "he might want to squeeze this place into his list of benevolent endeavors."

The thought of Jackson Montgomery sitting around with a bunch of kids, laughing and playing, seemed like the most normal thing in the world.

"Kids love him."

"I'll bet they do."

"Besides, once he sells his house he'll have plenty of time on his hands, between trips to the islands, that is. He's set to retire soon and this may be just the thing he needs to fill his days stateside. Anyway," Michael swiped a glance at his watch. "I've got to get running. Laurencia's waiting for me."

"Go, please," she told him. "Don't let me hold you up."

He leaned over and pecked a kiss to her cheek. "See you at the hospital."

"See you at the hospital," she replied, her mind still picking through Michael's remark. *Retire*? Was he serious? She stood immobile, her gaze trailing Michael across the parking lot as he hurried to his Mercedes. How on earth could Jackson retire? He couldn't be much older than her and she was nowhere near retirement.

Still sorting through the significance of Michael's revelation, Jennifer arrived home to find Jackson hard at work. Wednesdays were her half-day, the afternoons assigned to catching up with paperwork, attending to any personal affairs, and once a month, a trip to see her kids. But for Jackson, it was just another day on the job.

She parked and walked to the edge of her drive, but stopped. She wasn't about to soil her expensive leather heels in the black, inky dirt. Bringing a hand to her brow, she blocked the late afternoon sun and asked, "How's it coming?"

Jackson turned. Tucked into khaki shorts with more pockets than one had a use for, his white T-shirt was soaked through, muddy brown dirt smudged the small green emblem embroidered on its pocket. His legs were crawling with black grime, the sweat acting like glue for the dirt to adhere to his skin, his socks no longer white above tan leather work boots.

Retirement? Really?

I hear bartenders make pretty good money.

Sam may be right after all.

He straightened. "Hello, Dr. Hamilton."

"Hello." She took a quick survey of the area and noticed that weeds were gone, dirt was raked and organized into beds. It seemed he'd been busy, but did he really expect to complete this job himself? "Wouldn't it be quicker if you had help?"

"I did, but I have other jobs that need completing so I sent them there. I'm finishing up here today." He wiped the back of his hand against his brow. "But don't worry." He smiled. "We'll have it done on time."

Glancing around once more, she wished she shared his optimism. "Yes," she murmured. *One can only hope.*

With nothing left to say and more than a few questions swirling in her mind, she retreated into the house. Moving to a window hidden from view, she watched as he dumped a bag of dirt onto the ground, then moved it around with a metal rake. It looked grueling, and by the way his muscles were contracting and expanding, it seemed his body agreed.

His body. It was the first time she ever really looked at him, at Jackson the man, and here alone in her home and sheltered from view, she took the moment to linger.

Filling the back of his shirt was a large green tree, an intricate array of branches and leaves with the name *Montgomery Landscape* running across the bottom. The man was filthy and to look at him, one would think the stench would knock you down from ten feet away, but she had noticed none of it when he had stood nearby moments before. Not a waft.

Lifting and heaving what had to be forty-pound bags, Jackson was handling them as if they were filled with Styrofoam, as though he had the strength of a bull. Granted his arms were well-defined, the hard line profile of his broad shoulders and lean torso revealing not an inch of fat, but those bags had to be heavy! The rate at which he was working through them was incredible.

Impressive, really. And his hair, well, his hair never seemed to change. It looked as if the sun had raked its fingers through, massaged the mess, bleached the ends and pulled them straight out by the tips. She leaned against the wall.

Amazing. It struck her how different Jackson was from Aurelio. Slim and refined, his limbs lithe, his fingernails manicured, Aurelio was an elegant man—not a pile of brawn. He moved with grace, not the swagger of a bundle of testosterone.

Apparently finished, she continued to observe as Jackson tossed plastic bags into his wheelbarrow followed by his metal rake. Tugging the gloves from his hands, he pitched them in too. Then, wheeling the contents over to his truck, he opened the tailgate and put the bags in a heavy box, ostensibly his mobile trash bin, and followed with the rake and wheelbarrow, securing them with straps.

Another swipe of his forehead and he jumped into his truck, igniting the engine to life. As he threw it into reverse, the customary *pow* blew smoke from the exhaust pipe and away he went.

Moving from the window, she mulled over the enigma the man presented. Retirement. She couldn't imagine what that life would look like for him. And islands? What did Michael mean?

The telephone rang, pulling Jennifer from her thoughts. Strolling into the kitchen, she answered. "Hello?"

"Hey Jen."

"Hey, Sam."

"What's the matter?"

"Nothing," she replied, her gaze drifting back out the windows. "Why?"

"You sound like hell."

Jennifer blew a heavy sigh, slipping loose bangs behind an ear. "Well, if you must know, it's your bartender friend from Michael's party."

"What?"

"He's my landscaper."

"You lost me."

"He's the landscaper Michael recommended. Seems bartending is not his only skill."

"Well, I'll be damned!"

"Me, too," Jennifer replied, none to happy about the bouncing grin she heard in Sam's voice.

"He's a talented thing, isn't he?"

Jennifer spoke pointedly into the mouthpiece and said, "The jury is still out on that one, counselor."

"Not *this* jury. I can't wait to see him! What time should I be over?"

"Nice try, but he's already left for the day."

"Damn," she said, her voice laced with disappointment.

Jennifer brushed her hair behind an ear. "Was there something else?"

"No. Just called to chat."

She sighed. "Do you mind if we do so another time? I'm exhausted and want nothing more than to soak in a hot bath."

"You want to fantasize, don't you?"

"Please?" She hardened her tone. "I don't need this right now."

"No problem. I'll call you tomorrow."

"Tomorrow." Too tired to protest, she could only be thankful Sam let it go without a fight. But that was Sam. Easy on, easy off. Heading for the bathroom, Jennifer yearned for the same effortless state of mind. Yes, Sam had a legal career and dealt with hard and fast deadlines every day, but the stress was different. It wasn't personal. Dealing with someone else's problems was a heck of a lot easier than dealing with your own.

Chapter Eleven

Jennifer arose early on Saturday morning, more out of habit than necessity, but sleeping in had never been her style. Lying around in bed once she was awake was a waste of time. She had too many things to do and not enough time to do them and tonight was Aurelio's grand opening.

Pleasure coursed through her. Tonight marked the completion of years of hard work and she couldn't be more pleased. Completely naked, she strolled across hardwood floors, opening the back porch door on her way to the kitchen, inviting the sunrise and bird chatter to filter indoors. April was her favorite time of year. Days grew longer, temperatures were cool and the humidity relatively low; perfect for filling the house with fresh morning air.

Brushing tousled hair behind one ear, she turned on the coffeemaker, then poured herself a glass of orange juice. Roaming nude through her home was simply an indulgence, her privacy ensured by a wooded backyard, a thick overgrowth of bougainvillea reaching almost ten feet above the back wall. Especially important in her case. It wouldn't do for people to know the conservative Dr. Hamilton was a closet nudist! Enclosing her hands around her glass she chuckled and shook her head. *Wouldn't do at all.*

But moving about her house undressed gave her a sense of abandon. Liberating really, from the confines of her role and position of authority within the community. She strongly doubted anyone would suspect she had a free-spirited side, a wilder side, but she did. And the secret gave her great satisfaction.

Leaning comfortably against the counter, she gazed through the plate glass windows of her breakfast nook and noted the yard was clean, the dirt raked. Everything seemed to be coming together, but in time?

She took a sip from her juice and pushed the negative memories aside. Dawn was breaking overhead, the sun sprinkling its soft light through gracefully arched branches of an ancient live oak. Down below, a squirrel darted about in the dapple of light, collecting its treasure for the day. She smiled.

Morning was her favorite time of day. She enjoyed watching nature at work. It reminded her of the business of living, of getting things done. Despite her neglect, hers was a beautiful piece of property, though at the moment she had a hard time imagining Jackson's drawings as reality. Not in one month's time.

Sudden doubt pulled at her. *Was she deluding herself? Was it insane to believe it could be done?* This idea of landscaping a yard in a matter of weeks and expecting satisfactory results? It was nothing short of wishful thinking, wasn't it?

Something she was not prone to do.

The realization hit hard. But that's exactly what she was doing, wasn't she? Creating a scenario almost certain to fail?

Thoughts drifted to her mother. So frail, so hopeful...

Jennifer withdrew her focus from the yard, releasing it to a soft blur on the breakfast table. Her mother was so ill, yet so full of spirit. It shone in her eyes every time she spoke of the impending ceremony. She inhaled deep and slow, tempering the fleeting beat of her heart, then blew it out with a sigh. Wishful thinking or not, she had committed. She had chosen her course and must now see it through. It was the last gift she could bestow upon her mother and come hell or hurricane, she was going to get it done.

The coffee machine beeped three times. She only hoped the effort didn't blow up in her face.

Reaching into an upper cabinet she withdrew a coffee filter and filled it with dark, aromatic grounds; a specialty brand Aurelio secured for her from Colombia. Latching the cup into place she flipped the switch into the on position.

She caught movement out of the corner of her eye. "What the—" Jennifer froze. Her pulse skyrocketed. Jackson walked by her window. She dropped to the floor. *Did he see her*?

Conscious of the perspiration spray to her underarms, she burrowed her squatted body into the corner of her cabinets. Her heart pounded. She couldn't be seen like this!

Voices called back and forth. *What were they doing here on a Saturday*? Spotting the top of their heads walking around the back, she panicked. The back doors were wide open.

Now what? Make a dash for it?

She glanced at the back doors. Not a chance. There was no way she'd make it by without them seeing her. Her pulse skittered.

Seeing her naked. She groaned. Oh, wouldn't *that* be perfect. Dr. Jennifer Hamilton... She closed her eyes. Notorious streaker.

Her career would be ruined.

She popped open her eyes. What if they checked her open door? What if they poked their heads in and called her name.

She shuddered. That could not happen. Inching upward, she peered over the kitchen table. The man following Jackson had black hair and dark skin. He wore a loaded tool belt and carried a large white bucket. She briefly wondered what he needed a bucket for until they headed for the cracked wall. He must be the fellow Jackson hired to work on the back fountain.

Rising a tad higher, she scanned the perimeter for others. Seeing no one, she decided this was her best chance. She'd make a run for it while they were far enough away to miss her.

Crawling across the kitchen on all fours, she headed toward the living room; deeper into her house and further from view. Then, like a trapped animal, she made a dash for it. She yanked the blanket from the armrest when a man shouted.

Oh my God! Her heart thumped hard against her ribs. He sounded like he was standing right outside her door! Nearly tripping as she wrapped the material around her body, she flattened her body against a wall. Mostly hidden by an enormous armoire, she edged around the piece and checked for onlookers.

No one. Dropping her head back against the wall, she struggled for calm. Breathe. Breathe, darn it, breathe. Satisfied no one was in plain view she slid around the corner and ran to her bedroom. As she passed the back windows, she could see Jackson and the dark-haired man by the wall, but where was the other one?

Instantly alarmed that he must be outside the kitchen—watching her streak!—she slammed the door closed. Mortified as a guilty teenager, she struggled to catch her breath.

This was ridiculous! This was her home! Noting shades were still drawn, she thanked God for small favors.

Jennifer took more breaths to calm the rapid rhythm of her heart. Once back in control, she turned the lock on her door to assure her privacy, then reminded herself that the prospect of strangers in her backyard was something she was going to have to get used to—at least for the next couple of weeks anyway. Otherwise, the entire city will learn some interesting new tidbits about Dr. Jennifer Hamilton!

Shower. She seized upon the idea at once. Shower first, coffee second. She moaned, instantly craving her Java Mocha. A creature of habit, this wasn't going to be easy.

Forty-five minutes later Jennifer emerged from her bedroom a new woman. Dressed in khaki Capris and a sleeveless blue button-down, her hair blown-dry and complexion lightly made-up, she was ready for a taste of the heavy scent of coffee drifting through her home.

Peering out through the open patio doors as she ambled across the living room, she could see Jackson and his assistant smearing stucco over the wall. He seemed to be working as hard as his hired hand, causing her to wonder, did he put this much face-time in all his projects? Or was this one special, because Michael had insisted.

Pulling a ceramic mug from the cabinet she poured the coffee, replaced the carafe, and brought the hot liquid to her lips. She winced.

More cream. Setting the cup down on the counter, she fetched the carton of creamer and doused her coffee with a wallop. Must be what happens when coffee is allowed to sit, she mused soberly. Tasting it again and satisfied it was drinkable, she sighed. Oh well. Some things can't be helped.

It's not every day you find strange men lurking in your yard!

Plucking a pink grapefruit from the refrigerator, she grabbed a knife and plate and began to cut the individual sections. Though she had toyed with the idea in the shower—what if Jackson had seen her? A thrill shot through her belly. What if she had been inappropriately exposed? Would he have said something? Would they pretend it never happened? Jennifer shook the thoughts away. *Stop.* The man is here to work, not spy.

Her attention drifted from her task and back into the yard.

Definitely an industrious one, she'd give him that. At least on this job. Judging by his knowledge of plants and his skill at drawing, he could probably be successful—if he wanted to be. He need only apply himself and he could have a real business going where he wouldn't need to tend bar.

The question loomed heavy in her mind. Why settle for digging through dirt and part-time bartending, if you could do better? Was this a family business? She glanced back at him. Did he feel obligated to continue in this line of work?

Jennifer set her mug on the breakfast table and walked out the front door in search of her newspaper, only to crush it underfoot. Startled, she reached down and picked it up. How did the *Herald* manage to make it to her doorstep? But no sooner had the thought occurred, so did the answer—

Jackson. Well, wasn't that a thoughtful thing to do. She turned back into the house with a soft close of the door. Placing the paper on the table, she topped off her coffee mug and settled into a chair to eat—one that gave her a bird's-eye view of the backyard activity.

Jackson and his associate were laughing as they worked. Perhaps a funny tale shared over someone's cavorting the night before? Jennifer imagined men discussed those things, much like women did. Probably divulged a lot more detail, though. She experienced a mild shiver at the thought. Never do anything with a man you're dating that you don't want shared with his buddies, right?

Hmph. Perhaps one worried about that with other men, but not with Aurelio. He was a model of integrity; a man made from the cornerstone of honesty and respect. He would never talk in such a crude manner.

A half-hour passed as Jennifer enjoyed a leisurely breakfast, perusing the day's headlines. Jackson and his helper hadn't budged from their task, other than to change position along the wall. She was impressed. At this rate, they were making great strides, almost three-quarters of the way finished. Her mood lifted. Things were beginning to look up around here now that everything was under control.

Rising from her chair, she decided now was as good a time as any to check their progress. Refreshing her coffee, she slipped on a pair of leather slides she kept by the door and walked out onto the terrace. Across the quiet, she could hear the occasional metal clang against cement, the scraping as the men smoothed the wet cement mixture over the wall.

On either side of her yard, mounds of black dirt dotted with bright-orange flags and lined with string provided her only clue as to what lay ahead. Other than his phenomenal drawings of course, but paper and ink was one thing. Real life perspective was quite another.

She recalled that his plan called for a hedge between the driveway and grass and it was clearly marked as such, several holes already dug. The center aisle arbor that was to connect wall fountain and pool remained a vision in her imagination, as the space was currently free of any such markings.

Squatting to spackle the base Jackson turned, abandoning the wall for a moment to look in her direction. He smiled.

The unexpected spotlight of his attention caused a minor stir of self-consciousness. Jennifer waved and smiled back, slightly uneasy at being caught staring at him. But since he was doing the same, now was as "innocuous" an opportunity as any to make the first move.

Careful not to fill her sandals with dirt, she approached.

He stood, and without entirely deserting his work space took a few steps in her direction. Wearing khaki shorts and boots, no sweat on his brow, his appearance was neat, save for that stubborn mess atop his head.

"Good morning!" he called out.

"Good morning," she returned.

A patter of birdsong rang out as morning stretched into noon. The sun trickled in through the overhead oaks and while humidity dampened the air, it wasn't too heavy. The heat hadn't become oppressive yet thank goodness, or her makeup would be on the verge of melting.

A complication she didn't need when trying to put her best face forward. She gazed about the immediate vicinity in feigned indifference and sought comfort in benign conversation. "Do you always work on weekends?"

"Usually," he grinned. "But Sundays I keep for myself."

Not last Sunday, he hadn't. She came to a stop a good ten feet away. "So how's it coming?"

"Great. We're really making some headway on the fountain." Jackson turned to introduce the other man. "This is Carlos." The shorter fellow nodded a cheeky smile in her direction. "He's my masonry guy. He'll be forming the basin for the fountain this week, and then attach the fountainhead."

"Will he also be responsible for the tile?"

"No." Jackson shook his head as though the thought was absurd. "I have a special outfit I'll be using for the tile work. They specialize in international ceramics and I think you'll be happier with their selection and application process. The guy's going to call me tomorrow with his schedule. Then I'll have a better idea when I can get the sample books of tile for you to choose from."

Jennifer nodded, and Carlos stood.

"*Voy a coger mas.*"

"*Si*," Jackson replied. He placed his spatula on a temporary work table and proceeded to pull off his gloves.

Carlos gave another nod in her direction. "*Senora.*"

"*Senorita,*" Jackson corrected with a good-natured grin, tossing his chin toward Jennifer. "*No esta casada. Todavia,*" he winked.

"Sorry," Carlos said, his English thick, and aimed a sheepish smile in her direction.

Jennifer turned to Jackson in surprise. "You speak Spanish?"

He laughed. "Doesn't everybody in Miami?"

"No," she mumbled. It wasn't one of the subjects she had chosen to learn.

"A lot of my subs are Spanish so yes, I learned a little over the years. I'm not fluent, or anything close!" he added without an ounce of shame. "I speak mostly the nuts and bolts of the language, especially that which pertains to my business. It gets me by."

"It's more than I know," she said, bringing the warm cup of coffee to her lips.

"I plan on putting in the hibiscus today," he said, the change in subject brisk.

She withdrew her mug in surprise? "So soon?"

"The sooner I get them in, the better they'll look for the big day." Jackson smiled again, pleasure swallowing his eyes.

Something he did quite often, Jennifer noticed. In fact, smiling seemed second-nature to him.

Which she felt to be refreshing. She straightened a bit and cleared her throat. "Listen," she said, establishing a semblance of objectivity to her voice, "I realize Michael told you why I'm pressed to get this landscaping in, but—"

He held up a hand. "No explanation necessary. Nothing becomes a bride like a garden wedding." Gloves held in one hand, he hitched his shorts up a little higher then settled both hands to hips.

"Yes, well," she said, uncomfortable at revealing her personal affairs. "It's a little more complicated than that." Shifting her weight from one foot to the other, she mulled over the best approach. While she didn't want to give him the impression she was some foolish young bride who wanted what she wanted— when she wanted it—she did want him to understand why her situation demanded haste.

"Michael mentioned your mother," Jackson intervened, his tone dropped in reverence.

"Yes. Well, the truth of the matter..." she hemmed. "I could just as easily go to the Justice of the Peace, but it's not really an option and..."

Brown eyes filled with understanding. "I know."

The compassion in his expression closed her throat with a hard lump. Unable to speak, Jennifer didn't attempt to fill the pause.

"A bride is such a beautiful creature," he moved easily past the uncomfortable silence. "You can't waste that on a dirty government building. Your mother's right." His eyes softened. "A garden complements a woman in love like nothing else."

Beautiful creature? *Complements a woman in love*?

Jennifer had to work her almost certain gape under control.

But not him. His smile returned full force, opening his features in full appreciation. It was a combination that shattered her shell of indifference.

Swallowing, she grasped the mug more tightly within her hands. "My mother was an avid gardener you see...spent hour upon hour with her flowers, tending to them, nurturing them. I think she even talked to them," Jennifer revealed with a hint of insecurity. *Would he think that foolish*?

"Mine, too," he replied. "Every day of her life."

She looked at him more directly. "Really?"

"Absolutely. Plants are living things. They share the energy of life with us. It makes sense to connect with them, on all levels. From planting and nurturing, to pleasure and enjoyment." Jackson smiled. "We humans can't get along without the green stuff. The way I see it, we're all in this together and it would help if we would recognize as much." He followed with a grin. "Our lives would be a lot more pleasant."

It was strange, hearing a man like Jackson discuss the philosophical nature of life. He spoke of the garden as if it were an integral part of his existence, as though the two were intricately entwined to create the whole of his world.

And then she remembered. "You know, my mother probably did *live her garden*." As the phrase was intentional, she offered a small smile for his benefit.

"She probably did," Jackson replied, easily accepting the gesture. No victorious tone, no arrogance. He responded as though her comment were no more significant than if she had said the sky is blue. He slid his fingers into his front pockets. "It was my mom who gave me a love of nature. When I was growing up, my sister and I would spend hours outside while she pulled weeds and cut flowers. When we weren't running around like crazies, that is." He shook his head. "She'd assign us chores in the garden, to make us feel involved I think." The old trick registered with fondness in his adult eyes. "Like what we were doing was crucial to the survival of the plants, not to mention our very existence." He laughed. "My sister had a black thumb right from the start whereas mine, though it started out brown, gradually became as green as my mother's."

Jennifer couldn't help but smile as she listened to him. He spoke with obvious affection, and his eyes shone with pride. It felt like a dear friend citing shared experiences from the past, reinforcing a bond between them that had been initiated years before.

But they shared no such bond. She and Jackson were basically strangers. "I never really had the inclination to join my mother in the garden," she admitted, glancing away.

Her mom had invited her, but she never pushed. "It seemed like nothing more than a pile of work to me," she returned her gaze to his and funneled in her rationale, her defense. "I was focused on my studies, and there didn't seem room for much of anything else."

"It is a pile of work," he agreed heartily, placing an emphasis on the word work. "Or can be," he relaxed into a confident grin. "It's all a matter of perception. Like I said before—it's why I try to design a garden that suits the individual, one where they look forward to spending their time as opposed to avoiding." He pulled a hand from his shorts and gestured toward Jennifer. "Like your mom. She probably used hers as an escape, a therapy if you will. A physician's schedule is ruthless, demands shooting in from every angle. An hour sitting amidst the blossoms can distract even the most harried of professionals. Me, I'd say your mom probably topped that list."

Did he know her mother?

"Does she have a favorite?"

"Favorite what?" she asked, startled by the blunt question.

"A favorite flower."

"Gardenias..." Jennifer murmured. "Those are her favorites."

"Ah yes," his voice melted to silk, "the petals of velvet with an unforgettable scent."

An unforgettable scent. Her heart ached. And one etched in her mind forever.

"Nature is the center of the soul, Dr. Hamilton. It speaks to our senses on every level, reconnecting us with the spirit within."

Nature is the center of the soul. It was stunning to hear such sentiment uttered from his lips. Unexpected. "Yes," she uttered quietly. "It does. And please." She looked at him with a tentative smile. "Call me Jennifer."

Jackson smiled, seemingly pleased by her invitation. "Jennifer," he said, as though trying it on for size and liked it.

She smiled in return.

"My favorite thing about gardens," he picked right back up, "is they attract all kinds of life. Bees, birds, butterflies—all of them flock to the sweet bounty of the garden."

"My mom used to have a birdhouse in hers," Jennifer pitched in, enjoying their newfound camaraderie. "Actually, it was more like a bird *hotel*." She laughed softly. "Designed along the lines of a Victorian mansion, it was painted with extraordinary detail, bright blues and greens and scrolls everywhere. There was even a welcome home message written in script across the main entryway." Amazed by her vivid recall, she said, "The thing was fit more for a king than a bird!"

"I'll bet they loved it."

"They did." She paused. "In fact, she loved them." She looked at Jackson more directly. "The birds, I mean. She loved listening to them, watching them. Why, she could close her eyes and identify a bird simply based on its song." Jennifer allowed the warm memories to wash over her, and soothe her in their passage. It was a nice change when talking about her mother, to feel the fullness of her life instead of the impending loss.

"Passion comes in all forms."

Her pulse bumped at the mention of the word. "I imagine..." she replied with a slight nod.

"It's about following your heart you know, and living in the moment. Finding joy in the little things."

Relaxed, Jennifer's mind pulled away and drifted back through time. Two years ago, upon first diagnosis, her mother began sorting through her belongings. She preferred personal distribution as opposed to utilizing a will, and offered the elaborate birdhouse to Jennifer.

Which she refused. *Where on earth would I put a bird house? On the balcony of my condo?*

Her mother's smile never quit, Jennifer remembered but her eyes had given pause over the rejection. And that's what her refusal surely must have been; a rejection, of her mother's most personal and cherished possession.

Tears pushed at her eyes. How could she have been so insensitive?

Carlos returned then and Jennifer was grateful for the interruption. Resuming his work without delay, he dumped his bag in hand into the plastic bucket, added some water from the metal one next to it and began to mix the combination with a slow hand.

"I should let you get back to your work," Jennifer said, mortified her words sounded so weak, as though on the verge of breaking.

"No problem," Jackson replied, his genial tone giving her plenty of room to negotiate.

She turned back and headed for the house, overwhelmed by a sudden onslaught of heat. She hadn't been outside long, but it felt like the temperature had climbed ten degrees. The sun beat down on her as she crossed the yard, then straight up the steps into the house. She deposited her mug into the sink, realizing there would be no third cup this morning.

With a bolt of energy, she cleared the dishes from the table, rinsed and sorted them into the dishwasher, then went back to collect the newspaper scattered across the table.

Had she really been so cruel to her mother? Had she really? And why? Why couldn't she have seen what Jackson saw and realized it was important to her. Breaking focus, Jennifer looked out the window to find him hard at work plastering the wall. He wouldn't have rejected the birdhouse, she thought. He would have accepted it. Gladly.

Unlike her. She couldn't see past her own desires to empathize with those of her mother.

Jennifer reeled-in her thoughts. But it was a long time ago. She stacked the newspaper pages against the glass tabletop. There was no going back.

Her movements ceased, the newspaper flopping over in her hands. What kind of man was Jackson? Still mulling through their conversation, her mind hummed with his presence. What kind of man read a woman's needs and understood them, respected them?

Celebrated them. Slowly, she returned her gaze to the backyard—specifically, the back wall. Beneath his rough-edged exterior, his casual demeanor, she had glimpsed a sensitive side, an insightful side.

Really? Or had she imagined it, projected her thoughts onto his and engaged in an interesting conversation about life and gardening. She remained for a moment, watching his arms spread cement in wide, smooth arcs. His movements were swift and sinuous. Strong.

Jennifer withdrew her gaze and dropped it to the papers in hand. She smacked the *Herald* down onto the table, organized or not. She felt the sudden urge to move.

She could go to the hospital. Round on the few patients she had and then get ready for Aurelio's opening this evening. She checked her watch. Well after noon, her partner on call, Jennifer realized it would be a waste of time to go to the hospital.

She could go see her mother.

No, she thought quickly. A visit to the nursing home was the *last* thing she wanted right now. It would drain the positive energy that was flowing through her every cell—positive energy—and she didn't want to lose it. She ventured a glance toward Jackson. Arms moving with power and speed, she thought, yes...it is positive. And empowering, like the way his body moved. Reaching into the bucket for more cement, she watched him spread the heavy wet material high over the wall, his movements smooth and fluid, almost graceful. The man had a strength she wouldn't have guessed on first glance. From hauling heavy bags to handling a shovel, he moved with ease in everything he did, both inside and out. He turned toward her then and for a split-second, Jennifer thought he caught her watching him.

Her pulse quickened and she pulled her glance away. Moving from the kitchen, she headed to the front room, putting space between them. She didn't want to give him the wrong impression. Didn't want him to think she was interested.

Or give herself any more time to wonder.

Chapter Twelve

Carrying the bouquet of long-stemmed roses across her living room, Jennifer saw Sam's red Mercedes zip into the driveway and clip to a stop just shy of the front walk. Sliding out of the car she tossed the door closed behind her and with that long-legged stride of hers, breezed through the courtyard and let herself in.

"Aren't these beautiful?" Jennifer asked, placing the large vase on the coffee table. "They're from Aurelio."

"Gorgeous," she agreed flatly as Jennifer leaned over for her expected kiss. Sam smacked her with a solid one on the cheek and asked, "Speaking of gorgeous, where is Jax?" She glanced out the back windows, hunting for sight of him. "I saw a truck parked in the back."

"He's out there," Jennifer said, indicating the rear yard. "He's marking out the flower beds."

Sam strode to the back doors for a better look. "Oh... Be still my wanton heart."

Jennifer joined her and saw Jackson bending over, wrapping string around a stick that protruded from the ground.

"I think this is fate."

"It's not," Jennifer said. "It's your over-active hormones."

Jackson stood, massaged his lower back for a second then grabbed his spade. Raising it to a height above his shoulders, he thrust it deep into the dirt wedging it back and forth, then did so again. "God, I find manual labor sexy," Sam said, her voice a near purr. She rubbed her firebrick painted lips over one another. "The way his muscles jump and glisten..."

"He's sweating."

"Profusely."

"He probably stinks."

"Pheromones... An innate call to the wild."

Jennifer balked. "But he's dirty."

"I hope so."

Jennifer crossed her arms in a huff. "You're incorrigible."

"No," Sam swung her eyes to Jennifer, "I'm agreeable."

With that, she opened the door and let herself out. Jennifer watched from the anonymity of indoors as Sam trotted down the steps and straight over to Jackson. His recognition of her was swift, his reception friendly. Plunging the garden tool into the ground, he hitched an elbow atop the handle, resting a foot on the blade.

The two chatted with ease she noted, yet presented a startling contrast. Jackson donned his usual company T-shirt, soaked through with sweat, complete with his standard khaki shorts and boots while Sam was dressed in a stylish fitted skirt, sizzling crimson and cut just above the knee, accompanied by a simple coordinating jacket over a silk white tank. Her black sling-backs remained amazingly dirt-free.

How did she do it? How did Sam walk up to complete strangers and engage in lively conversation like old friends? Curiosity deepened. What could they be talking about? What did Sam have in common with Jackson, other than a healthy dose of lust?

Jackson threw his head back and laughed.

Jennifer felt a pinch of envy. It must be a skill honed in the courtroom. As a trial attorney, Sam was forever in front of people and her main objective: woo their hearts and minds to her client's side. What had become a winner's instinct on the job had become second-nature in her personal life.

Jennifer ran her hands down the sides of her royal blue silk dress, smoothing them over the soft material. She met new people all the time. She was friendly and amenable. She was known for her pleasant bedside manner and easy camaraderie with patients. That's what everyone said, anyway...

But watching Sam and Jackson, she realized theirs was a different connection. More than simple lust on a physical level, they seemed to share an ease of relations, and ease of communication. Every time she was around Jackson, she felt unsettled. Not uncomfortable really, but out-of-balance somehow. Flustered.

Why was that? What made him so difficult for her?

Seized by a prickly sensation of antsy, Jennifer glanced at her wristwatch. Well after four, it was time to go. Aurelio was waiting.

Jennifer opened the door. "Sam," she called out. "We need to get going." She felt stiff and severe, awkward.

"Okay," Sam nodded but didn't move, stirring Jennifer's impatience. She walked out and stood near the edge of her patio. She abhorred being late, especially on Aurelio's big night. "It's four-*twenty*."

Sam looked up at the same time as Jackson, but their eyes held contrary reactions. Hers was the usual, *okay, I hear you.* His was, *is there a problem?*

"Hey, Jen," Sam said. "Do you know an artist by the name of Bruce Marsh?"

She shook her head. "No, the name doesn't sound familiar."

"Jax says he's a Florida artist. Does a lot of water and nature scenes."

Jennifer looked at him, surprised he knew any artist by name. "No," she said again. "I don't. What medium does he use?"

"Paint," Jackson spoke up. "He paints some incredible impressions, where the entire canvas appears to be water, as though you're looking over the edge of your boat in the middle of nowhere. You'd swear the water was moving," he said, admiration painting a soft smile on his face. "The way he catches the play of light across the surface is unbelievable. He also does shorelines, waves against sand, some marshy areas. His work is exceptional and very distinct. Once you've seen one, you can recognize them anywhere."

"Maybe we can ask Aurelio," Sam suggested. "He should know."

"Maybe," Jennifer agreed, but what was the point? Was she really going to buy the latest and greatest of some unknown artist, based on the opinion of Jackson Montgomery?

Sam turned back to Jackson and said, "I'll check it out. Might be the perfect touch for my condo."

"Why would you want a painting of water hanging on your wall?" Her place on Brickell Avenue hosted one of the most enviable views in the city. "You stare at it through your windows all day long."

"For the nights," she grinned, encouraging the same from Jackson. Sam spun her focus back around to him. "But enough small talk. We've got to hit the road." She gave a firm pat to his shoulder and said, "Nice to see you again, Jax."

"You too, Sam."

Jennifer waited as Sam returned to the house. "You might want to wash your hand."

"Nah. I'd rather his scent linger a while longer."

"So, can I assume you two have a date?"

"Unfortunately, not." Her eyes held a faint defeat. "He's seeing someone."

"Oh well, better luck next time," Jennifer said, a strange disappointment grazing her mood. What did she care if Sam "struck out?" The woman had hordes of men, hanging in wait for her merest nod. One loss should not have the power to dampen her evening.

Nor hers.

With a swift tug of the front door, Jennifer followed Sam outside. She slipped into the passenger side of the shiny sports car and buckled herself in. Sam did likewise and ignited the car to life with a smooth thrust around the circular drive.

Unable to shut out thoughts of Jackson, she ventured, "So what did you two find so interesting a discussion?"

Sam slapped a grin on her face. "Art. The man's a connoisseur."

"Come now, be serious." Jennifer dipped her face, but kept her eyes fixed on Sam. "One memorized artist name does not make one a connoisseur."

"He knows his stuff."

"What stuff?" She drew back. "Art?"

"Art, use of color, the implicit subtext of emotion..."

"And you're the one to know the difference."

"I know a little. Enough to banter back and forth with him, anyway!"

"You sure he wasn't trying to flatter you?" she asked, bothered by the nip of jealousy she felt.

Sam laughed. "It wasn't flattery. He's a straight shooter, that one." Rolling through a stop sign, she accelerated her merge onto the highway and traffic closed in around them.

"And you know this how? As far as I know, you've spent all of ten minutes with the man."

"I read people for a living. I can spot the genuine deal when I see it."

"Hmmm..."

"What do you have against him, anyway?"

"Nothing."

"Is it the bartender thing?" Sam shot the question like an accusation.

Jennifer flipped her gaze back to Sam. "No. He's a landscaper, remember?"

"That's right. A service for which you're willing to pay dearly."

She crossed her arms. He's also about to retire she thought, her gaze touching upon the red Ferrari cruising past them while avoiding the driver's lecherous wink. But she said nothing. She refused to give Sam that kind of ammunition.

"I don't get it," Sam sailed over the pause. "He's a nice guy, hard-working, good-looking. As far as I see it, the only thing wrong with him is that he's unavailable."

She swiped a glance to her side. "You want to date him, now?"

"You bet I would," she said with a smile and a shake of her wavy hair. "Unlike you, I don't have such restrictive criteria for my prospective mates."

"You have no criteria."

"Oh c'mon, of course I do," she replied, and defiance sparked in her dark brown eyes. "But mine deals with the man inside."

"And mine doesn't?"

Sam waved her hand at Jennifer like she was a nuisance fly. "Don't get all fussy with me. I'm simply suggesting you pay more attention to the outside, the career, success, than you do the inside."

"You make me sound like a shallow gold-digger—which I'm not," she snapped. "I have high standards and there's nothing wrong with that."

Jennifer uncrossed her arms and resituated her position in the small leather seat. Staring out the window, traveling the highway, they were passing downtown Miami. Most buildings were tall and sleek, while others were short and sullied creating a mix of old and new, interspersed with palms and tropical foliage. Elevated about mid-level, the Metrorail wound oddly through them, like a space-train cruising through the air.

"You're not a shallow gold-digger," Sam said. "*Obviously*. You're a successful cardiologist. The point I'm trying to make is that you wouldn't date anyone who didn't make as much or more money than you. You hold men to the same bullion standard as gold-digging women do, but for different reasons. If they don't earn a good living like you do, then they're not worth your commitment."

Jennifer couldn't quite deny the accusation, but she didn't like the way it sounded. It made her assessment of men seem superficial when the truth was, she looked for a variety of traits, success being one of many.

She considered their education, their goals, both short-term and long. She contemplated their personal interests and hobbies, took into account the compatibility of their personalities and career choices.

Jennifer resented the insinuation that she was shallow. "I consider a myriad of aspects when considering a prospective husband, which is what I'm looking for in a man. To me, passing time with a man who won't meet my goals is pointless."

"Not everyone wants to get married, Jen. It doesn't make for a bad person." Sam whipped the car left, passing a bright-green VW bug ahead of them.

"No, but when you are considering the prospect of marriage," she pushed, "economic stability is a very important quality."

"You don't have to be rich to be happy."

"Similar interests and hobbies are important as well," she continued, ignoring the comment. "When two people come from entirely different backgrounds you are setting yourself up for disappointment."

"Jackson appreciates art, same as you and Aurelio."

Not on the same level Jennifer felt certain, but disregarded the comparison. "Then there are the long-term goals regarding career and family to consider. The short-term goals."

"Goals are good."

"When you marry," she emphasized, annoyed by the interruption, "the entire family must be considered."

"You might like his family."

"I'm talking about mine." Jennifer wouldn't do that to her mother. Her mother expected more, and more she intended to deliver. "All of this must be compatible." She spoke as teacher to student. "Jackson may appreciate a particular artist, but I assure you he is not interested in world travel, at least not to the same destinations I would like to explore. Nor is he the type to concern himself with which private school may best suit his child, or whether he wants children at all."

"How do you know that?" Sam fired back. "Have you ever discussed it?"

Jennifer returned a glare. "Obviously not."

"Well then you don't know, do you? All you have is assumption. Give him a minute of your time, and you might be surprised."

"I doubt it," she replied, slightly unnerved recalling their conversation from earlier today. Jackson had indeed surprised her, but only because she hadn't expected his vision to be so flowery, so detailed...

So *romantic*. The images he had created, the way he spoke of a bride... She had been more than surprised—she had been drawn in, eager to learn more about him, his past...

Like his mother. She was a gardener, much like her mom. And his sister had been married in a garden, like she was going to be. So they had a few things in common. Some interesting common ties. It was nowhere near enough to build a life upon.

"Stranger things have happened," Sam remarked with a mischievous gleam in her eye. "All you have to do is open the door."

Jennifer sealed her thoughts closed on the subject. Whether Sam was motivated by true belief or the spice of the battle she didn't know, but either way she always pushed, and right now Jennifer was feeling the shove.

She wasn't shallow. She wasn't judgmental. She was practical; a realist. She knew what she wanted in life and had a plan to get there. Her door had already been opened and she was walking through, hand in hand, with Aurelio.

There was no need to open up another door, nor did she hold anything against a man like Jackson for living his life by the bed of a pick-up.

Did she?

And why did it matter? Despite what Sam claimed, she accepted others as they were. Granted, she may not want to marry a man like him, but it didn't mean she looked down on his choices.

Did she?

Feeling uncomfortable in the tiny bucket seat, Jennifer hit the forward button on her mind play. This stream of thought was nonsensical. Why Jackson didn't make a good fit was irrelevant. She had found her perfect companion and there was no need to explore other possibilities.

Case closed.

Tonight was about Aurelio, not Jackson, and she couldn't wait to see him. This was a shining moment for her fiancé and she intended to fully support him, *without* distraction.

Putting the matter behind her, she noted the sign for their exit. A squiggle of nerves jumped in her belly.

Chapter Thirteen

Ten minutes later, Sam whipped her Mercedes to a tight stop in front of *Illuminations*, Aurelio's gallery located on Espanola Way. Neon lettering lit up the name in a calming blue, while spotless glass walls revealed standing room only. Cast in soft shades of color by interior lighting, patrons milled among the paintings and sculptures. Judging by the size of the group, it appeared his opening was a triumphant success.

"Hot damn," Sam exclaimed softly. "Who do we have here?"

Jennifer glanced briefly at the young valet while she applied a last touch of lipstick to her lips. Tall, slender and blonde, he looked to be all of twenty years of age.

Sam popped out of the driver's seat as he opened her door. "Hello, gorgeous..." she rolled out in a near purr.

Must she? Jennifer sighed. She replaced the lipstick into her slim purse and rose from the vehicle as the valet held her door. Breathing in the salt-misted air, she stepped onto the sidewalk of the narrow street and mentally prepared herself for the evening ahead.

"Take care of my baby, will you?"

"Yes Ma'am," he replied.

"I might be back for *you*," Sam whispered with a merry wink, then turned to Jennifer. "Damn, if this party isn't getting off to a good start!"

Jennifer grasped her by the arm. "Slow down, Casanova. You're scaring the help," she said, aware the valet's attention traced Sam's every move, especially her long, hose-free stride.

"I assure you, I am doing nothing of the kind." She chuckled wicked and low. "That boy is thinking of nothing but having his way with me this very minute—you can take that to the bank."

Jennifer rolled her eyes. Probably. But tonight was about Aurelio, not Sam's next score.

"Let's hope Slim-Hips has invited some manly men to his opening. I'm going to need all the distraction I can get after an eyeful of that little Kiwi!"

"Maybe you should pay attention to the art," Jennifer suggested. "You might just expand your horizons."

Grasping hold of the silver-plated handle, Sam opened the door. "My horizons are wide enough, thank you for noticing, but I was hoping for a little fun tonight." She stopped abruptly, as though from sudden thought. "Tell me it's an open bar."

Jennifer rolled her eyes. "Yes. Rest assured your liver won't shrivel up from inactivity."

"Good," she replied. "That baby needs regular exercise."

Jennifer shook her head in mock frustration, but chuckled nonetheless as she walked inside.

South Beach played a few beats faster than most, with edgy, trendy music spiking the atmosphere with an international flair. While she was partial to Coral

Gables proper, the beach provided a nice change of pace, a different flavor entirely.

Located in the heart of the art deco district, *Illuminations* was mere minutes from Aurelio's high-rise home on Ocean Drive. Organized and manageable, Jennifer envied the convenience. His entire life was contained within a few blocks—*almost* his entire life, she corrected herself. She lived a half-hour away.

And then there was Africa. Her gaze darted around the gallery. They would be here tonight as well.

Meandering among stylishly dressed men and women clustered in small groups of quiet conversation, Jennifer smiled as young artists enthusiastically described their art, talking color and texture. Aurelio had given them the opportunity of a lifetime with this showing and all were eager to describe the finer nuance of their creations and technique.

Standing here immersed in his vision, she felt proud to be Aurelio's fiancé. His was a generosity of spirit and one of the things she loved most about him.

"There sure are some crazy imaginations at work out there."

"Excuse me?"

"Look at that one." She gestured toward a painting off to their left. "It looks like paint splatter with photographs superimposed over it."

Jennifer considered the piece. Basically, it was exactly as Sam said, but from the selection of photos it seemed to her the artist was drawing contrasts along generational lines. "It's a statement on society."

"How do you figure?"

She turned to address her more fully. "If you look more closely, you'll notice each photograph represents a different era."

"You're reaching."

"Art requires an extension of the mind."

"Not all art."

True, none of these resembled the works Jax spoke about, the water and play of light, but that's because they were abstract, extreme.

"I prefer the play of light on water, thank you."

Caught by the coincidence of thought, Jennifer stammered, "Well today's young artist doesn't dabble in simple subjects like earth and sky." Both knew she meant water, and both knew she refused to voice as much. "They deal in imagination."

Sam grunted, but her eyes blazed with, *Caught ya*.

"Sweetheart."

Jennifer jumped.

Aurelio swept around them and said, "I'm so glad you're finally here."

"Aurelio..."

Sam's eyes flashed a shameless, *Yep, that's his name*.

Jennifer glared at her.

A picture of understated elegance in his brushed silk shirt of salmon, black slacks and shiny Italian loafers, Aurelio pecked a soft kiss on her cheek, giving an obligatory ditto for Sam. "Sweetheart..." He placed a gentle hand on her back. "I was beginning to get worried."

"My fault," Sam piped up. "I got sidetracked."

"Yes, well..." Aurelio arched a brow. "That does seem to happen with you, doesn't it?"

Sam shrugged, unaffected by the slight. "What can I say, I'm distracted easily," she said, thrusting another mischievous glance toward Jennifer.

She returned one of her own. *I will throttle you if you keep this up.* Then returned to Aurelio and said, "The gallery is breathtaking, darling. Absolutely stunning."

"Thank you," he replied, instantly aglow in light of her praise. "I am thrilled."

"Turnout's great."

"Yes," he acknowledged Sam's observation, glancing about the gallery. "The artists are very pleased. In fact, many have already registered their first sales, accepting commissions for more."

"That's wonderful!" Jennifer exclaimed.

Aurelio linked his hand through Jennifer's and said, "I have so many people I want you to meet."

"You go ahead," Sam said. "I'll make my way around."

"Okay." Jennifer turned to Aurelio with a bright smile. "I'm all yours!"

Two hours later, Jennifer strolled up behind Sam. "I see you've found the premier artist."

She whirled around at the familiar voice. "You call *this* art?" Pointing to the colorful canvas hanging from the wall before her, she suppressed a chuckle. "It looks more like a stack of party toothpicks!"

"That's by Armando and he's quite talented in the medium." Jennifer shifted her glance to the drink in Sam's hand. Shaped like a martini glass, a rainbow-colored line began at the stem and swirled up and around to the rim of the glass, inside of which a liquid the color of ripe melon shimmered. Definitely not her standard martini. "What is *that*?"

Sam turned back to examine the work. "A Cosmopolitan."

"I repeat, what is that?" No expert on liquor, Jennifer preferred wine, and held a large-bowled glass of Cabernet.

"I don't remember exactly, but it's downright tasty." She turned and extended the glass in hand. "Would you like to try it?"

"No, thank you."

Sam shrugged. "It's good." She brought the drink to her lips for a small sip.

"Any luck with the bartender?" Jennifer asked with a playful wink.

"You're having second thoughts, aren't you?" Sam donned a victorious smile. "You missed out on Jackson, but you see the potential now, don't you." It wasn't a question, but bait. "I see the fire steaming behind those otherwise cool, baby-blues. You want him, don't you? Your hunky yard boy..."

Jennifer smiled and moved her head back and forth in a methodical no. The wine was releasing threads of tension, loosening her earlier resentment. She harbored no ill will toward Jackson, or Sam's insinuations of gold-digging.

"Not quite," she said with a smile. Bringing her glass to within inches of her nose, she swirled the deep violet liquid and breathed in the rich scent of black cherry, plum and hints of tobacco. "And speaking of hunky men, Aurelio did invite some rather handsome ones tonight. If you're nice, I'll introduce you to one or two of them."

"Are they straight?"

She drew down her glass. "Of course they're straight!"

"Uh huh," Sam said, and arched her eyes toward Aurelio. She hitched her mouth to the side and shrugged her shoulders again. "I don't know... You know, he may have us all fooled."

"I assure you," Jennifer said in response to Sam's feigned skepticism. "Aurelio is as straight as a hat pin." She zapped her with recrimination. "He's sophisticated, a quality I realize you may be unfamiliar with in your men."

Sam grinned. "In a fruitful sort of way."

"Hush," Jennifer admonished, glancing around their immediate vicinity. "Just because he's refined and has a passion for art, doesn't mean he's any less of a man's man."

"Like I said..." Sam moseyed around the corner, on to the next painting.

Realizing she had played right into Sam's crude humor, Jennifer marched around the same corner and snapped, "This is the last exhibit you're invited to, I swear."

Standing in front of a mass of shrieking color, Sam's eyes grew wide. She spit out laughter, almost spilling her drink.

"Stop!" Jennifer scowled at her, followed by a quick check to see if the artist witnessed her awful display. "Stop it right now."

"I'm sorry, I can't help it!" She turned to Jennifer with a look of innocent plea in her eyes and pointed. "What *is* that?"

Searching again for onlookers, Jennifer looked to the painting. It appeared the artist threw every color from his palette onto the canvas, and then smeared them together before running his nails or the sharp end of his paintbrush across them, this way and that. Taken aback by the presentation, she murmured, "I don't know..."

She stretched her imagination in order to find something positive to say, but was honestly having trouble. The bright shades were nice on their own, but mixed together as they were and then scratched through like that, bid another interpretation entirely. A bellyful of nausea?

"It looks like someone was trying to depict a psychedelic meltdown," Sam declared.

This comment drew a few stares.

"This is *definitely* the last exhibit for you," Jennifer stated, concealing her complete agreement on the piece.

"Okay, okay, I hear you. But you've got to admit," she said, dashing another gander toward the painting. "That's really out there."

Jennifer rolled her eyes, refusing to give in. "Let's move along. Aurelio's expecting us. We have mingling to do."

"Not *this* we."

Taking Sam by the elbow, she directed her toward the rear of the gallery. Aurelio was waiting to unveil his prized subject; a sculptured nude of jade. "*We* is plural. That means both of us."

"I thought we were making an appearance, not spending the night."

"It's a party, and you're the *party* girl. Now let's go."

"I guess I do have a reputation to uphold."

"And then some. Besides, there are some very important people here and we need to put our best face forward."

"Important people?" Sam made a quick scan of the room. "What kind of people?"

"People who want Illuminations to be the first of many galleries of its kind. Worldwide, in fact."

Her eyes grew wide. "Aurelio's going global?"

"Yes. Africa, to be precise."

She slipped into a grin. "That explains the tall, dark and handsome stranger I met earlier."

Jennifer froze. "You didn't."

"Didn't what?"

"You didn't come-on to him, did you?"

Her grin turned mischievous.

"*Tell me you didn't.*"

She winked. "Not yet."

"Not ever. That man is here to help Aurelio establish galleries, similar to *Illuminations*, in Africa."

"*Africa?*"

"Yes, and it's a very important opportunity for him. If you do anything to interfere, I'll—"

Sam held a hand between them. "Got it. But let me ask you something. When did this Africa deal come up?"

"I don't know..." Jennifer eased them away from the small clusters of people beginning to fill the area. "He told me just the other night. He's planning on traveling to Africa—er, I mean, we're planning on traveling to Africa. After our honeymoon."

Sam's dark eyes honed in. "You're kidding me, right?"

"No. They need his expertise in setting up the first one." She glanced at the floor. "He's thinking maybe a honeymoon in the Canary Islands and then a short trip to the coast. The gentlemen here this evening are from The Gambia."

"Gambia?"

"Yes. The Gambia, actually. It's a small country on the west coast. They want to start there, but intend to expand the project to other countries on the continent."

"Nice." Sam shifted her weight from heel to heel. "Selfish bastard," she murmured.

"What?" Jennifer scowled. "Since when is there something wrong in following a dream?"

"With everything you have going on in your life right now, the last thing you need is to be hauled off to Africa for your honeymoon." Anger heated Sam's gaze. "You told him no, right?"

She tensed the grip on the bowl of her glass. "Of course I didn't tell him no. I'm his fiancé, soon to be his *wife*. My job is to support him in his endeavors, not act as adversary."

"Goddamn him." Sam gulped a sip from her bright-colored drink. "I can't believe he's doing this to you."

Careful to keep her voice down, Jennifer checked the immediate vicinity for onlookers. "I'd appreciate it if you'd keep your remarks to yourself. This evening means too much to Aurelio and I don't want you causing any trouble."

Despite the fact it would prove a blessing in disguise. The men she met this evening had been charming, the conversation stimulating, but each time the subject of Africa came up and she raised the question of time, it was batted away as meaningless.

This venture is too profound to limit within the scope of time. We are building a nation, a future.

Important is what she heard. Meaningful. And she couldn't disagree. But what about building a life for the two of them? With all Aurelio's talk of Africa, there was a part of her that couldn't help feel his dream would tear them apart in the process.

Aurelio approached. Sam spotted him and Jennifer's heart stopped. She placed her free hand on Sam's forearm. "Don't."

He pecked the cheek of a pink-haired young artist and breezed over. Completely ignoring Sam, he beamed at Jennifer. "We're almost ready."

"Good," she said, a rapid pulse shredding through her chest. She flashed a warning to Sam.

It went unnoticed. She was staring at Aurelio, her eyes narrowed to slits. "So, what's this I hear about Africa?"

"Sam," Jennifer whispered harshly.

He flicked her a look of disdain. "I don't think that's any of your business."

"Aurelio, *please*."

"What's the matter?" She brought a hand to her hip and egged him on. "I would think you'd be excited, want to gush all the juicy details. I mean, it sounds so provocative, so intriguing."

He smirked. "Would love to, but since you wouldn't understand the first thing, I think I'll save my breath for someone who would."

Painfully aware as the second head turned in their direction, Jennifer stood rigid between them.

"Nice display of consideration for your wife's personal life, don't you think? Asking her to leave the country when her mother's on her deathbed?"

"You know nothing of consideration." He glanced over her from head to toe. "It's a waste of time to have this conversation." Zeroing in on the drink in her hand he snipped, "Have another, Sam. You might get laid. I'm sure one of my young men will oblige you."

"Both of you stop—*this instant*!" Jennifer fought to hush her voice, but it was too late. People were staring.

Aurelio slid an arm around her. "Sweetheart, I'm sorry." He pulled her close and spoke into her ear. "Not another word, I promise."

Sam continued her redress with a fiery gaze.

"Sam?" she cried beneath her breath. "Let it go?"

With a roll of her lips, she nodded. But her eyes remained hot.

Jennifer heaved a tight sigh. Taking a long swallow of wine, she prayed it was over. For those still staring, she tried to smile. Nothing to see here. Move along.

The fact Sam remained by her side belied hope.

Chapter Fourteen

She needed to be with her mom. Last night at Aurelio's had drained her, emotionally and physically. She didn't speak to Sam again after the run-in with Aurelio. He didn't make matters any better. Acted like it never happened. No apology and no discussion. Instead, he insisted she stay until the last guest left, then drove her home himself.

Because she insisted. After his public show with Sam, she was in no mood for intimacy.

Odd that she should feel a sense of hope as she walked into the front entrance of Fairhaven, but hope it was. She waved to the volunteer on duty at the circular lobby desk. "Morning, Mildred."

She returned with one of her own and a smile. "Good morning, Jennifer. Early today."

She nodded in passing. "Early bird gets the worm," she replied in step. She heaved a ragged sigh. Couldn't sleep was more like it, but that wasn't this woman's fault. It was Sam's. Aurelio's. Come to think of it, maybe relief was a better word than hope. At least she didn't have to contend with Sam or Aurelio today. Or Africa.

Checking her mother's chart at the nurse's station, satisfied nothing of significance had changed, Jennifer pushed open the door to her room and poked her head inside. At the sight of the sleeping figure, she rapped softly against the door. Nothing. Ignoring the douse of disappointment, Jennifer lightly padded into the room. Even with blinds drawn, the room was light. You couldn't hold back the sun on a day like today. Brilliant blue, not a cloud in the sky, it was useless to try.

Well, at least she could sit with her for a while, soak in her presence. Jennifer noticed the wheelchair folded to a close and parked in the corner. Her outlook brightened. Perhaps her mom had been out for a stroll today.

Which meant she must be feeling better.

Warmed by the prognosis, Jennifer smiled. Three days this past week she had come by and each time her mother had been asleep. Fast asleep. She took her usual seat alongside her mother's bed, prepared to visit in silence, but like magic her mom's eyes opened.

Beatrice smiled, the sight of her daughter lighting up her face. It reminded Jennifer of a plaque she once read. *Children of any age care about only one thing; do their parent's eyes light up when they enter the room?*

Hers did. Parents were the driving force in their children's lives. Given enough love, a child would do anything for their parent. Plow through their studies, rise to the top of their class in medical school...

Jennifer heard her heart as it hit the floor. They'd even grant their mother's dying wish and get married in a beautiful garden setting, no matter how much they disagreed on the toll it took.

"Hello darling," came the faint greeting from lips too ashen for good health, despite the sheen of Vaseline used to soften the cracks.

"Hi, Mom." Jennifer reached for her hand. She caressed the papery skin with light strokes. "How are you feeling today?"

"Fine," she replied, trying to nod her head. "Fine."

"Did you go for a walk?" Jennifer's eyes indicated that she noticed the wheelchair.

Beatrice slowly followed her line of sight before returning her gaze to her daughter. "This morning."

"It was beautiful out, wasn't it?"

"It was." She paused to take a deeper breath. "I'm practicing...for the big day."

Jennifer leaned forward at the labored speech. "Mom, are you okay?"

"Fine," she rubbed her thumb back and forth across Jennifer's hand. "Just a little tired."

Angst fluttered against her ribs. Was this a turn for the worse? More pain? She didn't see any note in the chart, that her mother wasn't—

"Tell me..." her mother encouraged. "About your garden." She squeezed her hand. "How's it coming?"

"Wonderful," Jennifer replied. "I think you're going to love it." Determined not to ruin the visit with her worries, she allowed a genuine smile to form on her lips and filled her mother in on the progress thus far.

"It sounds lovely. I wish I had thought to put fountains in my garden."

"Why didn't you?"

"Never came to mind, I guess." She gave a tiny shrug, her eyes questioning. "I was so taken with my flowers, I never gave it a second thought." A smile spread across her face. "Closest I got was a bird-bath."

"Ah, your birds..." Jennifer thought at once of the birdhouse. "And the grand hotel!"

That sparked a flash of delight in Beatrice's eyes. "I did love my birds!"

"Little messengers from heaven."

"Not all of them," she corrected with a knowing grin, gaining energy as she added, "Some of them were down right pests! They'd hog all the seeds, then deposit their poop in the bath." Her eyes came to life at the memory as she swayed her head from side to side against the soft pillow. "They grew so greedy, it reached the point where I couldn't take even the smallest of snacks outdoors without fear they would swoop down and snatch some for themselves!"

Jennifer laughed. Knots loosened as her pleasure spread. God it felt good to laugh, to reminisce with her mom over the good times they shared. "How well I remember. You used to chase them, waving that floppy straw hat of yours, calling them all sorts of names!"

"Oh," her eyes sparkled, "but the neighbors had some fun with me, didn't they?"

"Much to Dad's chagrin."

"For such a wonderful man, he could be an old stick in the mud, couldn't he?"

"Educated people don't run around their yard fussing at the wildlife," Jennifer droned, mimicking her father's tone, reciting his words verbatim.

Her mom chuckled softly. "He never understood that." Her gaze drifted to the end of her bed where she paused, as though immersed in deep thought.

Jennifer gave her time, but it only took seconds before Beatrice turned to face her daughter once again. "Kooky nature buff is how he referred to me."

"You weren't kooky, Mom. You were a respected physician in your community who had a penchant for her garden."

"And a husband who didn't understand," she said, but rather than settle in dismay, defiant eyes danced around the notion.

"A husband who loved you," Jennifer defended, "despite himself."

Beatrice nodded, then her movements became somewhat shaky. "He did that...it's true. He tried not to judge what he didn't understand. He simply worked...to accept it." Her face grew somber, but her eyes continued to hold deep affection and persisted in the connection. "Which is why I'm so happy for you," she murmured, giving another light squeeze to their interlocked hands. "You're going to have a wonderful life, darling." She struggled for deeper breaths.

Jennifer wanted to lurch forward, but refrained. She wanted to help her mother breathe, ridiculous as it was, help her draw strength, but she couldn't.

Instead, she forced herself to remain calm and repeated her mantra, *she's okay, she's okay.*

This is normal, for a terminal patient.

After a moment, Beatrice smiled. "Love is the seed from which your garden will blossom...and your greatest dreams will come true."

Jennifer wanted to cry. She heard the sentiment as it filtered down to her heart, but couldn't quite coerce the emotion to join it. Caught between the ache of love and the distress of worry, she could only think of the end. Everything she looked forward to doing, from her marriage and family to her career and success, would be colored by her mother's passing.

And she would be alone, the last Hamilton, left to face the future by herself. Sure, she had Aurelio, and Sam, but no family. No blood. When her mother died, she would take a part of her with her.

Nothing would ever be the same.

At home that evening, settled in deep on one end of her sofa, arms wrapped around her legs, Jennifer contemplated her life. One of her favorite Spanish instrumentals swirled softly in the background calming her mind as she thought about where had she been, what had she accomplished, and where she wanted to go.

From the outside looking in, her life was on track. At thirty-six she was an established physician in her own right. She owned the home of her dreams, a superb automobile and fiscally conservative, was well on her way to a good solid retirement yet still had enormous potential and a host of professional goals.

She glanced about the living room and considered what the décor said about her as a person. If a stranger walked in, what would they assume? Here lived a doctor who enjoyed the nicer things in life, or here lived a woman, one who cherished family and friends and the good times shared between them.

Wood floors, warm colors, plush materials, nothing here was ostentatious or designer-influenced. Family photos, artsy ceramics, most items were gifts or mementos she had collected over the years. Jennifer's gaze roamed the room, lightly touching on possessions and memories until she landed on the colored-pencil drawing. It hung just above her writing desk.

More table than desk, the piece of furniture was made from Brazilian Rosewood, an intense and colorful grain sweeping through it that had garnered her attention the minute she laid eyes on it. She had discovered it in an off-color boutique in the Grove and was her first official purchase as a physician. A reward to herself that now sat mostly idle.

You'll be in veritable heaven, scouring their markets for the next interesting piece of furniture for our new home.

Will I? When will I have the time to enjoy them? Between work and travel, she didn't see much time left for anything else in her life.

The drawing drew her gaze. Full-color, the scene was half-jungle, half-coastline and could have been a rendition from Brazil or Spain, or a myriad of other exotic destinations. Sinking further into the imagery, she tried to recall exactly what she had been thinking when she drew that picture.

When had she done it? College? High school?

She shook her head. She remembered. It was the summer between high school and college, a time in her life when the full exhilaration of life's potential awaited her, enticing her to reach for the stars. Her acceptance to the University of Miami had been a given, since the majority of her first year classes had been completed during her senior year of high school—which gave her the freedom to explore, to live...to exist.

No demands, no worries, it was a brief window of time where she had lived in the moment. Her mother had suggested she spend the summer in Europe like some of her friends planned to do, but she had declined. Sam tried to lure her with an itinerary that would take her clear across the continent and back, but she remained adamant. Schedules were her norm. For once, she preferred the alternative; do nothing. Live, breathe, and savor the experience of doing nothing.

That was when she drew the scene. She peeled it from her imagination as clear as if she were sitting on the shoreline shaded by the canopy of vibrant green, peppered with luscious reds, brilliant orange, and of course, the sparkle of crystalline blue water as it lapped against the pink sandy beach.

Jennifer chuckled, warmed by the recollection. When Sam returned home from Europe and asked what she had done all summer, her reply was to simply unfurl her portfolio of artwork.

Sam's jaw nearly broke as it hit the tile floor. With utter disbelief, she gaped at her. "That's it? You drew pictures?"

"That's it," she said proudly. "Aren't they gorgeous?"

"Yes, sure..." She glanced back at the drawings. "But that's not the point."

"Isn't it?" Jennifer proposed. "Life is about living, Sam. From the inside out. You of all people should be able to understand that."

"I do." Sam's complaint dissolved. "I just didn't expect this." She leafed through the papers, her admiration clear. "They're good, though, really good." She turned. "I didn't know you could draw like this?

She beamed. "You know me, full of surprises!"

Sam smirked. "Speaking of surprises..." A naughty grin took hold. "Wanna know what happened to me in Italy?"

Jennifer smiled, and dropped her chin to her knees. Sam would be Sam. Some things would never change.

Her pleasure faded. But some things do. Like her life. And she wondered, rushing to marry, waiting for death. What was the goal? Everything could change in an evening. *Africa.*

Honeymoon in the Canary Islands. She peered more closely at her drawing. Would they be as beautiful? Would they be exotic? Longing pulled at her. Sam asked the question. How could he ask you at a time like this?

She wanted to know the answer to that one, too. Did he think she could just drop everything and follow him? She thought he respected her career. Understood what it meant to her, the time and commitment it demanded.

Perhaps Aurelio should travel alone. Solitude had been a friend to her in the past. It had allowed her imagination to run free and uninhibited, giving a satisfaction deeper than she expected possible. Why not now?

Something deep inside her closed. Because now her life was different. Solitude meant confinement— to her thoughts, memories. It was best to be avoided. At all costs. Her life was busy now, and busy made her happy. It was full. It kept her looking forward, outward, giving her no time to reflect. What she missed, what she lacked...

Even if it meant traveling halfway across the world.

Chapter Fifteen

Coffee in hand, Jennifer grabbed her briefcase and jogged down the patio steps. "Good morning, Jackson!"

Up to his knees in dirt—*literally*—he paused from his digging. "Good morning!"

"Do you have a minute?" Dressed in pink scrubs and pale blue Crocs, she strode across the dirt-covered yard, stopping just shy of the plump row of hibiscus; blooms of red, yellow and pink nestled close in a midst of vibrant green leaves, leaves almost heart-shaped in form and covered with a sheen of dew.

Jabbing the blade of his shovel into the soft pile of dirt, he swiped his brow. "I've got one right now." He slipped the work gloves from his hands. "What's up?"

She neared, surprised by the hint of woodsy spice clinging to the air around him and thought, that won't last long!

She enjoyed a private chuckle. "I was wondering...what kind of time frame are we talking to construct the fireplace up on the terrace?"

"Depends. I'd have to check my contractor's availability to do the work on short notice, but he's pretty good about coming through for me. Why? Are you interested?"

"Unless it's a problem. I can always add it later."

"No worries."

"And the railing?"

"Much easier," he laughed, his eyes crinkling dirt at the corners. "I know where to get it and how to put it in, so there'll be no waiting. You're good to go on that count."

She hesitated. "I hate to push, but do you think it could all be completed by the wedding date?"

"Absolutely." He relaxed into a smile, his teeth white against his dirt-dusted complexion. "So you're considering the idea?"

"I am," she confirmed, suppressing a tickle of anticipation beneath her rib cage.

"Fantastic. I think it will really make a statement. December to February, you won't want to leave that porch and come spring, you can place some ferns inside and enjoy the porch all year long."

Jennifer noticed that his eyes never wavered from hers, his expression never deterred from its friendly stance, and his smile, once he finished speaking fell easily back into place. "You may be right."

"Trust me, you won't be sorry."

She swallowed. *I haven't been, yet.*

"I set the ginger out front and will put the remainder in here before I go," he said, itemizing his progress report. "It's a variegated shell with fragrant white blossoms that will bloom during springtime. A real nice wake-up call after winter."

Plants weren't just plants with him, were they? Everything had a purpose. Like characters in a play, each plant seemed to carry a specific duty or manage a specific season. But then again, Jackson was more than a gardener; he was a landscaper extraordinaire!

"I've got the flower boxes ready for the front windows—but the Lantanas haven't arrived yet."

"Lantanas?"

Jackson's face opened into an enthusiastic grin. "I've ordered some real beauties for out front. A mix of orange-red and yellow flowers. A striking combination, like the most dazzling sunset you've ever seen. The nursery I use grows some incredible stuff, producing intense green growth and some of the richest color I've seen anywhere. They'll be the first thing you see when you drive in."

"Really..."

"After the fountain, that is."

Jennifer laughed aloud this time. Soft and friendly, Jackson genuinely loved his work. Plants and flowers, colors and analogies, he was everything Michael sold him to be. The man was pure genius when it came to the landscape.

Jackson swiped the back of his hand beneath his chin. "You're going to love the way the splash of water makes you feel when you come home after a long day at the hospital. It opens the door for chill time like nothing else."

She smiled. He was probably right. The cascade of water did have a way of relaxing the harried mind, especially important with a career like hers. When plants died or drinks spilled, you simply removed them. Not so with patients.

Jennifer sighed. "I think the yard is going to look great, Jackson. I appreciate all your hard work."

The compliment lit up his face. "Thanks, Jennifer. Have you decided what kind of flowers you want for the arbor? I was thinking mandevilla or wisteria. You could go with a climbing rose too, but you'll get a longer blooming season with the others."

Jennifer drew a blank and cast a glance toward the intended location. "I have no idea what any of those are."

Jackson smiled. "They're all flowering vines of sorts, with blooms that vary in color and shape. My personal favorite is the mandevilla. It comes in various colors, though my favorite is red. Wisteria in shades of purple or pink would also be nice." He focused more intently upon her. "What's your favorite color?"

"Uh..." she stammered, caught off guard by the question. "I like pink, purple..." She turned to the hibiscus, its brilliant blooms reminding her of the jungle drawing inside. "I also like bright and tropical colors. Red, yellow and pink, particularly when mixed all together... They seem so invigorating."

"I agree. When considering color, you want to gravitate toward the colors that resonate with your spirit, your emotion."

Jennifer gaped. *Resonate*?

"That way the garden will be a constant pleasure. Like I said before, when designing your garden I like to make it a place you want to spend your time. Bloom color is key. It can make all the difference in the world."

"Shouldn't the colors work well together, too?"

"Absolutely," he said, impassioned as a grade school teacher fawning over a student finally *getting* it. "It's all about the color wheel. From opposing to analogous, the placement of color has strong significance in any schemata."

Jennifer must have surely looked as ignorant as she felt, because Jackson jumped into further explanation. "Colors work together in different ways. Monochromatic is a range of one shade—which I *don't* recommend for your garden. Then there's analogous; colors side by side on the color ring that can be used to create a nice flow from space to space. But my favorite method is to use complementary colors. Like your house, for instance. Using colors that oppose each other on the wheel tend to be more striking, yet visually balanced. The dark blue of your awnings is a complement to the yellow-orange of your walls. A more complex variation includes the deep-green foliage that surrounds your house. Taking it a step further, would be a tetrad combination, otherwise known as using four colors equally spaced apart on the color ring." He smiled again. "Makes for a harmonious color theme which is why I chose those particular shades of Lantana. The red will complete the tetrad of your home's exterior colors, and really make a statement."

Jennifer was stunned. She had no idea his thought process was so involved. She figured he was choosing colors he liked, or plants that were popular. "Wow." It was all she could manage. "In the future, you'll be the first one I call for lawn emergencies." The cell phone at her hip vibrated. She unclipped it and answered, "Dr. Hamilton."

"Should we send for your patient?"

"Yes." She mouthed goodbye to Jackson and hurried to her car. "I'm on my way."

As Jennifer waved herself off, Jax watched her drive from sight. "Landscape emergencies." While he knew it was a compliment, the statement settled in him like a rock. Replacing his gloves, he walked back to his work area. He grabbed the shovel and thrust the blade into the ground. But that's what he was here for, right? Landscape.

Jax wedged the shovel deep and scooped the dirt free. That was the problem, working for a beautiful woman. There was always a part of you that wanted more. Whether it was because she was dressed casually in scrub clothes, or the fact she was warming up to him, her appeal had increased—*tenfold*. Compared to their previous encounters, the woman was becoming a whole football field easier to talk to.

And those eyes. Blue as Bahamas water and just as crystal clear. Those babies could lure a man in like a hypnotist's dazzling glass ball. They'd carry him right past that narrow, aristocratic nose of hers and straight to the heart. Straight to the core. A man could definitely lose himself there for a while.

Jax laughed at himself. Thank God he had experienced the first few days with the good and severe Doctor Hamilton! That lady was about as approachable as a cactus which provided excellent come-on repellent.

Particularly important in this case because Jennifer was exactly his type with her straight brown hair, soft clear skin. Her lithe figure, her muscles naturally firm.

And those eyes. He let out a soft whistle. Ocean blue was absolutely his favorite color, and a weak spot when framed in the face of a beautiful woman.

He shook his head and dumped the last fern into the hole, then proceeded to shovel the dirt back in around it. Getting lost in the likes of Jennifer

Hamilton would put a major kink in his life. Women didn't drop their medical careers to float around on the open sea for a month, no matter how attractive the man may seem.

He grunted a half laugh. He'd learned that lesson the hard way. Maria told him in plain English, the answer was no. She went so far as to add he was a jerk for even asking. Which he never did understand. Since when did asking someone to join you for the cruise of their life constitute being a jerk?

Old resentment soured in his stomach, but Jax allowed it to pass. Independent women liked to set the rules. They didn't follow and they didn't wait. Maria had been very clear: When you were dependent on someone else, you might as well call them master. *They would.*

Jax tamped the dirt down around the plant with his boot. He couldn't disagree with her which is why she left. With his blessing. Finished, he turned and headed toward his truck. At least in this case, the issue would never come up. This woman was off-limits.

Glancing at the house, he had to admit he was pleased. The fireplace was the perfect complement for the oasis he was creating out here and the fact she agreed made his job all the more rewarding. Battling with clients over design elements wasn't something he liked to do, though many times he found himself reminding them they hired him for a reason.

Incorporating their ideas into his vision and expertise usually made for a mishmash of plants and flowers. Jackson Montgomery Landscape brought yards to life. When he attached his name to a job, he wanted the end result to be a reflection of his artistry, not a jumble of plants.

Pulling his mobile from the dashboard of his truck, he was grateful on that count. Dr. Jennifer Hamilton now seemed content to let him handle the job. And handle it, he would.

# # #

Jennifer stood over her patient. Completely covered in blue sterile paper, save for the small opening at his groin, she held the catheter steady. "How's his pressure?"

"Steady, one thirty over ninety."

"How are you doing, Mr. Nunez?"

"Good," he mumbled from beneath his cover

"We're almost finished." Jennifer slid the catheter free and handed it to the awaiting nurse. "Everything looks great." She applied pressure to the incision area and patted his arm. "The nurse will get you cleaned up, okay?"

He nodded, though she doubted he was fully coherent. Most patients were able to follow and understand, but some, like Mr. Nunez, wouldn't remember a thing. He had been extremely agitated before the procedure, which required an extra dose of Versed and Fentanyl to calm him. But she continued to talk her patients through the procedure, whether they remembered or not.

Jennifer stepped aside as the male nurse took over, pressing a gauze where her hand had been. "Is the family here?"

"Yes doctor," he said through his mask. "In the waiting room."

"Thanks." Jennifer picked up the chart on her way out. She stopped in the control room and jotted down her notes. Slapping it closed, she left it on the counter and headed for the family. In the corridor, a blonde nurse hurried up to her.

"Dr. Hamilton—ER's calling you. Your patient Sarah Wiley just arrived by ambulance."

She stopped short. "What happened?"

"Paramedics called it in. Cardiac arrest."

"Oh, no." Jennifer bolted down the hall. "Get a room ready, stat," she called back and punched a metal plate on the wall. Double doors began to open. "C'mon, c'mon." She edged sideways through the narrow opening and ran to the emergency room. She strode past beds, checking each one. "Where is she?" Faces flipped up in question. "Sarah Wiley—which bed is she?"

"Down here, Dr. Hamilton!"

Jennifer hurried toward the voice at the opposite end of the room. Curtain shoved aside, paramedics worked with hospital staff to transfer the lifeless body from bed to bed. "One, two, three—move!"

Their pace was quick, controlled. A female nurse started attaching electrodes to Sarah's chest.

Breathless, Jennifer asked, "How is she?"

"Stabilized." The male paramedic hooked the IV next to the monitor and reeled, "Pressure's one thirty-eight over ninety-one. Rate's eighty-two. We ran a 12-lead. ST elevation. We gave her two milligrams nitro."

"When did this happen?" she demanded.

"About an hour ago. Daughter was with her when it happened. Gave her an aspirin." He pulled his sheet clear as the nurse laid another in its place.

Daughter. Jennifer ground her thoughts over the mention of the woman. "Is she here?"

The paramedic tipped his head toward the waiting room. "She's in there."

"Cath lab is prepping for her now. I'm going to talk to the daughter." Pushing through a glass door, Jennifer searched for Sarah's daughter. Comfortably seated in an end chair below the television, she was leafing through a magazine.

Jennifer marched up to her. "Your mother's in bad shape. She needs a stent. I need you to sign the papers for the procedure."

"Is she okay?"

So nice of you to ask. Jennifer crossed her arms and looked down at her. "Considering she almost died, yes, I'd say she's okay. But she needs a stent and she needs it now."

To her credit, the woman looked relieved. She lowered the magazine to her lap. "Are you sure she needs it?"

"I was sure she needed it last week," Jennifer shot back.

"I gave her an aspirin."

"That was wise."

"If you're sure..."

"She needs the procedure. Wait here. They'll bring you the paperwork." She turned on her heel. It was time to scrub.

In the darkened lab, Jennifer stepped on the floor pedal and studied the flow of dark liquid as it passed through the squiggly lines on the monitor above. The gray image moved in rhythm with Sarah's heart, beat for beat. Holding the catheter in place at Sarah's groin, she pumped more contrast dye and watched as it squirted through the coronaries, catching in the same spot. "That's it. Picture."

From inside the control room, technicians recorded the image. She detached the syringe-like injector and set it aside. "Balloon." She held her hand out as a nurse placed the floppy catheter into her palm. Checking Sarah's rhythm running across a separate monitor, satisfied she was holding up, Jennifer carefully navigated through stiff arteries, but the balloon stopped short.

"Ectopy."

Jennifer glanced at her patient's pulse monitor. It was to be expected. Poking around a sensitive heart was bound to create irritability. Checking the fluoroscopy image, she gently pushed through the calcified area until the balloon tip appeared onscreen at the location of the blockage.

Adjusting position, she inflated the balloon. Satisfied it was enough, she deflated the pressure and pulled the catheter free. The dye flowed through the artery with ease. "Picture."

"Got it."

"Stent." The next balloon was given to Jennifer, this one with a wire mesh stent wrapped around the balloon. Blood was beginning to collect on her gloved hands which made it more difficult to glide the catheters in. With short pushes, she advanced the stent into position. This time as she inflated the balloon, it expanded the stent. Deflating once again, she pulled the wire, leaving the stent inside the artery. "Picture."

"Got it."

Jennifer rolled her neck back and forth across her shoulders to release the grip of tension.

"V-tach."

She jerked her head forward. Sarah's pulse raced across the screen unchecked. "Charge!"

The scrub technician charged the external defibrillator. In seconds, it reached the standard 200 joules. "Ready."

Break, break, she willed the frantic bleeping to cease. Shocking Sarah's heart out of the irregular rhythm was the last thing she wanted to do. But if it was necessary...

Watching the monitor, Jennifer held steady.

No one in the room spoke. All eyes were on the monitor.

"Darn it, Sarah," she murmured under her mask, then said aloud to the technician, "Shock."

The patient's body jumped from the bed.

No longer racing, the green line on the monitor lay flat.

"Pace."

"Pacing, rate of eighty."

Instantly, the monitor came to life.

"Bring pacing down," Jennifer directed.

"Bringing pacing down to seventy."

Sarah was still dependent on the pacer. "Sixty."

"Sixty."

Sarah's heart began beating on its own. She sighed. Good girl. Jennifer looked at the gray picture image. Now she'd be forced to make sure the shock had not altered the placement of her stent.

Chapter Sixteen

As she pulled into her driveway, the sight of Jackson's truck warmed her mood a degree. Jennifer inhaled deeply and released her breath in one long, fluid sigh. She had missed him yesterday afternoon. Shifting the car into park, she collected her belongings and slid out of the vehicle. Funny how his presence was becoming something to which she looked forward.

Standing next to his truck, Jackson slipped a tool into the pocket of a black strap wrapped around his work bucket, then wiped a small triangular spade using a filthy gray rag.

Is he leaving for the day? Jennifer quickened her pace. "Hello Jackson!"

He turned at the sound of her voice and opened into his usual smile. "Hey, Jennifer." He gave her a brisk wave, but then continued with his cleanup.

"The flowers look great."

"I'm glad you like them," he said, lifting the cement crusted bucket from the ground and heaving it over the edge of his truck bed.

Her eyes jogged toward the house as she hesitated over the name of the flower. "What do you call them again?"

"Lantanas."

"Lantanas, yes. You were right. They really attract your attention when you drive in."

He nodded. "Good."

Jennifer watched as he dumped the contents of his garbage pail into the disposal bin in the back, then tossed it in after. Behind him, she could see brick pavers set neatly within wooden forms, the beginnings of her terrace. She took a few steps in his direction, but stopped. The humidity pressed in. Smoothing a hand over her hair, pulled back into a low ponytail, she said, "The patio looks wonderful."

"Thanks." He placed his tools in a built-in steel compartment box in the bed of his truck. "The guys did a great job." He flipped the tailgate closed and turned. "But let it cure for a good forty-eight hours before you walk on it." Wiping his hands clean with a fairly clean wet towel, he gazed at her, his pause pronounced. As though he expected her to say something more, or head into the house.

"So then your day went well?" Jennifer asked, struck by the routine nature of the question, as though it were old habit.

"Better than yesterday." He knocked a chunk of dirt from his arm. "The inspector showed up this afternoon, so we can get started on the fountain tomorrow."

"Well, that *does* sound good." She smiled, aware her heartbeat had picked up its pace.

"It is. Actually, it used to take a lot longer to get permits, but these days the internet facilitates the process. You can get them for simple projects in no time at all." He smiled. "Relatively speaking."

She nodded. "There's still the human element to consider, isn't there?"

"Always," he agreed, though his smile had dimmed. "How about you? Good day?"

"Tough. Too many patients squeezed into too few hours, plus two trips to the ER." Jennifer dropped her gaze, and scraped the bottom of her shoe over a small rock in the driveway. "I nearly lost one of them."

"Oh, no."

She lifted her gaze back to meet his, struck by the emotion swimming in his eyes. It was more than she would have expected from a stranger. "It wasn't good. But we're short-staffed at the moment. One of my partners has been out on extended leave and another's on vacation. The workload is taking its toll. My patients are getting shortchanged on their time with me and there's not a *thing* I can do about it. Nothing." Something that bothered her tremendously. "I can only schedule them so late into the evening... After that, you simply run out of time."

"I know what you mean. When everyone wants a piece of you, sometimes there's not enough to go around."

"Something has to give. Unfortunately for me," Jennifer frowned. "It's turning out to be my patients."

"Is your partner coming back on line any time soon?"

Her dropped her shoulders in a shrug. "We don't know. He had a massive MI and his recuperation will take a while. How long," she held up her hands in question, "is anyone's guess."

"That *is* tough."

"Life is short," she added, though not particularly sure why.

"That it is."

Allowing her gaze to wander, thoughts of Sarah and Aurelio and Sam and her mother swirled together. A light breeze brushed the back of her neck. "Do you ever feel like you can't keep up with your own life? Like you want to hit the rewind button so you know what's coming beforehand, giving you time to react?"

"Sure," he said. "I'd eliminate a lot of headaches that way."

"Yes." She glanced away. Heat seemed to collect on her forehead. "And heartaches."

Jax peered at her. "You seem a bit rattled today. Do you mind if I ask what happened?"

"Rattled," she said, letting loose with a ragged sigh. "I guess you could call it that." She smoothed the backside of her cotton scrubs, warm against her body in the afternoon sun. With a small smile she returned her gaze to him. "I had a patient land in the ER today. She needed an emergency stent. We succeeded, but she almost didn't make it."

Jax's jaw went slack. Beads of sweat clustered heavy on his brow. "Oh, no..."

"What's worse, it shouldn't have come to that. I recommended she do the procedure months ago, but her family waited."

"Why?"

Jennifer shook her head. "I have no idea. Her daughter wasn't convinced, she wasn't sure..." She looked into his eyes, as though she'd find the answer there. "I feel awful about it."

"You're not blaming yourself, are you?"

"Somewhat, yes." She gazed out over her yard and linked her arms together. "It's my job to convince her, isn't it?"

"You did everything you could. She's alive, right?"

Jennifer nodded.

"She has you to thank for that. Mike says you're the best of the best. She couldn't have been in better hands."

"She nearly died. I should have insisted. Long before it came to this, I should have insisted she have it done."

"People have minds of their own, Jennifer and sometimes, as much as we'd like to change them, they have their own ideas for living."

"Why anyone would wait? With all the technology we have today, why would anyone risk sudden death?" It was a concept she couldn't wrap her mind around.

Jax pulled a couple of plastic buckets from the back of his truck and set them on the ground with a thud, upside down. He lowered himself onto one and gestured for her to do the same.

She did.

He pulled a fresh cloth from his front pocket and wiped his forehead. "People have their reasons, Jennifer."

"What could they possibly be? When they know a simple procedure could save their lives, why would they wait?"

"Maybe she was afraid." He pushed the cloth back into his pocket. "There are risks associated with any surgical procedure, aren't there?"

"Yes," she answered, a hint of rancor to her voice, glancing at the ground. "But they are minimal when weighed against an almost certain heart attack. This family bet against the odds. They had all the tools at their disposal and still, they bet against the odds."

"I know what you mean. But it still comes down to choice."

"Irrational." She angled her shoulders away from him. "It's unacceptable."

"I agree." Jax laced his fingers together and dropped forearms to his thighs. "My mom lost the same gamble."

Jennifer looked at him suddenly. "What?"

Jax's soft gaze settled on hers. "She died of a heart attack."

"Oh Jackson, *I'm so sorry...*"

He fixed his gaze on the back wall and replied, "Yeah. It was a couple of years ago and like your patient, she knew the risks, knew what could happen if she did nothing, but she opted against them. Because she was afraid. More afraid of surgery than death." He turned to face her and Jennifer's heart twisted. "Needles and hospitals were never on her most favorites list. Hell, I'm not even sure she believed the doctor when he told her she had to have it done. Healthy her whole life, she barely missed a day of work." His voice dropped and he looked away. "She thought I was an alarmist."

Jennifer didn't know what to say.

"She blamed stress. Spent more time in her garden. She called it therapy. What it couldn't cure, didn't need curing, she used to say. What would be, would be."

He paused and Jennifer thought she detected tears in his eyes. It was all she could do not to wrap an arm around his shoulders. She folded them in her lap instead.

"I thought it selfish at the time."

"Heart disease can be a silent killer, Jax." She had never used his nickname before, but it just felt right. Straddling the line between professional and personal, she leaned toward him. "Especially for women. For some reason, they tend to put off their health problems. They ignore important warning signs, especially when it comes to their heart."

"Probably worrying too much about their families," Jax said, an edge in his voice. "My father had been battling ulcers at the time and instead of caring for herself, she catered to his every need."

"Probably," Jennifer agreed. "Women have a way of doing that."

He turned back to her, setting the palm of his hand to his knee. "You wanna know the worst part? She survived the heart attack, but died two days later in the hospital. The place she most feared. Spent her last forty-eight hours surrounded by strangers."

"The damage must have been severe."

"Yeah. But it was her choice to wait and she wasn't the kind of woman you pushed. She did things her way, end of story."

"That must have been hard on your father."

"Maybe." He slapped both hands to his thighs and looked at her, his eyes no longer vulnerable. "Look, the point is, there was nothing the doctor could have done to change the outcome. Today you made a difference. You saved a woman's life. Let that knowledge ease your heart a little."

With that he stood. "Listen, I'm sorry." He pointed toward the open holes of dirt by her bedroom. "But I've got to get that done before I leave. Tomorrow we plan to begin the bulk of the planting and Thursday the fountain for out front should be arriving."

Jennifer rose in response. Sitting here any longer would only prove awkward. It was clear they had stumbled onto a sore spot for Jax and he didn't want to talk anymore.

Which she understood. Not only from a professional perspective, but personal as well. A mother's illness, death surrounded by strangers. To love someone, yet be powerless to help...

It was a horrible burden to bear. "Everything is coming along really well," she offered, wanting to erase the hurt. "I want you to know that I appreciate all your effort, and I'm sorry if I've been difficult." She shoved as much cheer as she could manage behind her smile. "It means a lot."

He sighed. "You have nothing to apologize for, Jennifer."

Odd she should feel relief, but she did. "Thank you, Jackson," she said, delivering the words more softly than she had intended.

"No problem." He smiled. "Most of my friends call me Jax."

Brushing a wayward strand of hair behind an ear, she repeated, "Jax." Saying his name aloud invoked a smile deeper than she felt comfortable, a mix of nerves and satisfaction mingling in her midsection.

Jax returned to his spot beneath the pergola and sliding hands into gloves, grabbed his shovel and began to dig.

Jennifer remained stationary, the humid air clinging to her skin. They had connected, briefly, but the spell was breaking fast. She hadn't meant to resurrect his grief. He had only been trying to help, but the memory of his mother's death cut fresh wounds in his eyes, unearthing a hurt as raw as the day it happened.

Should she offer him some words of condolence? Offer him some relief, like he had done her? But one look at his rigid movements and it was clear: he was finished.

It wasn't her place to intrude. He had opened up to her. In his attempt to ease the burden of a difficult day, he had revealed a part of his past in hopes it would lessen her guilt.

But it had backfired on him.

He snapped closed tight as a clam the minute she mentioned his father. Curious. Grabbing her briefcase from her car, Jennifer hurried up her back steps. Letting herself in the house, the cool air was a blast to her senses. She closed the door, her hands remaining encircled around the knob behind her. Filling her lungs with a deep breath, the gesture strained and uncomforting, she blew it out. Sideways through the French door, she peered at his busy figure. His motions seemed to have taken on urgency, his muscles working against the clock.

He wanted out of here, because of her.

She mulled over the situation, allowing her gaze to wander his physique. Strong arms and legs, his body cut by hours of hard labor, his skin seemed kissed by the sun. Today, even his hair looked in place. Most likely matted down by sweat, but at least it looked more groomed.

She smiled at herself. Like what she thought mattered. The woman he was seeing probably fancied the wild hairdo. At the hospital, she had begun to notice the style was actually trendy with the younger generation. Her smile faded. Not that she was old, but at thirty-six she wasn't a kid anymore. Her tastes had changed, as had her behavior.

Jennifer turned from the window and made way for the shower. Leave the past alone, she warned herself. Behind you, where it belongs. She thwacked her forehead with tips of her fingers. *Move on.* Jennifer stopped suddenly as she entered her bedroom. Jax was right outside her window. On second thought, perhaps she needed a bite to eat.

Reversing direction, she headed toward the kitchen. She opened the refrigerator, not feeling an ounce of hunger, then closed the door. Perhaps a glass of red wine would do the trick.

Relax her mind, soothe her frayed nerves. Normally she would opt for a jog, but with Jax out back, she didn't want to leave. Didn't want to bother him but didn't want to leave him.

Locating a corkscrew, she opened a Malbec and filled a glass half-full. Ambling toward the sofa, one eye glancing through the back window, she settled down onto the sofa. Sweeping one leg across the other, she watched him move in and out of her line of vision. Sipping from her glass, she sank back into the cushions.

She savored the first swallow as it exploded across her tongue, swishing down her throat with an earthy blackberry plum finish. "Hmmm..." Usually a fan of the full-bodied Cabernet, she discovered this particular vintage while dining in a South American restaurant. Sam had suggested the place and from wine to food, it had been an evening to remember.

Sam. She'd have to call her. The two hadn't spoken since Aurelio's opening and they needed to.

The episode had to be addressed.   Jennifer took another sip, relishing the bite of pepper mixing with the fruits as it passed over her taste buds, she worked to empty her mind of tension. But she didn't have to think about it right now.

Sipping again, her thoughts wandered back to Jackson. Jax, she corrected with a smile. After all, they were friends now.

Uncrossing her legs, she set them on the sofa table. She glanced at the stereo clock. Five-thirty and he was still hard at work. She looked outside and caught sight of him dumping a bag of dirt over the newly-planted bougainvillea.

It wasn't fair. Her problem had become his problem and now he was working like a man with an ax to grind. How could she make it up to him? How could she set that grin of his back on track?

Glancing out once again, she noticed how the sun reflected across the pool, sprinkling the water with diamonds of light. It occurred to her that it was still quite warm outside. Hot, in fact. She leaned forward with a rush of idea.

Chapter Seventeen

Maybe Jax is thirsty. I could take him a glass of water she thought, and stood before the inspiration could pass. Yes. Unable to recall seeing a beverage around his workspace, she decided he needed one. Wineglass in hand, she head to the kitchen. She swung the refrigerator door open and plucked a bottle from the shelf.

She breezed outside onto the patio, pleased with her plan. "I thought you might be thirsty, so I brought you some water." Leaning over the simple wood railing, she extended the bottle in hand.

He turned to find it at chest level. "Thanks," he said in surprise and reached out a gloved hand to take it from her.

Graciously, he remained mute about the thermos she spied sitting by his tool bucket. "Is that the last one you have to plant?" she asked, indicating the lone vine of purple bougainvillea on the ground.

"Yep." He twisted the cap off the bottle.

"They really will look good out here, won't they," she said, not asking anything, simply intent on settling in for small talk. She folded her arms atop the porch rail and leaned her body into them. "Sort of a canopy of shade."

"I think so." Jax took a deep swig of water, one eye remaining on Jennifer. "Sheltered from the heat, it'll be your own private courtyard overlooking the pool."

Heat. It was a bit humid out here. Shade would be nice. "I'll have to shop for some lawn chairs to put out here. Those seem a little dilapidated, now that you've fixed up the area."

He chuckled. "They do look a bit worn, don't they?"

Bleached-out green plastic, most of the seats were cracked. "They're old," she said, instantly feeling better about his improved disposition. Whether he was being kind or actually felt relaxed, Jennifer found she cared little. She only wanted him to smile. "Do you have any suggestions?" she asked, hopeful for a new opening. "What style do people normally choose for patios?"

"Stone, tile. Teak is nice. Wears well, and would blend nicely out here."

"Teak," she repeated, trying the idea on for size. "Maybe some colorful cushions, a ceramic planter or two?"

"Now you're talking." He donned a grin. "But be careful," he said, slyly. "Don't make it so nice you won't want to return to the office!"

The word "office" had the potential to dampen her mission so she whisked past the reference with skilled aplomb. "Forget the office—"

She straightened with a smack of her hands on the railing. "I want to start looking forward to the weekends!"

"Now there's a sentiment I can relate to. Time off," he said, and knocked back another swig of water. "*That's* the key to good living."

"So what do you do for recreation, Jax? Any special hobbies?"

"Most of the time, I take to the ocean."

Of course, she realized at once. His retirement dreams on the high blue seas. Securing her grip around the wood rail, she pushed her weight against it, curious for more detail. "Do you sail much?"

"Every chance I get. I keep my boat at a marina in the Grove."

"You have a boat?"

"A real beauty," he said with pride. "Thirty-two feet of heaven on water that will take me anywhere I want to go, trimmed in some of the most gorgeous teakwood you'll ever lay eyes on."

He was like a kid describing his model boat, except it was real. *And expensive.* Wasn't teak one of the pricier woods? How could he afford such a thing?

"Thirty feet sounds awfully large to me."

Jennifer's face must have been a road map to her thoughts.

"It's not as expensive as one would think," he returned. "For less than the price of most houses," he tipped his bottle toward her. "You can buy yourself a very fine cruiser. I have a bedroom, living room, kitchen, and the best patio deck in the universe—no offense to yours, of course." He winked. "But my terrace opens to the world. And once out on the open sea, you don't need much money. You can catch your food, anchor in private coves for a restful night of sleep and entertainment..." Jax laughed. "It's life in the slow lane at its best. Just my style."

She imagined him splayed across the bow, his khakis soaked through after a dip in the crystal blue waters, his bare chest bronzed from a life in the sun. Funny, but it was the most natural image in the world. "Can you sail it by yourself?"

"Sure."

"It's not too big?"

"Stern cockpit allows a lot of flexibility. But if it was much bigger then yes, I could use a mate onboard."

Is that where his girlfriend fit in?

Jennifer swatted the thought from her mind. She wasn't going there. It was none of her business. "So when's the retirement party."

"Six months. Maybe less, to hear my real estate agent tell it."

"Six months?" She couldn't have been more stunned had Jax divulged he was a transsexual.

"Yep. She says there are a few things I can do to fix it up, but suggests we go ahead and get the house listed. That, and I've been saving up." His eyes danced with anticipation. "So yeah, I'd say in another six months I should be able to embark on the big one."

"How will you support yourself?"

"Bartending, if I need it." He sucked down another swallow of water. "Once I'm retired, that particular skill will come in handy, to keep the finances fluid."

"Where will you go?"

"Well," he grinned with delight. "I'll start by cruising around the Bahamas, maybe head to Puerto Rico for a while and practice my Spanish. Maybe spice up my Salsa, too, before I drift over to St. Thomas, St. Croix..." He beamed. "Who knows where I'll end up, and that's the beauty of it. Pure freedom."

She was dumbstruck. "You dance the Salsa?"

"Every chance I get!"

That was an image she couldn't contrive. This was a man's man, not a ladies' man. He worked dirt, not dance floors. She pushed away from the railing. "But Jackson. You can't just drift from island to island. What will you do all day long?"

"Enjoy life."

"Doing what? Other than dancing, I mean." Jennifer didn't mean to be rude, but he was still young with a lot of years ahead of him. How long could he spend floating around the middle of nowhere?

"Living. Breathing. The basics."

"But you're talking a long time. Won't you be bored?"

Jax belted out a laugh. "Bored?" he gaped. "How can you get *bored* when there are new discoveries waiting outside your porthole every day of the year?"

She could only stare. He had a point. A fan of exotic beaches herself she understood the allure, but there were other places she wanted to go as well. Africa came to mind.

She shoved the thought from her mind. "What about the old, 'You've seen one island, you've seen them all?'"

"Must have been a landlubber."

"Yes, but..." What gave his life purpose? What inspired him? At least with landscaping, he was servicing the needs of his fellow man. Who, but himself, would he be serving out in the middle of nowhere?

Jax must have sensed her verdict.   His enthusiasm dwindled. "Different strokes for different folks, I guess." Throwing back the last of the water, he chucked the empty bottle into a nearby bucket. "Thanks for the water, but I need to get finished up here."

Disappointment poured into Jennifer's heart. What began with good intention, collapsed in miserable failure. *Again.*

Jax's abrupt end to the conversation highlighted once again her propensity for stepping on other people's feelings—one she had no idea existed until now.

She heaved a sigh. At least not until now. It seemed every time she and Jax spoke, it ended on a disagreeable note and usually because of something she said. Or didn't say. No matter how unintentional, she always managed to pinch his spirit, extinguishing their rapport.

What was her problem? This wasn't like her. Rarely did she set out to deliberately offend anyone— unless of course that someone was Sam—and she usually had it coming.

But the proof was in his eyes. In his excuse for a sudden departure, his immediate subject change. She had pulled the plug on his enthusiasm. She had insulted him.

Again. Especially unforgivable today, because a part of her understood his desire to experience life on the most simplest of terms and a part of her wanted the same. It was that other part of her that kept getting in the way.

Frustration welled. But being a doctor was part of who she was, a big part and one she couldn't deny. Her life wouldn't be nearly as meaningful if she wasn't helping people. It was the part about Jackson she didn't understand. How could he float through life without purpose? Where did he derive satisfaction? Not mere pleasure, but the deeper satisfaction that touches the soul, connects one to humanity...

This was his problem. Jax lacked depth, purpose, serving a cause greater than himself. This is where their lives diverged in the starkest of terms. The difference she couldn't reconcile. The one she wouldn't even try.

Jennifer turned and went back into the house. Conversation may as well be over. She had to get ready for dinner with Aurelio later this evening.

# # #

"He has an amazing eye for color," Aurelio assured her, dark eyes coming alive. "And the way he plays them off the mind's anticipation is amazing."

Jennifer swirled the wine in her glass, the candle centered on their table casting it in a lustrous hue of blood red.

"In some cases, his mix is so subliminal, so intricate; one misses the scene within the scene. They're solely moved by the emotion of the piece."

It reminded her of Jax.

"True artists are experts in managing color. And this fellow," Aurelio smiled, "is an absolute genius."

Jennifer brought the glass of Cabernet to her lips, smiling as was expected, but her mind couldn't hold firm to conversation about debut artists, intricate plays of color, or the grandiose praise they were receiving post-opening. She was glad for Aurelio, and happy for the young painters, but her thoughts drifted, content to wander through the elegant bistro without focus.

At this late hour, the exclusive establishment had more shimmer than light, dimmed chandeliers reflecting golden against heavy brocade drapes and satiny-cream tablecloths. In the corner, the pianist played a mix of jazz and light classical, but she heard none of it, her mind recalling Jax's lesson on the color wheel. For a moment, she idled on his talent, his use of dual and tri-color groupings. Intriguing how the mind registered the combinations without realizing it, reacting as the artist intended; soothed by mellow blends, or invigorated by opposing. Then she recalled his and Sam's conversation. How he shared his favorite artist, the man's technique for creating a sense of light on his canvas, a hint of three dimensions...

In the quiet of her mind, she smiled. Jax knew a little something about art after all.

"How's the landscaping coming along?" Aurelio asked.

Jennifer blinked. "Good," she said, startled by the sudden change. "Fine. Many of the plants are already in and they begin work on the front fountain this week."

"Is it starting to make sense to you now?"

She set her glass down on the table. "Yes. The basin is formed and the spillover has been mounted on the back wall. They still have yet to tile, though."

"What colors did you finally decide on?"

"A mix of blue, yellow, rustic orange set against a white background. It sounds awful to hear it," she said in quick response to the dismay dashing his eyes, apparently none too impressed with the wisdom of her selection. "It's an Italian ceramic and is quite beautiful. Rather than listen to my description, you probably have to see it to understand how perfect it is. Jackson thought it was an excellent choice," she added, wondering why she felt the need to bolster her decision by mentioning his approval.

"I'm sure it is, love. Always a good idea to listen to the professional."

Why did Aurelio sound so patronizing?

Jennifer averted her gaze. Fiddling with the stem of her wineglass, the diamond on her left hand glittered with blinding clarity in the subtly lit room. Was it her? Was she being overly sensitive because this was to be their home, yet she was making all of the decisions?

Or because he was exerting artistic authority over her.

"It's not up, yet. Would you like to take a look, make sure it's adequate before they install it?"

"Good heavens, no!" Aurelio reached across the table with both hands and opened them, gesturing she place hers within.

Jennifer obliged, and as he closed his hands around hers, he said, "I know that whatever you choose will be perfect." He squeezed them with soothing reassurance. "Really."

Jennifer felt like a child being positively reinforced for doing something well. Something that really held no great significance for the adult, but was a huge deal for the little one.

"How do the plants look?"

"Fine," she said, feeling no desire to elaborate. "Jax is looking into the fireplace for the back patio, as well."

Aurelio pulled back.

Jennifer's hand froze within his clasp, self-conscious of the use of the nickname.

"Splendid. I agree. It's the best use of the space and will be a wonderfully romantic location come the winter." He smiled with a wink, yet the effect that he intended missed its mark.

"It will provide a nice barrier between the terrace and the driveway," she replied dully. Jennifer had suddenly lost her desire—for garden talk or romance. Her appetite, too.

"Maybe I can come by tomorrow and see for myself."

She felt a wave of ambivalence wash over her. "Tomorrow?"

"Yes." He looked at her curiously. "Is there a problem?"

"No problem. Let's see how my schedule goes," she evaded. "Can I call you?"

"Of course," he replied, tidily folding the question aside.

Dinner conversation slowed to discussion of catering arrangements. Jennifer had hired a wedding planner to handle most of the details regarding the actual ceremony and reception. Her job was the garden and Aurelio's...

What was his responsibility again? Show up on time?

Jennifer shook the rancor from her thoughts, agitated she was besieged by negativity this close to the wedding day. The big event was weeks away and here she was finding fault with her husband-to-be. Was this normal behavior?

Was she normal? Granted these weren't ideal conditions under which to be married, nor was theirs a rational timeline, but it was their reality. Her reality.

Her mother's.

"Listen, Aurelio. I want to discuss Africa."

"You've been thinking about the Canary Islands, haven't you?"

Jax and his dream of sailing the islands popped into her brain, but she brushed it aside. "Not exactly," she began, uncertain how to broach the subject. "I've been thinking about the time constraints of my schedule. You know Charles is out right now—"

"Yes, how is he?" Excitement swiftly turned to compassion. "Recovering well, I hope?"

"Yes, yes, he's doing fine." Her gaze dropped to her dessert coffee. Left mostly untouched, it had grown cold, the cream condensing in the center. "It's mine I'm worried about."

He pulled the silky napkin from his lap and dabbed both corners of his mouth. "What do you mean?"

"Well, what I mean is..." Jennifer rested her forearms against the table's edge. "I don't know how I'm going to manage a trip to Africa right now. What with my partner out, my mother..."

Aurelio's head tilted to one side. "Sweetheart. I understand this is a difficult time for you right now.

We can put off our honeymoon until you're ready. You know that's never been an issue with me."

"But what about after, Aurelio? I have a career—patients who rely on me. I simply can't go cavorting around Africa and ignore them."

"Well...there are other doctors you know."

"What?" The candle flame flickered. "Other doctors?"

"Sweetheart," he purred, calming his tone as though he were concerned with her emotional state. "Don't get upset—"

"I won't break, Aurelio. You can be direct. Get to the point. What did you mean?"

"I simply meant to state that there are other doctors. Your patients will not go untreated while you're in Africa with me. And besides," his glance grazed hers, "you'll have to make this decision sooner or later."

She ground her jaw closed. Pulling her hands from the table, she pressed them into her lap. Don't. *Don't do it, Aurelio.*

"Once we have children, you'll have to cut back your hours anyway."

She locked her brows together. "And you? What exactly will you be doing, sweetheart?"

He gave her a taut smile. "Well, I won't be bearing children, I can assure you."

The restaurant was near-empty. The staff hovered out of sight. While she and Aurelio rarely fought, she'd had enough. "Don't expect me to give up my career for Africa. It won't happen."

"And children? Does the same hold true?"

"It's completely different. Women manage careers and family every day and do so quite well, I might add. I don't anticipate a problem."

"I see."

"Especially when husbands pitch in and do their fair share."

Brown eyes became black as they seared into her. "Like your father?"

She pulled her frame up and nudged her shoulders back. "Yes. Like my father."

Aurelio pulled the napkin from his lap and carefully set it on the table. With a nimble wave of his fingers, their formally-clad waiter appeared tableside.

"What can I get for you, Mr. Villarreal?"

"Check, please."

"Very well." He hurried off to his station, tucked behind an embellished wall partition.

Jennifer glared at Aurelio. "That's it?"

"I think we should discuss this at another time."

"Now is fine with me."

"It's late. You're under stress. I don't want us to say anything we don't mean."

Jennifer detected no concern in the hard line of his mouth, the icy frame of his gaze. There was no heart in the sudden dismissal. She cleared her throat. Maybe it was better this way. He was right. She might say something she *did* mean.

Chapter Eighteen

Jax heard her car pull in and with it, felt a rise of anticipation. Without looking up, he wondered whether she would stop and chat as she had yesterday or bypass him altogether. Though he would never admit it, he positioned his schedule so he was here when she arrived home. Just in case. He may not harbor fantasies of them getting together, but he was a man.

And Dr. Jennifer Hamilton was a beautiful woman, as fine as they come, and he liked looking. Especially those ocean blue eyes. He jammed his shovel into the dirt around the post.

"Good afternoon!"

He turned at the opening. Lifting to a stand, he held the shovel aside and allowed himself full sight of her. Dressed in scrubs today, a lavender print, she looked natural, appealing. More college girl than career woman. Him, he'd take either one of her looks so long as she donned that beautiful smile of hers, the one she wore now. "Good afternoon, to you!" he called back.

Jennifer walked toward him, but as she drew near, he noticed the worn look to her eyes. Shades of exhaustion turned the normally vibrant cobalt he enjoyed, to a lackluster blue. Coming to a halt a few feet from him, she crossed her arms over her chest.

"The arbor looks great," she said, her voice on the weary side.

Freshly stained, the wood was light brown in color. "Thanks." While he wanted to know what bothered her, what could so completely rob the light from her eyes, it was none of his business.

"I like the color."

"Natural usually works well outdoors."

Could just be the weather. The sky held only a spattering of clouds. He swiped a gloved hand against his damp brow. April in Miami could be brutal, though her makeup appeared intact, not smudgy from the humidity. Her ponytail remained glossy brown, not the first sign of frizz.

She smiled softly. "That will be nice."

"I think so. Hey, I wanted to ask you, how's your patient?"

When Jennifer looked at him, he swore he saw gratitude in her eyes. "She's doing well. Went home today, in fact."

"That's good to hear."

"Yes," she said with a pause, as though debating what to say or how much. Ever the patient one, he waited, allowing her a smooth exit or an open door to conversation.

"I'm sorry about yesterday."

Not the direction he thought they were going, but replied easily, "Don't be."

"I didn't mean to insult your choices—"

"You can't."

She peered at him in question.

He didn't want to sound harsh, but he didn't want her to mistake his position, either. "I'm good with where I am in my life. The choices I've made, the decisions..." He smiled, crossing a leg at his ankle, boot tip resting on the ground. "No one has the power to take that away from me." Not even you, he mused soberly.

Unfolding her arms, she sighed. "It's just..." Jennifer glanced around the yard, her gaze drifting more than taking in.

He waited, impatient for where she was going with this.

She returned her focus to him. "I don't want you to think I'm making any sort of judgment."

Ah, but you are, he mused.

"Your life is yours and you have the right to live it as you see fit. I shouldn't have acted as though I..." She glanced at the ground.

Disapprove?

"It sounds exciting, really," she pulled her face up level with his. "To travel around, no cares, no one depending on you, no one to answer to."

Exciting?

"I'm envious."

Jax dropped his head back and laughed.

Jennifer drew back in offense. "What's so funny?"

"I'm sorry," he said, "but you sound about as excited as a woman headed for a walk on the plank!"

Finely shaped brows pulled together as she pursed her lips.

"Okay, okay." Uncrossing his legs, he stood erect. "Forgive me?" he asked, suppressing a chuckle.

She rolled her eyes, but lapsed into a smile. "This time. But next time when a woman tries to make amends, you should humor her and act as though it mattered."

"Aye, aye, Captain."

She grinned. "Now get back to work."

"At your service."

Jennifer shook her head and retreated into the house. As she did, Jax felt her absence. He definitely enjoyed her company and though short in duration today, at least he had removed the gloom from her eyes.

# # #

Sitting in silence by her mother's bedside, Jennifer waited for her to awaken. As the soft light of sunset faded, evening seeped in through sheer curtains, casting the room in sedate buttery tones. Tonight her mom wore blue. She loved the color on her. Brought out the life in her eyes.

Stroking the hand she held in her own, content with the connection of touch, Jennifer thought about Jax. Yesterday had been different. In defense of himself, he'd made a joke at her expense. She'd been caught off guard, but should she have been?

It occurred to her how little she knew about the man, the important things, like the fuel behind his desire, the emotional connection to his mother.

His father. How could a man be so close to his mother while at the same time, be estranged from his father? If he was estranged. She was making assumptions at this point, going on intuition. But the ties intrigued her. She wanted to empathize with him, his situation. She wanted to help him move past the anger and close the distance.

Struck by the admission, she questioned her motives. *Why?* Why did she feel the need to find common ground, to help him with his personal issues? What did it matter?

The epiphany was sharp. Because he had done so for her. His instinct was to reach out and help; console her, ease her heartache after the near loss of a patient. Whatever she needed, he seemed prepared to offer.

And when it was her turn?

She had robbed him. Jennifer's mind filled with his image; the sorrow in his eyes when he recalled his mother's death, the disappointment when it was clear she didn't understand his dreams. And then the distance.

Yet, he forgave her. She recalled his smile. With humor.

"Jennifer... Darling."

The whisper of voice pulled her back to the present.

"How long...have you been here?"

The fragile quality to her mother's voice scared her. She firmed her clasp of the elderly hand and tried to warm her skin. "Not too long. A couple of minutes."

Beatrice seemed pleased.

"How are you feeling?"

"Okay," she replied faintly.

"I brought you some flowers." Jennifer pointed to the bedside table where a bouquet of yellow lilies gently bowed from the hourglass vase. Lackluster in the dim lighting, they promised a glorious wakeup call in the morning.

Beatrice's eyes sought them out and brightened. Her gaze returned to her daughter. "They're beautiful."

Jennifer smiled, happy for any speck of joy she could bring to those dear blue eyes, a shade too gray at the moment. She leaned closer, the faint scent of Gardenia drifting up between them. "The yard is beginning to take shape."

Beatrice's eyes shone with pleasure. "Tell me."

She nodded. "Jax is doing a really fine job." Her mother looked confused. "Remember, he's the man I hired to do the landscape. The one Michael recommended."

"Oh yes," she laughed softly. "The...bartender."

The description curdled in Jennifer's mind. *The bartender*. That was how she had first described him to her mother. "Jax is first and foremost a landscaper, of immeasurable talent," she corrected with more vigor than necessary. "His bartending was a skill learned during his youth that served him through the years. His appearance at Michael's was nothing more than a favor to a friend."

Beatrice's brow rose, her quiet eyes appraising. "I see... Tell me more."

"He calls it a garden to live by," Jennifer said, a grin sweeping her face.

"What?"

"Yes. He's designed it around my lifestyle, my needs. That way, rather than looking out back and seeing one big chore, he says I'll look out and see a place I can't wait to spend time." She brushed a wisp of bangs from her eyes. "It's going to be incredible Mom. Jax is literally transforming the yard before my eyes."

"Hmmm..." she murmured, a suggestive tone in her reply. "What does...Aurelio think?"

She stilled. "He agrees."

"Well...that's good to hear, isn't it," she said, but her gaze assumed a faraway haze as it settled on the vase of flowers.

"You'd like Jax," Jennifer continued.

She returned her attention and patted Jennifer's hand. "Would I, now?"

"He learned everything he knows from his mother. She had a passion for gardening." She smiled and squeezed her mother's hand gently. "Like you."

Beatrice suppressed a chuckle. "Did she?"

"Yes." Jennifer's enthusiasm dipped. "But she died a few years back. Heart attack."

"Oh, I'm sorry to hear that," came the automatic response.

Jennifer nodded. "Jax took it pretty hard. Like I said, the two of them were quite close."

"I imagine he did," she replied, but seemed to drop with whatever thought she intended to follow. Beatrice took a deep breath and exhaled, holding a knowing smile in her eyes. "It won't be long now...before you and Aurelio begin your life together... As husband and wife."

Jennifer dropped her gaze fully, landing on their clasped hands. "Yes," she said, flat and non-committal. "It won't be long now."

Chapter Nineteen

Jennifer strode down the wide corridor, floors cleaned to a glossy finish, walls covered with cheerful murals depicting animals and children at play beneath rainbows and blue skies. Beverly Singleton's doctor had called. She was asking for her.

Taking the corner, she hurried down to the nurse's station. Men and women wore colorful scrubs, prints of flowers and teddy bears, fish and dolls, themes to entertain little boys and girls alike. She spotted the pediatric surgeon at once.

Closing the distance, she asked, "How is she?"

"Frightened. Nervous. The usual. I appreciate you coming by."

"Of course." As if she would consider otherwise. "Which room?"

He pointed down a well-lit hall to his left. "Thirty-three twenty."

She gave a quick pat to his shoulder. "Thanks."

Slowing at the open door, she peeked inside. The room was dim compared to the hallway, monitors prominent with their bright greens and blues. All systems go, she mused. In the center, the girl was reclined against a soft pillow, covers pulled up to beneath her arms.

Round eyes lit up at the sight of her, the smile instantaneous. "Dr. Hamilton, you came!"

Strolling up to the bed, Jennifer ushered forth a bright smile. "Of course I did." She spied the pink rabbit tucked close beneath the lightweight blanket. "Good evening, Poppy." She leaned over. "How could I miss an opportunity to visit the best crumpet chef this side of the United States?"

The little girl beamed.

Jennifer liked that her hair was done, combed and clipped with ribbons. This time they were sky blue and matched her eyes to perfection. She grasped the bedrails. "I hear someone's getting a transplant. That's wonderful news."

The frown was instant.

"Why, Beverly. What's the matter?"

With a flip of her lashes, she grabbed hold of Poppy and hugged her close. "I'm afraid."

Jennifer ran a hand over the child's forehead, her fingers caressing the silk of her hair. "It's okay to be scared, Beverly. Surgery is a big deal. But I know your doctor and he's the best there is. He's going to take real good care of you, you'll see."

"But Dr. Hamilton..." Her eyes darted to her stuffed animal. "I—"

"What is it? What's bothering you?"

She rolled them back up to Jennifer, tears lining the bottom. "Will another child have to die to give me their heart?"

Jennifer bit back a sudden rise of tears. There was no easy way to tell a child the truth, even if the facts were to their benefit. She ran her hand along Beverly's forearm. She nodded. "I'm afraid so."

She clutched the rabbit to her chest. "But that's not fair!" she cried and pressed her eyes closed.

Jennifer took a deep breath, blowing it out with calm and precision. She glanced around the room. Tubes were attached to the child's body, monitors recorded her vitals. She gazed at the girl. She was right. Life wasn't fair.

With a light squeeze, she whispered, "Beverly, listen to me." Touched by the warmth of her skin, she lingered, hating that any of this was necessary, but grateful they had the option. "Sometimes God needs angels, you know..."

The clenched expression relaxed.

"Sometimes, he needs to call back his children."

Slowly, she opened her eyes. Velvet blue in the darkened room, they reached into Jennifer's heart and begged her to continue.

"We don't know why, or when, we only know that it happens. Jennifer stroked the small arm beneath her hand, the fluffy fur of the stuffed rabbit. "It's not our job to make those decisions." She shook her head. "But it is our job to do the best we can while we're here. Life is a blessing."

She gazed at the innocence staring back at her and longed to encourage its trust. She stroked her curls, fiddled with the ribbon. "Yours has only just begun. You have big things ahead of you. Your family loves you, your friends..." She gently tousled her hair. "Besides, Poppy needs you."

Releasing her death grip on the rabbit, she asked, "Will it hurt?"

Jennifer smiled. "You won't feel a thing during the surgery. The doctor will give you medicine to help you sleep and then he'll fix everything."

"After?"

"A little. But nothing you can't get through. And I'll be here every step of the way. We'll have tea and make crumpets." She winked. "Now that you've introduced me to the delicacies, I'm hooked!"

Jennifer was rewarded with a small smile.

"My mom says I'll be able to go back to school soon."

"She's right. And before you know it, you'll be jumping rope, bouncing across the playground."

"I've never been able to jump rope."

No, she didn't imagine she had. "You will now, once you receive your new heart." Survival rates were good. Albeit the long-term outlook was uncertain, technology was improving and so were the odds.

"Mom says I'll have to take medicine." She scrunched her nose and mouth in disgust.

She laughed. "We've got great flavors, now. We can make anything taste good, even medicine!"

"Really?"

"Really." Jennifer pulled a small hand free from the rabbit and secured it between her own. Rubbing hers back and forth, she promised, "We'll get through this, Beverly, you'll see. Together. You'll never be alone. If you need me, all you have to do is call."

# # #

"What are you doing here?"

Sam ignored the paltry welcome and brushed her cheek with a kiss. "I'm great! Thank you for asking."

Jennifer stepped aside, and made way for her entrance.

"Thought I'd stop by for a visit on this bright and cheery Saturday morning, now that all's forgiven."

"You're on probation."

"Good enough." Spotting the sketch book in Jennifer's hand, she stopped and glanced at her in surprise. "I didn't know we were drawing again."

"I'm not. Not really," she evaded, self-conscious of the drawing. It was the first since the one she did of her mother. "Call me crazy, but it's been so long, I was curious to know if I could still do it."

"Judging by the looks of that one, you still got it, baby!"

Pleased by the compliment, she peered at the drawing in hand. Unlike her island themes, this one was a rendition of her garden. At least the way she envisioned it, once completed. Color everywhere, it was bright and happy and welcoming.

Sam sashayed over to the window.

Jennifer shook her head in amusement. "Did you say you were here to visit me, or Jax?"

The reference snagged Sam's attention and she glanced back over her bare shoulder, the light brown halter top blending auburn waves with tanned skin. "Jax?" She smirked. "There's still hope for you, yet." She returned her gaze to the back.

Surveying Sam's short black shorts and long legs, smoothly shaved and golden from the sun, Jennifer felt a snippet of envy. Most assuredly she would parade her wares outside, certain to garner Jax's full attention while she paled in comparison with her khaki Capris. "Well, he has been working here for nearly two weeks. You were on a first-name basis after two minutes."

"I work faster than you do."

Rolling her eyes, Jennifer set her pad down and joined Sam by the window. Jax and two other men were busy at work on the fountain wall. Pushing noon, they weren't very far into the project. Must have started later than usual, because they weren't here when she left to make rounds at eight.

"So why are you here?"

"I thought I'd swing by and see if you wanted to do lunch."

"Are you sure you want to invite *me*?" she smiled, amazed by Sam's one track mind currently running circles around Jax.

"He's one helluva hunk I'll give you that, but no Jen, I'm here for you." She winked and brushed overgrown curls behind an ear. "Right after I have a short visit with him."

With that, Sam disappeared through the patio door.

Jennifer followed.

"Hey Jax," Sam called out, as one would do to an old friend. She trekked across dirt without second thought, her sneakers well up for the undertaking.

He turned to see who called his name. At the sight of Sam, he smiled. "Hey there, stranger." When she drew near, he added quietly, "Hello Jennifer."

Sam's eyes moved between Jax and Jennifer. "How's it coming?"

"Great," he replied, then addressed Jennifer. "But you're the one we need to please. What do you think?"

"Perfect." Gaze touching upon the stone trim, she said, "I was skeptical about the travertine finish, but it blends so well with the ceramic, almost like they were made for each other."

Jax smiled. "It was your choice. You have good taste."

Sam raised a brow as if to say, *what's this*? She shifted her weight from hip to hip and said, "Good work, good taste. Sounds like a combination for success brewing around here."

Jennifer's cheeks burned with embarrassment.

"Once we get the paint on, this area will be a knockout," Jax said. "Especially when the arbor's complete."

"I agree," Sam chimed in. "I'll definitely be over to lounge by this pool. Skinny-dipping to the sound of splashing water—I'll think I've lost myself in a Roman bath!" She threw up her arms and mimicked a titter of excitement. "What will the Gods do with me? Oh, Heaven have *mercy*!"

"Sam," Jennifer admonished, her eyes singling out the workers, suggesting her comment was none too appropriate.

Jax let loose with a laugh. "Sorry Sam, but the chlorine's a bit harsher than silky milk against your skin."

"Better to kill those pesky STD's."

One of the workmen looked up with a grin, then quickly reverted back to task.

"They can be a bit of a nuisance," Jax agreed in stride.

Jennifer remained mum, zipped tighter than a drum.

Sam looked at Jax. "Awesome work, Jax."

"Yes, but don't let us interrupt you," Jennifer said. "We'll leave you to your work."

"Yeah, besides, you don't need two supervisors breathing down your neck."

"You're welcome to supervise any time, Jennifer."

"Thank you, Jax.

"We missed you yesterday."

Sam perked at the comment. "Yesterday?"

Jennifer glanced between the two. "Yes, well," she murmured, running hands down the backside of her Capris. "I was called over to St. Theresa's. One of the kids there was asking for me."

"Ah," he replied, as though he understood.

Though he couldn't. There was no possible way.

Unless Michael said something. The circle of conversation suddenly became too close. Jennifer hooked her elbow through Sam's. "Yes, well, why don't we stop bothering them and get to that lunch you came for in the first place."

"You bet. This heat is obscene, anyway. Ta, ta, Jax!" Sam waved off easily.

"Bye," he returned with a chuckle.

Sam kept a determined pace, clutching Jennifer's arm more tightly than necessary. "So fess up. What's going on with you two?"

"*What*?"

"You heard me. You and Jax. Is there something you forgot to tell me?"

"Don't be absurd." She stole a peek back at Jackson, only to find him staring at her. Whipping her attention back to the house, she picked up her speed.

Sam chuckled at her discomfort. "That man's attention is trailing you just as clear as if he ripped the white cotton tank from your back."

"You don't know what you're talking about."

Leaping up the steps together, Jennifer walked into the house ahead of Sam, hit first by the wave of cold.

"So you two have the hots for each other, huh?"

"Sam!"

"What's the matter with you? You look like someone pinched your nipple."

Jennifer planted hands on her hips and fired a warning glare.

"Okay, okay." She held her hands up in defense. "Sorry. I'm just asking what's up. Aren't best friends entitled to the truth?"

"I don't know what you're talking about. Nothing is up."

"You two seemed awful cozy out there."

"Cozy? Friendly is what you saw. Professional. There's nothing wrong with being nice to the help. And aren't you the one who insisted I shouldn't hold Jackson's position against him?" She looked past Sam and out into the yard, waving her arms about. "Bartender/landscaper—it should all be the same to me?"

"Yes," she said. "But I didn't realize you learned so quickly."

Jennifer remained mute.

"Listen, what I saw out there was more than friendly." She flipped a thumb toward the back. "At least on his part. That man is interested."

"He is nothing of the sort."

"*Trust me.* We're traveling my territory of expertise, now." Sam waved a hand toward the yard. "That man would like nothing less than to throw a saddle on you and take the ride of his life."

"Would you stop with the euphemisms? You're killing my appetite."

"There's nothing wrong with a ride on the wild side, Jen."

"As I recall, playing with cowboys didn't work for me quite like it does for you."

"What are you talking about?"

"Tony."

The name pierced the mood like a spear.

"My father was less than pleased with my behavior."

Sam winced at the implication. "Jen."

She turned her back on her and walked into the kitchen.

Sam followed. "You were a kid. Your father was only being protective, it's what dads do. It's their job. That can't be holding you back, now." She stopped. "Can it?"

Jennifer whirled around.

"C'mon." Sam suppressed a grin. "You can't be serious."

"Can't I? And why not?"

"Fathers are supposed to be upset when they find their seventeen-year-old daughter with her top off and her boyfriend's hand up her skirt!" Sam smiled, despite her best effort at brevity.

Jennifer refused to dignify her with a response.

"This is insane. You should worry if he didn't hit the roof, not that he did."

Jennifer fell heavy against the counter. Supposed to or not, the experience didn't help to encourage her appetite for adventure.

"My God Jen, you can't tie your life to one instance of poor timing. You were a kid. A teenager.

You act like you were out running the streets, selling your wares to strangers."

Jennifer glowered.

"This is why you've been so reserved all these years? Cooling the jets of some of the hottest men I've laid eyes on, all because you were caught in one naughty no-no with your teenage boyfriend?"

Nothing.

"You're being too hard on yourself. Your dad didn't know how to handle the situation is all. He lost control. He was surprised."

"Surprised?" Jennifer couldn't believe how Sam was minimizing the event. "Surprise is an understatement, to say the least. My father nearly had a coronary followed by a stroke!"

"He's your *father*. That's what they do. You've got to whip the sheet off that old ghost and let it fly— see it for what it is.

"There's nothing wrong with experimenting, Jen. All kids do it. You weren't any different than anyone else your age. You just got caught, is all. And your dad shouldn't have been so hard on you. He and your mom weren't playing dominoes in the bedroom all those years... They were getting it on!"

Anger turned to disgust as Jennifer crossed both arms over her chest. "That's revolting."

"But it's true, Jen." Sam softened her plea. "Your mom and dad had passion, the kind you could see and feel, every time you were around them."

"I never saw that."

"Because you were too busy mislabeling your own desires as dirty instead of the budding lust they rightly should have been called."

"When did psychiatrist Samantha pop in?"

"You know I'm right."

Jennifer pushed away from the counter with a shove. About to walk to the breakfast room window, she abruptly turned toward the refrigerator instead. Opening the door, she retrieved a bottle of water and twisted the cap free.

"I've seen your hot temper," Sam continued. "I know you've got the blood racing through your body. You're no different than me. A man could turn you into juicy mincemeat in a matter of seconds. It only takes the right chef—a man who loves to eat and knows his way around the pantry." Sam flashed a wicked grin.

"Aurelio and I have a wonderful sex life. We have buckets of passion."

Sam glanced around herself.

Jennifer slapped the water bottle to the counter. "What?"

"Either you forgot who you were talking to, or I just disappeared."

"Very funny."

"Not really." Sam's amusement faded. "You need to snap out of it." She poked a thumb in Jax's direction. "Why not give him a chance? Seriously. He's definitely interested, and you can tell he's got the fire. It's in the eyes."

"Is this about the other night? At the gallery?"

"I'm sorry, my A.D.D. must have kicked in."

"You don't have A.D.D."

"Yes, I do. I thought I was talking about Jax."

"You were and it's irrelevant. I'm engaged."

"But not married."

"For some of us, the promise is as good as the commitment."

"As good as, but not the same—not legally. Trust me on this one," she said with a straight face. "I'm a lawyer. I know the difference. It's not too late. You can change your mind."

"Life isn't that easy, Sam. Not when other people depend on you." Sure Tony had been fun. Lit up the nights like fireworks, packed her days with thrill, but he was the past. They were kids. Her life was different now.

"Listen, I only want what's best for you. Marriage demands more than compatibility. It demands want. Desire. The hot and deep, I-want-you-so-bad-I-would-walk-across-nails-for-you kind of desire."

Or travel to Africa for you.

The demand of reality halted her defense like a collision. She should be willing to travel to Africa. Should want to travel there. With Aurelio, her love.

But she didn't.

The high-pitched sound of a machine-saw cut through the silence. She glanced out the window to see Jax sliding a piece of tile through, white dust flying around his hands, his movement brisk but steady. She crossed arms over chest. Her mind tumbled between the stab of nails poking beneath her feet and the hot desert sand of Africa. Neither was appealing.

Sam broke the quiet. "You ready for that lunch?"

Chapter Twenty

"Good morning, love," Aurelio greeted softly as she opened the front door.

Jennifer tipped her cheek up for a kiss delivered with precise formality, and stepped aside as he entered.

"Are we ready for a fabulous cruise?"

Aurelio had hired a boat for the two of them to get away. He insisted stress was coming between them and they needed time alone. Together. To discuss their future.

Ambivalence zipped through her belly. "I can't wait."

He perused her attire. "You look ravishing."

"Thank you." Simple white skirt and navy striped halter, she had chosen navy topsiders to match. She was going for the nautical look by day, a silk tank dress and heels packed away in her bag for the evening.

"It's going to be incredible. The captain assures me we will be sailing across the clearest blue water you would ever want to lay eyes on."

"I'm sure it will be."

"And it's right off the bay," he said, his smile growing, "so we won't waste precious hours before our return home for a sunset cruise along the city lights."

Aurelio was clearly excited by the prospect. He had secured a yacht for hire and the two were set to enjoy a catered lunch on the open sea, followed by a return portside for a candlelight dinner cruise along the coast of Miami. He promised champagne and caviar, and lots and lots of coveted alone time.

She inhaled deep and full.

He took her hand and linked his fingers through hers, leading her to the back terrace. "I want to see the progress. It seems the landscaper has been making great time."

"Yes," she murmured faintly, slightly unnerved by his choice of words. "He has."

"I love the bird of paradise out front."

She nodded.

In his enthusiasm, Aurelio breezed through her home and out the back door, pulling Jennifer alongside. "Wow." He stopped briefly at the top of the stairs. "That wall is outstanding."

It drew the first real smile on her lips.

Descending hastily, he carefully made his way through the dirt until he was feet from the fountain. Scrutinizing the backdrop of tile, seemingly scouring the mosaic for some hint of error in pattern or placement, he stepped back. Crossing one arm over his chest, he brought the other to his chin. Curling a finger around his jaw, his brow rose. "The tile work is exquisite."

A mix of blues and terra-cotta with hints of yellow against a background of creamy white, the array was intricate without being busy. Forming an arc over the top it sloped down into yet another, wider arc as it created a graceful frame around the fountain and basin. She had been pleased with the result.

Turning his attention to her, he asked, "Did you say you created that design?"

Pride swelled. "I did indeed."

"It's absolutely perfect." He leaned over and kissed her full on the lips. Eyes hovering inches from hers, he said, "I couldn't have done better myself."

Her momentary gratification subsided.

Aurelio zeroed in on the back wall again. "The golden yellow of the house and this wall blend seamlessly with the tile. Striking yet subtle, the texture it adds to the area is sublime. What color bloom have you decided on for the vines over the arbor?"

Spotlights could have been burning hot upon her face, for the pointed inquiry felt the same. "Red," she responded without thinking.

"Perfect."

Funny, but his approval should have been more heartening.

Aurelio reached for her other hand and bringing the two together, he lifted them to his lips. His dark brown eyes were intent on hers, his focus complete. "The wedding will be a most enchanting scene, my darling." His lips pressed against her fingers in a light kiss. "Your mother will be pleased. She will rest in peace knowing that her one and only daughter is marrying the man who adores her, will keep her in sickness and in health, and never stray until death do they part."

If only she could share his vision so fully.

Aurelio drew her to him, enveloped her within his embrace, and kissed her. Overwhelmed by a sense of melancholy, Jennifer was torn. Caught between his tender advance and her own doubt, she sought reassurance where she should have returned affection.

Quiet and seeking, she slid her arms around his waist and yearned to feel desire. His hands brushed through her hair, increasing their pressure as they pulled her closer, his tongue delving inside. Moving her hands up his back, she felt the slender curve of his muscles, the narrow angle of his shoulders.

Hooking her hands over the tops of his shoulders, she took in the difference between his build and Jax's.

Aurelio pulled away, but kept her securely in his embrace.

Jennifer's cheeks felt hot.

"I love you."

"I love you, too," she blurted, praying she didn't look as embarrassed as she felt.

He kissed her again, lingering over her lips, rubbing his softly against hers. "Are you ready?"

No! She had a distinct need to collect herself. A need to dodge these distractions and concentrate on Aurelio—*their afternoon*. But she duly nodded, and followed his lead back through the yard, the house and into his awaiting Jaguar.

They were going on a cruise. A lovely, seafaring adventure that was incredibly romantic of him to plan and one that she was going to enjoy. A voyage to which Jax was uninvited.

And Jennifer had done well. Her thoughts had only diverted to Jax when they passed near Vizcaya and certainly because it was a Mediterranean-inspired mansion surrounded by lush gardens, much like he had depicted in his proposal. The second was out on the open water, when thoughts of his future drifted across her mind.

How could a man look forward to a life of nothing but wave after wave? He had to get bored. And what about family? He had been close to his mother. Didn't he want children? And what about his significant other? Was she joining him? Was she a restless soul like he?

As for Aurelio, he was behaving very unlike himself. It seemed the "spontaneous" bug had taken a chunk from his rear. Not usually one for public displays of affection, his arm had barely left her thigh as they sat on the plush leather sofa in the elegantly appointed cabin. Kissing her repeatedly, he told her again and again how beautiful she was, and how much he loved her. His fingers even found their way beneath the hem of her skirt, sliding the material up and exposing an indecent expanse of her skin!

Definitely unlike him. Granted the staff was discreet, almost nonexistent, but they did exist and could be anywhere, though Aurelio seemed quite heedless to this fact.

So much for Sam's insinuation that Aurelio lacked passion—the man was all over her! And now, nearing the turn for her street, he hinted he wanted more. Her hand clasped in his, he kept one eye on the road ahead and one eye on her, caressing her cheek with his gaze.

Leaning back against the headrest, she indulged her mind in the jazz flowing quietly from hidden speakers. A saxophone-led piece, it was wild and full, the tenor strong. Aurelio's cologne filled the interior of his car, a rich fragrance she enjoyed, one she had selected especially for him.

Slowing for her driveway, Aurelio handled the turn with a spin of the wheel, braking to a smooth stop. He flipped the ignition off and turned to face her. The expectant look in his eyes meant he wanted to be invited in, but he was too much the gentleman to insist.

She smiled. The day had been a good one. He retracted his earlier comments as rude and insensitive and promised he would partner with her in respect to the children. What more could she ask for? With a small tug of their entwined hands, Jennifer signaled she wanted the same.

Aurelio wasted no time and arose from the car in one fluid motion, rounding the front on his way to collect her. Opening her door, he lifted her hand high and pulled her free, pushing the door closed behind her.

Jennifer spied the bird of paradise standing proudly out front and experienced a touch of pleasure. Jax was right. It was a good choice. Something she would enjoy seeing every time she came home.

Aurelio unlatched the courtyard gate and ushered her in ahead of him. He waited by the front door as she unlocked the deadbolt, whereby the two made for her bedroom, their path lit by a small lamp left on in the foyer. Once inside, she set her purse down on the dresser and turned to find Aurelio's arms open and waiting.

Eagerly, Jennifer fell into his embrace, wrapping her arms around him. Slipping his arms around her he kissed the side of her head, the ensuing hug warm and full, lasting for several moments before he pulled away.

"I've had a wonderful day, my love."

"Me, too," she said, meaning it. It had begun slightly off-kilter, but she was over it now. And thoughts of Jax were to be expected. For heaven's sake, the man was here every day—of course he would cross her mind! Gary Gardener, Jackson Montgomery; did it matter?

Hovering close, Jennifer could see the love in Aurelio's eyes; a want that spoke volumes through the faint light. His was more than a simple desire for sex.

He cupped her chin and tipped it up as he kissed her. Sweet and soft, it was a sensitive gesture from a man in love. A man who cherished the woman he held in his arms...

And Jennifer relished the fact that she was that woman. Aurelio was a wonderful man and they were going to have a wonderful life together.

Her lips parted and his tongue slipped in, gliding around hers, probing her warmth, her easy reception. Jennifer anticipated his next move and stepped backward until the bed hit the back of her knees. Never losing contact with Aurelio, she lowered herself onto the edge and lay back, moving until the length of his body was halfway atop hers. Jennifer released one arm from around his neck and let it fall to her side, facilitating Aurelio's ease in undressing her.

Which he did immediately. Beginning at her shoulder he eased the dress from her body, then pulling the bedspread aside to reveal the soft cotton of her sheets, rolled his body close to hers. Jennifer surrendered to the moment, feeling his arousal hard against her hips. Somewhat impatient it seemed, Aurelio yanked his belt open, following suit with his trousers.

Unbuttoning his shirt, he pulled it open and moved between her legs. "I love you," he murmured as he flattened his body atop hers.

"I love you, too," she replied, and readied herself for his next move.

Lifting onto his elbows inches above her, Aurelio launched himself inside and promptly found his rhythm, settling into a docile sway, to and fro, side to side. His movements were easy and unhurried, his hands soft as whispers as they toyed with her hair, much like the feather kisses he was sprinkling across her cheeks.

While she listened to his breathing quicken, she relaxed into her own pleasure, her own feelings at the fullness of his body within hers. She closed her eyes and luxuriated in the union between lovers. The sensations their enjoined bodies produced were warm and sweet; exquisite. She relaxed further and her heart sighed. *Passion.* Love. They were beautiful things.

To feel his maleness deep inside her, full and content, she never wanted it to end... Her thoughts stretched like a lazy feline as she immersed herself in the moment. The hard ache as his hands glided across her breasts, the soft moan as his lips roamed her shoulder.

She wanted him. To touch her, to feel her, to move deep within her, she wanted him. She yearned to kiss that sweet smile, look into those warm eyes...to lose herself in the warmth of his embrace.

Aurelio mumbled something into her ear, and Jax's image popped into her mind. Jennifer's eyes burst open. Her limbs stiffened—briefly—though her lover never missed a beat, her mind cried out in protest.

But there was he was, smiling, the unmistakable look of sex in his eyes, drenching his grin as he looked at her. Looked at her...

Ignore it. She squeezed her eyes closed. It means nothing. *Nothing.*

Jennifer struggled to force thoughts of Jax from her mind and focus on Aurelio. She didn't want him to feel her distraction. Moving more quickly now, he was getting closer.

Intent on remaining in the moment, she picked up her pace to match his more frenzied movements. She wanted to be there with him and experience the ultimate release. "Yes, sweetheart..." she coaxed, blacking out her imagination. "That's it."

Aurelio's breathing became labored as he moved with determination. Yes, that's it... A little more and—

Aurelio exploded in climax, suspended above for several seconds before falling limp to her chest. Jennifer hadn't managed the same, and hated that she felt relief over his conclusion.

It shouldn't have happened this way. It wasn't fair.

Her spirits sunk. What should have been the perfect ending to the perfect day had turned into a colossal disappointment; a failure on her part.

Jennifer instantly began to berate herself for the unconscionable digression. *How could she do that to him*? What kind of fiancé allowed the thought of another man to intrude upon the lovemaking of her soon-to-be-husband?

Who must have sensed something was wrong, because he rolled off and asked, "Everything all right, my love?"

"Yes, of course," she replied, cursing the anxious quality to her voice.

"Did you?"

"Yes," she lied, feeling a jittery movement of her eyes. "It was wonderful, Aurelio, really wonderful." She forced a smile, unwilling to hurt his feelings— especially when he was so considerate of her own.

"You are the greatest lover I have ever known," he proclaimed, a satiated wave washing through hooded eyes.

"You too, sweetheart," Jennifer returned, closing her eyes to hide her shame. Her heart winced at the betrayal.

Chapter Twenty-One

Dusk cast the yard in shadows, dousing the colorful plants with grays and browns as Jennifer trudged up her front steps. There was no Jax this evening. A man couldn't work if a man couldn't see. Unlocking the door, she flipped on a light switch.

Walking to the kitchen, she glanced out the back windows and noted most of everything seemed to be in, save for the grass. New sod would be ruined by the traffic of activity and she knew he planned on installing it last. By the looks of her yard, it didn't seem like much longer before it would be finished, putting Jax well ahead of the schedule she had first proposed. Which meant she and Aurelio could be married sooner, and accommodate her mother's deteriorating condition.

That is what her doctor implied. They ran tests this afternoon and her blood counts were off. More significantly than usual. It explained her fatigue this evening, Jennifer thought, feeling a stab of guilt. The disease was moving with increased aggression through its final stage and it wouldn't be long before—

Dwelling on it would help no one. She understood the condition. She knew what was at stake. She jumped at the sound of her telephone ringing from inside the house. Hurrying up the steps, quickly unlocking the back door, she fell into a dash for the kitchen. She snatched the receiver from the counter and answered with a breathless, "Hello?"

"Jen."

"Sam," she said, recovering from the sudden leap in pulse rate.

"Hey, I need to talk to you."

The solemn tone alarmed her. Jennifer tightened her grip on the receiver.

"Blake's had a stroke."

Panic sputtered in her chest. "What?"

"Late last night—early this morning, I don't know. Patty called me this morning and I hopped the next flight to Ohio." She paused. "It's bad. The docs say he might not recover."

Jennifer slumped against the counter, heart sinking to the pit of her stomach. "Oh Sam, *I'm so sorry...*"

"Patty's a mess."

With four kids, who wouldn't be?

"She doesn't know what to do. I told her I'd call you."

"What happened?"

Sam answered, taking it from the beginning. He woke up with a splitting headache, took some aspirin, tried to go back to sleep, but couldn't. His speech started to slur, Patty called 911. From then on it was a nightmare. Her husband collapsed, the paramedics arrived and she rushed to the hospital where they delivered the bad news. She called Sam. The one person every Rawlings sibling turned to when in trouble.

"What can I do?"

"What can *she* do, Jen? She's freaking out. They're telling her Blake may not be able to function again. He may be paralyzed. He may not be able to speak! Or," her voice swung low, "he may pull through fine, with no long-term effects. It's all over the map. What the hell is she supposed to believe?"

The shrill tone was so unlike Sam. The panic in her voice... This was a woman normally in command of a crisis; the go-to gal when others stumbled. "It's all true, Sam. That's part of the problem. Recovery for stroke victims is a wait and see process. They simply don't know."

"But what's she supposed to do in the meantime? The not knowing is killing her."

"Be patient," Jennifer said. It was the same advice she gave to her patients' families. "Recovery will take time. Blake will need her support. Especially if the prognosis is good. Rehabilitation is tough work, but it can do wonders for his long-term prospects."

"Yeah, great. Except her nerves are like open wires getting rained on. I don't know how much she can take before she falls apart."

But this was a blow tough for anyone to digest.

Jennifer's heart reached out to her. "I'll call his doctor, Sam. I'll speak with him and find out what's going on." It was the only thing she could do—make sense of the medical jargon. Give Sam and Patty a starting point. A place from which to begin the arduous journey that lay ahead of them.

"Yeah, thanks."

A stump of appreciation, but Jennifer understood it was all she had. Sam was a dynamo in the courtroom, but when it came to matters of the heart her normal response was ejection. When emotions ran too close, she cut them loose. No commitments, no sappy love songs... She was a free spirit who refused to let anyone or anything tie her down. But she couldn't eject this time. Sam had to plug in, for Patty's sake. A challenge to say the least.

And not because Sam wasn't a loving person—she was. She stepped up to the plate whenever duty called. She'd walk you through the last mile. But Patty had four kids and they would need tending while she—not Sam—held vigil at the hospital.

Sam was kid-friendly, but not kid-competent. "It will be okay," Jennifer said. Both women knew she was referring to Sam this time. "Hang in there, it'll be okay."

For another ten minutes, Jennifer hung on the line with her, walking Sam through her feelings; her fears. She had cut out on two major trials to be in Ohio, but felt confident the partners could handle the load.

Didn't matter if they couldn't, because she had made her decision. Family came first in Sam's book, whether it cost her job, or not.

It was a sentiment that fused the two women at the heart.

"He's going to make it, Sam. I feel it in my bones, he's gonna beat this." Hope was the only salvation she could offer, the only thing capable of easing the pain.

"I hope so," Sam said, choking on her words. "Family is Patty's whole world."

"I know. And with you by her side, she'll get through it."

When Jennifer finally hung up the phone, she looked out over her backyard and allowed her gaze to drift. She saw everything and nothing. The pool, the wall, the plants...

It all blurred together in a landscape of nothing. It took a long while before she realized the arbor was up, though bare.

Pausing, she narrowed her focus on the structure. It felt entirely foreign to her present state of mind, while at the same time acted as a reminder that life goes on, with or without us, crisis or not. Moving nearer the window, she lingered on the light wood and thought it felt naked. Like a woman awaiting her frill of fine clothing and jewels, the embellishments that would transcend her from just another body to a magnificent creature of pomp and pageantry, the arbor was unfinished. Incomplete.

Jennifer tried to imagine it loaded with flowering vines arcing gracefully overhead as bride and groom made their way toward the fountain to take their vows and become man and wife.

A ceremony to die for.

Around five a.m., Jennifer finally gave up on sleep. Consumed with the plight of Patty and Blake, she needed to do something. They were hanging on the edge of prognosis, his condition liable to go either way. Even if he came through with honors and ribbons, it still meant a mountain of therapy. In the beginning, he'd probably struggle with minimal function, dealing Patty the added responsibility of child-like demands from her husband.

It would be a difficult road for Patty. Thankfully she had Sam by her side, but her sister could only stay on for so long. Eventually, Sam would have to return to her legal practice, leaving Patty to her own device.

Upon arrival at the hospital, she spoke with her colleagues regarding Blake's condition, but much to her dismay, she had given Sam the best advice she could have; it's a wait and see proposition. The first few days were crucial. The patient's inert body was solely responsible for driving the recovery.

Which didn't help Sam. She had called three times throughout the day and Jennifer wasn't sure if it was truly on Blake's behalf, or a compelling need to feel useful. Doing nothing was not on her agenda. Yet unable to give her more, Jennifer merely listened as the heartache spilled forth. Not much, but it was the best she could do.

Arriving home that evening, Jennifer was heartened to see Jax's truck by the garage. It would be a nice escape to talk about something other than Blake. But in a rush of realization, Jennifer knew she would have to tell him about Sam. Granted, they weren't close friends, but he was certainly familiar with her. It would be awkward to purposefully withhold the news as opposed to the more natural sharing of the day's events, as had become their habit.

At once, she opened her door and made her way for him. Standing beneath the arbor, he weaved vines through the arches elevated above. A distant rumble vibrated through the air as a cloud swept into the sun's path. It was a welcome rush of cool, the heat merciless during this late hour in the day, though Jax seemed oblivious.

Marveling at the difference a walkway between patio and pool made, she was beginning to be able to form a picture in her mind. She could easily envision her wedding here, chairs lining the lawn, filled with family and friends. A smile eased onto her lips. Jax was right. It would make an enchanting setting for bride and groom. *Or had Aurelio said that?*

At once perturbed by her muddle of memory, Jennifer batted the minor detail away. It didn't matter who said what, this will indeed be a wonderful backdrop for a garden wedding, period. Did it matter who received credit?

Jax moved around the wooden pillar, continually twisting the flowery climber, but waved when he saw her. She waved back, waiting for him to stop what he was doing and give her the routine progress report. Or something like that...

It was but a whisper from her heart, and one she refused to acknowledge. Making haste across the expanse of ragged lawn, she ignored the slight sink of her soft leather heels as she trekked over the dirt. It was more important to see how Jax was faring. She wanted to hear what he was planning, hear what he had done. She wanted to *talk*, something her subconscious wouldn't label so simply.

"Hello, Dr. Hamilton," he said, using her more formal address.

"Hello, Jax," she replied with a smile, refusing to do the same, though she wondered if her full suit was to blame. The cropped khaki blazer was one of her more casual ones. She didn't think it made her seem austere.

Did he?

"What do you think?" he asked, hands moving to his hips, an eye to his handiwork.

Absently brushing a loose strand of hair behind an ear, she smoothed down the back of her jacket. "That it looks fabulous. As does everything you do."

"Can I get that in writing?" Relaxed, easy, he chuckled.

A clear sign he felt comfortable with her. Jennifer knew the last thing he needed was a referral from her, but played along, "Not before my lawyer gets a gander."

"I know your lawyer." He grinned. "She's a shark. I'd be wise to sharpen my skills of survival before I face *her* on a dark beach."

"Jax." Her shift in tone was unmistakable. "Sam's in Ohio."

Question stopped his jovial brown gaze cold.

"Her brother-in-law had a stroke."

She felt the empathy immediately as his eyes filled with concern. "Oh no... How bad?"

"It's pretty serious. How bad..." She held out open palms. "We don't know yet. It's too soon to tell, but the good news is he's hanging in there."

"Thank God," Jax said, genuinely relieved.

Compassion, she mused. *Every day, with everyone.*

Pulling a glove from one hand, he wiped the sheen of sweat from his brow. Above them, the sky grew a shade darker, the air a degree cooler.

"At this point, Sam may be struggling the most," she went on. "She's taking charge of four children under the age of nine; a trice more difficult for her than criminal defense."

It seemed Jax glimpsed the irony in that, too, but his brown eyes buoyed. "She's a spitfire. If anyone can handle the challenge, she can."

Jennifer nodded and found it odd. He didn't know Sam that well, yet to talk about her with him felt like they were discussing a mutual friend, the trials and trauma for which both could appreciate on Sam's behalf. She sighed. "I hope so. Stroke recovery can be a long haul. Her sister's going to need all the help she can get."

"She's lucky to have Sam."

Her sentiments, exactly.

The wind picked up, blowing hair across her face which she brushed instantly aside, her gaze fixed on his in this moment of alliance.

"People need all the support they can get when pushed up against a wall. Family illness shoves hard."

"Yes," Jennifer nodded again, thinking of her mother. Indeed it did. With sudden realization, she thought of his mother. Jax was no stranger to family illness.

"My sister was the Rock of Gibraltar when my mom died. If it hadn't been for her dragging me back to my right mind, I might have sunk into a nasty depression."

Jennifer feared the very same for herself when her mother passed. It was as if he sensed it.

His gaze intensified and his voice softened. "My mom was the light of my life, Jennifer. But she always told me, life was about living, and nothing would disappoint her more than if I tossed mine into the gutter when she died."

"You two were close..."

"Like H-two and O. The basis of life. There didn't live a woman more dear to my heart, another human being who loved me more. Mother and child... It's a bond that can't be duplicated."

"It must have been hard on you..." she murmured, feeling at a loss to express her feelings more fully. But fighting the fear of losing the very same bond in her own life, she felt inadequate.

"She was the ground I walked on. The air I breathed. The day she died was the toughest in my life."

A tear slipped free from the corner of her eye, but Jax pretended not to see it. The air took on a cool mist, his expression turned warm and firm. "My mom was an incredible woman. She made me who I am today and I won't disappoint her by being anything less than the best I can be."

Jennifer nodded, a streak of pride bolting through her. How proud his mother would be if she could hear him now.

"Sam will be all right."

The depths in his eyes, the soft quality to his voice... His smile reached out to her, soothing as a caress on her cheek. So real, she could almost feel his hand on her face, his fingers trailing along her skin. The sensation stirred a need deep inside her.

"Sam has you, Jennifer, and you'll see her through."

She wanted to share his certainty, to feel it was true. "I haven't been of much help, really..." she protested feebly, rubbing her arms against the sudden chill.

"Just knowing you're here is enough." Brown eyes turned silken. "Trust me. When you're in the middle of a crisis, having someone by your side means everything."

Overhead, a black cloud cracked open, followed by a flash of light. Jennifer's head shot up. Her arms flung open. Rain fell in heavy sheets. Jax seemed just as surprised but was quicker to respond, making a mad dash for the house, gesturing for her to follow. Pelted by rain, the two ran up the steps and careened into a halt on the back porch.

"Whoa!" he shouted above the thunderous rain. "Where did that come from?"

"I have no idea!" she said, embarrassed by her sopping-wet appearance, amazed neither had seen it coming. She watched as he shook droplets of rain from his hair, then run a hand through it, rubbing out the remainder.

She missed it, because she had been so caught up in their conversation, drawn in by his words...

Words of empathy, one friend to another, that's what they were. "I didn't realize it was forecast to storm," she mumbled, tripping over the last thought.

That's what they were.

Words of empathy? Or were they friends...?

Puzzled by her own assessment, she stared at him. The battering overhead increased its intensity, but she heard none of it, her mind ensnared by the question.

"The weatherman probably didn't either. I think they usually guess," he added with a grin.

That grin. That irrepressible sign of self-possession of his was fully intact. Jennifer brushed hands over either side of her wet head. She smoothed her hair into place, squeezed the excess water from her ponytail. Empathy, self-possession, content-ment...

They were qualities in a man that held strong appeal, she could not deny. Beneath this man's rough exterior lay a heart of gold. "Would you like to come in?"

"Sure," he replied.

She meant until the rain stopped, but her words held invitation—like a first date. A sudden swarm of nerves rose in her belly. With a sideways glance to the yard, the rain, the pounding storm, she opened the door.

Unable to retract the invitation, and not sure she wanted to, she gestured for him to follow.

Chapter Twenty-Two

"Can I get you something to drink?"

Jax wiped the mud from his boots on the mat and entered. "Water would be great."

"Have a seat." Jennifer indicated the breakfast table, and quickly slipped out of her blazer. Her white button-down dry, she felt a tad more normal. *A relief.*

Hanging her jacket over the back of a chair, she retrieved two bottles of water from the refrigerator.

Jax was still standing when she returned. "I'm a bit wet," he said with a sheepish smile. "I don't want to ruin your chairs."

A fidgety tickle brushed beneath her ribs. "Don't be silly, Jax. A little water never hurt anything."

"I'm covered in more than a little water," he said, amusement dancing in his eyes.

She caught the implication. Dirt, grime. Somehow, she minded none of it. "They're made of wood. From the outside. I hear it's pretty durable stuff."

"I appreciate it, but I'm good."

Jennifer handed him the bottle, then fussed with the half-dry, half-wet tangles of her hair, patting them down for a more groomed appearance. The attempt was weak, but the effort made her feel better.

"Nice drawing." He indicated the sketch pad laying open on the counter. "You do it?"

A flush of self-consciousness swept through her. "Yes. I was, uh, playing around with some pencils the other day and—"

"You're good."

The flat statement of fact chopped off her attempt to downplay the drawing. She grazed the floor with her gaze before returning to him. "Thank you."

"You have quite a talent."

"I wouldn't go *that* far," she said, pride bursting in her chest. "It's just something I enjoy..."

A sudden boom of thunder engulfed the house, pulling her gaze outdoors. "It's really coming down, isn't it?"

She sways and rocks, giving herself to the passionate throes, then explodes, high above the landscape in a spectacular light show, releasing herself in a thunderous downpour, bathing the earth with her riches.

An involuntary smile crossed her lips.

"Something funny?"

"No," she said with a quick and determined grin. "No, there is not." Closing her fist around her water bottle, she tamped down the jumpy nerves in her chest.

Mildly confused, Jax took a swallow of water.

As she watched him, her mind considered the situation. On the one hand, she was grateful the storm had saved them from the slide in conversation. On the other, she enjoyed getting to know him. Especially the relationship with his mother. It was uncommon for mother and son to be so close. Again, the thought banged around inside her head. Why not married, with children? Wouldn't the two go hand in hand? "You said your sister helped you through your mom's death," Jennifer began, willing his openness to continue. "Are you still close with her?"

"Very. She's all I have."

"No other siblings?"

He shook his head. "How about you? Any brothers or sisters?"

"None," she said, careless to the drop in her voice, no longer guarded around him. "But Sam always had enough for both of us, with two sisters and three brothers."

"Wow. Sam's the lucky woman again."

Jennifer never thought of her friend in such terms. Lucky? Crowded, encumbered maybe—but *lucky*? She dropped a hand to the back of the chair and zeroed in on Jax. "Why no kids, Jax? If Sam's the lucky one, why wouldn't you marry and have your own? Don't you like them?"

He chuckled, clearly amused. "Oh, I *love* them, but like you and Sam, my sister has enough for both of us!"

"But that's different than having your own..."

"I realize that, but I get my fill. Believe me, Uncle Jax is a staple in the Bronson household. Like peanut butter and jelly, I'm there on a regular basis."

Jennifer cast an admonishing smile at his tease. "And no Mrs. Right?" she asked, acutely aware of the instant bolt to her pulse.

"Haven't met the woman who can fill those shoes."

"*Never*?"

He shook his head again, but this time his demeanor fell a notch. "That's a hefty order. The kind of love required to hold down a marriage, to weather the storms of life..." His eyes averted her gaze, making a distinct dodge to the living room. "No, I've never met that kind of woman."

Jennifer took a sip of water and analyzed the evasion. *Really* never, or was this the standard put-off from a man uninterested in sharing his private life.

"Besides," Jax said, forcing a smile to swipe away the unwelcome brevity as he faced her once again. "That's a walk the plank proposition."

She gaped at him. "What?"

"In my book, marriage is for keeps. Once you commit, there's no turning back. Sunny days, stormy nights..." A gleam entered his eyes as he glanced toward the backyard. While the rain continued its cold wet assault outside, the mood indoors had distinctly heated. Jax returned full board and secured her in his sights. "A marriage swallows you whole. From the inside out, two become one and a new journey is begun. For better or for worse," he added, a nip to his tone, a hitch up to his lips. "Like I said, it's an all or nothing proposition. Rain or shine, you better be damn sure of your intentions before you make that dive."

Jennifer liked what she heard. He wasn't a player. For him, it was about love, partnership.

Much like it was for her. "You're quite a philosopher, Jackson Montgomery."

He shrugged. "I guess. Life on the sea does that to a man. Gives him plenty of time for thought."

The reference gave her pause. Life on the sea awaited him. It would take him far away, their paths most probably never crossing again. Once he was finished here, he would be gone.

The deluge continued overhead as Jennifer retreated into the quiet of her mind. No place left to go with the subject, both seemed content with the silence.

Comforting. Simple companionship, it demanded nothing, yet filled the space with warmth, friendship. Jax was easy to be around, easy to look at—particularly so at the moment. Beneath the soft lighting, brown eyes gazed at her. Soft as suede, his laugh lines mellowed, he was private and reflective. It was a different Jax than she was used to seeing. More contemplative than usual, she felt a sense of depth, intensity. It was clear this man was solid through and through. No longer unnerving, she felt comfort in the privacy of his presence. Calm. Peaceful.

Except for his hair. It looked as though a bomb went off! The comparison tugged a smile from her lips.

It caught his attention and he smiled in turn, breaking the silence between them. "Can I ask you something?"

She nodded, eager to continue the intimacy, the warm connection running fluidly between them.

"Tell me if I'm out of line, but why don't you have your mother here," his eyes roamed about the room, "staying with you, instead of an assisted living facility?"

The question cut her in half.

Lightning exploded outside in several flashes of light, the expected round of thunder almost immediate. Around her, the kitchen turned a shade darker, the room a degree cooler.

Caught within his scrutiny, Jennifer crossed her arms over her chest.

"I'm sorry," he said at once. "That's none of my business."

With a shake of her head, she blurted, "It's okay."

"No it's not," he replied, eyes filling with remorse.

"She refused."

The point-blank statement caught him on the chin. "Refused?"

"My mom is a very independent woman, Jax. She didn't want to be a burden. She refused the suggestion outright. Short of taking her against her will, there was no way she'd agree." Jennifer sighed. "She said she preferred Fairhaven, because she felt more comfortable there. She'd have her own private room, grounds to stroll. The physicians were professionals—fully equipped to deal with her daily needs." She hugged her arms more tightly to her chest. *Where I wasn't.*

Across the room, a hefty pile of patient folders sitting on the bureau caught0 her eye. *I was too busy.*

"She wanted her own space," he said.

The statement drew a slow nod from her head. She peered at him more closely. Jax always seemed to *get* it, always seemed to have his thumb square on the pulse of the situation. "Yes, I imagine so..." But Jennifer knew there was more to it than space. Beatrice Hamilton wanted to maintain her dignity, her self-respect. She knew her presence would be an intrusion on her daughter's busy life.

"That must be hard on you," Jax said.

"It is," she murmured. Glancing away, she cursed the tears that threatened to spill.

"Parents get a little funny about their kids assuming the caregiver role. They think they have a corner on the market."

She shrugged. Soon, it wouldn't matter anymore. Her mother would be gone. A fact neither could avoid.

Chapter Twenty-Three

Damn him. Standing rigid, Jennifer was no longer the capable can-do woman, but instead a helpless child, deathly afraid of her mother's passing. It was a devastating emotion to feel helpless—powerless—and one he remembered all too well. If it hadn't been for his sister, he would have immersed himself in the isolation of grief—gladly—because the thought of life without his mother was unthinkable.

Why did he have to go and ask such a stupid question, anyway?

Transfixed by her immobile body, he wanted to take her in his arms. He wanted to chase away her fears, tell her everything would be all right. He wanted to brush his hand over her hair, her face, give her the warmth of another human being, the connection he knew she so desperately needed right now.

But that would be strictly out-of-bounds. It wasn't his place to console her, yet it was his fault she was hurting.

Angry with himself but determined to fix it, he took a slow, deep breath and limited himself to the power of words; his only tools available. They had worked for Delaney when she walked him off the ledge. They could work for him.

"My mom used to tell me... Look at the mother, you'll learn a lot about the daughter."

She turned, easing a wary gaze toward him.

"Your mom sounds like a strong and independent woman, Jennifer. Bright as the sun, solid as the earth. She has her own mind. Like *you*."

Her expression opened a sliver.

It was all the invitation he needed. "You're both doctors, right? You both care for people and about people... Both determined, you know what you want and how to get it. I've seen that first hand."

This earned him a small smile.

"I'll bet your mom knows what she wants, too. Probably knows what's best for you, and everyone around you—appreciated by those of us still searching for direction."

Her quiet chuckle relieved some of the pressure building in his chest. It was working. He was helping. "She loves you, Jennifer. She knows what's right. Moms generally do." He smiled, enjoying the sight of her relaxing, letting go.

Then he became serious. "You know what's right, too," he said. "And you're doing it. To the best of your ability, you're doing it."

Tears shone in her eyes, mixing vulnerability with gratitude.

Desire nearly leaped out of his skin—but he kept himself in check. The last thing he wanted to do was send her scampering off like a scared fawn. He wanted her with him, wanted her close. "Forgive me for intruding on your privacy." Her gaze clung to him. "I was a fool to even ask."

She shook her head, then turned away.

Jax gave her time. Speaking now would only be awkward and break the bond building between them.

Outside, the rain eased its battering, leaving pools of water hammered across dirt and grass. It was a mess. Finishing the arbor wasn't going to happen. Not today, anyway.

Settling his gaze on the structure, it was his rationalization for staying late. A feeble excuse, he knew, but admitting there was no place he'd rather be than here, with her, was not going to happen. Not aloud, anyway.

Dabbing her eyes with a finger, Jennifer returned to face him, her gaze as hard and direct as it was soft and knowing. "Your mom must have been a very special woman."

"She was." No question. No hesitation. "The best of the best."

"And your father?"

He stiffened. Though an innocent question, she might as well have kicked him in the gut. "What about him."

"Are you two close, as well?"

"No," he shook his head, the muscles in his jaw jumping.

"Does he live in Miami?"

"North Miami."

"Do you see each other often?"

"No," he replied and reached for his bottle of water.

Although her questions were the natural extension of their personal discussion, he didn't like the direction they were taking. There was a wrong-way road sign up ahead and he didn't want to drive over the cliff, simply because she didn't know they were headed for one.

Confusion flickered in her eyes. "I'm sorry, Jax, if I've said the wrong thing..."

Narrowing his gaze, emotion hardened. "It's not your fault."

Blue eyes pleaded. *What isn't my fault?*

"We don't get along. Basically, the man is a corporate suck-up with a foul-smelling nose."

She crinkled her nose at the depiction.

"The man never met an ass he didn't like."

"I got it," she said, raising a hand to end his elaboration. "Your description leaves little to the imagination."

"I'm sorry." He shrugged it off. "He never approved of my choices and I never approved of his."

"Landscaping?"

Jax took satisfaction in her surprise. "It would embarrass him to say his son was a landscape architect."

She balked. "Why?"

"Flowers are for sissies," he said, a bitter edge curling his words.

"But that's absurd! You have such talent!"

Mildly warmed by her offense, he clarified. "Because it's not a high-powered corporate position. Because I don't have a college degree. Because I don't give a damn about stocks and bonds. But mostly, he doesn't think it's respectable for a man to make his living planting daisies. Make that, his son."

Visions of their first meeting came rushing back to the forefront of his mind. *Like you,* Jax silently accused. *The woman who didn't want to hire a bartender doing landscape on the side. The woman who wouldn't trust her lawn to the likes of me.*

"Jax, there's more to success than a wall full of degrees. Paper doesn't matter."

Jax took a step away from the table. "It *matters* to some."

"Not everyone."

Though he detected no insincerity, he pushed back. "It matters to you."

Jennifer sucked in her breath. "Jax, I—"

"Doesn't it? If I recall, you wanted a landscape architect—*not* a lawn guy." The admission made him feel cheap. Resentful.

When she didn't respond, his body quieted. "I see."

With an edge sharp enough to slice through bone, he cut back, "Thanks for the water, but I've got work to do." He turned to go, but she protested.

"Jackson, wait."

He stopped. Though part of him wanted to keep going, to walk out that door and never look back, a larger part couldn't. He needed to hear her denial. Needed to see for himself where she stood. Turning, he looked her straight in the eye and felt the blade close to his heart.

Jennifer stilled.

He held his breath.

"You're right."

The tip inserted clean into him.

She took a step toward him, but seemed to think better of it and instead, grabbed hold of the chair between them. "It did matter."

The blade plunged. *So he was right.* Forget what he felt for her, how he thought they were connecting—he was wrong. She was as judgmental as any woman he'd met. Like his father, Jennifer Hamilton thought she was better than him.

Fine. Jax turned to go.

"But it doesn't anymore."

He whipped back. Angered by the visceral disappointment he felt over her rejection, the subsequent patronizing, he demanded, "And how's that?"

"I've learned."

"Had an epiphany, have you?"

Jennifer held her ground. "I was wrong, Jax, and I hope you'll accept my apology. I said unkind things to you in the beginning, when I didn't even know you. I had no right. I should have reserved judgment until I did. It would have saved me from acting like a fool."

His jaw slackened.

Jennifer inhaled deeply before continuing, "You are a creative, hard-working, *amazing* landscaper and you have every right to be darn proud of yourself. Anyone would be. *Would be*, if they had an ounce of sense."

Her reference to his father was clear.

"In addition to your many talents, you serve up one of the best wine spritzers I've ever tasted. Probably martinis, too, but those are..." a nervous chuckle escaped, "*thankfully* out of my realm of expertise."

Was she for real?

"Mr. Montgomery, unless you plan on walking outside and catching gnats with that orifice, I'd suggest you close it."

Jax couldn't believe the turnaround. Bringing lips together, he hesitated then stretched them into a smile. He wasn't sure if she was playing him or exposing true regret, but either way, he found he cared little. "You're funny."

"Not one of my more widely known attributes..." She briefly averted his gaze. "But thank you for noticing."

He brought hands to his hips and grinned.

She grinned.

God he wanted to kiss her. More open and exposed than he had ever seen her, Jennifer was humbled, but not disgraced. She had conceded, but not to defeat—far from it. She had conceded to victory.

His.

Never would he have guessed she had it in her. Never. But better than conceding to him, she claimed it for herself, and did so without conceit—an incredibly attractive feat.

Desire pulled at him. What he wouldn't give to crush his mouth over hers and slip past those clean, trim lips on that porcelain perfect face of hers for a taste of the woman inside... There was no doubt in his mind it would prove the sweetest delicacy on earth. He lingered over her face, her mouth. By far.

Jennifer glanced to the door. "It's stopped raining."

Eyes remaining solidly on her, he replied, "I see that."

She crossed arms over chest and assumed the tone of supervisor. Challenge leapt to her eyes. "Don't you want to finish up out there?"

"I should."

"May I join you?"

Excitement swiped the knees clear out from under him. "You may, indeed." With a slight bow he stepped back, laughter dancing beneath his breath. "Ladies first."

She brushed aside damp strands of hair, and offered a demure smile in thanks. Nearing him, he could smell the scent of shampoo in her hair, the sweet perfume remaining faint on her skin. Coupled with the small curves of her body sent a zing straight to his loin.

Suppressing his welling desire with pronounced effort, Jax reached an arm ahead of her and opened the door. "Chivalry still counts in my book."

"Mine, too," she replied, and her blue eyes softened, causing a stir deep within him.

He moaned inwardly. Spending time with her at this point without wanting more was going to take some doing.

"What do you have left to complete for today?"

The channel switch was innocent and jarring. Following her down the steps, he focused on plants and not the woman. "Just the mandevilla."

Which was tough. As she gazed across the lawn, her profile was delicate, alluring, her cheekbone begging for a slide of his hand along its fine line. Jax shoved both hands in his jean pockets.

Across the yard, a wave of light lit up the rain washed landscape. Leaves glistened golden in the evening light, red flowers still heavy with water. Hanging from the trellis in healthy clumps, the vine begged to be lifted and wound through the boards properly for good support.

"Looks like you're about finished."

He smiled. Not nearly. Well, with the job maybe, but not with her. "Actually, it's an intricate process, one that takes more care than first glance might imply."

"Can I help?"

His eyes dropped. "Not dressed like that."

She glanced down at her unsullied professional perfection. When she returned her gaze to his he met her with a grin. "But you can supervise."

Her satisfied smile held a hint of self-consciousness as she brushed tousled wet hair behind an ear. "I think I can manage that."

"Yes you can, Dr. Hamilton. Most definitely that is within your realm of expertise!"

She laughed, as did he, and walked alongside him to the arbor. Jax resumed his weaving of vine while she remarked on the color and how well it would blend. It was casual conversation about nothing, yet a major step toward healing.

"Cheer-cheer-cheer-purty-purty-purty!"

"What the...?" Jax turned at the abrupt siren-like noise.

"Cheer-cheer-cheer-purty-purty-purty!"

"What was *that*?"

Jennifer laughed. "Why, it's my finest rendition of the Cardinal, that's what!"

"The Cardinal?"

She nodded with an impish grin. "I used to mimic them as a kid."

Jax arched a brow. "You're pretty good, for someone who didn't spend much time in the garden."

"Well... I guess I spent a *little* more time there than I thought. At least when I was younger. But I wasn't weeding or picking through the flowers."

"No, just making friends with the wildlife."

She cocked her head in thoughtful recognition. "It passed the time."

"Why the Cardinal?"

Jennifer paused, her smile dimmed.

Jax feared he may have ruined the moment. Where her eyes held fond recollection, they were shadowed by sadness.

"I chose the Cardinal because I felt sorry for him."

"Sorry for him? How?"

"He couldn't fit into my mother's birdhouse."

Jax smiled tentatively, moved by the total seriousness of her expression. Was she kidding? *"For real?"*

She glanced at him. "Silly, huh?"

He shook his head. "Sweet."

Absolutely and completely sweet. *And beautiful.*

From the treetops above a bird called out and the two looked up in unison, then back to each other, a shared smile pulling them one step closer.

Chapter Twenty-Four

Tires screamed as the black limousine hurled itself around the corner, picking up speed with frightening purpose as it closed the space between them. Skidding to a stop, the car landed hard against the curb. A door swung open and a man approached.

Alarm bells sounded

His direction was clear. He was coming after her.

After her!

Jennifer rolled over in her bed. She gripped the pillow beneath her head.

The stranger was quick. He grabbed her from behind, wrestled her toward the vehicle and shoved her inside. The screech of rubber pierced the quiet morning. A blindfold was pulled taut around Jennifer's eyes. Her wrists were roughly tied together. A barrage of questions raced through her mind. What was happening? Who were they?

Time vanished, her pleas for answers were ignored. Transported from car to plane, then to helicopter. Men exchanged words, orders were given, and she was whisked through a series of doors before being settled into a plush sofa.

The blindfold was removed. Stunned, she realized she was on a boat. A bank of windows lined the expansive space, decorated like a gallery of fine

*art.   Except the thug was present, a rifle slung
casually across his chest.*

*But what she found more troubling, was the older
man seated in the center of the room.   Dressed to
perfection in a black suit, his light olive skin was
smooth, his features refined, save for a small scar
protruding from the edge of one eye.   Feet away, he
stared at her, an odd combination of quiet humor and
keen curiosity mingling in his dark eyes.   Whereas she
sensed familiarity on his part, she had never seen him
before in her life.*

"Welcome to my home, Jennifer."

*"Why am I here?   And what do you want with
me?"*

*"Ah, yes," he said with a sigh.   "You have
questions."   He flicked his eyes toward his sentry,
then to the door, before returning his gaze to her.
The man left without a word.   "I am sorry for my
methods.   They were unfortunate, but I had no
choice."*

*"What do you mean?"   Jennifer glared at him.
"That is absurd.   You have no right to take me against
my will.   Who do you think you are?"*

*"I am Constantine Pappas, a great admirer of
yours."   A gentle smile caressed his lips.   "You work
at one of my hospitals, and may I say, you are
magnificent."   His voice was tame, yet his intensity
was unmistakable.   "I had to be with you."*

*Her gut twisted.   "Be with me.   What does that
mean?"*

"I want you."

"I don't understand."

"For my own.   For always..."

The last word faded into the air between them.

He stood. "Freshen up. Dinner is at eight, on deck. I'll be waiting." With a small smile he was gone.

She bolted from the sofa. Scanning the horizon forward and back, nothing but sparkling blue-green water as far as the eye could see, Jennifer searched for shore. Nothing. Her spirits sank. There was no running from a ship at sea.

Jennifer rolled to her opposite side.

"Ah, my dear," Constantine murmured as she emerged on deck. "You take my breath away." He smiled. "That dress is my favorite. I knew you'd be stunning in it."

White and simple, made from the softest silk she had ever touched, it was cut to the curve of her body. The halter top was sexy without being blatant, revealing a mere hint of the woman beneath. Strappy gold sandals, completely foreign to her normal style, completed the outfit.

Originally she had no intention of joining him, or wearing anything he provided, but hiding in her room would get her no closer to escape. The only thing that mattered.

The table was dressed in white linen and silver, with vibrant red tulips arching lazily from a simple glass vase. Glancing about, she took note of the Cristal on ice, beads of water glistening from the golden bottle like morning dew. Fresh strawberries and grapes were piled high in a bowl accompanied by soft cheese, dark olives and a loaf of bread. A brilliant sunset filled the sky to her right with a gorgeous mix of pink and blue while a warm breeze danced across her skin. She filled her lungs with the crisp scent of the ocean.

"I'm so glad you decided to join me. I feared you might stay in your room and refuse."

She warily took her seat. *"Not much of a choice, is it."*

"May I pour you some champagne?"

She shook her head.

Constantine poured her some anyway and urged, *"Have something to eat, Jennifer."*

"Why am I here? What is this all about?"

"A few years ago, during a visit to the hospital, I suffered a mild heart attack. You assisted with my care." His eyes softened. *"You were extraordinary. So thorough and concerned, almost personal, as though I were a cherished loved one."*

Her patients. Jennifer's heart tightened at the thought of never seeing them again.

"You advised me to consider my lifestyle and make any changes necessary to ensure a long and prosperous future." Constantine smiled. *"I did as you recommended."*

"Forgive me," she said, *"but if you wanted to be with me, why take me against my will?"*

"I don't have the time."

She balked. *"We're sitting here, roaming around the middle of nowhere. Why not dinner in a restaurant?"*

"You may have said no."

"And..."

"I couldn't have accepted that."

The finality to his voice cut her to the quick.

Jennifer clutched her sheets to her chin. Images of the dream streamed through her mind, transcending time and place. Unbelievable visions, unacceptable positions, save for the safety of her sub-conscious.

The tepid breeze tossed her dark brown hair about her shoulders, blowing long bangs across her face. Careless to the other men on board, most of whom she never saw but was keenly aware existed as captain and mates, chefs and stewards, she walked out on deck and stopped at the edge of the table. The full-length lingerie was blue, like her eyes, with an intricate lace bodice that fit snugly at the breast. Her eyes were fixed upon his. Her old life was no more. Life would go on, had to go on, with or without her.

"Oh my..." Constantine swallowed hard.

"You are a goddess." Though not roaming up and down, she was certain his eyes were taking in her body in its entirety. Strange, but she was apprehensive, excited and hopeful at the same time.

"Well?" she prompted, seeking his approval. "Do you like it?" Wearing sexy underwear had never been her thing, yet here, with him, she found it titillating.

"Oh, I more than like it..."

The compliment caused a hot rise to her cheeks.

"You are the kind of woman men live and die for, Jennifer." Fire leaped to his eyes. "Come here."

Without a second's hesitation, she moved toward him, despite the uncustomary hardness to his voice.

"I have to touch you."

The words sent shivers racing through her body.

Lifting his hand, Constantine allowed his eyes to fall upon her chest. He touched her skin with his finger and skimmed the border of fabric along her breast. The tingles created by his touch turned her skin into a sheet of goose pimples, inflaming her want, swelling her loin with desire.

"You are so beautiful," he said, speaking a fraction above a whisper.

Frozen, her breath trapped in her chest, Jennifer dangled on the edge of his caress.

Constantine traced her curves as his hand slid down to her waist, stopped briefly at her hip, then stole behind her back, pulling her onto his lap.

With an ease of familiarity, Jennifer slid her arm around his neck. Where she had no idea as to what he might do next, she found that she cared little. It was a remarkable feeling and so freeing, to think only of the here and the now. It was not her nature. She drew comfort from having a plan. But nothing about her life here was normal, nor would it ever be. As far as she was concerned, Constantine could do whatever he wanted. She was prepared.

"Do you believe in love at first sight?"

Jennifer nodded with a smile, though not sure what she believed at the moment, her senses overwhelmed.

"I fell in love with you the moment I saw you. I knew right then, no other woman in the world would suffice."

The admitted reason behind her presence here fell limp against her craving for his touch. She had all but forgotten the reasons, the event surrendered to circumstances beyond her control.

Constantine's hand rose and slid across her cheek, his fingers stopping to entwine her hair within them. Drawing the long strands away from her head, he played with them as he gazed into her eyes. *"Are you happy?"*

She nodded in idle awareness.

Releasing her hair, he brushed it back and stroked her neck, then her collarbone, eyes trailing his route along the line of her body, stopping at the strap of her gown. Pausing, he rubbed his finger back and forth over the thin satin band, as though in contemplation. Suddenly, his eyes sprang to hers. "Stand up," he commanded.

Startled, she did as he asked.

"Step back."

She did so.

"I want to see you. All of you."

The statement sent shock waves through her body.

"Show me. Show me now," Constantine ordered, urgency coursing through his voice.

Jennifer prepared herself for the moment of truth. It was time to follow through with the prospect that had been lurking in the shadows of her desire. Hooking a thumb under each strap of her negligee, she pulled them down simultaneously, not stopping until she had passed the arc of her hip whereby the gown fell to the floor of its own accord.

It was a powerful moment. Wearing nothing more than a wisp of panties, she was excited by her nakedness, yet felt vulnerable in its exposure.

"Oh my..." Constantine's eyes engulfed her every inch, slowing over the small lace vee between her legs. Reaching for his glass of champagne, he brought the drink to his lips and sipped, unhurried, savoring the sight before him.

Jennifer waited, trembling with need.

"Turn around," he said on impulse.

She did so, without embarrassment, never more turned-on in her life.

"Take everything off."

The visual his request would create was almost more than she could bear, but she obeyed, causing Constantine to abandon his restraint and take her right there.   With his first touch, Jennifer's body experienced levels of pleasure she never imagined possible.

Jennifer bolted awake in a cold sweat. Her pulse thumped in her ears. Grasping for some sense of reason, she seized upon the bright red numbers piercing the darkness: 3:36.

Where was she?   Jennifer looked around the black room. She was in bed. Her hands twisted the cotton blanket into fists.

At home.

Alone in bed, in the middle of Coral Gables...not on a yacht with Constantine in the middle of nowhere. Pained by the realization, she dropped back to her pillows. A strange mix of disappointment and relief wound through her. It had all felt so real. But why? *Why was he back?*

Chapter Twenty-Five

Jennifer pulled the surgical glove off with a snap, followed by the second. In the harsh light of the cath lab, exhaustion burned in her eyes. It had been a dicey case. The patient's arteries were stiff as cardboard, about as pliable too. Another super end to a long day.

Tearing the scrub mask from her face, she made her way around the staff, now working to move the patient, grabbed the chart and flipped through the sections. Stopping at a steel table, she plucked the nearest pen, scribbled down her post-op note, then dropped the pen with a clang. Tossing a curt thank you behind her, she strode out of the cath lab without a word.

Smacking the metal plate on the wall, she proceeded through the automatic double doors, slipped through a side door to the stairwell and headed up to the fourth floor.

Last night had been another without sleep. But more than a nuisance, she had experienced an insane feeling of guilt when she awoke. Guilt—over making love to a fantasy—it was ridiculous!

Pulling herself up and around the third floor landing, Jennifer fought the absurdity. It was only a dream, for heaven's sake! A figment of her imagination.

But the lure had been strong.

The ideal man; the ideal connection. The psychologist had been clear in her analysis. More than body to body, she had allowed her tycoon access to the deepest crevices of her soul—once she moved past the initial impression, that is.

Once she got to know the man inside...

Jennifer stopped mid-stride. She grasped the cold metal door handle and thought, *the real Constantine*.

Moving beyond first impressions.

Jackson.

She pushed through the door and out into the hallway, her steps quick and determined, barely evading collision with a passing orderly. She made a beeline for the nurse's station.

"Hi, Dr. Hamilton."

"Hi, Angie." But it was Aurelio that Constantine reminded her of—not Jax! Looking straight through the people around her, she hurried to the rack of charts. She was losing it. Sure as she was standing here, she was going insane.

It was the stress. The stress of her mother, the stress of the wedding. The stress of pure exhaustion.

"Your patient in 402 is complaining about Wilson."

Again, is what Jennifer heard. The man was an excellent technologist, but his bedside manner left much to be desired. Grabbing a chart, she said, "I'll go and talk to her." Add stress from her job, stress from her partners, it was a wonder Jennifer hadn't lost her mind sooner!

Flipping back to the H and P she read: *Fifty-eight-year-old overweight Caucasian male, lifetime smoker, arteriosclerosis, suffering from acute angina.*

Why did people push their luck? Why did they hold life in so little regard?

She knew the risks and opted against any invasive procedures. Because she was more afraid of that than death.

Darn it, she fumed. Jax's mother had been too young to give up! Her son needed her. *Every* child needs his or her parent. But, no. She only considered herself. Jennifer returned her thoughts to the pages in hand. Like this man. She scoured the progress notes, fighting the urge to compare his situation to Jax's. Not only had this patient refused treatment in the past, he continued to smoke. Her outlook soured. And he expected her to fix it.

She was a doctor. "This patient needs a miracle," she muttered beneath her breath.

"You okay, Dr. Hamilton?"

Jennifer looked up.

The nursing supervisor shot her a look of concern.

"Yes, I'm fine. Just tired." And distracted.

"Aren't we all," the other chortled good-naturedly, the sound low, deep and merry. "And don't forget overworked and underpaid."

While you're at it, throw in confused and depressed, Jennifer mused. My future is falling apart, my plans are shattering at my feet, and my best friend is on a trip to hell. But Jennifer only smiled at the woman. None of it was her fault. The only good news was Beverly. Her doctor called to let her know they had a heart. Surgery was set for tomorrow.

Closing the chart, she shoved it under her arm and proceeded down the hall. The fracas in her head had to be stopped and the best way she knew how to achieve that was work. En route to her patient, she darted into room 402 for damage control.

Hours later, showered and ready to call it a day, Jennifer sat upright in bed. Dumping the latest medical journal to one side, she called to check on Patty and Blake.

She sighed. If only her exhaustion stemmed from a long day at the office. But it didn't. Not really. It was Jackson.

"Hello?"

"Hi Sam."

"Hey."

"How are you? How's Patty?"

"I don't know what she's going to do," Sam said, her voice tightly controlled.

"Oh no... Has Blake taken a turn for the worst?"

"He hasn't taken any turns—that's the problem. We keep waiting for some word as to what our next step is, what can we expect, but we get nothing."

"Do you want me to call and talk with his doctor again?"

"Thanks, but no. That's not the problem. The problem is he's not doing well, and I'm afraid for Patty."

Jennifer waited through her pause—afraid for Sam—but ready to support her in any way she could.

"Her whole life is wrapped up in Blake. She has no job, no skills. She makes babies and takes care of them. What's she going to do? She can't earn a living on that kind of resume!"

"*Sam*, slow down. It's too soon to make those types of assumptions. You're barely forty-eight hours into this—*anything* can change at this point."

Heedless to the advice, Sam barreled on, "Like you always say, Jen, we've got to have a plan. Right now, it's not looking good. Even if Blake does recover, and let's just say as full a recovery as one can, under the circumstances, she's still looking at months before he can return to work." She paused, her frustration audible.

"Let's face it. Engineering is a profession that requires the neurons to be firing full power in order to succeed and he won't see that kind of action for some time to come."

"They have no disability insurance?"

"None." Sam heaved a ragged sigh. "But it's not the money that concerns me. I can float her enough to keep them above water, but what I can't do, is handle the kids for that long. From what I can put together, it sounds like she's going to be living at the hospital while they work him through rehab. The kids have school, activities... She can't be in two places at one time. What's she gonna do?"

"I know it's tough, Sam."

"*Too* tough."

"You'll work something out. I know you."

"Right now I'd give my right arm to be on a beach in the Bahamas, stuck to my lounge chair sucking on a margarita as big as my head chock-full of pretty little umbrellas."

Jennifer smiled at the image. "You don't mean that. You don't want to be anywhere, but by your sister's side."

"No, Jen. I mean it. In fact, I'd give both my arms not to have to look her in the eye every day, and know, this may be as good as it gets. Ever. Her life as she once knew it is over. Either way, those days are gone."

Now *there's* looking on the bright side, Jennifer thought glumly, giving way to the swath of negativity.

"Marrying Blake was the happiest day of her life. With the birth of her kids, it only got better and then—POW—out of nowhere, all is lost."

"All is *not* lost, Sam. It's a bump in the road. She'll survive. They'll get through it."

"Bump in the road? The damn bridge is out! Blown to hell by some lunatic blood clot!"

"It's one of life's trials, Sam. Trust me. It will get better. I know it seems like a long time, but you've got to give Blake a chance to recover. His body has undergone major trauma. Patty needs your help to remain focused on the positive."

"I'm having trouble doing that, Jen." Sam's pace slowed as the exasperation dragged her down.

It was a normal cycle for patients' families to go through, Jennifer understood. But it hurt to hear it from Sam.

"Patty's hit hard, and I'm having a real tough time convincing her it's not as bad as it seems, because it sure as hell looks that way to me."

"I know." Jennifer said, winding the phone cord between her fingers. "But aren't you always the one who told me to embrace life's surprises. This challenge may be the beginning of a new and rewarding chapter in Patty's life. In *your* life."

Sam didn't say a word.

Okay. She needed time. Jennifer allowed her room to digest the concept. Starting over, starting anew; it was never easy changing habits and outlooks, especially not when you'd spent years ingraining them into your soul. This would take time. It would take effort.

It may take everything Sam had to get through this, and make it to the other side. Personal crisis wasn't her strong suit. Managing others' was her business, not handling her own.

"And how about you?"

"What about me?"

"Maybe you can learn something from this, too."

"Of course, helping you helps me, yes—"

"Life can surprise you, Jen. Just when you think you have it all planned, the tidy little package you've arranged for your future can unravel, leaving you with impossible chaos."

Her back stiffened. "Is this another attack on Aurelio?"

"Your picture-perfect image can be shattered—crushed—by oncoming traffic. What happens then? *And when you have kids*? Who will look after them?"

"Sam—"

"Will you expect your nanny to sweep in and clean up the mess? The hired help?"

"Sam."

"Because I'm here to tell you it's not the case," she continued, refusing to be interrupted. "Blake and Patty are prime exhibit number one. You need someone that worships the ground you walk on. Someone to stand by you through life's trials, 'cause let me tell you, it can get ugly. *Real* ugly."

"Sam," Jennifer said, a bit more cutting than she intended, but enough was enough. "I understand that you're under a bit of stress, but that is no reason to lash out at me."

"You're damn right I'm under stress! And you would be, too, but Blake's stroke should serve as a reminder to you. You can't count on sophistication to carry you through to that golden anniversary. Love and sacrifice do that."

"I appreciate the insight," she replied coolly, hating the rehash of old arguments. Sam should be focused on her current troubles. "But it's as I told you before. Aurelio and I are committed to a future together."

"Whitewash. You and Aurelio lead two different lifestyles, two different lives."

"How do you figure?"

"He's all about him and you're all about everybody else."

"You're wrong."

"I'm sorry, but it's true and you need to hear it."

"No, I don't." She steeled her nerves.

"Bullshit. Aurelio is more interested in serving his own needs and you—hell, giving to others is like speed for you. You'd go into withdrawal if you weren't helping some patient through a life or death crisis...

...or living your life to please someone else."

"*What is the matter with you*? Why do you insist on pushing?"

Sam remained mute.

Anger percolated. "I don't understand you!"

"You want a house full of children, running up and down those stairs, filling the halls with noise. I *know* you. In that traditional thinking brain of yours, you're still baking cookies, reading bedtime stories, painting that white picket fence...the one that lives deep in your heart."

"Aurelio wants kids..."

"He could live without them." Sam added quietly, "You can't." She paused. "The truth's a bitch, Jen. But at least she has your best interests at heart."

Chapter Twenty-Six

At the sound of her car, Jax turned his head in time to see the black BMW roll into the front driveway. Male instinct had warned him to be gone by now, but hunger for her company overruled. The other day revealed a fragile woman. A woman whose waters ran deep. A woman who needed the strong shoulder of a man.

His gut tightened. It was no good. Already slipping past his defenses, squeaking by his better sense, this woman was beginning to steal into his heart.

Where was the woman he first met, when he needed her? Judgmental, condescending—*that* one he could resist.

Jax watched Jennifer ease out of the sedan. Dressed in scrubs, her shiny brown hair fell loose around her shoulders and her skin, even from a distance, glowed in flawless ivory perfection. But it was her eyes that completely undid him; aquamarine jewels sparkling like crystalline island waters in the warm afternoon sun.

She looked for him and he stood. Struggling to recall those first days and the qualities he could easily dismiss was pointless. Unfortunately for him, she barely resembled that person anymore. Now, she was a woman he wanted.

Stupidity. They had no future. Forget she was engaged, they had different goals, different attitudes. She was a career woman, a doctor. She had structure and schedule. *Anchors*.

She waved at him and smiled—a smile that felt personal, more seductive than a full moon on the open sea. Warmth spread through his chest. He meant to be gone before she arrived home, but stayed—despite his better judgment. Falling for the good doctor was not in his best interest.

But enjoying the attraction? Where was the harm?

She headed toward him and he fell into step, moving in her direction. Nothing wrong with living in the moment. It was his life's motto.

She slowed to a stop, feet away from him. "Hello, Jax."

Damn. Though small, her smile had the power to blow his best defense to smithereens. He smiled in turn, and felt pleasure clear down to the tip of his toes. "Hey."

"How's it coming?"

"Fine." *Piss-poor, actually.* The damn inspector failed to show up and sign off on the job, throwing him another day behind schedule. And the longer he was here, the harder it was to leave.

Conscious of her glance to the sweat on his forehead, he swiped it dry. At least the sun had pitched back behind the trees for the moment. The heat today had been brutal.

Jennifer looked around, her features drawn into a soft expression of admiration. "The yard is in-credible..."

Jax followed her gaze. From the pergola outside her bedroom doors, cruising past the pool, past the hedge of hibiscus, he settled on the arbor and fountain in the back. Pleasure washed through him. He knew it was everything she wanted and more.

"I can't believe the transformation."

Collecting his gloves in one hand, he set them against his hip. "Amazing what two and a half weeks can do."

"It's amazing what you can do." She turned to him and his insides shifted beneath the point of her gaze. "These flowers were only just put in the ground, yet look at them." She swept a hand toward the plump row of hibiscus. "Healthy and full, they look as if they've been there for years."

"It's easy to set roots when the growing conditions are so perfect." Jax inwardly groaned. *Did he really say that*?

"You're modest." She smiled, as if she knew better. "I noticed the fountain out front doesn't have water. Do you have an idea when can I fill it? I'm anxious to start enjoying the sound of splashing water when I come home."

Jax frowned. "The inspector didn't show today and I don't want to fill it until he's checked off the electrical and plumbing."

"Oh," she said.

Her disappointment was deafening. "But as you can see," he worked to re-ignite her pleasure, "the yard is basically finished—*ahead of schedule*."

Crap. By the wounded look in her eyes, it was clear his pride in a job well done had taken the form of a dart. "I'm sorry—that's not what I meant."

"No," she said and held up a hand. "It's all right."

"I just want you to be happy with the job."

"I am, Jax." She fell back into her smile. "Your performance has been exceptional. I'd definitely recommend Montgomery Landscape to anyone who asked."

The compliment hung between them.

No uncertain terms, unequivocally, she made it clear her satisfaction. On one level, he felt triumphant. *Your performance has been exceptional.* On another...

It was a kick to the stomach. *I'm sorry, but you've wasted your time.* He could hear the words as if she had said them aloud today. Sure she had been nice of late, but that first meeting was all coming back to him. You're good enough to work here, he heard, but not good enough for more. You're a bartender doing yards on the side.

Jax clamped down on the well of resentment. He should never have let himself care. He knew this is where it would lead. He was a laborer. She was a professional.

The two worlds didn't mix.

He stepped away from her. "Yeah, well, all I'm waiting on now is inspection. Once the guy comes and signs off on the job, I'll fill the fountains and you'll be ready to take the big plunge." Jax didn't smile, despite the fact it would be required for a humorous delivery.

She rubbed her hands down along the backside of her scrubs. "Yes, well..."

While he thought she seemed uncomfortable, she didn't appear to be going anywhere. "So, what's next for you, Jax?"

"The usual" he lied. "More bids, more jobs."

"Are you still intent on sailing the islands?"

"If you mean, do I intend to sail around the islands and do nothing, then, absolutely. The answer is yes." Invigorated by the opening for a rebellious escape from his feelings, he added, "Can't think of a better use of my time."

It was his life and that's how he wanted to live it. It was also a subject he no longer wanted to share with her. "Enough about me. How about you. Good day, bad day?"

Jennifer looked startled by the question. "Fine, I guess. Stressful, busy." She brushed long bangs behind an ear and her gaze turned evasive.

"Spent it at the hospital, did you?" he asked, indicating her scrub attire.

She looked down. "Yes," she murmured, almost as though she was surprised to discover the fact herself.

Back in control, Jax settled into a carefree attitude; a safe and comfortable attitude, considering the circumstances. "Nothing life threatening, I hope."

Jennifer brought her face up to meet his, and stared into his eyes. "No, nothing life threatening."

The frail quality of her voice, the stark vulnerability etched in her eyes... "That's good news, right?"

He tried to leave it open, in case she wanted to elaborate.

But she did not. The conversation would have ended there, if left to its natural flow, but it didn't.

For some reason, Jennifer couldn't take her eyes from his. She seemed to be missing something. Searching.

It was then she noticed it. *The nick by his eye.*

The significance took her breath away.

Usually concealed in a bevy of laugh lines, the scar didn't stand out. But right now, Jax was uncommonly cool, unusually grin-free and the scar looked like a scar, protruding from the corner of his eye.

Like Constantine's. Her body went limp.

Jax reached out for her. "Hey—are you okay?"

"What?" Walls of blackness crowded her vision. An uncanny sensation trickled into her consciousness. Staring at him blankly, she tried to reengage. "Yes...of course..."

But mind-numbing shock squeezed harder. She felt strange, as if temporarily disconnected from her body. Suspended.

For a second, she feared she might faint.

"You don't look so good."

"I, uh," she stepped back to give herself some space. "I—it's hot." Consumed by a sudden pounding in her chest, a heavy ringing in her ears, she turned away.

"Let me get you some water."

"No."

"Please..."

The concern she saw flooding into his brown eyes undercut further objection. "Okay..."

"I'll be right back," he said, and jogged off.

Jennifer ran shaky fingers through her hair as she looked down at the ground. *This couldn't be happening.* It was a dream. Constantine was a fantasy.

He wasn't real. She was drawing simi-larities, making correlations, imagining things that didn't exist.

Pulling her head up, she turned slowly and trailed Jax's return. This was crazy. Nothing more than coincidence. But as he drew near, she thought she detected familiarity...

It was in the eyes. Unsmiling, they were dark and intense, like Constantine's could be when overcome by emotion.

Stop. *It's only a dream...*

Jax thrust a bottle of water toward her. "Drink this."

When she refused, he insisted. "It's hot out, Jennifer. Heat exhaustion sneaks up on people." His concern deepened, digging further into his eyes. "Please, drink some. You don't look good."

"I'm fine," she repeated, but to her embarrassment, her hand trembled as she reached for the bottle.

"Why don't you sit down."

It wasn't a question. "I'm okay, Jax, really I am."

"Why don't you let me be the judge of that," he said, and eased her down onto the nearby steps.

She didn't protest. Comforted by his firm hold, his body close to hers, she *wanted* him near.

But Jax maintained a respectable distance. Where he smelled of a hard day's work, it wasn't an offensive odor, rather a man's natural scent mingled with the hint of faded cologne.

Powerful, stirring, entirely male.

Jennifer sipped from the bottle, avoiding direct eye contact. Difficult, as his face hovered less than a foot from hers. So near, she could hear his breaths as he watched her. Side by side, she felt his shoulder graze against hers, his muscles strong and reassuring.

"Is that better?" he asked.

Yes. Everything was better this close to him. His presence was comforting, his concern heartwarming. She ventured a gaze toward him. Compassion swam in his soft brown eyes. Heat rose to her cheeks.

Jennifer closed her eyes. She was in trouble. Enjoying his nearness, wanting him to touch her, hold her.

She shouldn't be having these feelings. Shouldn't want these things.

"Are you okay?"

She gulped. *No.* I'm not okay. Not anywhere close. This—us, you, me. But of course he was referring to her physical health.

And waiting for an answer. "Yes. Thank you. But really," she tried to put him off, put some distance between him and her thoughts. "I'm all right. I've had a long day, I'm tired."

Tender eyes held steady. "Just take it easy, Jennifer. Give yourself a couple of minutes. You'll be okay."

She nodded, mesmerized by every word he uttered. This was a man who took care of those in need. She drank from her bottle, this time more slowly, her eyes daring to linger over his face.

He smiled then, a gesture meant to reaffirm he was here for her. Here. *For her.*

She flushed hot. Never had they been situated in such close proximity. Not for more than a moment.

Not under these conditions. Alone. Expressing care, concern...*desire*.

The connection was strong.

Worse—she enjoyed it.

Jennifer glanced away. She didn't want to look at him. Couldn't.

But she didn't want him to leave. It felt good to have him close. Good to have him here, by her side. She could imagine his arms wrapped around her, the feel of her body as it folded into the curve of his as he held her tight, consoling her until the trouble passed. She could imagine the ensuing kiss against her head, the gentle but secure hug that would surely follow.

Jennifer pitched her gaze to the ground. She shouldn't be having these feelings. She shouldn't wonder what it would be like to feel him against her, to yearn for sweet nothings murmured in her ear. She shouldn't ache for his closeness.

He shouldn't be allowed this role.

It should be Aurelio's arms she wanted wrapped around her. Aurelio pulling her close. Aurelio smoothing frazzled nerves. It should be Aurelio's shoulder she wanted for comfort, reassurance.

And if she had a speck of strength in her limbs, she would get up from these steps, march right into her house and put space between herself and this man. But lifting her gaze, taking in her beautiful yard, his phenomenal talent, she felt no desire to leave.

Dusk painted the yard in creamy tones of gold, a reminder the day was coming to an end. It was getting late. She had a lot of work to do.

Yet she felt no urgency. No compulsion to say, thanks, but no thanks. While I appreciate your kindness, I'm fine. I have to get going. No. Instead,

she wanted to savor this time with Jax. Enjoy their
time before it was gone. Gone. The job was almost
complete. His services no longer required.

But needed. Sorely needed.

Jennifer closed her eyes. She should go. This
wasn't good. Not good at all. Opening them again,
she breathed in and prepared to get up. It was the
right thing to do. Because if she stayed—

Wait a minute.   Her focus unexpectedly
sharpened, fastening on the bush with dark, shiny
green leaves. *Are those...*

Her breathing fell shallow, her pulse skittered.

But they couldn't be. They weren't part of the
proposal. They hadn't been discussed. "Jax."

"Yes?"

She turned and faced him directly. There was no
possible way. A wave of anxiety fluttered through
her chest. *Was there?* "Are those gardenias? Over
there," she pointed weakly. "By the ginger?"

He nodded.

Her stomach flipped. But how could they be?

"I know we didn't discuss them." Not a trace of
professionalism, his response was tender, personal.
"But I thought you'd enjoy them. They're covered in
buds. The blooms won't explode for another month,
but when they do, this yard will be filled with
fragrance." Jax grinned knowingly. "I tucked them
in all around the garden."

She wanted to cry. She wanted to throw her arms
around his neck and hug the last breath from his body.
She wanted to kiss him—*with abandon*—from his
generous heart to his handsome face and tell him how
much it meant to her.

It was a small detail, but one she'd forgotten. One she needed.

But she could hardly talk, let alone move. Fighting a wall of tears pressing behind her eyes, her throat hard and tight, she mouthed, "Thank you."

"You're welcome." Satisfaction swamped his expression. Rich and genuine, he made no attempt to hide his feelings. "Those beauties will bring you pleasure for years to come."

Years after I'm gone is what she heard. You will continue to enjoy your garden for years after I'm gone. Her mood plummeted.

It wasn't right. She shouldn't care that he was leaving to set sail on a one-way voyage to nowhere.

She *shouldn't* ache at the prospect. *Shouldn't* miss him before he even left.

But she did. Fool as she may be, Jennifer wanted to be by his side...wherever that may be.

Chapter Twenty-Seven

Lulled by the light kisses he feathered atop her forehead, Jennifer wanted them to go on forever. It had been a difficult day at the hospital and this was exactly the remedy she needed.

But he wasn't ready.

A knowing smile eased onto her lips. Jennifer didn't have to see his face. She could feel his intention with the more insistent press of his lips. The man had plans, and rolled her from side to back, placing his full weight on top of her.

Then she felt his naked hardness push into her thighs. She savored the feel of his skin against hers. Outstretching her arms like a lazy cat, she opened further to his advance. His lips increased their pressure as they moved along her cheekbone, down toward her mouth, lingering at its edge. He teased and toyed, then slipped his tongue inside.

Oh, how she loved the way he kissed her! Soft and supple, yet hot and persistent, hungry. He wanted more. Always more.

But so did she. Purring her desire, she gave herself to the roll of his tongue as it probed and explored. Need escalated. Desire mounted. Urgency took hold. Strange, to want someone so much, to crave their touch with every inch of your body...

Immensely overwhelming yet incredibly empowering at the same time. Want and need filled her to the very ends of her being, the core of her soul. She knew whatever he wanted, whatever he sought, she would give; readily, willingly—

Wantonly.

Abandoning her mouth he slid his tongue down her neck, along the line of her shoulder and encircled her breast. She moaned as her nipple hardened beneath the slippery swath, throbbing in protest when he slid away.

Sudden need pulled at her. She raked both hands through his hair, dragged them over the steel of his triceps and down the length of his arms. She pushed into him with her hips, urging him now.

This drew a wicked gleam from his eyes.

Parting her legs, she laced one over and between his and pulled him close. As he sank between her thighs, she wished he could swallow her whole.

More than anything, she needed to feel him, surround him—

—engulf him. Right now. He snaked his arms around her back and pulled her firm within his embrace. In seconds, she felt the jolt of stiff muscle plunge deep inside her.

Her groan was automatic. He pushed further, deeper, gently rocking their bodies in an easy sway.

But it wasn't enough. She hugged him to her and motioned faster, harder—more—until the two of them exploded in release. Her muscles melted beneath his weight, her insides flew high and away, her mind immune to thought. She could only feel. Only exist.

Feathering light kisses once again, he slowly drew her back to the moment, the present. "I love you, Jennifer."

The declaration flooded her heart with an amazing fullness.

"More than I've ever loved a woman..."

Nuzzling his cheek against hers, he pulled back, but not too far. Tilting her chin to face him, he urged her to look at him, hear him. "I need you, Jennifer."

"You have me," she whispered fiercely, meaning it with every inch of her soul. She eased her eyes open. "I'm yours, Jax."

Jennifer bolted awake.

Oh my God...

Her heart thumped against her ribs. Her pulse pounded between her ears. Comprehension staggered in. *It was only a dream?*

But it had been so real. *He* had been so real. She could still feel the sensation of his touch on her skin. His lips on her breast. His—

Shock trapped the breath in her chest. *What am I doing?*

Slowly her eyes traveled through the dark and locked onto the only tangible reminder of reality. Glowing red numbers told her it was 4:30.

She dropped her face into her hands. This shouldn't be happening. She shouldn't be dreaming of Jax. Forget she had been escaping to the yacht with *Constantine*, her fantasy lover! But now she was making love to Jax—a real-life person.

And she was enjoying it. Enjoying it more than she had ever enjoyed sex in her life, with anyone, at any time.

Dreams. They were blurring the line between fantasy and reality, allowing her to cross lines, go places and do things she wasn't supposed to do.

But they were lines she didn't know she wanted to cross. Or things...things she didn't know she wanted to do.

Images of Jax's body deep inside hers made her cringe.

This couldn't continue. Something had to give.

But what?

She stilled. Slowly, her hands slid from her face. There was no good solution here, no easy way out. No matter what she did, there would be loss. Someone was going to lose.

Would it be Aurelio?

Or would it be her. She could not deny what she had experienced. Making love to Jax had felt incredible. Granted it was a dream, but one that ended too soon.

Jennifer wanted to cry. She wanted to scream. *She wanted to run like hell*. Aurelio had extended his hand in marriage and what did she do? Escape into the arms of another. And she was so close to having it all; career, husband, family. Her wedding was two weeks away! Her mother was waiting and what did she do?

Slept with another man. Literally, figuratively, did it matter? It had felt real. *She had wanted it to be real*.

There was no way she could look Aurelio in the eye, knowing what she knew, feeling what she felt.

She had to tell them. Her mother, Aurelio, they had to learn the truth.

Showered by five-thirty, Jennifer gave up any hope for sleep. Forget that her body needed it, her mind refused it. She wasn't taking any chances the scene with Jax would be repeated.

Little good it did. Ever since she awoke, an incessant stream of images inundated her thoughts. She could see him. As clear as her own reflection in this mirror, she could see him, his face, his body, as if somehow she'd been working from personal knowledge.

Which was crazy. Yesterday on the steps was the closest the two had ever been. Yet he made her feel wanted, loved. Cherished. In every way. Even now, awake and rational, she could feel his touch, standing in the bright light of her bathroom, she could feel him.

Her attraction to him, her physical and emotional response was no longer something she could deny. Not to herself, not to anyone, though for an irrational moment in the shower she had tried. Desperately wanted to convince herself it was nothing; a fluke.

But she couldn't. Not even in the wide-awake daylight would she try. Jennifer uncapped her mascara and brushed the dark black color to her eyes. She would be honest with Aurelio. With herself. It was the right thing to do.

What she planned to do about Jax, she had no idea. The brush poked her lid, leaving a streak of black goo.

"*Darn it,*" she muttered. Smacking tube to counter, she yanked tissue from a box and wiped the mess clean.

His was the confusing part. There wasn't a list of physical features, though many appealed to her. It wasn't a handful of personality traits, for several were qualities he shared with Aurelio. It was something deeper, something hidden.

Jennifer inhaled, full and complete, and steadied her hand as she applied the remainder of her mascara. She would do what had to be done. On Aurelio's behalf. And on hers.

She couldn't marry him. For all of his kindness, his consideration, for his most sensitive outlook on life, Sam was right. Africa or no Africa, he wasn't right for her. The admission pulled her mouth into a frown. If he were, she wouldn't be fantasizing about Jackson.

Jennifer quickly dressed and dialed the number.

Despite the early morning hour, Sam picked up on the second ring. "Hello?"

"Sam."

"Jen?"

"Yes."

"My God—do you know what time it is? It's six in the morning!"

"I figured with a house full of kids, you'd be up."

"I am, *unfortunately*. The little beasts are scavenging the pantry as we speak."

"Do you need to go?" she blurted, a sudden skip to her pulse. "I can call you back at a better time."

"No, Patty's here. She's helping Mom organize breakfast duty while I stay locked in the guest room. Mornings are fine with me, except when my sleep is interrupted. Then, I'm down-right ornery."

Jennifer chuckled at the truth in her statement. "Kids can do that to you."

"I'll tell you what they can do to you—they can invade your bed like little night marauders! They roll and they kick and they carry-on without a clue to the destruction they wield!" Sam let out a heavy sigh. "Why they can't manage to stay in their own beds beats the hell out of me."

"They like to snuggle."

"That's what stuffed animals are for."

Jennifer thought of Beverly and her stuffed rabbit, Poppy. "True."

"So what's up?"

"I needed to talk to someone."

"And I'm it—oh, *lucky day*!"

"Sam," she cut in. "I'm having second thoughts about Aurelio."

Sam remained mute.

"I thought you'd be leaping for joy."

"Not with the tone of your voice, I'm not. What happened?"

"That stupid dream."

"*What*? What dream?"

"The Greek tycoon dream."

"That one? Big deal. I mean, you already figured out what it meant, right? I don't see the problem."

"Sam. It's about Jax."

Jennifer heard a low hiss of air escape at the other end of the line, but Sam remained mum. Taking a deep breath, Jennifer began, "I don't know what's happening to me—or what it means." *Liar*. "But last night, my dream began with Constantine and ended with Jax."

"Ah..."

"It wasn't the first time, either."

"Okay. You have my attention. We're dreaming of other men. Got it. But I need a little more to go on than that. For starters, what were you two doing?

Sailing around on his boat? If I recall, you mentioned Jax has a sailboat. Were you two cruising the islands? Could be a matter of simple association."

"We were making love."

Sam emitted a guttural sound, half-groan, half-chuckle.

"*Sam.*"

"So you guys *do* have the hots for each other—I knew it!"

Jennifer thought she sounded a bit too pleased. "Actually, it's worse. I know this is going to sound crazy..." It sounded crazy to her and it was her dream! She paused. "I think Jackson is Constantine."

"Hmmm... You're right. That does sound crazy."

"I mean it."

"Okay, okay. Let's take this point by point. They both like sailing around in the middle of nowhere. I see the similarity there. They both, uh, they both..." She paused. "Nope. I'm getting *nada*."

Jennifer felt foolish.

"Oops, no more similarities—but wait. Who cares? Except for the sex part. Now that, I want to hear more of."

"Sam, I'm serious."

"Who's kidding here? Not me. I want details, the gorier the better. *Trust me.* It'll be a welcome change from my current topics of conversation."

Jennifer felt the hit. They should be discussing Sam's issues, not silly erotic dreams. Sam and Patty were going through a rough time. She should be there for her friend, not dump a load of guilty pleasure at her feet.

"So tell me, why do you think Constantine is Jax?"

And why does it matter, she heard the silent follow-up.

Jennifer fought the urge to retreat. She needed to get this out of her system. "More than boats in common, Jax has a scar by his eye, just like Constantine."

"And?" Sam asked, unimpressed by the detail.

"You don't find that odd? Not in the *least* bit?"

"Not particularly. Before, you thought Constantine was Aurelio, their features strikingly similar, remember? Sounds more like a pattern of rationalization to me. *A reach.*"

"It's not. There's more." Jennifer paused. Sam could be so crass at times, but if she knew how important this was to her, she would give a genuine listen. "Hear me out, before you say a word, okay?"

"The witness is all yours, counselor."

"Saturday night I had a dream. It wasn't about Constantine. I was meeting up with Aurelio in the Bahamas, but feared I had boarded the wrong flight. The flight attendant assured me I had nothing to worry about, but my intuition screamed something was wrong. I woke up feeling like I'd blown it, confused the details because I was in too big a hurry to get there.

"When I woke up, I had an unbearable sensation of defeat. In the dream, my last thoughts were, how could I make it right?" She paused, allowing the information to be digested. "The next day, Aurelio chartered a yacht for us to sail around Biscayne Bay."

Jennifer explained how her thoughts had drifted to Jax and later, his intrusion upon their lovemaking. She continued by explaining in both the case of Constantine and Jackson, she had to move past the initial encounter, the initial impression, and get to know the man inside.

"Jax and I have spent a lot of time talking, Sam, about our families, about our thoughts and feelings. Then yesterday, when I came home, he was still here. He must have had a bad day, because he hardly smiled at all, and that's when I noticed the scar—and made the connection." She held her breath.

"Are we psychic now?"

"Sam," Jennifer quipped, but heard the commotion in the background. "What's that?"

"The screaming banshees racing down the hall to the brushing station."

"The *what*?"

"Nothing. Just another one of Patty's tactics for directing traffic around here."

"Do you need to go?"

"No, but I will shortly. I'm the bus driver this morning so I have a schedule to keep."

"Oh..."

"Now let me get this straight. Are you telling me that you think you envisioned Jax, years before you met him?"

"Stranger things have happened."

"Cut the theories. I'm asking do *you* believe that."

"Maybe..." Jennifer ventured. "I don't know. I'm not sure what I believe at this point! All I know is that my life is falling apart around me!"

"Why? Sounds to me like a case of mistaken identity. Swap the partners and move ahead with your plans." Sam chuckled. "I'm sure Jax would be amenable to a garden wedding..."

"Samantha Meredith Rawlings—would you be serious for one minute and help me?"

"I am!"

"Have you forgotten that Jax is seeing someone? Or that he intends to board a sea vessel and spend his future sailing around the middle of nowhere—*in six months' time*?"

"Dating is immaterial. As to his future, he's cruising around the Bahamas. I hardly call that the middle of nowhere. And six months is a number. Numbers can be changed—or manipulated."

"You're being difficult. I'm a physician. I have responsibilities. I can no sooner go cavorting through the islands with some man—"

"Love of your life."

"—some man I hardly know, based on the premonition of a silly dream."

"Some would call it spontaneous."

"I don't. I call it irresponsible. I can't drop everything I've worked so hard for because my imagination is running off in frivolous directions, doing unthinkable things—"

"He's that good?"

"—distracting me from what's important. What's *real*. I have a life. I have obligations. I have partners that rely on me, patients that need me."

"What about what you need? Doesn't that count for anything?"

Of course it did. That was the problem. What she *needed* and what she could *have* were two different things.

Two hugely *different* things.

"Jen," Sam plowed forward, the lawyer in her surfacing for air. "You need love. You need to let a man in. Remember the psychologist's words? You need to connect with a man on an honest level. Your mom..." Sam hesitated. "She isn't going to be here forever. At some point, you'll be on your own and as wonderful and exciting as I am, I am not enough. You need a man; a partner, *friend*."

Jennifer's objections began to slip.

"Jax may be the one, he may not be, I don't know. But don't marry Aurelio if you have even the slightest of doubts. Married life is hard enough when you love someone with every inch of your soul. You only have to look at Patty to see the truth in that." She paused.

Tears gathered thickly in freshly-done lashes.

"I know it's scary, Jen. I know you had a lot riding on this wedding, for your mom, yourself... *But is it worth it*? Really? When all is said and done, is it worth it to accept less than one hundred percent? I can't believe I'm saying this," she erupted with a chopped laugh, "but, give Aurelio a chance to find the right woman—the one that thinks he placed the moon and stars in the sky just for her." She paused. "If Jax can affect you like this, you need to explore the possibilities."

Jennifer's throat closed. Even if she wanted to agree, she couldn't form the words.

"Is marrying Aurelio for your mom's sake worth the years of heartache that will follow?"

No.

Sam misinterpreted her silence. "C'mon, Jen. I can help you through this. There'll be some adjustments, but we can do it—*together*. Just give me some time. Don't do anything rash."

Hot tears streamed down Jennifer's face as she managed a meek, "Hmph." *Too late for that advice*.

"You'll be better off in the long run. It'll be tough in the beginning, but you'll pull through, and you'll be stronger and happier for it. Aurelio will move on, he'll be okay. Trust me."

The "trust me" desperation was almost enough to make her laugh. If only everything she was saying weren't true...

"*I'm afraid*." The admission escaped from her lips, uttered almost involuntarily.

"Then you're normal."

"No, Sam. *I mean it*. I feel like I'm living in a land of make-believe, conjured up by my imagination. I'm afraid it doesn't exist anywhere but in my mind. I'm afraid I'm about to let go of everything real and end up with nothing. I don't even know how to make the step from here to there to find out if it's real!"

"One foot at a time, same as you take every other step."

"But what if I do? What if I do, only to discover it was all a dream. A figment of my imagination." After all, these were connections she was making with a man she hardly knew! "What if I try, only to have it blow up in my face?" Like a child's soap bubble, stinging her eyes. "What then?"

"Then you take it from there. You live life. You move on."

Like Aurelio will.

But her mother? Announcing there would be no wedding was akin to driving the last nail in her coffin. Without any reason to hang on, she would die.

Jennifer hung up the phone. She was going to have to face them; her mother, Aurelio. She had to tell them. Today. Soon. They had to know the truth.

Sweet Aurelio. It was like a sneak attack from behind. There was no way he could have anticipated such a move on her part. He had done nothing to deserve it. *Nothing to warrant her betrayal.*

And then she would have to tell her mom.

Chapter Twenty-Eight

By noon, Jennifer began to believe the fates were looking out for her. Morning clinic had been a breeze, allowing her to enjoy a full hour lunch—if she had an ounce of appetite—but sitting alone in her office, food was the last thing on her mind. Explaining her decision to two of the closest people in her life why she was about to turn *theirs* upside down was first and foremost.

Jennifer slumped back into her chair. Setting her left hand on the edge of the desk, she peered at the two-carat diamond ring glittering on her finger. Tears pushed behind her eyes as she moved her fingers, wishing she could appreciate its sparkle of perfection, the promise of commitment.

Everything she had hoped for, everything she wanted, Aurelio had given himself to her when he slipped it on her finger. In accepting it, she had done the same.

Until her subconscious betrayed her. *And she betrayed him.*

Wasn't it precisely what she had done? However unintentional, however figuratively, Jennifer had crossed a line and she wouldn't deny it. She didn't remember exactly where or when it happened, only that it had.

And that it was so unfair. Aurelio did nothing to deserve the punishment she was about to deliver. His only crime...

...was to pale in comparison to Jackson.

# # #

Jennifer sat like a dead weight on Aurelio's plush white leather sofa. From outside, the setting sun cast a soft palette of lavender and blue throughout the home, indoors and out blending seamlessly through a wall of glass. Perched high above South Beach, Aurelio's unobstructed view of the ocean was magnificent. Tonight, she observed, waters were smooth, calm, peaceful.

Unlike inside his home. She fiddled with the ring encircling her narrow finger and thought once again, how had it come to this?

"You're being selfish." Aurelio paced back and forth across his living room, a canvas of white from floor to furniture, the only color coming in the form of bold strokes of art placed strategically throughout the house, red tulips dangling over the edge of a vase centered on the dining table.

The stark salmon-pink of his silk shirt.

"Africa is a dream come true. It's an opportunity of a lifetime for me and what do you do? Spit it back in my face." He stopped. Raking a hand through long layers of black he stood there and stared. "You're using this against me. Why?"

Jennifer looked up at him. "I told you. This has nothing to do with Africa. I think it's wonderful, I do."

"Then why are you doing this? It doesn't make sense."

He didn't know the half of it! "I told you. This is about me, not you."

"What are you talking about?" He flung both arms out, slapping them to his sides. "It has everything to do with me!" He whirled around, stomping over to the glass doors. A lost silhouette, he stood there, staring out to sea. She hated that she had no explanation.

Aurelio deserved better.

"We love each other. I told you, if you want me to help with kids, I can. *I will*." He turned his head toward her. "If that's what it will take, I'll do it. Whatever I have to."

Anger is no way to raise a family, she thought. It must come from desire. But voicing as much would only aggravate the situation, more than she already had.

Aurelio dropped his head back. "You're giving me no alternatives here."

There weren't any good ones.

The separation settled between them, pushing man and woman farther apart.

"And what about your mother?" He turned around and leaned back to the wall. He crossed his arms and gave her a hard stare, fine features cemented in bitterness. "Have you thought about what this will do to her?"

Over and over and over.

Black hair fell from place, his jaw set. "This will kill her. You know that don't you? And it will be on your hands."

Once met with love and support by those deep black pools of his eyes, now she only saw bastard. With a deep breath, she slid the ring from her finger.

"If you take that off, don't expect a second chance."

No, she didn't expect he'd give her one. Strange, but he was the one man she thought capable of forgiveness. Jennifer set the ring on the glass table, careless to the tremble of her fingers. It dropped with a ping.

Rest in peace, she thought grimly. With one last look at Aurelio, her eyes filling with the familiar rush of tears, she mouthed goodbye.

Walking around his stone-still figure, she picked up her purse and went for the door. She didn't stop, he didn't protest. Sliding her hand around the cold metal handle, she made her exit, pulling the door to a soft close behind her.

# # #

Jennifer called her friend first thing. It was the only thing she knew to do. Spew out the pain, hash through her emotions. Get help making sense of it all.

Heaven knows, she couldn't.

Bless her heart, Sam didn't once interrupt. No snide remarks, no sage advice, she only listened. When there were no more words to describe her misery, she waited for Sam to step in.

"You need to call him."

Jennifer didn't speak.

"You need to tell him how you feel."

"He's not right for me." It was her new conclusion. Yes, she had ruined her life. Yes, she had courted the possibilities, but sanity finally intervened.

While it wasn't fair to tear Aurelio's world apart, it wouldn't be fair to undercut Jax's, either. He should have the freedom to pursue whatever life course he wanted. Resenting the Bahamas was no different than resenting Africa.

"You don't know that, Jen."

"I have a pretty good idea."

"Love is funny. It turns lives upside down. For better or worse. You can't predict choices of the heart."

"Maybe no, but I do know that I can't drop everything to sail through the islands."

"He might be persuaded to put that plan on hold."

"So now I'm changing who he is? How smart is that, Sam? The man wants his freedom. He has no ties here. He lives job to job." A lump rose in her throat. "I can't. My career is all or nothing."

"It doesn't have to be."

"Yes, it does."

"There's room for flexibility."

"What flexibility? I work out of hospitals, offices, not the bow of a boat! I can't save my patients without proper facilities."

"You save lives, Jen. You care for people." Sam paused. "They live in the States, they live in the islands. It's the *vo*-cation that matters, not the *lo*-cation."

"Sam."

"Jen."

The challenge hung between them.

"I would lose my practice, my career."

"You could lose the love of your life."

"It's a ridiculous risk."

"No it's not."

"He's probably not even interested."

"He's interested, *trust me*. I was there, remember?"

"But what if he's not? Then I've lost everything—I've ruined lives, broken promises—and for what?"

"Your freedom."

She could have thrown the receiver through her window. "I don't want my freedom, Sam!"

"Everyone wants their freedom, Jen. That's what living's all about."

Jennifer smacked the phone to her nightstand. Sam was wrong. Living was about more than freedom—it was about love, support; being responsible to those who needed you.

She thought about Beverly. Her surgeon called today and the news wasn't good. She had developed an infection. Jennifer closed her eyes. *One that could kill her.*

Chapter Twenty-Nine

"Mom?"

Beatrice's eyelashes fluttered at the voice. "Are you awake?"

"*Sweetheart...*" she murmured. "I'll see you soon..."

"Mom?"

Beatrice smiled at him. "I love you, too." She opened her eyes to her daughter Jennifer. "Oh—darling..." she said, and worked to adjust her focus to the dimly-lit room. The first rays of daylight filtered in through her blinds, curtains pushed aside, the air golden. And by her bed, in her usual seat, was her baby.

"Hi mom," Jennifer said, a slight quiver to her voice. "How are you feeling this morning?"

Beatrice's gaze relaxed as she settled in on her daughter, enjoying the warmth of her hands. She offered a smile. "Fine...just...fine."

"I brought you some tapioca pudding. The doctor said you're not eating."

"So sweet, Jenny..." She gave a feather squeeze to her palm. "Thank you."

"You need to eat."

Beatrice heard the concern. "I am... Don't worry..." But when her daughter's face remained grave, she seemed to detect something more than worry. "What is it?"

Jennifer's eyes dropped to their hands.

"Jenny?"

She raised her head to face her mother. "It's about the wedding. I can't—"

"Tell me," Beatrice insisted, a mix of confusion and apprehension crowding her intuition. "Jenny? Please?"

"I can't marry Aurelio," she croaked out the words.

Beatrice's heart fell.

Her daughter swallowed, hard. "I can't give you the garden wedding I promised."

She searched her daughter's gaze for direction, for meaning. But the glitter of blue revealed only distress. "But I don't understand... What's happened?"

"I'm having doubts."

Beatrice expelled her breath in a soft sigh. "Oh darling..." With pronounced effort, she reached over and patted her hands. "We all have doubts. It's normal."

Jennifer shook her head. "There's someone else."

Beatrice became very still.

"It's not what you think, Mom," she continued quickly, "it's...I had a..."

"*What*?"

Jennifer gushed out in one long sentence, "I had a dream and it's because of this I can't marry Aurelio."

Beatrice drew back. "A dream?"

And then she explained, from the beginning.

She did the best she could. From her slow and controlled speech, the unnatural state with which she delivered the story, Beatrice could tell this was difficult for her. And as she watched her daughter's face, eyes often dodging the elder's scrutiny, Beatrice heard a young woman under enormous pressure. Not from her profession, though she was certain it was a factor, but from herself. She had set a course of action and was following through, only to be tripped up by an unforeseen obstacle tossed in her path.

Beatrice smiled privately. Her baby girl always had been methodical in her choices, her decisions. She always kept an eye on the future, the goal.

Jennifer learned that from her parents. Arthur and she had always taught their child to have a plan. If she wanted to succeed, she must have a plan. One didn't make it, if they set no course. One would flounder, if they had no compass. Yet now it seemed the very lesson that had brilliantly advanced her career had failed her, personally.

The revelation broke Beatrice's heart.

And Sam. Her vivacious, fun-loving girlfriend, the one she and Arthur had never fully approved of had apparently doled out the best advice of all. Move past appearances. Look beneath the surface. Discover the man inside.

It was exactly what Beatrice had done with Arthur.

"Maybe Aurelio and I can make it work. Maybe this is only a temporary setback. I just need a little time, while I get my thoughts straight."

Beatrice gave a gentle shake of her head. Forcing her hand to be steady and strong, she reached up and brushed the tears from her daughter's cheeks. "I don't think so."

"But why not?" Jennifer asked, sounding perilously close to desperation. "For a successful marriage, people work through their problems, right? They overcome obstacles."

They don't run.

Both understood the unspoken sentiment. It was the antithesis of everything she was taught. Hamiltons didn't run from a challenge, they rose to it. But more than a challenge, Beatrice understood the deeper motivation at work. Jennifer feared disappointing *her*. Like always, she was trying to produce the results her parents expected.

Shame on them, Beatrice admonished herself at once. Shame on her and Arthur for not giving their daughter the power and knowledge to choose as well as they had chosen, the confidence to defy convention and love outside society's expectations.

Beatrice reined in her recriminations. Her bones ached, her energy nonexistent, but she rallied her strength. What's done is done. Right now, Jenny needed to know exactly the jewel her mother had found in her father, and how hard it had been to make their dreams a reality. She was going to need strength to go after this young man of hers, of that much Beatrice was certain.

Clasping her daughter's hand more securely in her own, she exhaled in a tired sigh. "Wrong."

For a long moment, she held her child in her gaze, allowing her to digest the unexpected. "You're not marrying him, because you don't love him...*enough*...in the right way."

"What?"

Beatrice shook her head at the disbelief swirling in her daughter's eyes. "And it's okay."

"But what about the wedding?"

She shook her head again. "I didn't want a wedding."

Jennifer gaped at her.

"I'm sorry I pushed. I only wanted love...for you. The kind your father and I shared." She paused, heart strung by her daughter's stricken look. "Help me up, sweetheart. I'd like to tell you a story." She smiled and dipped her chin. "A love story."

Jennifer did as she was told. Propping her mother slightly higher in bed, she adjusted her pillows and tucked in her blanket. It took only a few moments, but gave both a chance to gather their thoughts. As the day began, sweeping in the beams of sunlight, Jennifer turned off her bedside lamp.

With her daughter perched on the edge of her bedside chair, Beatrice gestured for her daughter's hand. More than the physical connection, she was warmed by its presence. Its love. She felt it in every touch, every caress. Doggedly devoted, Jenny had been relentless in her loyalty. It wasn't until now that Beatrice realized it was flawed.

And needed correcting. Beatrice started at the beginning. "Your father and I met in college..." Visions of a youthful Arthur swirled in her mind. Quiet, unassuming, it was a miracle the two ever spoke. But fortunately for her, they did.

She smiled, bathed in his memory. "It was a whirlwind courtship...and one neither of us expected."

Beatrice went on to describe both students as ambitious, their minds equally inflated with the idealistic brand of youth. Each wanted to pursue a career in medicine, each had an eye on the ultimate prize—their doctorate—but through the years, a difference began to emerge.

"Your father was so intelligent, passing his classes with near-perfect scores, piling on extra credits, just for the fun of it. I held my own, managing to stay in the top tier of my class, but I preferred labs. I liked to get my hands dirty," she added with a playful grin. "Digging through the guts and gore, really set me on fire!"

Jennifer smiled, nodding she could relate, but remained quiet.

For Beatrice, it felt good to remember. Like a shot in the arm of much-needed energy. They were some of the best days of her life—before giving birth—and she wanted her daughter to understand...understand husband and wife came first. They stood by one another through the childbearing and rearing years and once the kids were gone, they remained by each other's sides.

Until death do us part.

Tears pricked at her eyes as Beatrice rubbed her thumb back and forth over the soft warm skin of her child's hand. She wanted to remember this, too. The feel of her slender hands, the touch of her skin. Mother and child was a connection like no other and one she wanted Jenny to experience for herself.

But she needed to understand the difficulties involved. The sacrifice. "Along the way, it became apparent we had very different directions in mind for our careers."

Jennifer appeared confused. "But you're both doctors."

"Yes, but I was a woman, studying in a male dominated field. Your father... Well, he was showing tendencies toward the academic."

"You make it sound like that was a problem."

Beatrice fell back through time, landing in an era when it was indeed, a problem. "Oh darling, you have no idea... The bias women had to overcome in my time was enormous. Women physicians were not as accepted as they are today. Why, Harvard didn't even open its doors to us until the 1940s!" She paused, settling into the memory. "But I was determined to make it. Your father, well, he had positions waiting for him...with the best groups in town. All he had to do was say yes."

"But he didn't."

Beatrice shook her head. "He didn't."

"Why not?"

"Because his heart had found its love in academics, in teaching. He loved seeing the lights go on in the minds of his students...the excitement build as they connected the dots. The heated exchange when they challenged him... And research. It became his passion."

"His passion?"

"His passion. Other than me, of course." She nodded her head, slow and easy, amused by the mild embarrassment in her daughter's eyes. "When we weren't focused on each other, he submersed himself in data, I with people. I wanted to make a difference on a human level, in the lives of sick people; the ones who needed my care the most." Beatrice stopped. She narrowed in on her daughter. "Like you."

Jennifer responded with a timid smile.

"Your father was an amazing parent. There for you every step of the way, he never missed a beat." She paused, her mind overwhelmed by sudden apology. *Unlike her.* She had missed entire days, special events, school picnics...

Because her career had demanded it. Staring at her child, it was with mixed emotion she considered her advice. *Change a thing?* Beatrice couldn't say that she would. Arthur had been the love of her life. Jenny a gift from God. The three of them had made a good life, but it hadn't been without hurdles. Much like her daughter was experiencing now. But to advise the same? "Our life together almost didn't happen."

Jennifer's mouth fell open.

An older gentlemen pushed open the door to her room and slipped his head inside. "Ready for breakfast, Dr. Hamilton?"

"Not yet." She glanced at Jennifer. "Can you give me an hour?"

"No problem. I'll check back." With that, he disappeared from sight.

"But why not?" Jennifer jumped back on course. "What happened?"

Beatrice paused. "Your father and I faced a bit of... Opposition, shall we say?"

"From who—*your parents?*"

"From our parents, the community at large..."

Jennifer's expression assumed a stance of defiance. "Why? It sounds to me like you two were meant for each other, right from the start."

"We thought so, too," she said, warmed by her daughter's adamant defense. Sharing the moment, she patted her hand, pleased by the alliance. "But your father was assuming the role of teacher and I the role of physician. Why, in those days, he may as well have called himself Mr. Mom for the impression was the same."

"You've lost me."

"Those who can, *do*. Those who can't, *teach*. Men are capable. They provide. Women are powerless. They support."

Jennifer bristled and Beatrice smiled. "I was under a lot of pressure to choose a partner *more suitable* for my future, as was he. It didn't matter that we loved each other to the very core, that we couldn't imagine a day go by without the other by our side..."

"But dad was brilliant. He received national acclaim for his research from both the academic and the scientific community. How could anyone view him as unsuitable?"

"I agree. I, myself, always considered it an asinine premise. When you think about it, where did good physicians come from, but from good professors?"

"So how could anyone consider a medical professor incompatible with a medical doctor?"

"Because I am a woman and he was a man." She paused. "Our roles were reversed."

"But that's ridiculous." Jennifer was becoming agitated. "Who cares who did what—you loved each other!"

"Exactly."

It was all Beatrice had to say.

The implication made its mark. *Who cares*.

Jennifer became very still-. Her eyes grew sharp with comprehension. Beatrice caressed her daugh-

ter's hand with a feather-soft brush, but didn't utter a
sound.

Let her draw her own conclusions.

Jennifer rose from her seat and went to the
window. Separating the blinds with her fingers, she
peered outside. As the campus awoke, residents
crossed the expansive lawn, some pushed in their
wheelchairs by nurses, other taking heavy steps, their
efforts supported by walkers or canes. A few seemed
too young to be here.

Taking her time, she digested the information
revealed. Her mother had offered her a glimpse into a
side of her past she hadn't known existed. Until now.
Private, intimate, they were the details of love.
Behind the scenes workings that made a marriage
succeed, ones she had been wholly unaware of.

Jennifer dropped her hand from the window and
turned. "It doesn't matter."

Beatrice shook her head with a hint of rebellious
challenge. "No, it doesn't." She smiled. With a pat
to her bed, she said, "Come. Tell me about Jackson."

Her tone was teasing, yet daring refusal.

Jennifer couldn't help but smile at the coax.
"Jackson. *Jax*."

Thoughts of describing him gave her pause.
Where to begin? "Well, he's a genuinely nice guy..."

"Handsome?" her mom's eyes sparkled with
mischief.

It was the first time Jennifer had laughed all day.
"Handsome doesn't begin to describe Jax!" Pleasure
filled her insides as she returned to her chair. "He's
sexy—in the most physical way—if you like your

man's muscles strong and chiseled, glistening in the sun after a hard day's work."

Which she did. At least, she did *now*.

"*Good*." Beatrice's smile mirrored her daughter's delight. "Does he have brown eyes, like your father?"

"He does. The most incredible pools of warmth and compassion you'd ever want to lose yourself in," she said, absently moving her hand upward along her mother's forearm in sweeping strokes as she considered him. "He has a smile that doesn't quit. The kind of smile that reaches out and holds your hand...rubs your back when you've had a rough day. He senses immediately when something's wrong and sets right out to ease the upset."

"Jackson sounds a lot like your father..."

Jennifer's heart filled with his memory. Her gaze drifted through the quiet room and she thought about her dad. He had been the sweetest, most sensitive man she had ever known. Except for one black day, when he discovered her and Tony in the backyard, he had been nothing but understanding. Ever the "man of the house," Jennifer had no idea others saw him as less for the choices he made; choices that fulfilled his passion for life, the work that made him happy.

Shame crept into her heart. All those years, while she had seen him for who he was, she had mistaken him for a title. Dr. Arthur Hamilton had been the king of her existence, the epitome of what a man should be. Yet she had missed the real man. Not only in her dad, but when seeking her ideal husband. Distracted by polished appearance, she overlooked true worth.

"Maybe I can meet him sometime."

The statement cut open Jennifer's reverie. "What?"

"Maybe I can meet this Jackson."

And sliced her heart in two. It was a casual remark, as though she had all the time in the world. But there was no Jackson "to meet."

Theirs was a relationship which existed in fantasy. "Sure," she lied, gutted by the reality of her farce. "Maybe you can..."

Chapter Thirty

Relax, she counseled herself. Jax has no idea anything has changed. Only you know the two of you made love. Her vision tunneled slightly. *Hot, steamy, no holds barred love.*

Standing at the edge of her drive, he brushed his hands against one another, freeing them of dirt, his smile easy and comfortable.

Closed in her car, she gathered her things. Nothing has changed between you. He knows nothing.

His eyes turned expectant.

She pushed open the door and lifted free, hit by the humidity of the day. The heat felt magnified by her light blue Oxford button-down. Oppressive, damp, she groaned inwardly.

"Good afternoon."

"Hello, Jax," she said. Remaining behind her door, she took advantage of the momentary barrier it provided. "How's it coming?" she asked as casually as possible.

"I'm finished, but I wanted to be here to make a final inspection."

"*Finished?*" The statement sucked the breath from her lungs.

"Ahead of schedule," he said proudly. "The inspector comes on Monday to sign off on the

plumbing and electrical and then we're good to go."
His eyes dodged back toward the yard behind him.
"What do you think?"

Fighting a crushing mix of anticipation and
despair, Jennifer reluctantly followed his gaze, willing
it not to be true. Finished? *Already*?

But what she saw siphoned the strength from her
limbs. Painted across the pool surface was a splash of
light, cherubs dipping their toes in its crystal clear
water. Hanging from the arbor were the first blooms
of mandevilla. And there, right in front of her, a new
carpet of lawn.

Though she had completely missed it. Thick and
lush, it appeared as though it had been there for years.
Up on her patio, tucked behind a cluster of giant,
white bird of paradise, was her outdoor fireplace.
Funny, but she couldn't recall exactly when it had
gone in. Allowing her gaze to fall around her, she
realized her yard was reminiscent of a Mediterranean
paradise.

The perfect setting for a garden wedding.

She pulled her gaze up to meet his. Or in her
case, a wonderful place to spend the summer *alone*.
"It's fine..."

His expression reflected the hit. "I thought it
turned out well..."

Hating that her limp compliment nicked his
pride, Jennifer fumbled to recover, "It did, it is, but..."

It was clear by the glaze of detachment sliding
over his eyes, Jax wasn't listening.

But struggling against the shift in tide, the finality
of the moment, it was all she could manage. He was
leaving! But he couldn't—she wasn't ready for her
job to be finished, for them to be finished...

This was to be their beginning.

"Keep water on the grass or it will die," he said flatly, as though it was just a yard to her, as good as any other in the neighborhood, though both knew he worked overtime to make this one special. "I'll mail you my invoice." With that he turned to leave.

"Jax—*wait*." Instinctively, she reached out to stop him but smacked into the car door. "Don't go..." *Please. Not yet.*

He turned, his jaw set in a rigid line.

"I thought maybe, we could..." she stammered, uncomfortable with his stare that cut right through her. What was she supposed to do now? *Ask him out? Confess her feelings?*

Jax remained mute, expectation settled square in his eyes.

Jennifer shrank beneath his glare. He felt cold, distant. There was none of his usual warmth, none of the tenderness from her dream, none of the love and desire in his eyes...

She wanted to slap herself. *What did she expect?*

It was a dream! A dream, darn it! Jackson Montgomery wasn't some figment of her imagination—he was a *man*—with an agenda, *feelings*.

Jennifer felt cornered. She was trapped by her fantasy, trapped by foolish desire. It was one thing to dream about a man, it was another entirely to face him—in the flesh!

The space between them quickly became awkward.

Jennifer blurted, "I can write you a check. Right now. If you'll come inside—"

"That won't be necessary."

"It's no problem," she assured. "I have time..."

"Don't go to any trouble on my behalf. I don't need it."

Ouch. "Really," her shoulders slumped, "it's no problem."

"Mail it."

"Sure," she mumbled. So much for her musings...where the two of them exchanged nervous smiles, both interested in pursuing the possibilities, yet uncertain how to begin.

Hesitant, but interested.

Jax was interested in one thing. Leaving.

"Thanks for the business." The kick to her stomach was swift and sure as he turned, and stalked off to his truck.

So that's it? No asking for referrals, no call me if you need anything? Jennifer couldn't believe it. It was over. Just like that. The job was finished and so was he.

Disappointment shattered inside her, like shards of delicate crystal. Interested?

No, this man clearly wasn't interested.

But hadn't he said that from the start? Hadn't she said as much to Sam? Watching him climb into his vehicle, Jennifer knew the answer. Fantasy was a fool's game.

Jax slid onto the bench seat, slamming the door closed behind him. He gunned the engine to life, heedless to the explosion of exhaust as he threw it into reverse. No need to tie up loose ends. His tools were cleaned up and packed in the bed of his truck.

He had only been waiting to see her.

Without another glance in her direction, he barreled out of her drive, cursing himself for looking forward to her arrival, a glowing reception of his work. Dr. Jennifer Hamilton was hard to please—he had known *that* going in—but he deserved better than a lackluster response.

Hers was an insult.

But worse, he actually thought he'd made a dent in that shiny exterior of hers—especially after the compliments she doled out the other day. The woman sounded like she meant what she said. While he may not have a shot in hell for anything more serious, Jax believed they had become friends.

He believed wrong. Today's paltry response proved it. Not only couldn't she find it in herself to say the words "good job," or "thanks for finishing it a week ahead of schedule," she had quickly dismissed him. Eager to pay her bill, it boiled down to money.

In her eyes, he was one more laborer to pay.

Bitterness churned deep. *You're a lawn guy. I'm a doctor.*

Friends? *We aren't even in the same league.*

Jax wrestled with old disappointment, battling the similarities between Jennifer Hamilton and most women he knew. Women today were shallow. Most wanted something from him, expected something from him.

Like his father. Jax tried to shake the correlation, but he couldn't. It was always there, lurking in the background of his mind. To some extent, he guessed it always would be. His father would never accept him for who he was, not until he chose to fall in line with his expectations, his ideals, that is.

Something he never intended to do. Jax would not change who he was—not for his father, not for a woman. Not even for Jennifer Hamilton, the woman he had begun to believe might prove different.

Chapter Thirty-One

Monday dawned and with it, a most startling development. Her mother decided she wanted to see the garden. Today. No wedding, no rush, she wanted to visit. *Today*.

Jennifer had been stunned. Jax was due by sometime today to meet with the inspector.

Maybe I can meet this Jackson.

What if her mother asked questions, made innuendos? Jax had no idea of her feelings. No idea she had broken off the engagement. The entire situation could unravel.

She would look the fool.

Caged by her thoughts, Jennifer felt cornered. She couldn't refuse, but could she delay? Could she persuade her mother to wait a day?

What if she didn't have another day? At this point, there was no reason to hold on...

The doctor in Jennifer knew her mother's condition was a pendulum. It swung between good days and bad. This visit to the garden could mark the final pass.

As she marched through the lobby of Fairhaven, Jennifer's emotions flipped between fear and dread; fear for her mother's well-being, dread they may run into Jax.

She couldn't face him. Not with her mother present, not after she had revealed *everything*.

She'd have to prepare her mother. She'd have to ensure her silence. But the minute Jennifer tried to visualize the discussion, the absurdity hit. *Who was she kidding?*

Beatrice Hamilton would do as she pleased.

Jennifer groaned as she rounded the nursing station. Well, the likelihood of Jax being there when they arrived was slim. It was getting late.

She checked her watch. *Four o'clock.* He'd most certainly have met with the inspector by now. City employees didn't work overtime.

Jennifer hurried past elegant oil paintings lining the walls, seeing not a one. Her mother was waiting. For her visit.

"Dr. Hamilton."

Jennifer whirled around at the call of her name.

"May I have a word with you?"

Fear scurried into her heart. Her mother's attending physician. "Of course."

Dr. Roberts walked toward her. "I understand your mother will be visiting your home this afternoon."

"She is."

"You need to understand her condition is fragile. Her bones are compromised, and can be broken easily."

Jennifer's emotions turned to grit. Her teeth clenched together. She understood what was at stake. His warning was out of line. "We will be extremely careful with her, Dr. Carter." She slipped her hands into the front pockets of her coat. "This trip is to buoy her condition, not break it."

"Yes," he said, eyes patently masking thoughts to the contrary. "I only wanted to make certain you were aware of the risks. Which are numerous."

"I am. We have arranged for special transportation, a wheelchair, including a nurse for assistance in moving her to and from the backyard. She's taken her pain medication, but we're taking more in case she experiences the need. Is there anything else you would recommend?"

"I think that about covers it." His curt response underscored his disapproval.

"Thank you, but if you will excuse me, it's getting late. I need to be on my way."

"Yes, very well." He turned and walked off in the opposite direction.

Jennifer went to her mother's room and found her already seated in her wheelchair, ready to make the trip. Fussing with her silk blouse, her hair curled, makeup done, a bright pink lipstick had been applied to her lips. Beside her, a nurse finished pumping the last dose of medicine through her IV.

"Jenny!"

Jennifer fought back tears at the sight of her mother's excitement. The way her eyes lit up only served to twist the blade. This was a visit.

Not her wedding day.

"All ready?"

"Yes, Ma'am."

The next half-hour was spent loading her into the patient transport van, Jennifer wincing with pain over every step her mother took. No longer taken for granted, walking had become a grueling event. Climbing stairs; excruciating.

Yet as she helped lift her up and inside, Jennifer could feel the determination in her mother's grip. Taking her to see the garden was the right thing to do. *It was.*

Chatting as though they were two women out for a drive, her mother ignored the white elephant riding with them. Beautiful outside, it seemed she was enjoying the moment, savoring her time away from Fairhaven.

Sitting beside her, Jennifer couldn't shake an uneasy feeling. Like the last meal, finality wedged in hard. There would be no future rides, nor future visits. Bittersweet, both knew this was the end of the road.

As they turned into her drive, Jennifer placed a hand on her mother's arm. "We're here," she announced quietly, anxiety spooking a flock of nerves into flight through her chest.

The van made a wide slow arc around the fountain before coming to a stop. Her mother gasped. "Oh, Jenny!" She clasped onto her daughter's hand. "It's beautiful!"

Splashing with life, the tiered fountain reigned prominent in the front yard. More than making for a regal entry, it proved a wonderful welcome home.

Exactly as Jax intended.

Jennifer spotted the tail end of his truck in the back and trepidation closed her throat. "There's more." *Much more.*

"But the fountain is gorgeous," her mother admired softly, "and the flowers..." She turned to face her daughter, eyes glowing in approval. "They are *incredible.* I love your choices. The tropical flavor...it really suits your home."

Jennifer could only nod. Jax suggested them.

The van nurse retrieved the wheelchair as Jennifer rose to help her mother from her seat and down the few steps. Beatrice was shaky, but anxious to begin her tour. "Let's get to it!"

Once outside, the nurse allowed Jennifer to take control of her mother's wheelchair, while she hovered in the background. Jennifer understood. She was available, if needed.

Beyond the fountain, the lantanas' hues of sunset stole the attention, their tricolor blooms soaking up the late afternoon sun filtering in through the treetops. Beatrice pointed to them. "What a nice, homey feel those give to the house."

Jennifer acknowledged the remark, but kept a keen eye out for Jax. "They've filled in considerably since planted."

"The selection complements your home to perfection."

"I've learned it's a complicated process," she replied absently, preparing herself for his appearance any second.

"Not when you know the basics of your color wheel." Placing elbows on her armrests, Beatrice looked up at her daughter and smiled. "Then it's only a matter of choosing what appeals to you."

Jennifer nodded, anticipation strangling her pleasure.

"I want to see the back."

Of course you do, she rued. Pushing her mother's wheelchair, the three made their way around the front drive to the back—and undoubtedly—where Jax would be.

"Oh darling, I love the hibiscus!"

One eye on the hunt for Jax, she replied, "They are beautiful, aren't they?"

"And they're so full..."

"Yes," she murmured, glancing about the yard. *Where was he?* That was his truck, though she saw no sign of an inspector's vehicle.

"Jennifer, push me to the back."

The sharp command pulled her back into the moment. Crossing into open yard, Jennifer felt like she was approaching an awaiting firing squad.

"Oh, it's lovely..."

Jennifer followed her mother's gaze to the arbor. Positioned before the fountain wall, laden with red-flowering vine, it was an utterly perfect setting for bride and groom.

Jennifer swallowed a lump of regret.

"It looks as though it were made for the occasion..."

"It was," escaped the soft admission.

Beatrice turned to her daughter in surprise. "He knows about the wedding, then?"

"Yes." Guilt flipped in her belly. "He designed the entire area with that in mind."

Beatrice clasped her hands together, then allowed them to fall to her lap. "How thoughtful of him."

Yes. Jennifer's heart sank. The man was thoughtful to a fault. Unlike her.

"Dr. Hamilton!"

Beatrice turned at the sound of the male voice.

Jennifer froze. Her heart stopped.

She eased around to see him.

Dressed in his customary Montgomery Landscape shirt, khaki shorts and work boots, his hair the usual mess of tufts, Jax stood by her bedroom window. A look of mild surprise brushed across his features.

Jennifer swallowed hard. *Judgment day.*

He smiled.

Her heart split.

"Shall we?" her mother prodded.

Jennifer's pulse sprinted through her limbs. No. Let's not go anywhere near him.

Beatrice fussed with her hair.

Forcing her body to react, Jennifer pushed the chair toward him, but not far. As usual, Jax met her halfway.

When he drew near, his smile dimmed. Taking in the elderly woman before him, brown eyes filled with curiosity. He turned to Jennifer. *Your mother?*

Beatrice spoke first. "You must be Jackson."

"I am," he answered, his comprehension complete. "You must be Dr. Hamilton."

Jennifer cringed. Short and sweet, she prayed. Better yet, *short* will do. In a defensive stance, she took up position by her mother's side.

"I am," Beatrice replied, her cheeks blushing like a schoolgirl.

"Jackson Montgomery," he declared, and reached down to take her hand in formal introduction. "It's a pleasure to meet you."

"And you." Her gaze drifted over the yard then returned to Jax. "The yard is *wonderful*... You've really gone to a lot of trouble."

He looked directly at her mother, his reply soft and intense. "I'm always glad to work for a worthy cause, Dr. Hamilton."

Jennifer gulped.

"And good news," he said, turning to her. "The inspector signed us off. Congratulations. You're good to go, anytime," he added, though his eyes held no pleasure at the prospect.

"Great," Jennifer said dully.

Beatrice drew in a sharp breath. "Oh, my!"

Jennifer's heart thumped. She bent over at once. "Mom, what is it? What's the matter? Are you okay?"

"Where did you ever find that?" Asking no one in particular, Beatrice pointed.

Chapter Thirty-Two

Jax's smile returned.

Escaping the sudden fear that had taken hold, Jennifer's gaze leapt in the direction her mother pointed. That's when she saw it. Situated off the corner of her bedroom, rising high and free on a pole above the clump of lush plumbago, sat a Victorian birdhouse.

She noted the extraordinary detail bore an uncanny resemblance to her mother's old one, except the color scheme was different. Rather than painted with usual pastels, this one mirrored the colors of her house.

Jax spoke solely to her mother. "I found it in a specialty store. Your daughter described one that she remembered while growing up, one you had in your garden. She mentioned it was a real beauty, fit for a king." He smiled. "I checked around and a friend suggested where I might find one similar." He paused, his expression open, filled with the innocence of a child's. "What do you think?"

Tears filled her mother's eyes. "*I love it...*" she whispered fiercely. She turned upward to face her daughter, her eyes hopeful. "You remember that?"

With a lump in her throat the size of a boulder, she could only nod. *Jax remembered.*

Evidenced by her mother's smile, years of hurt melted away. Though he had no idea his role, Jax's thoughtfulness repaired a bridge between mother and daughter; a gaping rift torn by the harsh words of a self-centered young woman, healed by the deeds of a compassionate young stranger.

While Beatrice had no idea this was the first time her daughter had laid eyes on the thing, Jennifer knew. She glanced at him. Jax knew.

Dabbing the corner of her eyes with a crooked forefinger, Beatrice collected herself. She pulled herself a little taller, a little stronger and said, "Jackson, I love what you've done here. Will you be so kind as to show me around the rest of your beautiful creation?"

"It would be my pleasure, Dr. Hamilton."

"Call me Beatrice," she said, warming to his charm.

He cast a glance toward her, gauging her reception.

The noose encircled Jennifer's neck with a yank. If her mother became too cozy, if he learned of her feelings...

She would absolutely be the fool.

"Jenny?"

"Yes, please," she mumbled, and grasped hold of the chair handles with a white-knuckled grip.

"I want to see the bird house up close," Beatrice declared.

Jennifer's ego and heart tumbled over one another. *Of course you do...* But she duly followed Jax's lead.

"It's an amazing piece of artwork, both in craft and creativity," he shared as they walked. "A true custom job."

Nearing the bedroom patio, the three of them slowed.

"In fact, if you look close, you'll see it's outfitted with a special entrance on the side."

Upon closer inspection, Jennifer could see he was right. The birdhouse appeared hand-painted, the woodwork fancy enough for a human's home, let alone a bird's.

Over Beatrice's head, Jax shot Jennifer a quiet smile—one so brilliant and so powerful—she couldn't avoid its intimacy.

Even if she tried. And held within his gaze, one with all the familiarity of a close friend, she heard, "The side entry was made large enough for a Cardinal." Her grip tightened.

"Cardinals?" Beatrice asked, glancing to him, somewhat confused. "Why, I don't believe I've ever seen a birdhouse made for Cardinals."

Jennifer couldn't breathe. The gesture was so intimate—so private—she feared her eyes betrayed her.

But Jax grazed past the question with barely a hesitation. Turning to focus on her mother, he replied, "They're a common visitor around here. I didn't want them to feel left out. And their song is outstanding, especially in the calm, after the rain..."

Beatrice laughed softly. "That's sweet."

Jennifer's heart ached. You have no idea.

Lacing her fingers together, Beatrice settled in as Jax began a narrative of the yard, the planning that went into it, the changes along the way, directing his comments entirely toward her mother—to which Jennifer was grateful.

She didn't know if she could survive any more of his attention. Not with any semblance of indifference, that is.

What had he done! Jax never mentioned a bird-house, not once. What was the meaning of it? Was it significant? Warmth flushed through her cheeks. Could it mean Sam was right?

Did she dare believe...he was interested in her?

Watching as he discussed the yard and plants with her mother, amiable and personable, he acted as though this was the only job that mattered.

After their cool farewell from yesterday, Jennifer couldn't imagine him feeling anything so personal, doing anything so thoughtful.

But he had. She ventured a peek toward her bedroom. The proof stood clear, perched outside her window.

"The mandevilla is a perfect choice," her mother said.

Jennifer pulled her thoughts inside out. Jax picked it especially for her.

He stopped shy of the arbor. "Throughout the summer, the red blooms will really light up this space."

The three of them stood by the pool, the still water reflecting their image in buttery yellow tones. Retiring for the day, the sun had cooled to a soft glimmer. Behind them, the wall fountain added a subtle splash of peace to the air.

Jennifer's eyes lingered on their mirror image, thinking how they appeared three individuals out for a leisurely stroll.

It was far from reality. Far from the more accurate description of a woman on the verge of death, her daughter mired in reservation, the man caught in between.

"I think this area is my favorite," Beatrice said, her gaze resting on the fountain, the wrought iron bench nestled nearby, beneath an umbrella of shade. "It's relaxing."

"Exactly what we were looking for when we designed this fountain."

Jax's eyes sought Jennifer for confirmation, and while she met his gaze, she couldn't agree. There was no "we" involved in the decision. It had been his. All his.

And it was perfect.

Beatrice looked to her daughter, her eyes gentle yet appraising. "It will be a wonderful place to begin your new life, Jenny."

Jennifer stared mute.

She turned to Jax, assessing the man before her. "I commend you, Mr. Montgomery. You are a true master. An artist."

Pride illuminated his smile. He nodded in response, the gesture more bow than nod.

Beatrice glanced between Jax and Jennifer, pausing, as though she intended to add something more, something of significance. Jennifer held her breath, a thousand emotions hanging on the outcome. Jax waited in respectful silence.

Tranquil blue-gray eyes settled on Jax. "I once had a garden... A garden to live by," she said, nudging a sly smile toward her daughter. "It was my retreat. My private haven tucked away from the pressures of work." She folded her hands in her lap.

"I used to spend hours there, fussing with my flowers, weeding, pruning, savoring my privacy..." Her smile seemed to reach out, and wrap itself around Jax. "Heaven on earth."

He looked at Jennifer, his gaze dark and penetrating. *You told her about my mother*.

Jennifer felt her bare arms turn to gooseflesh.

"One of the purest connections with our Father is through the Mother," Beatrice continued. "From the riches of the earth to the heavens above, Mother Nature takes part in everything we do." Beatrice's eyes were intent, serene against the ravages of time, focused on the man before her.

Jennifer was amazed to witness Jax's expression turn meek as a kitten. His eyes had stilled, almost mesmerized as he spoke. "It makes sense, doesn't it?"

Jennifer wondered at his question.

"Complete." Beatrice gave a sad nod. "It's the cycle of life."

But she suddenly understood. Jax was feeling his mother's absence. Within a small space of time, his world had been flipped by the soft words of her mother.

Instinct wanted to fill the void for him, to soothe the hurt that must be coursing through him, but she resisted. Grief was a space nothing could satisfy, a hole no word could plug.

"Love is everlasting, on earth as it is in heaven," Beatrice murmured, a bare wisp in the hollow of evening.

"For ever and ever," Jax whispered, his tone coated in sorrow. Dusk descended upon them, casting shadows across the lawn. No one uttered a sound, each content to listen as the water flowed into the basin below. A sense of inevitability hung heavy in the air. Surreal and weightless, it reminded the end was near, yet promised love would endure.

Life was fleeting, attachments were temporary, grief worked its way in and out through time. Death made no judgment, snatched without quarrel.

Her chest tightened. Left one vacant without qualm.

Jennifer's eyes met Jax's and for an instant, recognition passed between them. He understood.

All she could do was wait.

Unfortunately for Jennifer, the fingertips of death crept quickly, slipped around her neck, announcing themselves with the shrill ring of her telephone. Bolting to life, she grappled through the black of night.

2:14.

A bone-chilling trepidation poured into her heart. The hospital paged her. *Fairhaven called her at home*. Hand trembling, she picked up the receiver. "Hello?"

"Dr. Hamilton?"

"Yes." Her heart tripped, knowing immediately what came next.

"Your mother is asking for you."

"I'll be there right away." She smacked phone to its cradle. Fear wound through her limbs. Your mother is asking for you. Wasting no time, Jennifer hurried to dress. Unsteady hands rendered a simple task difficult, but her mind pushed. She couldn't be late. Please, she prayed.

Don't let me be late.

Twenty minutes later, she stood staring at her mother's still body through a blur of tears. Painted in soft light, the cream cotton blankets appeared velvet, her nightgown more satin than cotton, her ivory skin...

Pasty by comparison. Jennifer hurried to the head of the bed and reached for her mother's slender hand. Startled by the touch of ice, her heart skipped. No...!

Chapter Thirty-Three

Beatrice's lashes fluttered. With that uncanny sense of hers, she opened them and turned toward Jennifer. Reaching out through the silence, her gaze deepened to a lucid blue.

"Mom," Jennifer whispered, heart pounding with relief.

She'd made it. She wasn't too late.

"Jenny..."

Her mother's speech was near indiscernible. Jennifer leaned forward, closing the space between them to inches. "Yes, mom, I'm here." One hand clutched around her mother's, she lightly rubbed the other across her forearm—for warmth, for connection, for something constructive to do. "You asked to see me."

Beatrice's smile never made it to her lips, but shimmered lovingly in her eyes. "I love you... More than life... I love you."

The words sliced her heart in two. "I love you, too." Grief rendered her hand limp. "So much. I love you, too."

"You have...a beautiful life...ahead of you..."

She moved to caress her mother's cheek, to brush the hair from her face. She wanted to scream—don't go! *Not now.*

I need you!

"Look...beneath the surface..." Her voice but a feather of sound, Beatrice's speech was labored but clear. "That's where your true love lies..."

She closed her eyes.

Denial warred with reality. No—not yet. *Please not yet.*

But they proved to be her mother's last words. Jennifer's face twisted in anguish. She pressed the thin hand hard against her lips. She hated the feel of skin and bones, but she needed the connection, the union. She needed her to remain.

Jennifer rolled the hand to her cheek, squeezing her eyes shut, she fought the fear coursing through her. She can't go. There's too much to live for. Too much she needed to do.

But as she reeled, deep inside Jennifer knew this was the end; an end she had already prolonged for too long. She hung on, because of her daughter. As if she could delay the inevitable.

But it was irrational. Beatrice Hamilton's life was over. Her mother's body was shutting down, turning out the light on life, returning to her husband's side.

Leaving Jennifer alone. Aurelio summarily rejected, Sam a thousand miles away, and Jax...

Her heart broke as their recent weeks, filled with new beginning and life-changing moments evaporated from her thoughts. Jax may as well be a thousand miles away. No ties, no connection, he was but a blip on the screen of her subconscious. A dream.

Jennifer's shoulders shook as she began to sob. She dropped to the bedside chair. Once her anchor, the cushions now felt rigid, like foreign objects. No longer a place to ease into the visit at hand, this was her post for the death watch.

Still breathing, her mother had lapsed into a coma.

Through the night, Jennifer nodded in and out of sleep. But as dawn seeped in through the blinds, her mind crawled to an awakened state. With a light brush across dry powdery lips, she determined her mother was still alive.

Allowing her hand to fall, Jennifer prepared herself to sit out the duration. She would not leave her mother's side.

She had alerted her partners hours ago, grateful for their response. *Take all the time you want. We'll manage your patients from this end.* Next she had called Sam, now bound for the next flight out of Ohio.

Which gave Jennifer comfort. She would help her carry this burden she had no idea how to bear.

Vigilant nurses moved in and out of the room, offering assistance and words of support. Jennifer appreciated them all, but refused their advice to break from her vigil. She couldn't leave. Wouldn't. Her mother was all she had and until she took her last breath, she wanted to be with her.

By noon, the doctor stopped in. He warned her it could be days before Beatrice finally let go. At this point, the best thing she could do was keep up her strength. Go home. Get showered. Eat something. They would call her if anything changed.

Reluctantly, Jennifer agreed. Since being roused from the dead of night, she had not eaten a morsel and admitted a shower might do her good. If only to renew her energy, enable her to resume her position.

Releasing the frail hand, it was settled. Jennifer would return within two hours' time. If need be, they were to call her cell phone directly.

# # #

"Jennifer, *I'm so sorry*."

Jax had been waiting for her. Leaning against his truck, patient, determined, he had been here. Waiting.

She stared at him blankly. But how could Jax know?

"Sam called me this afternoon." His words were rushed, as though he couldn't get them out fast enough. "She couldn't get a flight out until this evening and asked me to check on you—I told her I would."

That explained it. Darn her, bless her, but that's exactly something Sam would do. Caught between surprise and relief, Jennifer's mind numbed to the courtesy of decorum and simply nodded she heard. Above them hung a low ceiling of gray. It dulled the beauty of her yard, but nourished her mood.

"Are you all right?" Jax swore under his breath, and brushed a hand through his hair. "*I'm sorry*—that was stupid." He blinked hard, concern swimming in his eyes. "I *meant* is there anything I can do? How is she?"

The question unleashed a flurry of tears.

He cursed again. "I'm sorry."

"It's okay," she said, not wanting him to struggle. Jax was here as a measure of good deed. He should know she appreciated it. No matter how mixed her feelings were at his presence, how much thoughts of her mother hurt, he should know she cared. "Thank you for coming." She wiped fingers along the lids of her eyes. "Her condition hasn't changed."

"Does her doctor—" he asked, but dumped the question as he stared at her. Brown eyes heavy with doubt, he seemed at a loss, but intent on being helpful, there for her.

"Her doctor doesn't know..." Jennifer evaded the persistence of his gaze, unable to bear the yearning pulse of her heart, the desire to release her troubles and allow him the role of support. *Lover*.

The air temperature dropped by a noticeable degree. She rubbed her shoulders. "No one has any way of knowing," she said abruptly. "Only time will tell."

Sprinkles began to fall. Jax looked up, but before either could make a move, a crack of lightning cut across the sky, followed by a deafening roar. Rain fell.

Jax grabbed Jennifer by the arm. He slammed her car door closed and pulled her into a sudden sprint. Sailing up the steps and onto her back porch, he steered her toward a dry spot near the house. Shaking the water free from his hair, he released her arm. Allowing his gaze to settle on hers, he waited for direction.

Twisting straight dark hair into a makeshift ponytail, she gave a quick squeeze and release, wringing the water loose. The rain pounded overhead, fell in droves around them. It filled the silence with its beating.

"Jennifer?" he probed softly. "What can I do?"

Need gnawed at her. There was so much she wanted from him, but not the first idea how to ask.

He understood what she was feeling, understood the connection, firsthand.

Jennifer turned and wrapped her arms around her body. There was so much she wanted—from him, from life—but not this way.

A lonesome feeling, the likes of which she had never known, encircled her body like a pack of hungry wolves. She felt lost in the present. Nowhere to go, no one to turn to. By her own hand, she had committed herself to a life of solitude.

Absorbed in her grief and guilt, she had almost forgotten Jax was there until his arms slid around her body. Startled, she made no protest as he secured her within his embrace, cradling her against the warmth of his body.

Surprise evaporated as longing washed over her. Immense longing. The muscled wall of his chest behind her, the gentle rest of his head against hers... Never before had she needed the touch of another human being as much as she needed it now. Like a child seeking reassurance, everything would be okay, the world was not as scary as it seemed, she needed his touch.

She sank into his body. If only for a little while, she would steal this connection and claim it as her own.

If only for a little while...

The sound of rain filled the afternoon.

As the two stood in silence, their common tie threaded through her chest, around her troubled heart, and laced them tightly together. Firm within his hold, she brought her head back and rubbed her cheek lightly against his. He drew her closer and swayed them back and forth in a subtle, calming motion. He stroked her hair, caressed her cheek. He kissed her. A simple kiss, delivered at the side of her head, the way one would do to ease the troubled heart of a friend.

She didn't object. It felt good. *Right.* The two were crossing boundaries never before crossed. What should have felt awkward, felt perfect.

Meant to be.

Rain hammered the rooftop, blocking out everything beyond this porch, beyond this moment, as his lips stole their way down to her ear. Moving with feather-light pressure, he drifted to her cheek. He ran a hand up and down her arm, her skin erupting into gooseflesh beneath his fingertips. No longer crying, she moved further into the contour of his body. Matching his rhythm, she swayed, back and forth, back and forth.

She breathed in slow and deep. He pulled her closer and she gave in, into his strength, into his desire. Yes. This felt right. She turned.

She parted her lips in invitation. As she hoped, he dropped his mouth to hers, barely grazing, his movements hesitant, unsure. Dry and bare, her lips pulsed with desire. She moaned. Friendship was no longer enough.

She slid her arms around his waist and met him with a quiet seeking. *Kiss me, Jax.* She pulled him closer. Kiss me.

He slipped his tongue inside her mouth and groaned.

Longing consumed her. More powerful than she imagined. Like her dream, she ached to fill herself with this man. She abandoned reason and gave in to the kiss.

His desire swelled low between them. His tongue delved deeper, his moves fluid and sure. She grasped hold of him tighter. The sensations streaming through her body were succulent, sweet. Hot. Her loin melted. Her breasts tingled.

Jax moved deeper, harder, his mouth eager, searching.

Surrender. Give in. *Let this happen.*

He peeled himself away.

Her eyes moved back and forth across his. Jax?

The magic melted, replaced by instant doubt. The repulsion Jennifer saw in his eyes turned her stomach. *It had been a mistake.* The warmth spreading between them, the emotion she felt pouring from his soul...

He hadn't meant the kiss.

Only she had wanted it. Standing face to face with the man she had fantasized over, claimed as her own...

He closed his eyes and allowed his head to fall forward.

It was clear Jax regretted it.

Jennifer's hands flew to her face. She whirled around. *What a fool*! Harboring fantasies, playing make-believe he wanted the same...

Acting upon it in the flesh. She had made a terrible error in judgment. Jax wanted nothing of the kind. An image of Aurelio surfaced and tears sprang to her eyes. She had cheated him—cheated herself—and for what? A dream, a fantasy. But how?

How could she have been so stupid?

Jax's hands settled on her shoulders, his touch firm, yet gentle. The move stopped her heart. He stepped closer and her breathing ceased. His forehead dropped against the back of her head. *"I'm sorry."*

The choked quality of his voice splintered through her, spilling a ridge of hot tears onto her cheeks. *Sorry.*

"I'm so sorry, Jennifer."

He began to massage her shoulders, her neck, working the tension that gripped her thin frame. Jennifer dragged hands down her face, but stopped short at her mouth, shy of abandoning their defense. Jax didn't say another word. Despite the fact she needed him to say something, he remained mute.

Say something, her heart urged. *Anything.* Her world was careening off a cliff and she needed him to grab tight, else she'd plummet to the depths below.

But Jax said nothing. His hands stilled. The rain ceased.

Silence stood between them. Heavy moisture filled the air. But neither spoke a word.

Without warning, Jax turned Jennifer around to face him. Powerless to maintain the barrier, she dropped her hands. The repulsion in his eyes was gone, replaced by pain. But the implication remained the same. The kiss had been a mistake.

"Jennifer," he said, the effort strained. "I was so far out of line...so unbelievably stupid..." He paused. "I can't even begin to ask your forgiveness...I..." Though his hands maintained a warm hold on her shoulders, his expression closed. "It won't happen again."

Jennifer's heart fell into the pit of her stomach. He asserted the last statement with such ferocity, such sincerity, Jennifer wondered who was most sorry, him...

Or her.

"I only came by to help." Emotion folded into the depths of his brown eyes, now safely tucked beyond her reach. "Sam didn't want you to be alone and I agreed. You shouldn't be."

Through her eyes, she pleaded for him to stay—to hold her—to continue as he had been. She wanted his help, in his touch, his desire.

There was enough remorse in her life, enough apology.

All of which she had been able to forget, if only for the briefest of moments. Because of him. Jax had given her that escape. To have it stripped away so abruptly was a shock to her system. She hated to beg. "Please..."

But she had run out of options.

"Do you need anything? Anything at all?"

She would have sworn he almost reached for her hair, but his hands didn't stray from her shoulders.

Though she ached for them to do so. Yearned for him to hold her, kiss her...

"What can I do?"

Kiss me, hug me, hold me like you want me the way I want you. Tell me we have a chance. Convince me opposite lifestyles can overcome the odds, circumvent schedules, obligations...

Silly and as unrealistic as it is, tell me we have a chance, Jax. Before you walk away. Regret lodged hard in her throat. And leave me to myself.

She shook her head. More tears threatened, but she wiped at her eyes and forced them back. She steeled herself for what came next. In real life. The truth.

Jax was leaving.

Rain dripped from gutters. Strands of sunshine brightened the landscape. Sunset eased free from the weight of clouds.

The worst had passed. From the shelter of the porch, she understood. This was Miami. The Gables. Showers swept in and showers swept out. Consistent, steady, she could count on afternoon thunderstorms.

Much like the roll of life, there was a season for everything; life, death, joy and sorrow. And she'd had enough.

Expectation, disappointment, fantasy, reality...

She'd had enough. It was time to be alone. Nurse her grief in solitude, move on with her life. It was time.

Time for acceptance.

Inhaling slow and deep, Jennifer steadied her gaze. Busying trembling hands, she straightened her shirt. Raising her head as high as she possibly could, she cautiously put thought into words. "I'm fine, Jackson. I appreciate you coming by, but there's nothing you can do here."

"Are you sure?"

"Yes, thank you." She managed to exert a faint smile. "Your concern means a lot."

Her appreciation did nothing to lighten the weight of his gaze. "Your mother is a special lady. She'll always be with you." A sheen of tears glistened in his eyes. "You know that, right?"

Jennifer nodded, the motion difficult, like slugging through quicksand. "I do."

"Like you. You're an amazing woman, Jennifer Hamilton. Your fiancé is a wealthy man, in more ways than one."

Jax withdrew his hands from her shoulders.

In their place, Jennifer felt a distinct absence, a heavy emptiness. He turned to go and she nearly reached out to stop him. He should know about Aurelio...that it was over between them.

There may be a chance. Hope.

The impulse faded.

Who was she kidding? Telling him now would only complicate matters. Force an already awkward situation.

The irony stung. Had she disclosed the impending breakup with Aurelio during their last visit, when she knew, this moment would have been the most natural way for them to come together.

If he were interested. If there was no one else.

But there was someone else in his life. She could feel it. It explained why he was so ashamed of his behavior. He had betrayed someone. A woman he loved. To turn the tide on him now would be more than uncomfortable. It would be unfair.

"Goodbye, Jennifer."

As she watched him hurry down the steps to his truck, she couldn't help feel the possibilities of a lifetime went with him. Then he gunned the engine, the sound of which cut through her chest. The fantasies she entertained went up in a puff of smoke, much like the spit of his exhaust. It was over.

Everything. Her wedding, fantasies of crazy love, the bond between mother and daughter...

It was all over.

Jennifer dissolved into tears.

Jax tore out of her driveway, his truck lurching to its side at the sudden speed. He smacked his hand to the steering wheel. Dammit—*how could he have* taken advantage like that! *How could he have betrayed her trust?*

A million regrets slammed through his body, a trail of loathing following in their wake. He clenched his jaw closed. He whipped his head. She deserved better. Far better than his thin guise of support, she deserved a friend she could trust.

Not that he didn't want to comfort, *he did*. But he wanted so much more. He wanted to hold her and kiss her, to chase away the demons. *Jax wanted to make love to her*. He wanted to wrap her in his arms, plunge deep inside, and take her for his own.

But he couldn't. She wasn't his for the taking.

Jax pulled his truck over. The grass was rough beneath his tires as he jerked the gear shift into park. He sat.

He couldn't drive, couldn't focus. He calmed his breathing. Recalling her eyes, red and bare, her pale face, no makeup, no defense, Jennifer remained the most beautiful woman he had ever seen. Delicate. *Vulnerable*.

He should have stuck to his original plan. He told Sam he would be there for Jennifer and give her support, a willing ear.

But damn it if she hadn't lingered. Stood so close he could smell her perfume. Hugging her to him had been the most natural thing to do. But the wet strands of her hair did something to him. Pulled him to her in a way he couldn't control. And he kissed her.

Jax shook his head slowly back and forth. He shouldn't have done it. But the slender feel of her body, raw vulnerability...

It was more than he could resist. He thrust his head back against the headrest and closed his eyes. One stupid move had ruined everything.

Chapter Thirty-Four

"Has there been any change?"

Jennifer looked up from her bedside post, swamped by relief. Dressed casually in slacks and blouse, her hair a mess of curls, her mascara smudged, Sam looked like she slept the entire flight down. But to Jennifer, she was a beacon; a light in the night, a sense of direction, a tower to lean on. Forget the room full of flowers, glorious bouquets of color and fragrance, sympathy cards, genuine and heartfelt...

Having Sam by her side made it easier to say, "No, nothing's changed."

"Damn," she muttered, and lifted Jennifer into a powerful hug. Though both knew it was to be expected. Once Beatrice succumbed to the coma, death was only a matter of time. Sam pulled away, and scrutinized her pal. "You don't look so good. Those black craters beneath your eyes tell me you haven't slept."

Jennifer shook her head. "I'll sleep later. When it's over."

"Running yourself into the ground isn't going to help your mom, Jen. You need to eat. You need to sleep. Did Jax come by like I asked him?"

Jennifer tensed. "He did."

"Was that a problem I called him?"

"No."

"Well..." Dark brown eyes flashed around the room in question, as if she expected to find him here, by her side. "Was he of any help?"

Jennifer turned back to her mother. Reaching over with calm precision, she took the delicate hand between her own, and gently caressed the deathly pale skin. "There's nothing he can do." Still smarting over the incident, she wasn't ready to divulge what happened. Not yet. She had to get past it herself, first.

"He's a warm shoulder and a sympathetic ear—both exactly what you need right now."

Without looking back, she said, "Neither will help."

Sam pulled up a nearby chair and plopped herself down. "Well they better, cause they're all I've got."

This drew a small smile and Jennifer turned back to Sam. "From *you*, they will." Her expression turned serious. "Thanks for coming so quickly, Sam. I hope Patty can cope without you for a while."

"She can and you're welcome." Sam brushed long bangs from her face and tucked them behind an ear. "Blake has stabilized and is beginning to make progress in his rehabilitation therapy. Patty actually insisted I come. If you ask me, she's had her fill of sisterly love. I think I was beginning to grate on her nerves a bit."

Jennifer dropped her glance aside. "Oh come, now. You?"

Sam pressed her lips together and donned a sheepish grin. "Yep, sweet little old sweet-pea-me. But don't worry. My mom's there to help fill in so I won't be missed."

Jennifer chuckled—*for real*—and it felt good.

Leave it to Sam. An elixir for the grief, a respite from the pain, she was glad Patty had had her fill—if that were truly the case—which she doubted. She needed Sam. And bless Patty for letting her go. She owed the woman a thousand thank yous, but *later*. Right now, she needed to get through the night. Number two, and counting.

Sam rubbed Jennifer's back, but offered nothing. No words, no jokes, she knew her role, knew what was needed. She was here for her friend, whatever it took.

Jennifer appreciated the caress. It was a far cry from the touch of Jax's hand, but it was safer, reliable. Real.

Your fiancé is a wealthy man, in more ways than one.

She couldn't let the statement go. Jax sounded so wistful, so forlorn when he said it. Insanity, she knew. It was nothing more than a compliment. A nice guy saying nice things. But still. It felt so wishful. *Envious*, even.

Frivolous mind-play, of course. She doubted he'd keep in touch, let alone pine for her. His job was complete. He had plans for his future, plans that would take him miles from land, miles from her, eons away from possibility.

And it would keep him there. Jackson Montgomery had no interest in a life lived with mortgages and bills, a job filled with responsibilities and obligations. No. His job was a means to an end. He had a dream and he intended to follow it, wherever it may lead. Willful, passionate, his was a spontaneous vision.

She felt the pinch. *Now who was envious*?

Gliding her hand across the soft skin of her mother's arm, Jennifer thought about her own future. For her, nothing would change. A tiny ache worked through her heart. Other than there would be no marriage. No wedding, no children. Her life would remain as is. She would do as she always did. She would heal others the best she could.

Sam continued to rub her back, and the touch of a friend never felt better. Well, not counting Jax. That was better. *That had been incredible.*

Jennifer passed the next three days, tossed about between sleep and phone calls. Dr. Beatrice Hamilton had many friends and colleagues, all saddened to hear the news. Sam made a continual trek between her bedside and the cafeteria, insisting she eat, despite her protest, a spatter of work calls made along the way.

But Jennifer couldn't eat. She could only pray, willing the end would come soon. Slowly, she grew accustomed to the idea. It was time. It wasn't right for her mother's body to waste away in a place that meant nothing to her. She had lived a full life and it was time to let go.

Out with the old and in with the new. Wasn't that her motto?

Tracing a finger along the delicate outline of her mother's hand, Jennifer recalled the familiar sentiment, though it didn't seem right it should apply to a person's life. Used appliances, worn out clothes, maybe, but not to the most important person in her world.

"Hey."

Startled by Sam's soundless entry, she turned. "What?"

"C'mon." She walked over and tapped her on the back. "You're coming with me."

"No," she replied without thinking.

"Yes. You need a break and you need to eat."

"I'm fine."

"You're not, and you're coming with me."

"Sam..." But when she glanced up, the feeble dissent was easily overcome. Sam wasn't taking no for an answer. Gently hoisted up by the arm, she allowed Sam a victory.

Back home, Jennifer stared enormous brown bag. "You bought too much food, Sam."

"A meager start to replenish a certain bag of bones I know."

"I am nowhere near a bag of bones." Jennifer pinched her side through the light cotton tank. "See? Plenty of fat to hold me through the winter."

Showered and dressed in tank and boxers, she felt ages better, and privately thanked Sam for pushing. Her mother wouldn't want her to spend the rest of her life waiting for her life to end. She had to focus on moving ahead with her own.

A concept she was still getting used to.

"Lucky for you winter is months away, or you'd freeze into a pile of icicles. Look at you," she stuck out her hand. "Your legs look like toothpicks sticking out of those shorts!" Sam turned serious. "Which is why you're going to put a dent in this feast. If you won't, be forewarned. It won't be pretty when I start shoveling it down your throat."

Jennifer shook her head. "You never were the reasonable type." She poked her nose over the edge of the bag and asked, "What do you have in there, anyway?"

"*Arroz con pollo, frijoles negros, plantanos maduros y tu postre favorito. Flan.*"

Jennifer was impressed. "Your Spanish is improving."

"Pesky new South American paralegal at the office—an unbelievably sexy new hire while I was away in Ohio."

She chuckled. "That would explain it."

Sam stopped. "I'm sorry."

"For what?"

"You know for what—Aurelio. Considering the circumstances, I don't need to be reminding you of South American men."

She waved off the mention. "Don't worry about it."

"Come here." Sam pulled Jennifer into a bear hug.

No resistance, she slid both arms around Sam's waist, and relaxed into the embrace. There was no changing Sam. Men would remain first, last and everywhere in between on her list and it was okay. But aside from facts, *truthfully...*

The mention of Aurelio hadn't bothered her. He felt like a distant memory—as unfair as that may be—one without the power to hurt. Where she should feel sad, she didn't. She felt indifferent. Unfortunate.

Jennifer pulled away. "Let's eat."

Playing hostess in her home away from home, Sam retrieved plates from the cabinet, silverware from the drawers. "Can I pour you a glass of wine?"

"That would be great."

Watching as Sam poured the wine and set the table, Jennifer realized how much she needed her ready ear. Sam would listen all night, if that's what it took. A gurgle of confession bubbled inside her. And she deserved to know everything.

Strolling closer, a zing of anticipation zipped across her abdomen. "You'll never guess what happened between Jax and me." Jennifer smiled. The look on Sam's *face was priceless*.

Chapter Thirty-Five

"So, we're back to square one."

Wedged into the corner between two large cushions, legs crossed Indian-style, Jennifer allowed the Latin instrumental to caress her senses with its gentle play of guitar and soft chimes of percussion. "How do you figure?"

"It seems to me, there is no other woman. Jax wants you."

"Are we engaging in wishful thinking now?"

"Not me, pumpkin pie. I engage in nothing shy of hard-core reality, you know that."

"Perhaps you've had a wee bit too much wine," Jennifer said, her own glass near empty. *But it was working.* The sharp edge of her mind had dulled. She wasn't crying, her heart didn't ache. It was exactly the relief she needed.

"I can handle my liquor, thank you very much," yet her tone implied, *perhaps someone else in the room could not.* "This is a simple analysis of the male species, 101—a subject in which I happen to score off the charts." She grinned with a wink. "And I'm telling you, the man is interested. While there may have *been* someone else," she raised a brow, "though I'm not entirely convinced there was, there is no more. It's like I said—"

"I know," Jennifer cut her off. "You read people for a living."

She smiled. "You're damn right and I'm damn good at it and I'm *telling* you what I saw transpire between the two of you that day. There was an electrically charged cord connecting you at the hip! You guys were popping like fat on bacon, working up an appetite for some sizzling sex."

Jennifer shook her head and sighed. "Where do you come *up* with these analogies?"

Pleased with herself, she flashed a grin. "I have an active imagination." Then erased it in an instant. "But it doesn't change the facts."

"Highly colors them?"

"You know what your problem is?"

A soft laugh escaped as she replied, "No, but I bet you're going to tell me."

"You want Jax. More than you're willing to let on, even with me, you want him. Admit it. Despite he represents the opposite of everything you *thought* you wanted, you want him."

Jennifer's eyes stilled.

Steadying her aim, Sam went straight for the heart. "But you keep it hidden, because a relationship with him scares the hell out of you."

Dick Tracy.

"His bank account isn't stocked with six figures. Not a degree to his name, he *works* social functions— not *attends* them. Jeans and beer over suits and champagne, he gets his hands dirty, his brow sweaty. He's a laborer. A working stiff."

Her voice wasn't accusatory, but pointed. And Jennifer felt the cut.

"I'll bet part of you thinks he's not good enough while the other knows *he's the best damn thing that's ever walked into your life*."

Jennifer couldn't utter a word in protest.

It was all true. Except, Sam neglected to mention the qualities that made Jax so special.

The ones that lay beneath the surface...

Her mother's words drifted to the forefront of her mind. Her mom knew the qualities. Witnessed them firsthand, packaged, painted and delivered in the form of one exquisite birdhouse.

"You have me, counselor. On all counts." Sudden need clawed at her. Tears welled in her eyes. Hook, line and sinker, she was caught. "Now what do I do about it?"

"You go after him."

Jennifer mildly flinched. It sounded so forward, so Sam.

And so unlike herself. "I will not chase him. I wouldn't intrude on his life like that."

"*Intrude*? Are you kidding me?"

It did sound silly, but she didn't go after men. She didn't seek them out and hound them for a date. Men asked her. If Jax was truly interested, as Sam suggested, he would ask her on a date not the other way around. Save for one small detail.

He still thinks she's engaged to be married.

"Jen. You have the man at your fingertips. All you have to do is curl one hither and he will jump. *Believe me*. He will come running."

Jennifer chuckled at the image, causing a tear to spill forward, hot on the flush of her cheeks. She couldn't imagine him jumping for any woman, let alone herself.

"It's simple, Jen. You open the door. Invite him in."

Simple. Her pulse picked up. Until she imagined actually doing it.

"You want *me* to call him?"

"No. Absolutely *not*." Heaven only knows what Sam would say to the man. She shuddered. "I can handle this on my own, thank you." She glanced at Sam. "Okay?"

"Sure."

"*Sam*?"

"What? I said sure, didn't I?"

"You didn't say yes."

Sam shrugged. "Same thing."

"Not in a court of law, it's not. Do I need to have you swear under oath?"

"Nah." She waved her off and took a sip from her wine.

Jennifer kept a wary eye on her friend as she considered the situation. She did want Jax. She could admit that much. And she did want to try—*but how*? How did she move their relationship from professional to personal? How did she inquire about his current state of affairs?

Could she really push herself into his life? Going after the man was one thing, losing her dignity in the process was something else. "Jax's so far out of my league. His future, his goals... They're completely opposite to mine."

"They don't have to be. Those are details. You work them out when the time comes. Right now, you need to focus on coming together. The rest will happen...*naturally*."

A sudden sweep of nerves flew through her. "That's easy for you to say—you run through men like a delinquent school boy runs through spit-balls!"

"Whoa, save the personal attacks for divorce court. I'm trying to help out over here. Like the Calvary, you know?" She thumped her chest. "I'm one of the good guys, remember?"

Jennifer corked her attitude. "I'm sorry." Sam wasn't the enemy—wishful thinking was. "But darn it, Sam, I don't want to sit here and convince myself this is feasible when it's not. I've had my fill of heartache. The last thing I want is to add a breakup with Jax to the mix!"

"No risk, no reward."

"One in the hand is worth two in the bush."

"Not good enough."

"My mother's gone, Sam." She frowned, ambivalence tearing through her. For all intents and purposes, anyway. "I want to grieve the loss and move on. I need to find peace of mind, some equilibrium. If I try for Jax and fail..." Jennifer shook her head, ignoring the loose bangs falling across her face. "I'll only compound the pain."

"It doesn't have to fail. You two can make a great team."

"Like Oscar and Felix or Clyde and Costello..."

"You're being negative."

"Realistic," she defended, but evaded Sam's disapproval with the close of her eyes. A great team. Partners. Could she really envision a future with him?

Did they have enough in common? Did they have similar values? Did they want the same things out of life?

"Don't give up, Jen. It's not what your mom would have wanted. She understood life is worth living. It's at least worth a try."

Fidgeting with the stem of her glass, Jennifer struggled against the onslaught of emotion. It was exactly what her mother wanted. She wanted her to find happiness. She wanted her to know true love.

Beatrice Hamilton understood that sometimes, true love defied convention, yet survived the odds. True love prevailed.

"Are you afraid he'll turn you down?"

"It's a possibility," she said, a quiver stealing into her voice.

"So is the part where he says yes, and takes you into his arms, makes mad passionate love to you."

Vivid images from her dream came flooding back, mixing with memories of their real-life kiss. Powerful yearning pulled. That was her greatest hope, her greatest desire. Evading Sam's heated knowing gaze, Jennifer glanced away.

More than she had ever wanted it before, more than she could believe it herself, she wanted to be held in his arms again and finish that kiss—all the way to physical completion.

She wanted Jackson Montgomery mentally, emotionally and physically. *But could it really happen*?

Apprehension, excitement, fear and naked desire skirted through her making a total mess of her insides. More than a dream come true, it would be the best of all possible worlds.

Jennifer's beeper pierced the quiet of early morning. Stationed by her mother's side, she grabbed the pager from her waistband. Heart pounding, she pressed the green button. The number displayed.

It was the service. Catching her breath, she reoriented to her location. *Why were they calling her*? She peered at her mother. Undisturbed, she lay peaceful; a lifeless remnant trapped in placid suffering.

Her eyes dropped to the pager in hand. She needed to inform them the pages had come to her in error. She heaved a sigh. Now.

It might be important.

Jennifer covered her mother's hand with her own and gave a light squeeze. This would only take a minute. She'd be right back. Rising abruptly, she grabbed her cell phone and headed out into the hallway for privacy.

The sudden realization hit. Privacy from comatose? There was no need. Jennifer swallowed the bitter dose of reality and dialed the number. Her mother's life shouldn't end this way; dragging through the days, oblivious to those around her. It felt more insult than blessing.

An operator answered on the second ring. "This is Dr. Hamilton. You paged me, but I'm off call. You need to send it to one of my partners."

"I'm sorry Dr. Hamilton," came the polite reply, "but we were asked by your office to page you specifically."

"Me?" She rubbed the sleep from her eyes. "What for?"

"There's an emergency at Baptist Hospital. The E.R. asked to page you, stat."

"Who told you to call *me* with this?"

"Dr. Miller."

Why would he do that? she wondered almost aloud. Senior partner, he knew where she was. There must be a reason. A good one. "Okay," she said, not bothering to disguise her fatigue. "Give me the number."

Chapter Thirty-Six

The operator rattled it off and Jennifer dialed.

"E.R."

"This is Dr. Hamilton. You paged me?"

"Yes, Dr. Hamilton. We have a patient of yours on the way to the E.R., as we speak. Cardiac arrest. The family has requested you be notified."

"Who?"

"Bronson."

It didn't sound familiar. Normally a rolodex of memory, her mind couldn't locate this one. She glanced around the quiet corridor, moving aside as a gentleman wheeled a cart filled with the first round of breakfast trays. He acknowledged her with a silent nod.

"Are you sure they're asking for me?"

"Positive. The guy is adamant. He wants no one touching her, but you. And the situation is acute. It sounds like she needs immediate intervention."

She hesitated, but only for a minute. "Page Dr. Miller for me. Tell him I'm on my way."

Grabbing her purse from her mother's bedside, she placed a soft kiss on her forehead and whispered goodbye. "I love you." Lingering only a second or two, Jennifer hurried out of the room.

On her way out of Fairhaven, she informed the nursing staff of her plans and how to reach her, should anything change.

Driving to the hospital, she called the hospital and gathered information. Bronson was a young woman, late thirties, with a family history of cardiac arrest.

It was a classic story. Jennifer heard risk factor, near sudden death, time was of the essence. Next, she called the cath lab and placed them on notice.

Mind whirring at high speed as she plowed through a side entrance, she ran through potential complications; how much damage was done to the heart, cardiogenic shock, arrhythmias, the amount of underlying heart disease, calcification...

Hustling down a wide corridor, she pushed through double doors leading to the emergency room. The collision jarred them both. Jennifer gaped in disbelief. "Jackson! What are *you* doing here?"

Stark fear scored ridges deep into brown eyes, his expression shocked blank.

"*Jax?*" When he didn't utter a word, she hesitated, but only for a second. Professionalism kicked in, launching her body into action. There was no time to waste. She shoved her personal affairs aside and hurried into the emergency room.

It wasn't until she realized he was following at her heel that it made sense. Stopping at the edge of the bed, she whirled around. "She's with you?"

Jax nodded. A look of pure desperation poured from his eyes.

His response knocked the wind from her chest. It explained the page. Glancing back to the attractive blonde with a tube stuck down her throat, a blood pressure cuff pumping to life on her upper arm, it was clear she was in serious trouble.

And just as clear she was with Jax.

"Pressure's 130 over 90. Rate's a hundred and fifteen."

Jennifer grappled for reason. *How could this be?* With her mother in a coma, her engagement in ruins, Jax's dying girlfriend shows up at the hospital and *she's* supposed to save her?

She scanned the faces around the bed. *Was this a bad dream? A cruel joke?*

She snapped back to the situation at hand. Enough. No more dreams, no more fantasy. This was her life. "Talk to me. What have we got?"

"Thirty-six year old Caucasian female called 911 approximately seven a.m.," the attending paramedic reeled off. "She complained of a burning sensation in the abdomen. Patient took two aspirin and experienced loss of consciousness before we arrived on scene at seven fourteen. CPR performed immediately, but no pulse—patient shocked at 200 joules for successful defibrillation, then intubated. IV access secured with one dose of Epi, administered on scene before stabilized and transported. Non-smoker, no previous MI, family history of high cholesterol. Father still living. Mother deceased; cardiac arrest. Current medications; 40mg Atorvastatin, 81mg aspirin. No known allergies."

"V-tach!"

"Pressure's dropping," barked another nurse. "Hundred over eighty-five!"

A frantic bleeping blasted from the monitor.

Jennifer registered the information. This was definitely not a dream. This was real. This was bad. *And she was expected to fix it.*

"She's coding!"

Jennifer shut Jax out of her mind and clicked into rescue mode. She had to focus every cell of her attention on this woman if she was going to save her life. "Defib!" she commanded.

Nurses flew around the patient, pulled handles from a machine and called back, "Defib's charged."

"Stand back."

Everyone moved as paddles were slapped to the woman's sides. "Clear!"

The patient's body leaped from the bed as the first shock was administered. The furious pace of the ECG line swept up, then down, reduced to a flat nothing.

Seconds passed like years for Jennifer. *C'mon, c'mon.*

Ready to shock again, the line spontaneously jumped back to life. "Cath lab ready?" Jennifer asked to no one in particular.

"Yes, doctor."

"Get her prepped." Jennifer turned in place and came face to face with the ashen expression of Jackson Montgomery. It cut through her heart like a knife to see him so afraid, so desperate. It was obvious he cared deeply.

She shoved her emotions into a back compartment and slammed the lid closed. This was a patient. He was the closest person to her. She had to move on. "It's bad. I need to open up her arteries, get some blood flowing into the heart." *Or she will die.*

Frozen, he managed a meek nod of his head.

The faraway look in his eyes reminded Jennifer of a child. Helpless, powerless, he was completely out of his element. Resisting the urge to stay, and counsel him through the details, she couldn't. *There wasn't time.*

Tamping down her desire to comfort, ambivalence shooting through her system, she turned back to her team. "Let's get moving."

# # #

"Use extra tape to secure the dressing," Jennifer instructed, wanting double precaution against infection—like the kind that killed Jax's mother. Losing another loved one to post-op infection might throw him over the edge.

It would her.

Stepping back, Jennifer allowed room for a nurse to move in and take over breakdown of the sterile environment. Yanking blue paper from posts, the younger woman started talking to the patient. "Ms. Bronson, can you hear me? The procedure's over."

Pulling the gloves from her hands, Jennifer dragged the mask from her face. It was time to talk with the family.

Or in this case, *loved one.*

Jennifer inhaled a chest full of courage, and slowly, purposefully, exhaled her anxiety. It was time to talk with Jax. Pushing through the lab door en route to the waiting room, her stomach cramped into a mass of knots.

You can do this. She's just another patient. He's just another—

Jax rose from a chair the minute she opened the door. A heavyset man in the corner looked up in unison.

Jennifer locked eyes with Jax.

"How is she?"

Always the first question. "Jax," she began, her professionalism giving way in one fluid breath of nerves. *Who was she kidding?*

This was personal.

And painful.

"Is she going to be all right?" It was more plea than question. As if his entire future hung on her answer, and he was afraid it would be wrong. He ventured closer, the movement alien to his usual ease and confidence.

"Yes."

One little word, he visibly crumbled with relief. Apprehension was replaced by joy. So obviously happy, he didn't try to hide his tears.

"Thank God..."

And it broke her heart. Everything she would never have seemed to crystallize before her very eyes. With one moment, the kiss that should never have been, the friendship that moved too far into her heart...

Tears threatened her façade of cool. Jax would never be hers. He was taken. Unavailable; consumed with the welfare of another.

"I think she's going to be fine," Jennifer said, pressed with a driving need to quell the emotion churning inside. She'll be fine. You'll be fine. Everyone will be fine. *Just fine.*

"Thank you."

The raw gratitude in his voice caught in her throat, lodging high and tight. She couldn't speak. She couldn't move. They stood in silence, separated by a chasm of loss. Despite the stranger's presence in the room, she and Jax were alone.

Her heart teemed with grief. She understood his pain. She could identify with his fear. She could console him—if only they were standing on the same side of suffering.

But they weren't. Jax felt miles out of her reach. He was not hers. Never had been she reminded herself, a touch of anger trickling into her heart. It was stupid of her to have believed otherwise.

Courting chance is a game for fools. The odds stacked against her, she made a ridiculous bet, and lost.

The house always wins.

"She's got a tough road ahead of her, but she's young and strong and I think she can make it." She hated that her voice fell short of her usual crisp, competent tone, but these were unusual circumstances.

She was lucky to get words out at all.

Jax ran his hands over his hair, flattening the unruly tufts, then dropped them to his hips. "Thank you." Eyes cast downward, he sighed, his relief palpable. "For everything." Lifting his gaze to meet hers, he said, "I know this is a difficult time for you. I'm sorry to have bothered you, but you were the only one I knew to call."

You don't know the half of it! she wanted to scream. Eyes burned as tears pushed forward. *Not even close.*

But Jennifer refused to let him see her pain. She was a physician. This was her job. There was time enough later to fall apart. "She'll be in the hospital for a few days, so we can monitor her. She may need an ICD, but we'll need further evaluation before any decisions are made. I can refer you to an excellent EP. Adjusting her medications may be necessary but other than that, adhering to a proper lifestyle should see her through the next forty years." And the two of you can live happily-ever-after. Producing a smile, careless to its fragile quality, she was finished here.

She had met her obligation.

"Jennifer..."

He whispered her name like a caress. Intimate, personal, it felt like a balm to her soul. Her pretense quickly began to collapse. She turned to take her leave.

"Jennifer, wait—"

She couldn't. Self-control was disintegrating, *fast*. Slipping out through the waiting room door, she hurried down the hall, dodging for shelter in the first stairwell.

Safely behind the steel door, willpower buckled. Sorrow deluged, tears flowed, and her heart broke in two. "Oh God," she whimpered, closing her eyes. *Why is this happening to me?*

"*Why me?*" She had jeopardized it all and for what? Smacked down by facts, shot down by reality, it couldn't be any more clear. Jax was in love with someone else.

Sam was wrong. She was wrong. She gambled her life on a dream and lost. Everything she wanted had been at her fingertips—fiancé, storybook wedding, the final gift to her mother...

A week ago, she had everything.

And still would, if Jackson Montgomery had never walked into her life. The sudden image of the blonde popped into her mind. Despite the wires and electrodes, Jennifer could tell she was an attractive woman. Young and beautiful.

And lucky. Not only had she flirted with death today, might do so again, but she had Jax by her side and that made her lucky indeed. Strong loving arms, a warm affectionate embrace, he would see her through any crisis.

Jennifer felt an unexpected pang of physical desire. And once healthy, he'd fill her nights with pleasure, her days with adventure. On the high seas, wandering through the islands, discovering new people and places...

He'd make her life complete.

A man dashed down the stairs past her, shooting an inquisitive look in her direction, but disappeared through the door in seconds. Startled by the proximity of the stranger, Jennifer tried to collect herself. Swiping hot tears from her cheeks, she willed the flow to cease. She was a doctor, *darn it,* not some bleary-eyed teenager, devastated by a high school crush. She had things to do. Lives to save.

She shook her hair, brushed stray strands behind her ears. She had responsibilities.

Breathing in the stale warm air, filling her lungs until they could take no more, Jennifer released in one long, controlled sigh. She had to get back to her mother.

Grasping hold of the cold metal railing, she hastened down the stairs, avoiding any possibility of running into Jackson. Emerging from the stairwell on the first floor, she exited through the first door and felt a small semblance of strength.

Fresh air, a swallow of water, she would be fine, ready to resume her place alongside her mother. The pager blared from her waistband. Dropping her hand, she unhooked the black device and checked the number. Her heart stopped.

Her body froze. Flimsy limbs fell to her sides like rubber. It was Fairhaven.

Spurned by adrenaline, Jennifer forced herself to make the call. A woman answered with a mechanical, "Nurse Benson."

"This is Jennifer Hamilton."

"Dr. Hamilton. Dr. Carter is standing by to speak with you."

Fear and expectation rolled in the pit of her stomach.

"Dr. Hamilton."

"Yes?" She heard the words before he spoke them. "I'm sorry, but your mother passed away a short time ago."

The ground gave way beneath her.

Chapter Thirty-Seven

Her mother was dead. In a blur of crisis, a few hours spent saving the life of Jackson Montgomery's lover, Jennifer missed holding the hand of the most important person to her as she passed.

It was a moment in time she could never retrieve, one she would remember forever. Beatrice Hamilton had died, alone.

Standing by her bed, numbed to the world outside this room, Jennifer peered at her mother's motionless body. Much like she had left her this morning, she appeared a woman sleeping, free of concern, free of pain.

Free of life.

The first rays of sunlight crept into the room, washing furniture in soft creamy gold. Rather than signal the dawn of a new day, it felt more like an intrusion. An illumination of loss. Jennifer hadn't been here.

The only solace she found was that her mother was back in the arms of her greatest love; Dr. Arthur Hamilton. Today they were reunited. It was something.

Something. Jennifer cupped her mom's hand. Saddened by the clammy chill to her skin, the finality it denoted, it was so unlike the woman herself; the one who scooped sunshine into a hug, wore stars in her eyes...

The woman whose smile could light up a room.

She closed her hand around the one she held and squeezed. But no more. It was over. A mother's love, a mother's counsel... They were gone.

Except in her heart, where she would savor them forever.

A heavy tear fell from Jennifer's eye, splattering atop their entwined hands. Beatrice Hamilton, mother to one, inspiration to all, would always remain in her heart.

Leaning down, she placed a kiss on her mom's forehead. Lingering, she breathed warmth into the delicate skin. Jennifer drew in her last scent of floral perfume, the one she dabbed on her mother's temples last evening.

Goodbye. I'll see you... We'll meet each other again.

Pulling herself back to a standing position, Jennifer heard the familiar whisper. Live, darling. Move on with your life.

The advice wrenched her face with pain. She knew it was the right thing to do. She knew there was no other choice.

Soft as an angel, firm as a chief, her mother would always watch over her. *Love, darling. Live.*

Be happy.

Jennifer nodded, tears streaming. Yes, she would try. The living she could manage. But the happiness...

It would take some time.

# # #

Thankful she had someplace to go, something to *do*, Jennifer scanned the charts lined in a row behind the nurses' desk. Jumping back into work made sense for her. Gave her purpose.

"Is this the chart you're looking for Dr. Hamilton?"

Jennifer eyed the name marked on the binder spine as the nurse neared. "Yes, that's it."

"Sorry," she said with an awkward smile. "Someone left it by the monitors."

"No problem." Taking the chart from the thin brunette, she carried it around to a vacant spot on the counter. Flipping it open, she zeroed in on the progress notes, quickly scanning through them. Dizzy spells, shortness of breath. She examined the attached copy of the Holter monitor. Documented episodes of ventricular arrhythmia. Jennifer ran through the list of his medications, making mental notes to vary dosages.

Work. Helping people—at least those she could—would see her through. It would also help distract her thoughts from Jax.

She wondered if she'd see him, today. Part of her wanted to, part of her didn't. Part of her knew it was inevitable.

Replacing the chart into the shelf file, she pulled the next one free. Part of her wanted to forget.

"Dr. Hamilton?"

Jennifer looked up from the chart. Standing beside her was a tall, distinguished-looking gentleman, with deep brown skin and jet black hair. He was a complete stranger to her, yet called her by name. A fellow physician, perhaps?

"Yes, I'm Dr. Hamilton."

His features relaxed into a smile. "I wanted to thank you for saving my wife's life."

"*I'm sorry?*" Jennifer allowed the chart to close on her hand.

"I was told you're the doctor responsible for her care. And that it was your expertise and quick actions that made the difference in her survival."

"I apologize," she said, drawing a complete blank—unusual for her, but under the circumstances, feasible. "You must have me mistaken for someone else."

"Bronson."

The name exploded through her conscious.

"Delaney Bronson. The young woman from this weekend. That was you, wasn't it?"

She balked. "Did you say she was your *wife?*"

"Yes." He extended a hand toward her. "I'm Pete Bronson."

"Why was Jax with her?"

With the queerest look in his eye, he ventured, "Um, because he's her brother?"

"*Her brother?*"

The man nodded, his expression one of mild embarrassment. He dropped his hand and placed it in a pocket. "Yes. I was out in California when she wasn't feeling well. The family has a history of heart problems, so she knew not to waste time when it became severe. She called him first thing. I jumped on the next flight out and arrived late last night."

"*Oh my God...*" She dropped her gaze to the chart in hand, the past twenty-four hours thrusting her mind back through time.

The frantic desperation she had witnessed in his eyes—the panic—*it was his sister*. Realization swallowed her whole. It made perfect sense. He must have been beside himself with fear.

"Is something wrong?"

She looked up to find Pete Bronson's face filled with concern. "No, I only..." she stumbled through her response, suppressing the urge to sit down, to run. The woman wasn't with Jax—she was this man's wife! Where she should have felt jubilation, she only felt sick.

Did that mean he was available?

He peered at her in expectation, shifting the gears of professionalism for her. "She was smart to have called him when she did."

"Yes, *very*."

"And you. Jax says you saved her life."

Her backpedal was swift. "Well... I didn't do anything any other competent physician wouldn't have done. It was the paramedics on the scene who really made the difference."

The man nodded. "He said you were modest." Then he smiled. "And that you were the best."

Embarrassment rose hot to her cheeks. Jennifer instinctively dodged his gaze, knowing full well her feelings would be splayed across her face. These were feelings she couldn't deny, emotions she couldn't conceal.

He grew serious and extended his hand again. "Thank you."

Taking his hand this time, she wondered at the close of his around hers, drawing her closer with a familiarity he should not feel. "I don't know what I would do without her. What we would do. We have four kids."

Doctors crowded near, phones rang. It was business as usual at the nurse's station. Business as usual—for everyone except her. It was all she could do not to hammer the man for information, but yes—she recalled something about children.

Jax had his fill with his sister's kids.

They must have been scared out of their wits to see their mother sent away in an ambulance! If Jax hadn't been there, if she hadn't called him in time...

The image of his sister dead on the floor with children as her witness scored a jagged gash through her heart. The family would be devastated. Thank God, Jax had been there. "I understand," she said, desperate to regain a more professional demeanor. She was the *doctor* here, not a family friend. She had to maintain perspective, control. "How's she feeling today?"

He laughed. "Like nothing ever happened. She's chomping at the bit to get back home, but I told her that wasn't a good idea. Besides, she should stay here where she can be waited on. It'll only be chaos after calamity at home."

"I bet that's all she wants right now," Jennifer said, a strange wistfulness taking hold.

"You're right." A fondness entered his eyes. "You must have kids of your own."

"No," she said, her voice quiet. "I don't."

"Well, you have a keen sense of my wife. She can't wait to get home. Hospitals have never been one of her favorite places."

"No." Jennifer was sure they weren't. Didn't Jax say the same of their mother? "But if she progresses as expected, she should be able to head home tomorrow."

"The doctor who stopped by this morning said as much. Nice guy," he said, a hint of question hovering in his tone as to why it hadn't been her checking in on his wife. "Delaney's already pressuring him for sooner rather than later."

Jennifer tried to smile. Her delegating responsibility for this particular patient to her partner was something this man couldn't have known. "Her cardiologist contacted me. He wants to keep her in to run some other tests—on account of her history, of course." She hated to raise any more flags for the family, but her physician wasn't doing anything she wouldn't do faced with the same situation. "I'll talk to him and see what we can do."

He grinned. "Thanks. We'd appreciate it."

She wanted to ask after Jax. She wanted to know if he was in the hospital. She wanted to know what the kiss meant, and where they were headed. She wanted to know if he was taken.

But didn't ask the first one. This wasn't the place. This wasn't the time. Let him deal with his sister first. Then she could—

Nerves jangled like bells of warning. Then maybe she could approach him. Tell him how she felt. Jennifer glanced at her watch. But first things first. She had patients waiting for her at the office and one more to see here. She needed to get moving. Excusing herself, she finished with her charts then headed for the exits. Any longer here, she may run into him.

Jennifer checked the text on her phone screen as she waited for the elevator. A family joined her, their conversation muffled, private. The chime rang, the doors slid open. She looked up and Michael Kingsley walked out.

"Oh!"

He smiled at the sight of her. "Hey, Jennifer."

"Hello, Michael," she said, stepping back, watching the doors slide to a close behind him. Dressed in full suit and tie, he was the consummate professional during work hours.

He placed a hand on her shoulder and asked, "How are you?"

"Fine." She tamped down a sudden swell of grief. "I'm getting through it."

"Do you need anything?"

"No." She looked around the hallway and said, "I think work is the best thing for me right now."

"It'll do you good." He rubbed her shoulder. "Get your mind off things."

"Yes."

"Laurencia's going to call you. She's got plate-loads of food going in the kitchen and plans to deliver it—whenever it works for your schedule, of course."

"Of course, yes." The spectacle of more food was the last thing she needed, but she understood it was a gesture meant to support. "That's sweet of her. Thank you."

"Did you hear about Beverly?"

She smiled, rolling into the more pleasant topic. "I did. They moved her out of CICU."

"Yeah, she's really doing great. Gus told me she's taking to her meds no problem."

"Her nurses told me she's eating well, too."

He nodded. "It's really great news."

She agreed. "I'm going to see her this after-noon."

"Bearing gifts, as usual."

She chuckled. Already had one picked out and sitting in the backseat of her car.

"Hey, did you see Jax?"

Jennifer quickly shook her head. She slid her hands into the front pockets of her lab coat and replied, "No, I haven't."

"He's upstairs with his sister. I just came from there."

She nodded.

"Sold his house."

Her heart stopped. "He did?"

"Yep. Got a pile of money for it, too."

Pulse thundering in her ears, she moved aside to make room for a rolling steel cart of food trays. The man commandeering it leaned over and pressed the button for the elevator.

"He's real excited."

Did that mean he would set sail soon? Leave on his journey and never look back? "I imagine so..."

How could she insert herself into his life so quickly? It would be awkward, strange—she'd only broken up with Aurelio a week ago! There was no time to take up with Jax. He was leaving.

Michael stepped forward and pulled her into a strong hug. "I gotta run, but call me if you need anything. Anything at all."

Hope fell away. Disappointment filtered through her limbs. Secure within Michael's embrace, Jennifer inhaled the scent of his cologne. Spicy, distinct, his was familiar. Comfortable. He didn't mention the wedding. Didn't ask if she had plans to postpone. Nothing. He only offered his unconditional support.

Grateful for the reprieve, she whispered, "Thank you, Michael." She squeezed him. "Thank you."

Elevator doors slid open. Eager to follow the steel cart as it slid inside, she pulled away.

Michael released easily and said, "Catch ya later."

"Goodbye." She waved him off and stepped into the elevator. Slipping to one side, she pressed the button for her floor. It lit up immediately. As the doors closed, she stared at the glowing circle. Jax's image appeared in her mind.

He's sold his house. *Now what was she going to do*?

Driving beneath the canopy of banyan, Jennifer couldn't get home soon enough. Deriving no joy from the ride through the Gables, she noticed none of the natural splendor of her neighborhood. The only bright spots in her day had been Sarah and Beverly.

Sarah had come to see her, accompanied by her daughter, and had been radiant. She felt great, had no pain, no complaints and said she owed it all to her doctor. Whatever miracle Jennifer had performed was working.

Even her daughter conceded the fact.

It had been the boost she needed. She was making a difference in the lives of her patients, helping people as she was meant to do. This was her calling. Like her mother, she was meant to be in the center of strife, saving lives, restoring futures.

They were the same. Isn't that what her mom said? Mother and daughter, their hearts thrived on the same satisfaction? But it was Beverly that moved her the most. Despite having undergone major surgery, the child emanated energy. When handed the plush yellow rabbit, a sister for Poppy, she was exuberance personified. From her curls to her smile, the only sight that gave Jennifer more pleasure was the pink hue to her skin.

Her life would not be cut short. She would make it.

She would live.

Slowing for the turn into her driveway, she pulled her car around the fountain and placed it into park. Splashing water surrounded by beautiful foliage, an oasis meant to relax—

Stressed. Because of him. Instead of plants and flowers, and the sparkle of water, she saw Jax. Everywhere she looked, she saw his hand, his touch. *Him*.

Jennifer ambled toward the house, her movements slow and heavy. She paused at the bird of paradise, drawing her fingers along the underside of waxy buds. She lingered over luscious shades of orange-red, a hint of blue as they burst forth in bloom. Admiring the masterpiece of Mother Nature, it occurred to her that this flower indeed resembled a bird. Proud as a peacock, it stood guard outside her courtyard, flaunting its bright plumage, warning passersby of its presence.

She smiled at the comparison. Like Jax, she was beginning to see more in plants than a simple array of leaves and blooms. Today she saw works of art, reflections of life, symbols meant to inspire.

Yes, today was different. Today she saw Jax in every plant, flower, and blade of grass. In the serenity of her fountains, the tranquility of her pool, he was there. Longing wound through her. This home would be a magical place to share a life to-gether...

With him. As it was, it was half his, anyway.

She dropped her hand from the flower. Jennifer filled her lungs with moist, warm air, and repressed the melancholy welling within. She had a funeral to plan. Accompanied by friends and distant relatives, she would pay her last respects to the woman she adored, say her final goodbyes to the woman who had been her everything. Though how one actually did that, Jennifer had no idea.

Chapter Thirty-Eight

Wading through her second glass of Cabernet, dressed in T-shirt and boxers, feet tucked beneath her legs, Jennifer sat alone. From the stereo, an earthy Flamenco swayed through the dim light, weaving its instruments through the room, coaxing her mind to let go.

Gaze fixed on the candle glowing from within the amber hurricane glass, she felt defeated. The news regarding the sale of Jax's home knocked the wind from her dreams. She had expected time. She had expected a chance.

Something. Anything.

Jennifer brought the rim of her wineglass to rest against her lips. She thought she had months before he sold his house. Even convinced herself she could do it. Make the first move and open the door. Life was short. Seize the moment.

With Sam, it all sounded so easy.

Jennifer loosened her focus from the soft flicker of candlelight. It could still be easy. If she were Sam, someone like her... If she were bold and direct, she could still do it. Time be damned, she could go after him.

The problem was her. Reserved, withheld, she was her biggest enemy. Pulling the glass from her mouth, she allowed the admission to settle deep in her chest. She was the problem.

The song's tempo slowed. Guitar strings were picked one by one as the delicate solo tiptoed through the room, like a secret. Suddenly a quick strum of lower chords thrust into the rhythm. Together, it was a rich harmony of emotion, a depiction of need... Jennifer could almost see the woman taking long, graceful strides as she moved across the moonlit path, the dance still in her but the drive to leave strong; urgent.

Another drum of chords, another pick of strings... It was a sexy rise and fall in rhythm, a sinuous quality of guitar sound creating a visual artistry in her mind.

Was it a lover? Was she called to see him? In the silk of moonlight, the secret of night, did *need* drive her?

Or had she been called back by obligation. Duty.

Jennifer's vision closed. Duty. For too long it had defined her life. It had tied her to schedule, limited her horizons. She cradled the glass in her lap. Sam was right. She needed to break free, go after what she wanted.

Jax. Go after him. With all the pain and loss and near death she witnessed, she of all people should understand the value of living.

She did. She did understand. And she wanted to live. Free and unencumbered, she wanted to experience everything life had to offer.

Taking a deep sip of wine, inhaling the smoky plum aroma as it filled the oversized crystal bowl encircling her nose, she decided. She would do it. Whatever it took, she would try.

The sound of tapping against her door stopped her cold.

"What the—" She yanked the glass from her face. Heart pounding, thoughts colliding, she suddenly remembered: *Sam*.

Sam was coming by. She called earlier to forewarn she'd be making her nightly rounds. Setting her wineglass on the coffee table, she breathed in to catch her breath, then lifted from the sofa and headed for the door. She grasped the handle and opened. "Lost your key at—"

"Hi, Jennifer." Jax stood on her doorstep, a slip of a smile in his eyes.

She couldn't speak, couldn't move—except for the race of her heart.

"I hope it's not too late."

"I don't understand," she stammered, instantly crossing arms over braless chest in a stark rush of embarrassment. She hadn't been expecting company. He on the other hand, appeared freshly showered and shaved in T-shirt and jeans. "What time is it—what are you doing here?"

"I was hoping we could talk." His voice was satin soft, his eyes windows of emotion.

Sanity scrambled for cover as she stared, speechless.

"May I come in?"

Jittery legs backed aside, giving him silent permission to enter.

Jax closed the door behind him.

"I was just—would you like a glass—"

"Jennifer." He reached out and tugged a hand from the locked grip of her arms.

Resistance melted.   When he reached for the other and secured the shaky hand within his own, her surrender was complete. She couldn't move a muscle if she tried.

"I hope you don't mind my coming here.   If you'd rather be alone, I'll make it short."

That was the last thing she wanted! "No," she blurted, scared he would leave. "It's okay." It's more than okay. *It's amazing...*

"I'm sorry about your mom."

She nodded.

"And I'm sorry about Aurelio."

The admission stopped her heart.

"Sam told me you broke the engagement."   He paused, his eyes hovering as he seemed prepared to meet protest.

But Jennifer offered none. She couldn't.

She had none in her.

"I can only hope you believe me when I say I am truly sorry it happened."

What? If he was sorry to hear about her breakup, then why was he here?

"I don't wish that sentence on anyone."

Jennifer swallowed, the lump in her throat hard and sore. He was being nice. But she needed answers. "Why are you here, Jax?"

"You."

With arms that felt like straw, she pulled free from his grip and moved away, putting space between them. She needed to be clear. She needed to understand. Willing her arms to regain strength, she crossed them again.

Jax held steady. "I'm here because of you."

"What does that mean?" she implored, and took a step back. She desperately wanted it to mean what she wanted it to mean—but she kept her mind on guard. Suddenly, she needed him to make the first move.

"These last few weeks have changed things for me."

What kind of things! Tell me!

"Over the course of this project," his eyes wandered to the back windows, waded into the darkness of night. "My priorities have shifted." His face was soft, open. He spoke in supple tones. "Cruising the islands doesn't seem so important anymore." He returned his gaze to Jennifer. "Having family close... That's what's important to me."

This was about his sister. Delaney's experience had scared him. He was reaching out. To a friend. Someone who could sympathize, help make sense of it all. "I understand," Jennifer said, quick to cap the well of disappointment overflowing in her heart. "Life can be a delicate balance," the doctor in her replied, hating the lovesick fool inside coming to blows with reality. But Jax had been there for her and she was going to be there for him.

No matter how much it hurt. Holding her arms close to the breast, she continued. "It's about finding the right mix of living for today, for yourself, and spending time with your loved ones. The challenge is in the not knowing," she ran on, grasping for the comfort she usually found in consoling people in difficult times. "You never know if death might be waiting around the next corner—for you, for *them*."

The blade cut deeper. "I know you don't want to squander your time with family, Jax, but you can't stifle your own dreams, either."

Jax took a step toward her.

Her antennae shot up. Alarms sounded.

"You're right. But I learned there's something even more important."

Her breathing became shallow, her ears razor sharp.

"Love."

With that one word, he closed the distance between them to mere feet. Her breath came in spurts, her senses on fire.

"I want a love of my own. *A woman of my own*." He ventured closer. "And over the last several weeks I've gotten to know a very special woman. One with a heart of gold, a will of steel." A smile tugged at the corner of his mouth. "She's honest and forthright and *beautiful*. The most beautiful woman I've ever met. From the inside out."

His eyes never moved from hers. His voice never wavered. "She's a better friend than I could ever ask for, always willing to listen, and lend her support. All you have to do is call. She'll come running."

He stilled.

She could smell his cologne, his fresh masculine scent as it filled the space around her.

"But there's one problem."

Jennifer gulped down a blistering knot of anticipation. All breathing ceased, her limbs a rubbery nothing.

"She's smarter than I am." He moved a little nearer. "She has more degrees than I have clues." He tried to grin, but abandoned the attempt. Instead, he turned somber. "I'm afraid she won't have me..." He paused. "Because I don't measure up." His eyes mellowed to a creamy daze. "Which is unfortunate."

He lifted a hand to her cheek, caressed the skin with the back of his fingers, a palpable longing hanging in his eyes. "Because I've fallen in love with her."

The declaration was but a whisper, yet swept the legs clear out from under her. *Jackson wanted her.* Warmth flared low in her belly. *He wanted her.*

Running his fingers under the curve of her chin, he drew one forward. "Could there be a chance?"

Chapter Thirty-Nine

The tremor in his voice roused a need deep within. It was real. No longer limited to the fantasy of her mind, he wanted her.

Exploring a future with him would be a risk. A big one.

And she could lose. But she needed this man. Beyond explanation, beyond sensibility, this connection had to be investigated. "Yes," Jennifer murmured, arms unwinding in a slow slide down her body.

"*Yes*?"

The shackles of self-discipline hit the floor. The last wisp of fear took flight. She was crossing the line of no return. If she consented, her life would never be the same. "Yes," she responded softly. "We have a chance."

"You won't regret it," he said in a powerful whisper. He tipped her chin upward and her heart hammered in expectation.

She knew what came next and she was ready.

Jax brought his lips to hers and feathered them back and forth. Mesmerized by the intensity of his touch, the sensation of his lips as they glided across hers, she closed her eyes. His lips were tender yet laden with want. He grazed his nose against hers, trailed it faintly along her cheek—as if he were savoring her skin, her every inch—and rested it near her ear.

The music came into sharp focus. Bold and romantic, the gypsy-inspired melody evoked an urge to move, to feel...

To let go. Sam's words wound quietly through her conscious as the tempo kicked up, the guitar pulsating through her veins.

Feel your way through life... Let yourself be courted by desire. Yes. It was something she wanted to do. Now, with him.

Jennifer opened her eyes and through the quiet glow of her living room confessed, "I've been so afraid."

A startled surprise crept into his eyes. "Of me?"

She nodded. "Of you, of us, of what it would mean."

"You have nothing to be afraid of. I won't ever hurt you."

His fierce refute made her chuckle. The thought of Jax hurting her was absurd.

"Something funny?"

She peered into his eyes and realized no, this wasn't funny. It was serious. "No. Jax...I only meant..." Jump in. Dive in, heart first. It was time. Jennifer took a deep breath and said, "I've been afraid for far too long. Of myself, of my desires... I didn't know what I truly needed." Jennifer paused, then smiled. "Until you showed up and everything I thought I knew was turned upside down."

He smiled and slid his arms around her.

Body to body, his embrace felt right. "I mean it, Jax. I had no idea a man like you would be right for me. It never occurred to me to even consider someone like you."

"Looks can be deceiving," he replied, delivered without the slightest hint of wound at her insult.

"I know, but—" Admitting she had judged him so harshly, hurt. A lot. After all, he was the last person to deserve it. She deserved it more.

Jennifer glanced down at his chest. Outlined beneath his T-shirt was a mound of muscle, a reminder of his solid build. No, she had never considered dating a rugged man, a man who made his living with the power of his back.

But she couldn't deny her attraction, or her need to be held by him, though only weeks before she had cringed at the very same thought. Jax was a laborer. Unsophisticated.

A drifter.

She brushed old thoughts from her mind. So close, so near, this was no place for shame, or regret. This was about new beginnings. It was time to move on, forward.

Within the soft strength of his arms, she brought her face back to his. Swaying and building, the music reached inside her. Warmed by the candlelight, it streamed through her body, unlocking the last of inhibition. "I love you, Jax. Whatever that looks like, I love you."

Naked desire blazed in his eyes. He grasped her head with both hands and crushed his mouth to hers. Reaching around his waist, she pulled herself against him. Yes, yes. Parting her lips, she gave in to desire. When his tongue slipped inside, seeking, searching, she pulled him closer. Whatever he wanted, she wanted. The deck of Constantine's yacht materialized in her mind. He was a man to whom she had given herself fully; a combination of raw lust and warm affection never since matched.

Jax's mouth pulled her back to the present. Greedy, demanding, his need swelled between them.

Until now, that is. Tonight, she would match it and then some.

He pulled away. Brown eyes hot and hungry on hers, he murmured, "I want you, Jennifer."

The words seared into her, deep. Permanent.

"*Right now*, I want you."

A nod of her head sent his mouth to her neck. His tongue moved lower, quickly, his hand covered a breast. Jennifer groaned with pleasure as he gently squeezed it through the flimsy cotton fabric. Fluid desire surged hot between her legs.

Without warning, he returned his lips to hers. Slowing the motion of his kiss, his breath warm against her lips, he slipped a hand under her shirt and caressed the delicate skin of her breast, rubbing feather-light circles around the tight fleshy point.

The sensation was incredible—but unnerving— as though it was the first time, thrilling and new. She felt off-balance, yet fully engaged. She was scared and excited and impatient for more.

Jax withdrew his hands and placed them solid on her shoulders. Secure in his grasp she stared into his eyes, eyes she was getting comfortable staring into. It looked as though he were about to say something, but he remained silent.

For a moment, neither made a move. Gazes locked, a torrent of emotion passed between them. Both were where they wanted to be and with whom. Both knew what came next and both wanted it.

His eyes moved to her lips, skimmed her jaw line, where his fingers followed suit. "You're so beautiful," he murmured, gently sliding a hand down to the hollow of her neck. "And incredible. I was beginning to believe you didn't exist."

Her lips curled into a slow smile.

"I've never wanted anyone like I want you right now."

Pleasure enveloped her. "I feel the same."

He smiled and scooped her into his arms, the transfer of weight effortless. Without hesitation, he walked to her bedroom. There wouldn't be any objection.

Crossing the threshold, he kissed the side of her mouth, and she couldn't help but feel a sense of familiarity. Of experience. As though what was about to transpire was the most natural course of events.

Easing her down onto the bed, Jennifer laid back and welcomed him alongside her with a kiss that erased time. No more questions, no more doubt. This was meant to be.

She didn't know how long they remained in the embrace, entwined in the kiss that didn't seem to end, but she did remember his hands as they slipped off her shirt, and the titillating arousal she felt at the newness of being revealed.

As with Constantine, she was excited by the exposure, turned-on by the liberty he took with his possession. Moving to remove her shorts, Jax led the way with his tongue. Helping him disrobe, she marveled at his build, the sinewy muscles she had admired from afar, the fair skin of his stomach so different from the tan of his face.

Running her hands along the ridges and valleys, she guided his body onto hers, flesh against flesh, immersed in satisfaction as the two came together as one.

When he returned his face to hers, Jennifer's fingers sought the nick by his eye. Constantine. Lulled by the slow and gentle sway of his body, she caressed the tiny gnarl of skin and recalled the images from her dreams, the feeling of lack when she awoke. There would be no more.

Jax paused, a question in his eyes.

She smiled. He had no way of knowing how much she had wanted to find a man like him, like Constantine, the kind that could move her body to distraction, caress her heart with love.

Only she knew. She would follow him anywhere, God help her, wherever that may lead. No plans, no goals, without reservation—even if it landed her on the deck of a boat in the middle of nowhere, surrounded by nothing but sparkling blue-green water. Kissing the spot beneath her fingers, she lingered. Maybe life really was an extension of the mind, dreams a bridge from the soul, the path to discovery.

Perhaps they were messages; signs from the powerful subconscious to direct one along the path to finding their true desire. Had hers whispered, Stop. Take note. Dig beneath the surface and see what you find.

Yes. Jennifer felt certain to the core of her center. Jackson Montgomery was the man of her dreams.

# # #

Amidst crumpled sheets, Jennifer rested in the folds of Jax's arms, at ease against his naked body. She had opened her patio doors, inviting the sounds of dawn to prance around her bedroom. Not yet humid, the temperature was comfortable as a range of chirps and calls filled the space around them.

Last night changed something inside her. Fluent in the wants of a woman, Jax was a generous lover. But more than physical union, he had committed. With the sensitive character she had come to know, he offered his heart without attachments, without expectation. He assured her there would be no demands, no expectations and then, with the smile that rivaled the sun, he predicted they would walk hand in hand, swim side by side, until they were old and gray.

He was sure of it.

Warmed by the image his unflappable optimism presented, she could hardly disagree. And from deep within her heart, an understanding emerged; the decision was theirs. To have and to hold, for better or worse, they would face the ups, the downs, and they would do so, together.

And children. A wave of excitement rolled through her belly like a flock of birds lifting for takeoff. Jax wanted children—*as many as she could stand*—for whom he intended to be a hands-on dad. Jennifer turned her head up and pecked the underside of his chin with a kiss.

"What was that for?" he asked in a lazy tone, his hair an endearing mess of tangles.

"Just because."

He hummed against her ear, and ran his hand along her thigh. Responding to his touch, she covered his hand with her own. From the outside looking in, we may be different, she mused. But on the inside...

On the inside we hold the key to love.

Jennifer's mind drifted, her gaze meandering about the backyard. Bursting with color, flowers burgeoning with life, her mother had been pleased. It was everything she wanted for her daughter and more.

Beatrice Hamilton wanted love for her child, not a ceremony. She wanted a life filled with happiness. Had she known Jax would be the one? Her subtle comments, the spark in her eyes. Could she have predicted this outcome?

Jennifer's smile returned in gentle recognition of her mother's wisdom. She was an amazing woman. The birds outside seemed to agree, increasing the volume of their song, one fluttering to a landing on the bird house right outside her bedroom. Darting pecks, a sudden flap of wings, the bird took flight and a second took its place.

A Cardinal. Red, gallant, he was magnificent. Perfect in every way. As was the birdhouse, as was her garden. More than a gift from the heart, more than a beautiful backdrop for a wedding, they were heaven on earth. And they were hers.

# # #

Standing shoulder to shoulder with her best friend, Jennifer peered down at her parents' adjoining headstones, the first mist of winter nipping at her skin. The two women were alone in the cemetery, the hour early, but it was Jennifer's favorite time to visit.

Through the quiet of dawn, she would talk to her parents, certain they could hear. Amidst the chirps and waking sun, she would share her life, her latest adventures.

Numerous, now that Jax was in her life.

But today was about the upcoming nuptials. She wanted to be with them and share this momentous occasion in her life. Arthur and Beatrice Hamilton, may they rest in love, would miss her wedding day. Her father would not walk her down the aisle, her mother would not cry in joy.

A tear poked at the corner of her eye. It would be the most important day in her adult life and they would be absent. Absent physically, but not emotionally. She had learned over the last months that love crossed lifetimes. It didn't accept the boundary of the physical plane, the limits of physical thought. Jennifer understood now. Love endured. It persisted. Each and every day she felt her mother's love as strong as when she was alive. And better yet, she had opened the connection to her father. Jax had opened the connection.

Sam squeezed Jennifer to her side. "I'm proud of you. You set your sights on something and went for it."

"That's nothing new," she replied, not quite understanding, her attention divided.

Sam chuckled. "*True*. But tangible goals like diplomas and jobs are easy. With those, you know if you begin with a-b-c, you'll eventually reach x-y-z."

Jennifer lifted her head and turned to Sam, tugging her focus to the present. "What on earth are you talking about?"

Sam grinned. "I'm talking about love."

Jennifer arched her brow.

"It's unpredictable. It's inexplicable. You can run the entire alphabet of love, memorize it backward and forward and still end up with nothing. Yet you still tried, and *that's* why I'm proud of you."

Tears filled Jennifer's eyes. She wanted her mom to be proud of her. She wanted her dad to be proud of her. But Sam... A lump lodged in her throat.

"Going part-time with your practice took a lot of guts, but I think you did the right thing."

"Shouldn't we see if I'm seaworthy, first?" Jennifer asked, an attempt to lighten the moment.

Sam laughed. "You'll do fine. Jax will see to that! I have a lot of faith in the man. He'll take care of you." Her expression calmed. "You're going to help a lot of people, Jen, and you're going to have fun in the process. That's an impressive combination in my book."

Butterflies swarmed in anticipation. For their honeymoon, she and Jax were sailing to the Bahamas in their first official capacity for a Florida-based organization whose mission it was—through training and technical assistance—to improve environmental, social and economical conditions throughout the Caribbean. She was going as volunteer physician and Jax as agricultural specialist. It was an adventure they were excited to begin and one for which her partners had given their blessing.

Portside, island-hopping, she was a physician either way. And one they didn't want to lose. They agreed to hold her position within the firm so she could practice when she found herself land-side.

Jennifer settled her gaze on Sam. And if it wasn't for her bull-headed, interfering, know-it-all best friend, she wouldn't be looking forward to *any* of it. She smiled, allowing the tears to spill onto her cheeks. "I love you, Sam."

With her arm draped around Jennifer's shoulders, she kissed the side of her head. "I love you, too."

# # #

About the Author:

Dianne Venetta lives in Central Florida with her husband, two children and part-time Yellow Lab Cody-boy! An avid gardener, she spends her spare time growing organic vegetables, surprised by what she finds there every day. Who knew there were so many amazing similarities between men and plants? Women, life and love and her discoveries provide for never-ending fun on her blog: BloominThyme.com.

Look for Dianne Venetta's next novel:
LUST ON THE ROCKS

She has what he needs, and he won't stop until he gets it. Trouble is, what begins as a matter of death, becomes a matter of life.

# # #

One case away from partnership, Samantha Rawlings is forced to share her high-profile case with a sexy younger man, whose eyes are on a different prize. In the best interests of her client, Sam opens the door to his strategy. Turns out, a little too far...

Victor Marin has ulterior motives. The defendant in her case holds the key to his revenge, and his last chance for justice. But as he chases old demons, he uncovers a powerful woman with no inhibitions, one he wants to possess for himself. But decidedly single, Sam wants no part.

Until Vic walks away.

Excerpt from Lust on the Rocks

Chapter One

"I want you to consider Victor Marin for the Perry case."

Samantha Rawlings stiffened, without altering her seated position, forced her fingers to finish removing the dark fuzz of lint from her cream linen skirt. With cool precision, she settled both arms along the wide fabric armrests of her chair and locked onto her boss, Raul Martinez. "Not necessary, Raul. It's covered."

"He has experience in the area."

"As do I," Sam replied, wondering why he would suggest involving a new hire on the firm's powerhouse complaint. He may be the senior partner, and he may have authority, but this was *her* case.

"I'm merely suggesting you take advantage of his insight. It may prove fruitful to your case."

"I'm always willing to listen."

Raul's dark brown eyes registered the deflection. "But not inclined to include him for trial?"

The Perry Fitness case was hers, and there was no room for the new guy to work it with her. She might want to get close to Victor, but only in the most *personal* of terms.   Her business affairs were something else entirely.

"Victor won a substantial settlement from a casino out of New Jersey. One of their patrons died on the premises." He paused. "From sudden cardiac death."

Sam shifted her weight and fought a rising tide of misgiving. The chair at her back felt hot. Heart attacks were not rare occurrences. People collapsed in all sorts of places unfortunately, casinos not-withstanding. "I'm well versed in the arena, Raul, from the statistics to the complications and I've already consulted Diego on the case."   Diego Rodriguez was her in-house ally and extremely skilled in trial work. "We're still working up the history now, but if Perry has been found culpable before, as I suspect, it's going to cost them." Cutting corners to boost profits shouldn't come at the expense of people's lives.

Not in her courtroom.

Raul interlaced his fingers and set them to rest on a manila folder. Despite the steam of summer, his formality seldom changed. From his cufflinks to the perfectly formed knot in his silk tie, the man reigned supreme over Baker, Schofield, Martinez and Brown in both title and appearance. A full head of gray hair and expensive cut only accentuated his vitality.

"I know you and Diego work well together, but he's heavily involved in the Esposito trial. You may need the extra hand."

"Diego says that'll be wrapped up within the month."

Curiosity churned in Raul's eyes like a storm on the horizon. "Is there a problem, Sam? I was under the impression you were pleased with Victor's performance."

"I am. He's sharp, aggressive, and I think he'll make a great lawyer someday."

Raul's brow raised in question.

Sam pulled her top leg in, braced her body against the chair and leaned forward. "While I'm always willing to help show the new hires how it's done, I want to nail this one, Raul. It's an important case and likely to be precedent-setting. I can't be distracted by training the new guy—not on this one."

"I see."

"Besides, my understanding is that as soon as we tie up Morgan-Baxter, Vic's digging into an HMO case. Vic doesn't have time to work Perry with me." Nor the experience, but voicing that would only insult Raul.

"I'm not asking you to recuse yourself. Simply bring him up to speed and consider what he has to say. Listen to him. Allow him to assist you with discovery, pre-trial motions, sit alongside you in court when the time comes."

Alarms started to sound. Was Raul out of his mind? She needed no assistance. *Where was this coming from*?

"It's worth a listen. His experience could prove invaluable."

She heard a distinct retreat in Raul's voice.

Good. Sam pulled back into her chair and relaxed her demeanor. The air-conditioner kicked on, her tension eased. "I appreciate the advice Raul, and

I'll take it into consideration. I'll talk to him. But I reserve the right to try this case my way."

He smiled. "As always."

Though he had given in, Sam didn't like the note of victory she detected in his voice. It meant the discussion wasn't over. "Listen, if it's all right with you," she rose from her chair. "I need to get back to work."

"Of course."

Taking no comfort in the concession, her mind launched into high gear. Something was going on around here. Like a pirate too close to the plank, she knew something was lurking beneath the surface. *But what?*

Good sense evaporated. "Raul, is there something—"

"Yes?" he asked with soft expectation.

The glimpse of premeditation staring back at her sent Sam's body shock-still. His tone was too cool, too deliberate. There was more to this—more than his pretense of helpful unity among associates, the man had an agenda.

She held his gaze. "Nothing, Raul."

He pulled his hands from the ebony desktop and set them on the smooth leather armrests of his chair. His smile was nothing if not gracious, accommodating, befitting that of a patriarch. "If you're sure."

Sam wasn't sure about anything at the moment. But she knew how to avoid a trap. "I'm sure."

"Very well."

Without another word, Raul waited for her to make her exit. No more arguments, no more questions, he was giving her lead time. For what, she didn't have a clue, but experience taught that he'd be back.

As Sam headed back to her office, speculation consumed her. Had Diego miscalculated? Was that what bothered her? Or was she ornery, because Raul had interfered with her caseload. Veered into her lane like oncoming traffic, blind-siding her with a full blast of headlights.

Passing her secretary with an absent nod, Sam strode into her office and rounded the corner of her desk. She stopped short. Unable to indulge in her prized view of Biscayne Bay, glittering like a sheet of diamonds out the thirty-first floor windows, suspicion gnawed. Something wasn't right. She shuffled through a stack of new phone messages, interested by none.

Maria Jimenez breezed into her office, the tight maroon skirt wrapped around her hourglass hips moving with unbelievable ease, she carried a stack of files hugged close to her chest. "What's the matter with you?"

"Nothing." Ditching the pink sheets of paper, Sam glanced about the office. Regal blue lampshades and plush navy carpeting, diplomas organized on her wall, it looked like any other in the firm.

Maria dropped the folders onto the edge of the desk. "These are the files you requested."

"Thanks." Whipping a hand to her hip, Sam asked, "What's up with Diego's schedule? I thought he and Stevens were almost finished, but Raul says they're still deep in it."

"I don't know." Saucy eyes sharpened and her Spanish accent thickened. "You want me to find out?"

Sam shook her head. "Don't worry about it." She wasn't sure what she wanted or from whom. No sense sending Maria out unarmed.

"So what did Raul want?"

She looked at Maria, the question crystallizing in her brain. What did he want? Was he setting her up? Did he have an agenda? Sam's gaze wandered to the red leather chaise sequestered in the corner. A bit loud and far outside the dignified image Raul was cultivating for the firm, it was the only piece of décor in her office that hinted to the woman within.

She insisted it gave fire to her thought process and was largely responsible for her wins. Who could argue with such logic? Certainly not Raul, so he allowed the one item to stay.

Why was he challenging her now?

"Never mind. None of my business," Maria murmured, but her black eyes blazed the third degree.

"Actually," Sam sighed. "I have no idea." Had he wanted to revoke confidence with her performance? Express disapproval at her budding interest in Vic? He frowned upon office relationships, but usually allowed her wiggle room on the subject. But pushing another associate on her, overriding her authority...

It wasn't his style.

"You think it's good news or bad?"

Misgiving pinched her chest. Sam couldn't answer that one. "You tell me," she pitched back. "He wants Vic to assist on the Perry case."

"*What*? Why would he want to do something crazy like that?" she whipped back.

"My question exactly."

"Is it Diego's schedule?" She packed on a matter-of-fact attitude and waved a finger through the air, gold bangles jingling. "I'll call Suzette right now. She'll tell me what's going on over there in *two* seconds."

Sam surrendered to a small smile. Maria; her paralegal-secretary-extraordinaire. The woman was a pint of sass packed into a Latin man's voluptuous fantasy: long black hair and big brown eyes, full pouty lips and enough makeup to make a cosmetician swoon. Damn sharp when it came to following instructions though, making Maria the best assistant since Moses. And indispensable. No doubt she would plunder the information in no time if asked. "Don't bother, Mare. I'll ask him myself."

"You sure?"

"I'm sure." Sam dropped to her chair, careful not to disturb the neat stacks of paper she had arranged on her desk in the form of a triangle. She was visual and these piles represented the three litigants in her current case. Details she needed to close for the conference call she was about to make. When the lies took wing, she intended to swat them like flies, pulling facts and figures from the sheets at her fingertips.

Sam pulled a business card from the top pile and handed it to Maria. "Get these guys on the phone for me, will you? They're expecting my call."

"You got it."

"Beep in when you're ready."

"Yes Ma'am."

As Maria exited the office, Sam began formulating her plan of attack—at present, aimed at securing her settlement. Soon enough, she'd target

Raul's sudden generosity *and* his chosen benefactor. Taking her place among the elite group of women perched high atop their male-dominated fields was the crown of her achievements and she wasn't about to jeopardize it. Not for anything or anyone.

Sam stilled.

Wait a minute. Maybe Raul's suggestion for including Vic on the Perry case was a test. She looked up from her notes. Her mind slashed through the possibilities. Maybe he wanted her to do more than consult him on strategy. Maybe Raul wanted to see how she handled the role of mentor to a junior associate. Speculation mounted as pressure built inside her. Senior partners carried out the task every day, right? Makes sense they'd want to see how she'd do before they granted her full partnership.

Her breathing paused. Sam squeezed her eyes shut. Shit.

Did she screw up?

Chapter Two

"I told you!" the elderly woman cried from the stand. "I set up no such meeting between the two of them!"

Victor Marin leaned over the partition. "That's not what your phone log says. It says you made several calls to the Senator in the weeks leading up to the transfer of funds and several the day of. Two of them were to his cell phone."

"It was fundraising!" Delicate cheeks flushed bright red within a frame of perfectly-coiffed silver hair. Like a trapped animal, she sought the judge, counsel, anyone who could help rescue her from the jaws of interrogation.

Samantha Rawlings' focus shot to the jury, taking satisfaction in how deeply engaged they were in the process. Each and every one of them sat riveted upon Vic's every move. Throughout the entire proceedings, it seemed they couldn't get enough of him.

She savored a private smile. An allure she understood all too well. Pushing six-four, he had a striking presence. Not only his size, it was also his eyes. Almost black, yet lit by sparks of fire. Factor in his short-cropped hair, sharp-featured nose, and the chiseled edge of his jaw line and Vic reminded her of a bird.

A falcon. Yes, she thought, pressing the tip of her sleek silver pen into the yellow note pad spread open before her. If he were an animal, he would be a bird of prey. Struck by the assessment, Sam felt an odd alliance with the jury. One couldn't help being drawn to him. Wary, but mesmerized.

Another smile pulled at her.

Definitely mesmerized.

Vic hovered closer to the witness and scowled. "You're lying."

Petite within the confines of the witness stand, Morgan's secretary recoiled, but Vic wasn't buying her lamb-on-the-butcher-block routine. "Covering for Morgan can send you to jail," he said. "For years."

The gavel slammed the room into silence.

"Enough!" Judge Chavez flashed an angry look to the twelve men and women seated to his left, a gust of speculation blowing across the packed courtroom.

Vic grazed her with warning, "It's a favor he wouldn't return."

"The jury will disregard the defense's last statements," Chavez said to them, then swung his wrath toward Vic. "Not another word, counselor."

Sam was on her feet. "Your Honor, may I approach the bench?"

A muffled wave of whispers rippled through the gallery behind them, packed full today because this case had been feeding the front pages for weeks. Hijacking an employee pension fund was bad enough, but a senator?

Vic cast a glance toward her in an appeal for support, but her glare told him to back off. She had seniority here and he'd better respect it.

Judge Chavez approved her request with a nod of his head, but just over his reading glasses, his cold gaze burned a path straight for Vic.

Sam strode over to the elevated perch which towered over the federal courtroom, Vic close on her heels. Chavez's black eyes were popping mad, his lips set in a hard line. Even the brown of his skin seemed to redden with fury.

Damn, she mused. Vic did have an effect, didn't he?

Opposing counsel joined them.

"Your Honor," Sam controlled her tone as she eased into her appeal. "First let me apologize for my associate's egregious violation of your courtroom. I assure you it won't happen again."

Chavez cupped a hand over the microphone and leaned forward. "You're damn right it won't."

"Your Honor," Vic interjected. "The witness is holding back."

"Another word from you," Chavez growled, "and I'll have your butt hauled out of my courtroom by force." Then he addressed Sam. "He's finished here. I want him out."

The air in the courtroom grew thick with speculation, silently clinging to her backside.

But she wasn't bothered. She had been here before and enjoyed the pressure. It meant people were paying attention. Sam turned somber and leaned in. "I understand, Your Honor. I'll take it from here." She paused, tempering the charge of battle coursing between them. "But if I may be so forward as to ask your permission that he stay on as an observer?"

Vic opened his mouth to reply, but Sam clamped a hand on his forearm.

Chavez balked. "*What*?"

"He's a good attorney, your Honor, just a bit overzealous at times."

"Overzealous is an understatement, Sam." His gaze hardened behind the black rim of his glasses. "Even a first-year law student knows not to harass the witness."

Sam lifted her shoulders in an attempt at forgiveness. "He got carried away?"

"You're much too generous on his behalf." Judge Chavez allowed a small smile for her benefit, then cut back to Vic. "As for you. You, young man, are severely lacking in good judgment. Harassing an old woman on the stand not only injures the dignity of my courtroom, but it breeds contempt for our entire system of justice."

One of the attorneys next to them chuckled under his breath. Which had to grate on him, Sam thought. But to Vic's credit, he remained immobile. And in control, she noted, with another rush of satisfaction. The man *is* good.

"Don't play guessing games on my time," Chavez belabored. "You have questions, you ask them. Can't get a witness to answer? Get smarter."

Vic bristled, but pasted a smile on his face. "Yes sir."

"Very well," Chavez said. With his look of distaste securely intact, he held Vic in his scope for several seconds more before returning to Sam. "Maybe he can learn something from watching a seasoned professional such as yourself."

Sam smiled, warm and personal. "I appreciate it, Your Honor. And I promise, you won't hear another word from him today."

"Let's hope not." The judge sat back, spitting out a round of nasty condescension, "Or he will find himself a guest of the state hotel."

With that, the group of attorneys returned to their respective tables while murmurs fluttered back to life in the room behind them.

"Sam—"

"Your Honor," she started, plowing right over Vic's quiet plea. "If it pleases the court, I have no further questions for this witness."

"Sam," Vic whispered harshly. "You can't let her walk!"

But she ignored him.

Judge Chavez spoke to the witness. "You may be excused."

Like a timid kitten, the secretary fled the chair in the witness box. Refusing eye contact with Sam and Vic, she clutched a shiny black purse to her chest and hurried up the aisle to a set of double-doors leading out into the hallway.

In her case, the hallway to freedom.

The judge gave two rapid smacks of his gavel. "One hour recess for lunch." He pushed himself up from his seat. "*If* I can rally my appetite," he grumbled aloud.

Everyone rose as the judge exited through a side door, the jurors followed, filing out through another.

"What the hell was that about?" demanded their client as he jumped up from his seat. "You trying to mangle this case more than it already is?"

But Sam didn't flinch. "Nothing more than courtroom antics." She gathered her files and began to shove them into her briefcase. Behind her, the commotion of mass exodus began as reporters raced to file their stories, others more eager to report the lurid gossip.

"What the hell were you doing?" he railed into Vic. "I *told* you she wouldn't break."

"She's been the executive secretary at Morgan-Baxter for twenty years," Sam cut in. "We had to try."

"Try, hell—you fumbled the goddamn cross-examination!"

Vic stepped forward to defend himself, but the man's finger landed in his face. "If you screwed this case I'll have your ass in a canister, you hear me?"

Something inside him clicked.

Around him, people were shuffling about, stacking papers, making phone calls, the bedlam of a courtroom as it emptied, but Vic held steady.

Then there was Sam, staring at him. He could feel her scrutiny. Hovering like a helicopter over a hostage scene, she was waiting for him to lose his temper and tear into the client.

"I've got a lot of money invested in this suit and if you've blown it..." The man's neck vein seemed about to burst through his skin, his anger was palpable. "You're *done*. You hear me? Done."

Sam lifted a hand to cease the man's tirade. "Enough. Morgan-Baxter knows nothing about where we're headed. When the trial resumes, we go in for the kill. I'm calling Dave Brenner to the stand, first thing."

The corporate bag of wind deflated. "Dave?"

"Dave," she repeated the name. "He's the key to the whole case and I intend to rip him open when we return. Once I fill my belly." She winked. "Snake meat tends to curdle on an empty stomach." Stuffing the last of the folders into her case, Sam slung the long leather strap over her shoulder. Looking to the men, she asked, "Anyone care to join me?"

"I've got phone calls to make," her client replied, then plowed into the sea of bodies making an exit out the back.

Sam turned to Vic. "How about you?"

"Fine."

# # #

Sam's choice of restaurants was located just around the corner from the courthouse. On a humid day the walk was unbearable, but this morning it wasn't too bad, thanks to the breeze whisking in off Biscayne Bay. It tamed the vicious heat rising from the sidewalks, but did nothing to alleviate the sweat climbing up the back of his neck. Vic sighed. But this was Miami, the tropical moisture something you tolerated.

Suit coat folded over his arm, Vic opened the door to Finkle's Deli and Sam waltzed inside ahead of him. Baskets overloaded with fresh-baked bread lined the top of the display case, the rich aroma of coffee and grilled meat saturated the air.

Sam paused. "Save room for the Key Lime Fantasy Fest."

"No thanks. Not a fan of sweets."

"Me neither, but that baby is pure fantasy when it comes to desserts."

"Whatever."

"What'll it be?" asked a heavyset man behind the counter.

"Reuben," Sam responded.

"Make it two."

"You's got it."

Hearing the tough, northeast accent reminded Vic of Philly. So much, that eyes closed, he could have sworn he walked indoors from any street corner back home, ready to order up one of the city's finest.

Sam plucked a plastic tray from the stack and reached for a glass. "Water?"

"Fine," he replied, returning his attention to the counter. Too bad he wasn't hungry. After his court-room fiasco, food was the last thing on Vic's mind.

At the soda fountain Sam filled two glasses, placed them on her tray then pushed it along metal rails, stopping before a young cashier. Vic followed behind and yanked the wallet from his back pocket and flipped it open. "How much?"

Sam eyed the twenty in his hand. "Don't worry. I got it."

"Take it." He shoved the money toward her.

About to refuse, she accepted the money with a shrug. "Have it your way."

The cash register clanged to life, the girl changed the bill and Vic pushed the remainder into his wallet and back into his pocket. He trailed Sam to a table and pulled out a wooden chair. When she hesitated, he fired a warning flare not to refuse the gesture. She sat. He tossed his suit jacket onto the back of the other chair and Sam did likewise with hers. Dropping to his seat, Vic ripped the paper from his straw.

Sam leaned back into her chair. "Can't say I remember the last time I saw this place so clean."

Vic loosened his tie with a yank. "Tends to happen when you're the first one here."

"Good point." Running a hand through her near shoulder-length waves of auburn, she fluffed them off her neck, airing the skin beneath with the blast of air-conditioning blowing from the ceiling vent. Wearing no red today, the feminine shade of yellow softened her strong features, enhancing the female in her.

"Chavez was in some kind of hurry, wasn't he?"

Vic didn't appreciate her idle commentary and pinned her with a glare. "Are you enjoying this?"

Sam zapped him with a feisty smile. "Who, me?"

"Yes, you."

She gave a few quick tugs to her silk blouse. "Why, Victor Marin. I am not so callous a woman that I derive pleasure from the pain of a fellow human being."

"No sale."

"You doubt my word?"

"I suspect your motives."

"Is it my fault you got carried away with your witness?"

Vic expelled a grunt. "I didn't get carried away." He grabbed his glass of water. "Joe Morgan is guilty."

"I agree."

Knocking back a swallow of water, he said, "And that woman knows it."

"I agree."

"Chavez was too quick to her defense."

"Mmmm..." Sam fudged with a grimace.

"You think I was badgering the witness?"

"Borderline."

"Give me a break. The judge was out of line. Her little old lady act was a sham." He glowered, every muscle in his body so tight they were about to snap. No judge in Philly would have come down on him like that. Quite the opposite. They would have thrown him some slack so he could hang the lady.

Bare elbows hit the table and Sam leaned forward, linking her forearms together. "That may be true, but how you go about extracting the information is something else. Not everyone caves under intimidation. Especially experienced corporate felons."

"I'm not a rookie," he spit out. "Check my record. I'm good at what I do. *Damn good.*"

"You may have an impressive track record to show for your years with Gilbert and Wiley, but we play with the big boys down here. You're not the big fish in the big pond, anymore."

"That's big fish in the small pond."

"No," she corrected. "Big fish in the big pond. Philadelphia is no cracker town, I'll give you that." She shook the hair from her face and narrowed her gaze. "You've got your mobsters, your crooks, *but it ain't no Miami,* either. You're in the ocean now, where the sharks swim." Brown eyes sparked. "They swallow fish like you whole," she said, "without even noticing the lump of your carcass as it passes through. When you're dealing with the sums of money we are, the rules change. The players don't play nice. They lie, cheat and steal. Morgan-Baxter has been around a long time. They've gotten good at winning the game."

"And you should know."

"A piece of advice," she said, a smile creeping onto her lips. "You want to sneak up on someone? Sneak up on the sloth, not the fox. It's why I'm calling Brenner to the stand."

Vic's resentment pooled in his gut. Forget Brenner. Where he came from, there was no "sneaking around" about it. Sam may think she has all the answers—and when it came to Morgan-Baxter—she may. But where he came from if a guy interfered in your business, he took a cruise—straight to the bottom of the ocean.

He shoved the subject from his mind. Let her play her games. There was only one case he was interested in and it wasn't Morgan-Baxter. It was Perry.

And it was hers.

A wave of determination swept over him. Something he intended to change and soon.

Lunch suddenly landed between them. Two plates piled high with golden brown bread, layered with meat, cheese and sauerkraut were delivered without fanfare. Thick, fat French fries surrounded the sandwiches, several enmeshed in the drippings of piping hot Swiss. Both plates boasted mammoth pickle wedges.

"Do you guys need anything else?"

"Not at the moment," Sam answered, sucking in a chest-full of the aroma steaming from her plate.

"I'm good," Vic echoed the sentiment.

"Enjoy your lunch," the server quipped and disappeared from sight.

Sam sighed, and threw the paper napkin in her lap. "God am I hungry." She grabbed one enormous half of her sandwich and brought it to her lips for a bite, but as Vic watched the first chunk of sandwich vanish, he knew she wouldn't give up Perry without a fight. It was her ticket to partnership and from what he could gather around the office, she wasn't sharing.

But Sam was gonna have to change her mind. Resolve filtered through his system. *Because it was the only reason he came to Miami.*

Taking his time, Vic reached for his sandwich and grasping it with two hands, rested forearms against the table. Time to change the tide. "So tell me. If you're such a rainmaker, why haven't you achieved partner status?"

Sam offered a gentle smile. "Deflect the attention from yourself. Nice." She nodded. "I like it."

"You're avoiding the question."

Swamped by a shit-eating grin, Sam only stared at him.

"Well?"

But she said nothing, only stared with a decisive gleam in her eyes.

Vic felt a sudden zing.

The woman wasn't talking business anymore, he'd be willing to bet. Her thoughts were going underground.

Then, with surprising skill, Sam extinguished the flirtatious hint in her eyes. Like it never happened. "I'm on the edge of partnership, as we speak."

Whoa. Did he imagine it?

Not likely. *No.* No possible way. You didn't mistake a look like that one. But with no room to pry, he returned to his question, though his edge had been considerably softened. "More than ten years to make partner for a hotshot like you? I'm surprised."

"Don't be." Sam swiped the napkin across her lips and took a quick sip from her water. "I took some time off after high school."

"Why?"

"Why not? Nothing wrong with taking advantage of one's youth, much like you're doing now," she reminded him with unwarranted thrust. "Miami's a long way from Philly."

Vic tensed. *Did she know something?*

But he refused to rise to the bait. There was too much riding on it. "Backpack across Europe, did you?"

She smiled. "Not my cup of chi."

"Chi? What the hell does that mean?"

"It's complicated."

Shrugging it off, he asked, "So what *were* you doing?"

"Having fun."

Did she always speak in half-baked terms? "What the hell's that supposed to mean?"

"Fun?" She grinned. "What's not to understand about fun?"

"Sounds like someone was avoiding responsibility."

She wiped a drop of grease from the corner of her mouth. "No, Vic. I needed a little space and I took it. A simple recipe for a simple life."

"There's nothing simple about you, Sam Rawlings," he said, his gaze making a quick dodge toward the door. "You're about as complicated as they get."

"I am not," she shot back, but then laughed. "Not really," she said, softening her tone. "I'm a simple woman doing a simple job. I fight for the good guys. I right wrongs."

Vic almost choked on his sandwich.

"Funny."

Sam pushed her lunch aside and looked him square in the eye. Customers pushed in across the black and white checkered floor, crowded the front counter as they called out orders, many met with a shouted reply. Most were obvious professionals, a few construction workers, but Sam seemed oblivious. At the moment, she only had eyes for him.

"You did well today, Vic. You didn't win your argument, your performance was a little overpowering, but you did well." She slid a hand across the table. He would have sworn she was about to touch his, but instead, her fingers curled around the stem of her water glass. "Chavez was out of line. It's his M.O. Whenever there's a new attorney in his courtroom, he parades power like a peacock. Don't take it personal."

No longer sparring, Vic noted her removal of armor.

"You're good. Really good. You have phenomenal energy in the courtroom—I mean you *had* the jury." A smile crept onto her lips, a gesture which reached deep inside him. "I was watching. Each and every one of them followed you around that courtroom, your every move, your every word, they were right there with you. They didn't believe her either."

"Then why won't you include me on Perry?"

Sam's breath caught in her throat. Trapped beneath his gaze, the question echoed Raul's.

Around her, the noise level rose as lunch hour officially reached full sprint. People shouted orders, metal cash registers clanged in action, but she focused solely on Vic.

Her suspicion returned. Because I don't need any help. Because I don't want the distraction.

Because I'll be damned if some unknown hotshot comes in and tries to strip the prize from my hands regardless of how good, or how good-looking he is.

Sam's spine locked straight. All her life she had to work twice as hard, run twice as fast—because she was a woman. As an adolescent, her parents forced her to share an overload of responsibility for the care of five younger siblings, despite the fact her brother was scarcely a year behind her. In college she was offered more sexual advances than internships with law school providing more of the same.

Sam sighed. Baker, Schofield, Martinez and Brown had been the one interview where she felt wholly respected; wholly appreciated for her talent and *not* her looks. Because of Raul. He focused on her abilities and she responded. From there, the man taught her everything she knew, from the law to the lowdown, and groomed her into the legal shark she was proud to be.

Her thoughts chilled. Yet now, he was encouraging interference on her caseload from the new guy. It didn't make sense.

Sam honed in on Vic. "Give me one good reason I should include you on Perry."

"You said it yourself, I'm good."

"So am I."

"It's a big case. More than one attorney can handle."

"I have Diego."

"I have experience."

"So I hear." Sam lifted her glass from the table, but never took her eyes off him.

"It could work to your benefit."

"I work to my benefit."

Vic eased his neck from the snug fit of his collar and reached for his glass. "I'm offering to help, Sam. Most attorneys would jump at the opportunity."

"If you hadn't gathered by now, I'm not most attorneys." Sam took a sip from her water, noting his sudden discomfort. Was he agitated? Squirming? "Vic, help me out here. Is there something I'm missing?"

"Missing?" he asked innocently, but his expression took the hit. "Like what?"

"You're working Memorial, right?"

"Planning to." Vic sat back in his chair.

"So why Perry?" She gave a terse shake to her head. "What's in it for you?"

"Nothing's in it for me. Diego ran a few details of the case by me and I said I'd help." He shifted about in his chair. "Forget it. Sorry I asked."

Sam pulled her arms into a cross over her chest and smiled thinly. "I didn't just roll off the mango truck."

"What? What the hell are you talking about, mango truck?"

"You know, mangoes...beautiful golden red on the outside, luscious tasty sweet on the inside?"

Vic looked at her as though she'd lost her mind.

But she hadn't. Not even close.

Sam flicked a glance to his plate. "Finished?"

He slugged back the last of his water then smacked the glass to the table. "Yeah, I'm finished."

But Sam felt the distinct sense this was far from over.

# # #

8802322R0

Made in the USA
Charleston, SC
16 July 2011